CRASH ON THE BRIDGE!

In the helicopter, the pilot was too busy to think, operating on pure reflex and barking commands into the radio. “Mayday, mayday, clear the deck for emergency landing!” His voice was rock steady as he reminded himself he'd been in worse spots than this one. He and the copilot wrestled with the stick as the rear rotor assembly wiped out the bridge, throwing the rear of the helicopter back and forth even as the copilot cut shaft power. Too late. Before the rotors could slow, what was left of the rotor assembly tore itself loose. The heavily laden rear of the CH–46 dropped like a stone.

On the CH–46, Nolan felt the rotor assembly give way and knew he was going to die. With his bird still too high to drop safely, he had one option. He poured more power into his front rotors and tried to pull the helicopter out over the water. It did no good. The weight of the two engines and the extra fuel were too much. The back of the helicopter dropped while the forward rotors kept elevating the front of the helicopter.

Those who survived and saw it would forever after talk of the picture. One kid with nerves of steel and a video camera actually caught it on film. A CH–46, with SEAL team aboard, upside-down as, from seventy feet in the air, it dropped onto four uploaded F-18 Hornets.

LANDING PARTY

T.J. McFADDEN

LEISURE BOOKS NEW YORK CITY

To my wife, Helena, for getting me through this. And to the men and women of the United States Armed Forces without whom this country could not have been.

A LEISURE BOOK®

November 1999

Published by

Dorchester Publishing Co., Inc.
276 Fifth Avenue
New York, NY 10001

ISBN 0-8439-4627-X

Printed in the United States of America.

LANDING PARTY

Chapter One

Cruising the Western Mediterranean on the seventh month of a six-month deployment, the guided missile destroyer USS *Kimmel* cut through waves turned to molten copper by the sunset.

It was 563 feet of metal, a floating city shaped like a sword blade. Inside it were four jet engines, kitchens, weapons, ventilation systems, fuel tanks, ammunition lockers, and living spaces for its crew of 350 men and women. Nearing the end of a working day, it was about to commence a working night.

On the bridge, the captain took one last look at his orders. He still could not quite believe what he read. In the hangar, the flight crew finished preflight checks. In Combat Information Central (CIC), the gunnery officer entered, brushed the last bits of dinner from her hands, and relieved the watch officer. On the mess decks, sailors finished their evening meal.

One of those sailors was Seaman Dave Halloran. He was a broad-shouldered man of average height, solidly built, with eyes that went from pale blue to dark gray depending on his moods. On this ship, his eyes were most often the dark gray of brewing storm clouds. His crewcut hair was brown, fading to premature gray, his skin pale where it was not sunburned. His uniform of white T-shirt and blue dungaree jeans was clean but worn.

Halloran was a deck seaman, one of the ''non-rate'' sailors on the ship who did the jobs no one else wanted. Tonight he was starting the three months of duty in the ship's mess—mess cranking—that all sailors did sometime during their first year on a ship. He was working the beverage line.

Halloran looked over the mess decks and checked his watch. Another five minutes and he could start cleanup, he hoped. Then it would be time to find a quiet corner with some friends for an evening of war gaming. Another mess crank walked past, gingerly holding a stack of trays still steaming from the dishwashers. ''Is this going to take much longer?'' Halloran asked.

''Not much,'' answered the other sailor. ''The last man's off the mess decks, the Chief's mess already sent their dishes through, and wardroom does all their own. Just hope Davis doesn't want us to wax the decks tonight.''

Halloran gritted his teeth, then froze.

Over the 1MC public address system, someone was ringing the ship's bell, a rapid ringing done as fast as the bosuns mate of the watch could swing the clapper. The ringing stopped, and a voice barked out.

''General quarters, general quarters, all hands man your battle stations! Set condition zebra throughout the ship! Go up and forward on starboard side, down and aft on port! Reason for general quarters: possible air attack! This is not a drill!''

The mess decks exploded into motion. Halloran was booking for the nearest ladderwell before the bell stopped ringing. He'd been hearing the rumors all day. Something real was up. Around him, the narrow passageways suddenly flooded with crewmembers running to GQ stations. Some ran for the engine rooms, others for damage control lockers where they would outfit themselves as damage control and firefighting parties. Some manned the gun and missile mounts, or replaced watchstanders who had their own GQ stations to get to. Watertight doors were slammed shut and secured all over the ship, turning *Kimmel* into a honeycomb of watertight spaces, virtually impossible to sink.

Halloran passed others already in flash gear, lunged up a ladder to the top level of the superstructure, emerged from the pilot house, and ran to the aft lookout position. The lookout who'd been on watch was hopping back and forth nervously. He threw off his sound-powered phones as Halloran approached. ''Nothing in sight, no air or surface contacts, gotta go, Chief'll have my—'' Slamming metal shut off his words. Gears squealed as the hatch was dogged shut.

First, Halloran bloused his bell-bottom dungarees into his socks to keep the bell-bottoms from snagging on anything. Then he went to the hatch from the helicopter control tower. It was already shut, but before the tower crew had dogged the hatch they had shoved out his GQ gear. He threw on a blue, long-sleeved denim shirt he'd stuffed into his gas mask bag, rolled down the sleeves, and buttoned it up. The long pants and shirtsleeves were hot, but they would protect him from flash burns in the event of explosion or fire.

Next he pulled his cloth flash gloves and flash hood out of the gas mask bag, put them on over hands and head. The hood smelled stale, sour from sitting too long stuffed into the bag. He ignored it. No gas alarm yet, so the gas mask went back in its bag. Now his entire body except his face was protected from flash burns. The entire crew, from newest seaman recruit to the captain in his seat on the bridge, wore the same rig.

On went the sound-powered phones. "Aft lookout, on line!" he barked, then listened, strapping on his gas mask bag as he did so.

"Aft lookout, aye!" The bridge, responding. Now they knew he was there, and he knew they were listening. Next, on went the phone talkers' helmet, made huge to fit over the ear pieces of his head phones. Finally, he picked up the binoculars the lookout had hung over the railing. He looked through, adjusted focus, scanned the aft 180 degrees of the horizon around the ship, then the sky, then the ocean close in. As the man had said, no air contacts, no surface contacts.

That done, he spared a minute to look at the aft weatherdecks of the ship. Empty, except for the flight deck, where the ship's helicopter was being rolled out. Then he saw the missile launchers. Looked closely. Olive-drab missiles were on the launch rails.

That was when it really sank in. Unknown to Halloran, a smile crept across his face. Excitement, tinged with a bit of fear, made his heart pound in his chest. "Well, there's something you don't see every day, McGee," he muttered to no one in particular. He began scanning again. Horizon, sky, near ocean.

"Attention, straight shooters! This is the captain speaking!"

"Big surprise," muttered Halloran. Sound-powered phones only worked if you held down the button, which he most assuredly was not doing.

"Many of you have heard rumors today about our course changes and some unusual message traffic. Here's the situation: A Libyan pilot and an American agent are defecting from Libya on a helicopter. We are waiting for them in international waters. We intend to land their helicopter on this ship. Expect the helicopter to come in under radar. All lookouts are to stay alert,

particularly the Big Eyes.'' On top of the pilothouse, signalmen high-fived each other as they manned the outsize, pedestal-mounted binoculars called ''Big Eyes.''

''*Libyan aircraft may enter international airspace in hot pursuit of this helicopter and attack it, or us. We have been authorized to use all available force in self-defense, or to defend the defecting helicopter. We only know the general direction of approach of the helicopter, so we have to keep our eyes open to catch it. This may take all night.*'' For once, Halloran didn't mind a planned game being canceled by ship's operations. ''*This is an opportunity to excel. To prove that* Kimmel's *reputation on the waterfront has been well earned.*''

Halloran smirked at that. Given the choice between three hours of sleep or a good reputation on the waterfront, he had a pretty good idea which the crew would take. ''Yadda, yadda, yadda,'' he muttered. ''Get this show on the road, you royal pain in the butt.''

''*So stay alert and remember your training! This will be a fitting finale to an outstanding med cruise. I will keep you informed as information comes in. This entire operation is classified, so do not mention it in your letters home until you have been cleared to do so. Further, all radio calls home are canceled until we get back to Norfolk. Stay alert, straight shooters, and good luck!*''

Halloran began scanning eagerly, all frustrations put aside for now. This wasn't one more training exercise. This was real!

Two hundred miles to the south, it was all too real. Major Abood, late of the Libyan Air Force, checked the controls of the Mi-8 HIP one more time. Everything was running well. Below them, the land north of Benghazi was green with the new irrigated farms. Patches of desert gleamed pink in the setting sun. The sun was setting over the Gulf of Sidra, glowing orange fire in a turquoise sky. The beauty of it made Abood's heart ache. Then the land slid away, replaced by the blue waters of the Mediterranean.

There was a noise behind him as the American came up from the cargo cabin, stuffing papers, maps, and photographs into a plastic bag. Majors was red-haired and light-complected constantly getting sunburned, his hair worn a little long, his bushy mustache carefully trimmed. Abood was the classic dark Arab, taller, movie-star handsome, complete with the Ray-Bans that indicated he was Somebody. In the Arab world, you were nobody if you didn't have Ray-Bans.

Abood spoke over the roar of the twin Isotov turboprops driving the helicopter. "We have not been followed. I radioed in a mayday before I dived below radar. They will believe we have crashed. You are satisfied with the papers?"

Majors checked the package one last time before sealing it in the waterproof bag. Then he smiled. "Congratulations! You have just won the defector's grand prize!" said Majors, in an odd accent Abood could not recognize as an imitation of a game show host. "Instant American citizenship! A new name! A new job! Along with the thanks of a grateful nation, your own luxury condominium in Langley, Virginia, and the right to be audited by the IRS!"

Abood looked back quizzically and shrugged again. The American sat in the copilot's seat and watched as Abood fed power to the rotors and flew west, skimming the waves of the Gulf of Sidra. It was a far cry from when they had met that morning in Benghazi. He wondered what the American had thought of their meeting.

The Benghazi streets had still been cool from the desert night. The smells of food, of camel dung and goats and exotic spices lay heavy in the air. Majors looked across the street to the shade of the coffee house, squinted.

Abood was there, dapper in his Libyan Air Force uniform. Majors glanced around casually. Nobody watching. Trying to shake the feeling of cross hairs centered on his back, Majors crossed the street, sat at an empty table next to Abood, and ordered coffee.

Abood turned to face him. "Excuse me, are you an American?"

Majors coughed and tried to slow down his heart. "Excuse me?"

"I said, are you an American? Come, sit with me."

What was this lunatic doing? "Uh, no, I'm Canadian. I sell oil-pumping equipment. I, uh, I don't want to be a bother."

"It is no bother!" Abood grinned, showing a mouthful of perfect teeth. "Sit with me! We will have coffee and talk. I meet so few foreigners." Reluctantly, Majors went over to Abood's table and sat down. The waiter, eagerly serving anyone who paid in hard currency, brought his cup of coffee. It was served in the Arabic fashion—very strong, and sugared to almost syrupy sweetness. Majors had developed a taste for it. He sipped it to calm himself.

Abood smiled and spoke. "Don't worry. The Secret Police are busy at the Western embassies, or shuttling around the press. Those Sword of Islam dogs really stirred it up this time." Majors recalled his briefing on Abood. The Libyan Major was a hotshot at piloting and, apparently, everything else. The man prided himself on his command of American slang, picked up from black-market videotapes. Utterly fearless, as befitted the longest-lasting indigenous contact the CIA had ever had in Libya. Majors wished the man was a little less fearless. As a non-card-carrying field agent of the CIA, he hated flamboyancy when practiced by allies.

"So what's the big deal?" Majors kept scanning the street. "The plane's blown up, the hostages are dead,

Sword of Islam has a few more martyrs. Why are the Secret Police worried now?"

"Because the hostages aren't blown up." Abood watched Majors's reaction, grinned, and ordered tea.

Majors thought a second as he stared into the Libyan's Ray-Bans. Damn. Couldn't read the eyes through those. Maybe the overpriced sunglasses weren't such a bad idea after all. He took another sip of hot coffee to steady his jangled nerves. "What happened to the hostages, then?"

"Sword of Islam has them in a training camp, all thirty-two of them. They were taken off the airliner when it was stuck in the sand at the end of the runway, out of view of the cameras. They want to use them to negotiate the release of prisoners. That's why the Secret Police are working so hard to keep your press at a distance."

Majors's head spun for a moment. Thirty-two was the magic number. He began running through options in his head. "Why is Khaddaffi still saying they died?"

"It is a big mess. Sword of Islam wants hostages. Khaddaffi still remembers your F-111s bombing his house. He wants nothing to do with any more hostages. He says to just shoot the hostages and bury them in the sand, so everyone forgets about it. No muss, no fuss, no bombers." As Abood spoke, his hands waved in the gestures of pilots worldwide. How do you silence a pilot? Majors thought to himself. You tie his hands.

"So why aren't they dead and buried?"

"Sword of Islam pitched a bitch about it. They say they will slip them out of the country. Khaddaffi gave them five days to do it. Four days now. Nobody else will take the hostages. Their nuts are in the meatgrinder on this one." Spoken in a thick Arabic accent, the slang was comical but clear.

"How do you know so much?"

"A friend of mine flew them to the camp. Here is the

straight skippy.'' The Libyan handed Majors a grainy Polaroid. In it, Majors could see two children—a boy and a girl—and an older man sporting a black eye, in the cargo bay of some aircraft, guarded by a man with an AK-47.

Majors studied it closely. If this could be confirmed . . . ''Where's the camp?''

Abood grinned. ''That is for me to know and you to find out, buckaroo.''

Majors looked at the children in the photos. Their fear came out, even in the grainy picture. Anger put an edge on his next words. ''What do you mean by that?''

''I am tired of Libya. I wish to defect. I can bring the location of the camp with me, full information and maps. They were . . . lost during the flight in.''

Majors shook his head. ''That's no good. If what you say is true, we have ninety-six hours before the terrorists kill the hostages. We need that information in time to plan a rescue. Or we can use it to expose this, and at least make the hostages public, so Khaddaffi can't kill them.''

''You cannot expose it.'' Abood shook his head mournfully. ''Orders have already been given. At the first mention we have the hostages, they are to be immediately taken out to the desert and shot. It's a big desert. Easy to lose a few bodies in.'' Abood shrugged.

''So our only option is a rescue. For that we need the maps in time to do some good. It takes time to put these things together.''

Abood nodded. ''I have a solution.'' He checked his watch. ''Tonight I must fly a training mission over the Gulf of Sidra. Instead, I will land my helicopter on the coast road, five kilometers north of Benghazi to pick you up and fly to a U.S. Navy ship which you will have waiting outside Libyan waters. I will have the maps with me. You will then have three days to use them to plan the rescue.''

Majors's mind ran through options, staggered by the audacity of the Libyan's plan. "You've thought this out, haven't you?"

"You damn skippy I have." Abood reached into a pocket, pulled out a pack of cigarettes. "I told you I was tired of Libya. Tired of watching these idiots kill each other and trying not to be caught in the crossfire. Khaddaffi is not getting any younger. Just more nervous." He lit the cigarette, drew deeply. Exhaled. Suddenly, he didn't seem so jaunty. Just exhausted.

"What if I can't have a ship waiting there?"

"Then I make the training flight, four days pass, and the hostages die. Or your Navy gets too close to our coast, Khaddaffi panics, and the hostages die. Or word is leaked to the press—"

"—And the hostages die," Majors finished. "I get it."

Abood finished his tea in one long drink and stood up. "Dusk, on the coast road, five kilometers north of Benghazi. It is the only way. Can you have a ship waiting or not?"

That had been this morning.

Now, Abood looked across the empty ocean and hoped the promised ship was where it should be. He was still flying under radar, almost skimming the wave tops. The American spoke. "Abood, what if you were spotted?"

"The MiGs will catch us before we go a hundred kilometers."

"What if they catch us before we make the ship?"

Abood got his jaunty grin back. "Your ships have shot down our planes before. What is a few more between friends? Besides, those jet pilots are stinking dogs anyways, and ass-kissers too." Abood concentrated on his flying and listened to the radio. Frantic queries filled the airwaves. As he'd hoped, his radio silence had them already assuming he'd crashed. He reached under the instrument panel, made sure he'd disabled the IFF beacon. It broadcast an identification code in response to radar. Now all he had to do was keep his helicopter under radar to avoid detection. The lack of response from his beacon would help in the deception.

Behind him was home. Behind were the Secret Police, the disappointment, the fear. Ahead of him was the West. An end to fear. Perhaps even something he could believe in. If even America disappointed him . . . Well, if there was nothing to truly believe in, one might as well be an unbeliever in a comfortable spot. He could already taste his first Tom Collins.

Back on land, unknown to Abood, a security patrol had stopped on one of the dunes. Its commander was already on the radio reporting that the crashed helicopter he had been told to look for was heading out into the gulf, skimming the waves. That message was passed on. A training flight of MiG-23s loaded for a ground-attack run were vectored in.

On the bridge of USS *Kimmel*, Lieutenant Jimmelle Washington, Ship's Gunnery Officer, adjusted her gas mask bag—the damn thing had a tendency to slide down below her knees. Then she focused as Lieutenant Commander Wendell Scott—Operations Officer, or simply, OPS—read their orders a third time. His whole manner was tense, matching the atmosphere on the bridge. The officers present had each gone over the orders at least twice. This was a new situation and nobody wanted to make any mistakes. OPS excelled in not making mistakes.

"It seems clear," OPS said in his reedy voice. He was a tall man with thinning sandy-colored hair and mustache. "We stay in international waters, conduct air-sea rescue of anyone who needs it, and defend ourselves if attacked. I've never seen anything like this before, but it happens."

Commander (SW/AW) Matt Reisling nodded. The commanding officer of *Kimmel* was a short, athletic man, a fanatic about physical fitness, with dark brown hair and eyes and a perpetually eager expression. "Outstanding. If we're all agreed, I think this is an excellent training opportunity." He turned to Washington. " 'Guns,' I want all weapons hot, the whole nine yards."

"Live birds are on the rails, sir," snapped Lieutenant Washington, checking her list. She was a young black woman, her hair cropped close to her skull, uniform creased razor sharp.

Reisling thought a moment. "I also want the men with the keys standing by C-WIZ at all times during GQ."

"Yes sir," she snapped, and scribbled some lines into her notebook to make it look as if she were changing something. The Close-In Weapons System, CIWS or C-WIZ, was a 20mm Gatling gun designed to shoot down incoming missiles or aircraft. The problem with C-WIZ was that, left to itself, it would track and fire on anything within 2000 meters—seagulls, their own helicopter, anything. It could only safely be switched on during actual attack, so personnel with arming keys had to stand by the weapons if they were to be used safely. What annoyed Washington was that they'd been doing this for seven months now. It was SOP, yet Reisling was still micromanaging the job like they were on their first workup.

"OPS, I want the Search and Rescue swimmer and the boat crew standing by for recovery, in case we have to pull someone out of the water."

"Not a problem, sir." That was peachy with OPS. Washington sincerely believed that if the CO had told OPS to have Deck Division tap dancing naked on the quarterdeck at 0200 hours, that would have been peachy with OPS too. "Guns, I'll need one of your people there with a shark gun."

The term "anal-retentive control freak" occurred to Washington. "Yes sir."

OPS checked his own notebook. "Sir, there's a lot of maintenance to be done. How late should this run?"

"Don't worry. We'll finish this tonight. It won't interfere with normal working hours."

OPS laughed at that. "Sounds like good training, sir."

Washington spoke up. "How long do we expect to have the crew at their GQ stations, sir?"

"As long as it takes, Guns." Reisling cocked an eyebrow. "Why?"

Go ahead, Jimmelle, said a little voice inside her head. Tell the Captain who's failed two promotion boards that his crew is running on the ragged edge of exhaustion. Tell him his people are an accident waiting to happen. Advise him to secure from General Quarters at first opportunity, so they can get some rest. Then go on down to your quarters, take your lieutenant bars, and frame them. Because after you tell him, the CO will write you a performance evaluation that will make sure lieutenant is the last promotion you will ever see. "Should we break out the night vision gear, sir?"

Reisling smiled. "Outstanding idea! Make it happen, Guns. The quartermaster of the watch says we'll hit the operations area about 1945 hours."

Washington left the bridge and went to the combat information center.

CIC looked like the set from a science-fiction movie. Eternally dark, the only light permitted came from dozens of computer screens and radar scans. In a time when weapons had rendered armor almost irrelevant, CIC was still kept deep within the superstructure, with other spaces beside, above or beneath it acting as its protection. The bridge could be replaced if taken out. So could the berthings and the officers' quarters. CIC could not be replaced if *Kimmel* was to remain a warship.

The men and women in CIC, faces lit phosphor-green,

all wore flash gear. They scanned radio and radar waves, plotted sightings both visual and electronic, checked the status of the ship's weapons.

"Target package loaded and confirmed for harpoons." These were cruise missles, capable of hitting ships or ground targets. "Targets as follows: Benghazi sea scan radar, designation alpha tango, harpoon one. Commo center designation bravo uniform, harpoons two and three. Radar facility—"

"All lookouts on line."

"All standard missiles green, tracking enabled." Two missles on each launcher, live and on the rail, waiting for the information that would send them to their targets at twice the speed of sound.

"Mount five-one, manned and ready." The forward 5-inch gun.

"Mount twenty-two, manned and ready." The rear 20mm C-WIZ.

"Nixie checks green, ready to stream on command." A sonar jammer the ship could trail to distract sonar-guided torpedoes. Just in case.

A thousand and one checks were made, a multitude of systems tested. Then they waited, as *Kimmel* skirted Libyan airspace, listening and looking. OPS came in and tried to get them to start a training scenario on the computers. The captain started calling down every fifteen minutes. The senior enlisted man present, Senior Chief Carter, went over to the watch desk and fell asleep sitting up.

After an hour and forty-five minutes, the air scan radar operator spoke. "Spa-48 detects six aircraft, squawking MiG-23s, Libyan, bearing 165 true." The SPS-48 Air Search Radar, or Spa-48, was the ship's primary set of electronic eyes, linked with the SPG-51 (Spig five-one) targeting radar. Computers linked with the radar read their target's IFF (Identification, Friend or Foe) beacons and identified them, putting the information on the radar screen.

"Target angle 351, range ninety miles. Altitude 3500 meters, airspeed 350 knots. Air contact designation Mike." From now on, the Libyan jets and their pilots would be referred to as Contact Mike. Unless shooting started, in which case they would become Vampire Mike and, shortly afterward, dead.

On the plotting board, a sailor grease-penciled their new contact in. Lieutenant Washington watched the scene, grinning nervously. She wasn't eager to fight, but the adrenaline was pumping. "OS1, I want all our passive electronic counter-measures on them. Let me know the minute they light off targeting radars."

"Aye aye, ma'am" rasped Operations Specialist 1st Class "Black" Bart Ingalls. With slick black hair, narrow black mustache, and squinting dark eyes, he looked like nothing so much as a villain from an old Western. The impression was furthered by a voice made raspy by the smoke of a few thousand cigarettes and at least as many shots of whiskey drunk in dozens of nations. "Should we light off Spig five-one, illuminate them for the missles?"

"Negative. Rules of engagement say we only fire in self-defense. They're in international airspace. They might panic and open fire."

"That's the idea, ma'am." OS1 Ingalls grinned and looked at the screen, analyzing it in a moment while the OS3 was still trying to read the computer prompts. "Still in Libyan airspace. They'll enter international airspace in a minute." He raised his head, barked at the OS's. "Does anyone pick up anything that might be a chopper? Probably a Soviet model?"

Silence from the OS's. The phone rang. Washington answered. "CIC, Guns here."

"Guns, this is the CO. You're tracking Libyan aircraft?"

"Affirmative, sir, but no helos. Recommend we steer clear until we can spot our defector."

"Sounds good, Guns. CO out." The phone clicked off. A few seconds later the deck tilted as *Kimmel* adjusted course. Washington thought hard. The Libyan IFF beacons were working fine—squawking, in OS slang. Intended to avoid having one's own missles shoot down friendly aircraft, they actually helped *Kimmel*, made it easy for the OS's to spot them. Which bothered Washington. If that defecting helicopter was over the gulf, they should be picking up its IFF beacon. She looked over the OS3's shoulder at a screen filled with images, each solid image tagged with its electronic identification.

"Ma'am!" The OSSA handling communications with the radio room spoke up. "Commo has clear channel broadcasts in Arabic from those planes. We don't have a translator, but they've said helicopter several times."

Washington nodded. "Pass that on to the bridge. Let me know if the Libyans sound excited."

"Has radio said anything about a mayday from our chopper?"

"Negative."

"No surprise," said Washington. "If our defectors used the radio, it'd just lead those jets to them."

"Aye aye." Now they waited. The Libyan jets split up into pairs, searched a wider area, were redesignated Mike Alpha, Mike Bravo, and Mike Charley. There were frantic air contacts from the port lookout, instantly canceled. False alarm. Sonar picked up something, tried to identify it. Passive Electronic Counter Measures, or ECM, detected the Libyan coastal radars lighting off. The Libyans, detecting the radar emissions of *Kimmel*, were now lighting off their own radars.

"Mike Bravo lighting off targeting radar!" called the man at the ECM board. "Going for missile lock!"

"On what?" snapped Washington. She turned to the

console for the SPS-48 surface scan radar. "Anything on Spa-48?"

The OS3, as cocky as OS's always are, answered, "Nothing but those MiGs."

A cold chill clamped on Washington's heart. "Where is Mike Bravo?"

"Mike Bravo has target lock on! They're reading a low-level air contact!"

Ingalls looked over the OS3's shoulder at the radar screen. "You idiot! They're right on top of an air contact!"

The OS3 sputtered. "That's a cloud! It doesn't have IFF or a beacon! It's just a shadow!"

Sick with sudden realization of what had happened, Washington grabbed the phone, called out. "Light off targeting radars! Target all Mike Contacts!"

Operational specialists hardly ever actually read their radar screens anymore. Computers did that, then filled the screen with computer prompts identifying what they saw. Identification was achieved by scanning the target's IFF beacon. Normally the only things without IFF beacons were clouds, which were ignored. Only the oldest OS's remembered when all a radar screen gave you were images which you had to figure out yourself.

Ingalls snarled, threw the younger OS from his chair and took over the screen. "Boot, if you're trying to escape someone, you disable your IFF! That's why they didn't squawk!" Furious, Ingalls concentrated on the screen, mentally cursing arrogant punks who were incapable of reading a radar screen without computer assistance. "I have target vector, location as follows!"

Ingalls gave them the location of the defecting helicopter.

Thc CO called down for information, ordered a course change.

The Libyan jets fired their missles.

The SPG-51 targeting radar acquired targets.

Ingalls reported multiple hits by the Libyans.

Washington watched it happen, excitement replaced by a sick, helpless feeling. "Missiles locked!" she called over the phone to Reisling. "Do we fire, sir?"

"Contact Mike Bravo and Mike Charley passing over crash area, believe they are doing strafing runs," said Ingalls, shooting a venomous look at the young OS3.

No word from the CO, thought Washington. He was probably deciding whether it would do any good to shoot down the Libyans now. She knew the answer to that. But she had to do something. "Spig five-one, illuminate all Mike contacts with everything you have! Strongest pulses, multiple. I want their gold fillings to melt! Spig six-oh, do the same." If they knew they were targeted, they might break off.

Washington held her breath as the radars pulsed. The phone from the bridge spoke. "Guns, this is the CO. For the record, we cannot be sure that is our pickup. Do not fire."

Dang, thought Washington. Reisling was actually putting his usually well-covered butt on the line here. "Aye-aye, sir."

The Libyan jets split away from the crash site, hit the deck, and headed for home. On full afterburners, judging from their speed. Washington spared half a second to imagine every threat detector in their jets going off at once. Then she sighed. They might just be going home because their job was done.

A horrified silence filled CIC, broken by OS1 Ingalls glaring into the screen and chanting his own furious mantra. "Shit, shit, shit, shit." He realized what he was saying, grew silent. Leaving them all in silence.

Broken by the 1MC.

"This is the captain speaking." Washington had never thought she would miss Reisling's eternal cheerfulness. She missed it now. *"Stand down from GQ stations, with the exception of CIC and lookouts. We are*

shortly going to go to flight quarters.'' A pause. The silence was deafening. *''Libyan jets may have caught the defector before we did and shot him down. It is also possible our pickup is still out there. Every lookout must stay alert. We will proceed to where the Libyan jets shot down an air contact, and rescue anyone we find. This is not over yet. We should get to the location in two hours. That is all.''*

Washington looked around CIC. ''You heard the CO. We're still looking for that helicopter! I want everything reported! Rowboats, seagulls, flying fish, anything! I don't care if it squawks as Noah's Ark! Get to it!'' They got to it.

Ingalls turned to the OS3 who'd been handling surface scan. ''Harrison, you are relieved. Report to berthing and stay there.'' Harrison left.

''Well, that was a lovely little goat rope,'' Ingalls growled.

Washington nodded. ''It's going to be a long night.''

It all depended on your perspective, thought Majors.

He'd flown over the sea many times, seen it as a gleaming surface, speckled with waves. He'd gone swimming in the sea, where it jutted against the land. Now he was in it and the sea was huge. A vast, roaring, damp infinity, stretching off into darkness forever, rising and falling and showing him how completely helpless he was.

He checked his life vest. Still working. He worked his fingers through the pilot's harness he'd taken off Abood. Flares, a spare magazine for the pistol, a flashlight, other things.

The Libyan pilot had taken them down to wavetop level when their threat detectors screamed, then halted the helicopter in midair when the first missle went shooting past—a miss. They'd both bailed out then, diving into the churning waters twenty feet below seconds before a missle blew the helicopter to flaming scrap. Majors had delayed inflating his life preserver, diving under the water repeatedly. Eventually, the jets had gone, leaving the sea full of broken bits of helicopter. That was when he'd swum to Abood. A cannon shell had torn a massive hole in the man's chest. The man had inflated his life preserver as soon as he'd hit the water, trapping himself on the surface.

Majors didn't waste thought on how bad his situation was. In places like this, you concentrated on one job at a time and let the universe take care of itself. Majors had stripped the man's body and consigned him to the deep. His lungs punctured, Abood's body vanished into the depths. That done, the CIA agent got about the business of surviving. Sooner or later, someone would come to investigate the crash site. The question was, who?

If it was Americans, he needed to be seen. He held the flare and the flashlight ready as he floated.

If it was Libyans, well, he still had Abood's pistol, a Makarov 9mm. He'd take a few of them with him before he died. Not that dying appealed to him, but torture in a Libyan cell appealed to him even less.

Dusk turned into night. The stars came out. He floated. All perspective vanished. He was floating between the stars above and the darkness below. The water was cool but not cold, so he managed. He spared a moment to wonder if there were sharks in the Med, then shoved that thought from his mind. The sea felt very big and suddenly, he felt very small. Unbidden, thoughts of the girl in the picture came to mind. One of the hostages he hoped to save.

He'd grabbed Abood's package in the gym bag on his way out the door. With the cold logic he picked up in moments like that, Majors had stuffed the package into a plastic bag before he jumped out of the helicopter. Now, air trapped in the bag helped keep him afloat. With the picture of the girl inside it.

His fears rose in the darkness. He thought of that girl, of how terrified she must be, and his fear suddenly seemed a small thing.

She didn't look a thing like the girl in Leningrad.

The men he'd killed never haunted him. But the people who'd died because he screwed up? The physicist in Leningrad, arrested by the militia because Majors missed a contact? The man's entire family had been "disappeared." Including their daughter, whose round slavic face didn't look a bit like the girl in the picture. Except for that expression of fear, as she was taken away.

Could there be absolution for that?

Maybe it was unprofessional, but he wanted to rescue that girl, wanted to see her eyes light up as someone took her from danger to safety. He'd seen so much suffering, so much pain and death he could do nothing about. This, he could do something about. He'd planned to try to go in with the rescue team.

Now he'd be lucky to survive the night.

Was that a helicopter? Or crashing waves? No telling. He had two flares. He fired off one.

Hiss, pop, tiny orange sun arcing into the darkness.

A moment's light and it was gone.

The helicopter? Couldn't hear it.

One flare and a flashlight left. He turned the flashlight on, clipped it to his harness. It flickered and went out.

Damn Russian garbage. He hit it. It flickered.

Noise of a helicopter again . . . maybe. Far off. Couldn't see over the wave tops. It was amazing how the waves cut off the horizon when you were floating up to your neck in sea. He listened again.

There! He was sure he heard it! The second flare now.

Hiss, pop. His last flare gone into the dark. Noise of a helicopter getting closer. They'd seen the flares! But now it was dark. How would they see him in the ocean?

The helicopter was closer now. He could see the glow of its searchlight over the wave tops. He fiddled with the flashlight. It came on, a glorious, beautiful column of light reaching into the darkness. Answered by a blinding flash, a searchlight off the helicopter. Now it was close, and downdraft was whipping up the sea around him. Descending like an angel, someone in swimming gear was lowered from the helicopter. Majors readied his pistol. Now he would find out. Rescue? Or sudden death, and the long fall into the abyss?

"Are you the CIA agent?" yelled the swimmer over the roar of the helicopter. "Put your arms in the life rings, and they'll pull you up!"

Majors dropped the pistol, struggled into the canvas rescue harness lowered by the chopper. He grinned as he heard the helicopter's winch. "I'm coming to save you, little girl," he muttered to himself. "I'm on my way." Sea spray whipping around him, he ascended into the light.

Chapter Two

The night winds whipped over the superstructure of *Kimmel* and the dozen or so crewmembers who huddled there, trying to smoke. Released from GQ, many of the crew had come out to catch a smoke and discuss rumors. Dusk had turned to night as they stood there.

Halloran adjusted the focus on his binoculars to scan the ocean. Something had gone wrong in CIC, he knew that. The phone circuit the lookouts used went to CIC, where an OS was supposed to use their sightings to maintain a continual plot. The OS's had a marked tendency to ignore lookout reports. They were being very attentive now. They were also surlier than usual.

Halloran had heard the warning bell for the aft missile launcher and ducked for cover. The missile had never launched. Flight quarters had been called and he'd ducked under cover. Then the ship had changed course and gone to flank speed. Now the voices from CIC sounded elated.

"Attention, straight shooters!" The CO was back to

his usual cheerful self. *"Our helicopter just rescued the CIA agent we were looking for. Unfortunately, the defecting Libyan officer with him was killed when Libyan jets shot them down. Despite that, our mission has been a success!"* He heard cheers, actual cheers at that, loud from the smokers, faintly audible from the boat deck and from within the ship. Come to think of it, Halloran felt like cheering himself.

Reisling continued. *"However, straight shooters, our mission is not complete. We have been ordered to stand by for the time being and await further orders. Something is up. I will keep you fully informed. In the meantime, catch up on your sleep if possible. Good night, straight shooters, and good work!"*

The 1MC clicked off for a second, then clicked back on. It was the normal GQ bosuns mate of the watch. *"Set condition yoke throughout the ship. Make yoke reports to the bridge. Now set normal underway watch. Watch section three has the bridge. Officer's section two has the conn."*

Halloran went back to keeping watch, waiting for his relief. As he stood watch, he removed his flash gear. The night air chilled his hair. He suddenly noticed he was soaked with sweat. He just hadn't noticed it in the excitement. He stuffed his flash gear into his gas mask bag. He knew he had a long time to wait. Whoever relieved him would be standing the midwatch, from 2300 hours to 0300 hours. They wouldn't be eager to take his place.

As usual, his expectations were wrong. Toombs tapped him on the shoulder a few minutes later. "Yo, Halloran, z'up? I'm your relief."

"Tombstone? Cool! I thought I'd be stuck up here 'til after mid-rats." Halloran started handing over the lookout gear. "How'd you get up here so fast?"

"I'm messenger of the watch of GQ. You have anything to report?"

"Nah. No sightings. What happened on the bridge?"

"CIC messed up. Nobody wants to talk about it, but I think the OS's did it. The Libyans shot down that helicopter before we could get to it. The CO was pissed, but he's all smiles since they rescued that guy off the helicopter." His face grew thoughtful. "You the man with the college degree. Do you think this guy is really CIA?"

Halloran grinned as Toombs threw on his watch gear and adjusted his binoculars. "I don't think the CO could make this up if he wanted to. You know the real reason why he's happy, don't you?"

"Why?"

"Because he's keeping us out here another week." That got a flash of smile from Toombs. "Take care, Tombstone."

Halloran stowed his GQ gear in the now-empty control tower and went below. Now it was time for sleep. He wound his way down to the mess decks, checked the beverage line. Everything had been put away. Bormann, his partner at this station, must have come back when he was released from GQ. Outstanding!

Halloran turned to head for his rack.

"Halloran!" It was Podlogar. "C'mon man! Midnight rations start in thirty minutes. We have to get the steam tables going."

Halloran gritted his teeth and headed for the galley. He'd forgotten it was his turn to serve midnight rations.

"He didn't have a right to call me an idiot! That's abuse! And he laid hands on me! I don't got to take that!" OS3 Harrison was using what Washington had always termed the "punk" defense. Namely: If you've screwed up, try to distract people from your mistake by accusing everybody else of having made their own mistakes.

"You *are* an idiot, and you got a man killed because you do not know your freaking job!" snapped OS1 Ingalls. ''Does that even matter to you? Do you even comprehend that a man is dead because you didn't do your job?''

''You don't have no right to lay hands on me!'' replied Harrison. ''That's abuse! I'm reporting this!''

''Stand fast, both of you!'' Senior Chief Carter was in a foul mood, not least because he and Washington had been royally chewed out by the captain.

Harrison had always been taught that you didn't learn from your mistakes, you denied them. ''He used verbal and physical abuse on me!''

''Shut the fuck up, or you will spend the next three years chipping paint in Deck Division!'' growled Carter. Harrison finally shut up. Carter went on talking in a more reasonable manner. ''Nobody is writing up anybody. Harrison, if I hear anything about this from you, you will be brought up on charges of dereliction of duty and the murder of that man who died on the helicopter. I shit you not, if you want to go to Leavenworth, say one more word about this!''

That finally sank in with Harrison. ''OS1 Ingalls, I believe OS3 Harrison needs further instruction in using the Spa-48. Make sure he gets at least two extra hours of training a day after normal working hours. Harrison, you are now responsible for cleaning the passageways outside CIC. You also will be cleaning our berthing for the next month.''

That almost got a response from Harrison. Then he looked at the other three people in the room and stayed quiet.

Washington tried to think of what you could do about people who used the ''punk'' defense. The idea of beating him bloody with a dogging wrench kept popping into her head. Senior Chief Carter looked over at her. ''Anything to add, ma'am?''

''Just one other thing, Senior Chief. Harrison, before you get any stupid ideas about a letter to the CO, keep in mind that his promotion was riding on that pickup. It's your fault it went wrong, and he will not be sympathetic with any letters you write to him. The senior chief is absolutely correct about us being able to charge you with murder. So for once in your ignorant life, stop being hard-headed, start listening, and learn how to do your job. Dismissed.'' Harrison left. Washington looked at the two men. ''Do you think he'll learn anything?''

''Why learn when you can make excuses?'' OS1 Ingalls answered. He closed his eyes and rubbed his forehead. ''Man, I am so tired of these punks coming in off the streets.''

''We'll bring him along.'' Senior Chief Carter got up, headed for the door. ''Or we'll bust his skinny little butt into deck division. OS1, I know it was an extreme situation, but with all these jailhouse lawyers we got, you have to remember, keep control of your temper at all times.'' Carter left. Ingalls slumped into a chair.

Washington spoke. ''So what do you think, OS1?''

''I think that little punk should have been washed out in basic training. Do you know how hard it is to wash someone out of basic? Other than for drugs?'' Washington shook her head. ''When I was an instructor at Great Lakes, we had people recycled through basic training six, seven times. Sooner or later, even the dumbest recruit realizes all he has to do to graduate is keep his mouth shut for a month or two. Then they go out to the fleet and, what, they magically become good sailors?'' Ingalls shook his head. ''No, they pull the same shit, and ruin everybody else's work while they do it. Man, I'm glad I have retirement in six months.''

''This ship won't be the same without you, Black Bart.''

Ingalls grinned. ''You bet it won't.''

The Seasprite's engine sent a deafening wave of noise through the air of the cabin, counterpointed by the pounding of the rotors. The whole helicopter shook and rattled in flight, the interior of the cabin dimly lit by red lights that protected the occupant's night vision. In a corner of the passenger compartment, Majors huddled in the blanket the search and rescue (SAR) swimmer had given him, leaned back against the cabin walls. The SAR swimmer, still in his wet suit, sat next to him.

An older man in khakis tapped Majors on the shoulder and shouted over the noise, "We'll be on *Kimmel* in ten minutes! Do you want some coffee?" Majors nodded. The man pulled out a huge, battered old thermos, poured a mug of coffee, produced a small silver flask, and offered it. Majors nodded vigorously, watched as his benefactor added a generous dollop of something to the coffee. Then he took it and drank, welcome heat spreading through his body. Brandy flavored the coffee.

"I thought Navy ships were dry!" he shouted.

The man in khaki, Chief Hamner, grinned. "We are! That's just old fruit juice! Yo, MacKenzie, you want some?" He turned to the SAR swimmer. "You don't get the fruit juice, though!"

"Thanks Chief! Coffee's okay!" It was curious, Majors thought, everybody having to yell just to be heard. The swimmer pulled the headpiece of his wet suit off, gratefully took the cup of coffee, and drained it. Even in the dim red light, Majors noted the man didn't look like a MacKenzie. More like he ought to be on the Great Plains, hunting buffalo. Thick-boned, strong features, straight black hair, dark eyes, jutting nose.

With the odd, out-of-place curiosity that seemed to rule his life, Majors asked, "Was one of your parents Indian?"

The swimmer shrugged, grinned. "Both of them were, I guess. I'm adopted. My adoptive parents are the MacKenzies. Why?"

Majors shook his head. "No good reason. Thanks for saving my life. I was getting nervous back there!" He shook hands with Mackenzie, looked up as the Chief tapped his shoulder for attention.

"If you want to look, *Kimmel*'s just off to our left!" Chief Hamner stowed away his coffee thermos. The flask had disappeared. Both men looked out the side window of the helicopter.

Majors's first thought was that someone had a Christmas ornament dangling out the window. Then he realized he was looking at the running lights of a ship, so far below it looked like a toy. Three lights outlined the ship, framing a small square of pale lights towards its end. Then the helicopter turned so that he couldn't see it. "Strap in!" bellowed Chief Hamner. "Be a shame to get this far and then break your neck landing, wouldn't it?"

He helped Majors strap himself in. Then all they could do was sit in the noisy, vibrating, red lit space that had become their world. Majors tried hard not to think of how small the ship had looked from the air.

In the pilot's seat, Lt. Mary Steiner tried to suppress memories of another night, to concentrate on the tiny square of lights to her front. She was a tall, slender woman, with curly hair tied back severely and watchful brown eyes. Thoughts of smashing into the sea kept popping into her mind. She gritted her teeth, tried not to overcontrol, tried to smooth out the flight of the helicopter.

Beside her, Ensign Freeman watched the controls nervously, listening to chatter from the control tower. They had observed radio silence when they went out on the rescue. It wouldn't do to tip off the Libyans that they had an interest in this wreck, or that any survivors were rescued. Now, close in, short-range communications were possible. "Kilo One, this is Kilo Three. We have a package. Over." He looked over at Steiner. She was fighting the controls, her whole body tense, fear in her eyes. She never talked about what had happened to her on *America*, but he knew she had been trapped in a helicopter crash.

The destroyer's flight deck was approximately half again the size of a convenience store parking lot, which in itself wasn't too bad. It did make both pilots miss the vast expanse of a carrier's flight deck. What made it really difficult was that *Kimmel* had to maintain speed to keep control of maneuvering. Its huge, boxy superstructure seemed to have been designed by people who were trying to see how far they could defy the laws of aerodynamics and still have something that would move. That structure caused vast updrafts to swirl around it as the ship moved, leaving pilots the added joy of having to find the narrow aisle of calm air that remained for anyone trying to land.

"Kilo Three, this is Kilo One, confirm. You have the package? Over."

Freeman took off the radio headset. "Ma'am, do you want me to take the stick? I think the tower wants to talk to you."

"Don't bullshit me, Freeman," growled Steiner. "Tell the tower I'm ready for the green light. I've made plenty of night landings." Both pilots could now see a red light on the control tower and the signal lights held by the ground controller. Freeman would have felt a lot steadier if the Chief was guiding them in rather than sitting in the back, taking care of their charge.

Steiner would have felt a lot steadier if she never had to fly at night again.

Her subconscious was whispering in her ear as she struggled to control the helicopter. It told her what would happen next. Just like before. A sudden cabin fire. The horizon would turn sideways as the helicopter slammed into the sea tumbling in updrafts and crosswinds. She would be slammed into the windshield, whipped from side to side as they crashed. Then the water would pour in, dark and cold, filling the cabin before she could take a breath. Her safety harness would jam—

She pushed the fear to the back of her mind, fought it as she fought the crosswinds. Hating the fear, hating the way the stick tried to jerk out of her hands, she kept control and brought her charges in.

The signal light went green. "Green light!" Freeman called into the radio. "We're coming in!"

A sudden gust of air jerked the helicopter to the right. "Don't worry about landing!" Hamner was shouting to be heard, the red lights giving a satanic cast to his glee. "I've gone over this with our ground control a million times! He'll do it right, even if he did lose his last one!" Panicked, Majors stared at the Chief, who shrugged. "Hey, anybody can make a mistake!"

"We didn't lose the whole helicopter, Chief!" chimed in MacKenzie. "They salvaged most of it! Shame how the crew got all mashed up, though! But it wasn't Roswell's fault he guided them into those wires!" Majors stared in panic at MacKenzie as the helicopter dropped twenty feet.

Hamner shook his head, glanced out the window. "I hate these night helo landings! That's where all the crashes happen!" Another air pocket, another heart-stopping drop. Hamner pulled a thin, flat can from one pocket, unrolled the top with a key. The smell from it made Majors's stomach churn even worse. "Do you want something to eat?" He offered the can to the terrified CIA agent. "Sardines with mustard! Good stuff!"

Slam! They hit something solid. Outside, red lights came on. "Damn! We're going in!" shouted the Chief. Majors struggled with his straps, trying to escape before the helicopter exploded or sank—then looked at the SAR swimmer and the Chief. Both grinned back at him.

Which was when he noticed that the helicopter had stopped moving. Mostly.

Suddenly, all he could do was laugh right along with them.

He whooped with laughter, nervous tension pouring out, laughing until he cried. When he could speak again, he shook his head. "You sons of—"

The Seasprite's door was thrown open. Sure hands unfastened belts and guided him out of the helicopter towards a small, red-rimmed door. Around him, he could see people in multicolored turtleneck shirts running up as the helicopter wound down. All night vision gone, he simply stepped into the red glow. It was the door to an aircraft hanger, lit by more red lamps, like the helicopter had been. Thunderous cheers shook the room. He saw dozens of sailors against the opposite walls watching him come in. They cheered as they saw him, whistling and clapping and throwing hats in the air. A trim, athletic man in khakis walked up to him and shook his hand. "Welcome aboard the USS *Kimmel*! I'm Commander Matt Reisling, the CO. Follow me."

The next few minutes were a jumble in Majors's memory, passing dozens of dungaree-clad sailors, surrounded by a wedge of khaki-clad men and women, passing through a tangle of narrow, red-lit hallways that passed through small doors every twenty feet. Majors stubbed his feet three times and banged his head twice before he figured out that there were watertight doors in steel walls, raised up from the floor and lowered from the ceiling.

By the time he realized that, he was in a small room. A desk was against one wall, a table against the other. Through a door, he saw a bed that suddenly looked very inviting, as well as a small bathroom. Normal lights were turned on, blindingly bright after the dim red illumination of the passageways. Four khaki-clad individuals were in the room with him. The door shut. Sudden quiet.

For a second, no one had anything to say. Majors noted that they all looked at him as if he were a hard-won prize. Which he guessed he was. "Hello. I'm Vince Majors, CIA. I sure hope you're my pickup."

Everybody laughed at that one, Reisling most of all. Majors noted he had silver oak leaves on his collars. Reisling spoke. "We just hope you're *our* CIA agent. It's always so embarrassing to pick up the wrong secret agent!" More chuckles. "If you don't mind, I'd like to introduce my staff." He introduced the XO and OPS and Guns and each of them had a name, but in Majors's present state he simply noted that everybody seemed to have swapped their names for acronyms.

When introductions were done, the XO stepped forward.

"We're standing by to transmit your information," Lieutenant Commander Kendricks said slowly, observing the man's exhaustion. "Have you sorted out the information yet?"

Majors nodded, tore open the plastic bag, and burrowed into the gym bag. He produced a map from it. "Could I borrow a magic marker?" One was handed to him. He marked the map, handed it to Kendricks. "Here you go. Langley should be able to produce satellite photos of it on demand. I was told the terrorists have around fifty effectives there."

Kendricks jotted the numbers down in a little green notebook. "Will they be ready for us? Do they know that we know?"

Majors shook his head. "Negative. Abood—my contact—was not directly associated with the effort. He heard about it from someone else and stole this information without being caught. I'd recommend you steer clear of the crash site, to avoid tipping the Libyans off that we have any interest in this."

Reisling nodded. "Already done."

Majors leaned back. Kendricks spoke. "I'll have the

radio shack send this out ASAP. Anything else?''

''Could I have the map back when you're done? I want to keep this stuff together if possible.''

''Certainly. Good evening, Agent Majors.'' Kendricks left.

Majors looked back at the other three smiling faces. ''What happened to the pickup? Didn't they authorize you to use force to protect us?''

Reisling shook his head. ''I'm afraid your pilot did his evasive flying maneuvers too well. Flying under radar as he did, we didn't pick him up until the Libyan jets had locked onto him. By then, it was too late.''

Majors noted the anxious glance that the black woman—Guns, Reisling had called her—shot at the CO. Was there more to this than they were telling him? Well, too late now.

Reisling sat down at the only other chair in the room. ''You've got to be tired. Are you hungry? I could have the galley send up some food, coffee, whatever. Or would you rather get some sleep?''

''Food sounds good, then sleep,'' answered Majors. He rubbed his forehead. ''Could I get some dry clothes?''

Reisling nodded, smiling. ''Already taken care of. OPS, have the galley send up sandwiches and coffee, whatever they've got. I'm sure the two of you have a lot to do.'' Guns and OPS left. Reisling went on, every inch of the genial host. ''This is my inport cabin. You'll stay here while you're on *Kimmel*. Our master at arms will post someone at the door to keep crewmen from bothering you. You're free to move around the ship. Your escort can take you anywhere on the ship.''

Reisling opened a drawer heaped with clothes—underwear, unmarked khakis, etc. ''Our supply officer drew several sets of clothes for you. We didn't know your sizes, so we put in some of everything. Take what you need. While you're aboard *Kimmel*, please wear the khakis. This is a military vessel and uniformity is important. The khakis will keep our bluejackets from bothering you. Uhm, bluejackets are junior enlisted personnel. We've got some outstanding people on board, but there are always a few who would get distracted. Here's a little souvenir of your stay on our ship." He handed Majors a navy blue baseball cap, with "USS *Kimmel*" and the outline of the ship embroidered in gold on it. Reisling had a similar one, with gold braid stitched into the brim.

Reisling collected his thoughts. "Our supply officer also broke out six pairs of flight deck boots, again of varying sizes. I'm sure one pair should fit. All footwear on the ship must have steel toes for safety purposes, so please don't wear your civilian shoes."

Majors looked at his two-hundred-dollar Italian shoes still dripping salt water. Ruined. He shook his head. "Thank you. I guess I should change out of these. Does your ship have a laundry, or . . . ?"

Reisling laughed at that. "We can even starch and press your clothes. But if what you're wearing needs to be dry-cleaned, you're out of luck."

The CIA agent looked at his silk shirt and suit. He'd dressed formally before leaving the embassy, trying to mislead people as to his purposes in going out. "I'll just toss this. I can bill the Agency for it."

Reisling got up, shook Majors's hand one more time, said a few more words of welcome, then departed. Alone, Majors undressed. Once he had dumped his soaking clothes, he towel-dried himself, dressed in his new clothes, then pulled out the papers Abood had brought and began studying them.

"Ravioli? Ugh!" Seaman Apprentice Mitchell looked at what was left of the midnight rations—mid-rats—and made a face.

Halloran refrained from throwing the serving of ravioli into his face. "It's what we have left. Everybody stayed up to watch that CIA agent come on board. Do you want it or not?"

Mitchell muttered and left with an empty tray.

"I'll take that as a no." Halloran dumped the ravioli back in the pan. Mid-rats had been hell tonight. Normally only the watchstanders and the most dedicated chow hounds stayed up until mid-rats. The people in Supply and Administration didn't stand any watches, so they tended to stay up late if anything was going on. Tonight it had been all of them, plus the air detachment, and what seemed like half the crew. Podlogar had used the last measure of desperation of a mess specialist—he'd opened the ravioli. Whatever brand the military used, it was a tasteless, vile mess that Chef Boyardee wouldn't have touched with a ten-foot spoon.

Well, they were almost done. Mills was cleaning up in the back. Podlogar had just been called away by OPS. The chow line was gone.

Correction. The chow line had one more member. Seaman Woodall stepped into the galley and picked up a tray. As always, Halloran let his gaze rest on the statuesque blonde for a moment, drinking in her beauty. For the thousandth time, he considered making a pass at her. For the thousandth time he reminded himself, shipboard relationships were poison. Whoever got dumped first invariably tried to make life hell for the other. Since women had joined the crew, it had been one long soap opera.

As he looked at Woodall now, though, he noticed she seemed more depressed than was usual for the crew. "Hey Woodall, is something the matter? All that damage control stuff wearing you down?"

She shook her head. She still hadn't met his eyes as she spoke. "No. Uh, just give me whatever you have." As always, her soft southern accent made his heart skip a beat.

Halloran spooned out some ravioli, added a serving of corn. ''We've got bread and jelly. The peanut butter ran out fifteen minutes ago.'' She nodded silently. ''Woodall, if you ain't complaining about a crappy menu like that, something is wrong. What's up?''

She looked up, angry. ''Leave me alone!'' She stomped off.

Halloran watched her leave with mixed thoughts. A corner of his mind that hadn't changed since adolescence still noted that Navy dungaree slacks had an uncanny ability to fit every magnificent curve on the right woman. The practical side of his mind told him he had enough problems on his own plate, that he couldn't force anybody to accept help from him if they didn't want it. The final portions of his mind noted that Podlogar had come back to the mess line.

''Halloran, we're closed! OPS wants us to send a plate up to that CIA agent. What have we got?''

Okay, Podlogar was tripping. ''Not much. Ravioli, some corn, bread, jelly—''

Podlogar shook his head. ''No good. Follow me.'' They ducked back into the galley. The other mess crank on duty, Mills, had just finished cleaning up. ''Mills, grab a pitcher of bug juice and a pitcher of coffee.''

''But I just cleaned all the pitchers!''

''Do it!'' The mess specialist opened the meat locker, took out a canned ham, started up the meat slicer, and started slicing off thick slabs of ham. ''Halloran, go to Malone, get some of whatever he has that's done. Get the mustard and mayo from the ward room mess while you're at it.''

Halloran got the items. MS2 Malone, the night baker, had just finished a tray of cinnamon rolls. Halloran snagged two. When he got back, Podlogar was already making up the sandwiches. ''Why aren't the wardroom cranks doing this? This secret agent's their guest.''

''Because OPS would have to find the wardroom

cranks and wake them up!'' Podlogar added an apple and some carrot sticks to the tray. Mills returned with two pitchers, plus some sugar and creamer. ''Sure hope this guy likes ham. Halloran, you better take it to him. He's in the captain's inport cabin.''

Halloran picked up the tray, looked at the opened, partially sliced canned ham near the meat slicer. ''Are you going to cut the rest of that ham? If you don't serve it, you'll just have to throw it away. The people out there for mid-rats would eat it up.''

''Fuck 'em.'' Podlogar had, Halloran noted, made a sandwich for himself.

''I'll get it,'' said Mills, picking up the ham and starting the meat slicer. ''It'll be good to have something decent for mid-rats.''

Halloran took the tray and wound his way through the passageways. The mess decks were lit with regular fluorescents. His eyes took a second to adjust to the red light of the passageways at night. A gunner's mate was waiting outside the Captain's inport cabin. ''This where we have our secret agent?''

''Yeah. You got a spare sandwich there?'' Halloran looked at the tray. Podlogar had made three ham sandwiches, which did seem a little much. He nodded to the gunner's mate, who grabbed one. Then he knocked on the door.

''Come in.''

Halloran went in. The CIA agent was an unremarkable man on the younger side of middle age, strongly built, with a mustache and longish hair. Dressed in unmarked khakis, he was sitting at the desk reading papers and looking at photographs. ''Sir, I hope you like ham. I also brought coffee, bug juice—that's navy-ese for Kool-aid—an apple, some other stuff. If you have any requests . . .''

''No, that's fine.'' Without looking up from his papers, the CIA agent shoved a coffee cup towards Halloran. "Could you give me some coffee? No cream, four sugars."

Halloran made the coffee, looked over the agent's shoulder as he handed it to the man. He saw something he recognized in one picture. "Hey, an M-48A5! I thought these guys were Libyan!"

That got Majors's attention. He fixed an annoyed glare on Halloran. "These are Libyan. And that's an M-60 tank. I think the terrorists are using it for training."

"Wonder where they got it." Halloran looked at the picture again, then shook his head. "No, that's an M-48A5 main battle tank. It doesn't have a fifty-caliber cupola on the top—it'd look like a little, miniature turret." It was an overhead view. Halloran looked closer. "Look at the front slope of the chassis. It's curved instead of being a straight line."

Major looked a little less annoyed. "Any other differences?"

Halloran shrugged. "Depends. If it's American, then the coaxial machine gun—the one mounted inside the turret—is a piece of garbage called the M-219. The world's finest single-shot machine gun. If it's German, they'd have an MG-3 in it. Good equipment. There are mounts for light machine guns on the loaders and track commander's hatches—the ones on the turret. What we used to call "John Wayne" mounts, ones you have to expose yourself to fire. A diesel pack, 105mm rifled cannon, pretty decent night vision gear—all infrared though. It's not too different form a regular M-60."

"How do you know?"

"I was in the Army National Guard for a while. I crewed M-48A5s, then retrained on the M-1 Abrams."

Majors nodded, smiled. "Okay, thanks. I'll pass your information on." He sipped the coffee, slumped back in his chair. "Jeez, what a day!"

Halloran nodded and glanced at the floor. Then he

looked again at the small heap of boots. "Holy cow! Are those flight deck boots yours?"

Majors glanced over at the boots. Five pairs remained of what the Captain had left there. "Uh, your skipper left them here. One pair of them fits me. Why, are they something special?"

Halloran picked up one pair lovingly. "Man, these things are impossible to get. They cost ninety bucks at the PX. The soles are insulated against electricity and fuel, they have steel toes, they're reinforced—these are the only things I've seen the Navy has that are better than the Army. I've been trying to scam a pair of these for months. I only have one pair of boondockers left, and they're about beat to hell."

Majors chuckled at the naked greed in the sailor's eye. "Tonight's your lucky night. Grab a pair, if you can find any that fit you."

"Man, this is great! Thanks!" Halloran searched through the boots, picked out a pair that fit, laced them, and put them on. Majors really looked at him for the first time. The sailor had silver-gray hair and an older face than most he'd seen on this ship. Yet there were no stripes on his sleeve.

"Are you an NCO here?" asked Majors.

"Nah. Just an ex-paratrooper who was stupid enough to join the Navy. Now I'm studying to be a gunners mate, if they ever let me out of deck division." Halloran stomped the boots on gleefully, and tied the laces. "Great! Once I get these broken in . . ." He looked up at Majors, smiled. "Thanks. I appreciate this."

Majors nodded. "You're welcome. Now get out of here so I can get some work done. It looks bad if I let some ex-anybody do my photo intel, capish?" The gray-haired seaman nodded and left. Majors went back to his studying, grabbed one of the sandwiches, and took a hefty bite. He smiled. It had been a while since he'd had ham. Then he sipped his coffee and went back to work.

* * *

Kimmel cruised onward through the night, watchstanders at their stations. Radio messages burned up the airwaves as information was relayed.

At Norfolk, it was just past midnight when Seal Team Six gathered for the first briefing on the upcoming operation. In Libya, the commander of coastal defenses informed the Great Leader the American imperialist pigs had turned away from the coast, and that the search helicopters had found no survivors of the crash. In a base camp ten miles in from the coast, thirty-two people shivered in the cold night air, locked in stone buildings. North of Malta, on the aircraft carrier USS *Thomas Jefferson*, the captain ordered all strike aircraft loaded. If the operation kicked off early, *Jeff* would be ready.

On the bridge of *Kimmel*, watch section two was standing the dog watch, the watch that followed the midwatch. All was dark outside. The only lights on the bridge were the dim red and green lights of the controls. In the center of the bridge stood the helmsman, steering the ship, and the lee helmsman, who talked to the engine room, controlling the speed of the ship. The quartermaster of the watch kept track of their location on the charts while central relayed reports from CIC over sound-powered phones. The bosuns mate of the watch, bosuns mate third class ''Skater'' Mayes, read the POD for the upcoming day. The messenger of the watch was on a vital mission.

The only two individuals on the bridge of higher rank than a third class petty officer were the officer of the deck (OOD), Ensign Pullman, and OOD-UI (under instruction) Ensign Milt Jeffries.

''Helm!'' said Pullman, carefully gauging his voice so that it wouldn't be heard in the CO's at-sea cabin near the bridge. ''Right five degrees rudder, steer course 315.''

The helmsman, five months out of boot camp, repeated the orders, exactly like she'd been trained. "Right five degrees rudder, come to course 315, aye, sir." She adjusted the helm and watched the ship's heading begin to shift. "Sir, my rudder is right five degrees, coming to course 315." A few moments later, she gently straightened the rudder, checked the magnetic compass that kept track of the ship's heading, and compared it with the inertial compass, that tracked the location of true north, rather than magnetic north. "Steady on course 315, sir. Course 315 checks 317 true."

"See?" whispered Jeffries, so only Pullman could hear. "Even you couldn't screw that up."

"Annapolis pansy," muttered Pullman, grinning.

"That's Lieutenant J. G. Annapolis pansy, thank you very much," answered Jeffries. "Don't you ROTC pukes know anything?"

Pullman chuckled, picked up his binoculars, and scanned the ocean. They both stood there, bored out of their minds. Jeffries smiled and said in a low tone, "This is a drill, this is a drill. Happiness, happiness! Outbreak of morale on the mess decks. Morale suppression teams, report to despair locker two."

Pullman grinned, picking up the game. "Now deploying OPS. OPS deployed, time: 0215."

"Morale out of control on the mess decks. OPS not effective."

"Deploying CO, time: 0217. Morale suppression team one is at morale."

"CO is effective. Morale has been suppressed."

"Morale suppressed, time: 0218. Set rehappiness watch with OPS."

"Rehappiness watch set. Have morale suppre—"

The door to the bridge opened. Red lights from the passageway flashed briefly. Then the door closed and was dogged shut. The smell of fresh-baked bread wafted across the bridge.

"H-how many l-l-loaves you get?" asked BM3

Mayes, the BMOW, trying to see in the dark.

"Two loaves, and butter, G-Money!" answered Chambers. "Trust the maestro of the hookup!" Chambers dug out his knife, carved off a chunk of bread and spread a thick slice of butter on it. Still hot, the bread began melting the butter almost instantly. "Hey, Skater, since I done so good, what you say I stay on as messenger of the watch for the next hour?"

"Hey, Skater!" whined Mayes in an imitation of Chambers's bantering tone. "You know y'all overdue for rotation. Get to port lookout!"

Chambers stomped off to the port door from the bridge. "Ugly, ungrateful, no-shave-chit-havin'—" His voice was cut off as the door to the port bridge wing slammed shut.

Mayes took a slice of bread and butter, bit into it, rubbed deeply stubbled cheeks as he mumbled, "I got me a no-shave chit, motherfucker, and two more stripes than you!" Mayes's permanently stubbled cheeks were testimony to a permit he had filled out by the ship's medics every week.

One by one, everyone on the bridge helped themselves to the fresh-baked bread and butter. At two AM, anything tasted good, and fresh baked bread was one of the few advantages of spending most of your deployment at sea. The bread from *Kimmel*'s bakery was a heavy, faintly sweet loaf and more than one crewman skipped meals by picking up three or four slices of the bread and some butter.

The door to the bridge opened again in a brief flash of red light before it shut. Mayes didn't bother to look, knowing it had to be the new relieved aft lookout. "Took you a long-ass time gettin' up here!"

"Not as long as you might think," answered the CO's voice.

Mayes jumped, tried to bark "Captain on—" but inhaled when he should have exhaled and began choking on a piece of bread. He coughed furiously.

"Captain on the bridge!" called the helmsman, newly rotated onto the helm. He grinned at Mayes in the darkness as the struggling BM3 cleared his throat.

"As you were," snapped Reisling, watching his BMOW to see if he would have to perform the Heimlich maneuver on the man. Mayes eventually got control of his wayward food. "Boats, are you going to be okay?" Mayes nodded, still crouched down, no longer gagging. Reisling shook his head, grinned, felt rather than saw Jeffries and Pullman walk up to him.

"Good evening, sir. What's going on? Is there an emergency?"

Reisling nodded with satisfaction. "No emergency. I just decoded our orders. The SEAL team doing the rescue will stage off *Kimmel*. We will provide fire support for it, in and out. We're going to rendezvous with *Savannah* for underway replenishment at 0330 hours. We'll move reveille up too. That'll give our people more time to prepare for the SEALs. I want those SEALs to see a clean ship, ready for action. I also want CIC doing nonstop drills."

"What time do the SEALs arrive, sir?"

"1630 hours tomorrow. Plenty of time. Roust out deck division and make sure the gear is laid out for underway replenishment. Then wake me when we rendezvous with *Savannah*. I'm going to grab a little sleep." Reisling left the bridge.

"Captain off the bridge!" gasped Mayes.

"Shit!" muttered Villanueva. The two ensigns went to work.

Chapter Three

He woke in the darkness.

Swimming up through the muzziness of sleep, Halloran stared into the dark. Around him he could hear the endless whirring of the fans, sense other men in other racks. The dark was always there, always waiting in the guts of the ship, down where the crew slept. Lights could come on, could banish it to the corners where it would wait. But deep within the ship, the dark always waited.

Finally he forced himself to move, turned on the light in his watch: 0345 hours. Almost two hours left to sleep. He smiled, turned to go back to sleep as the light in his watch went out, leaving him in a darkness that had become warm and welcoming.

"Now man all unrep stations! Now man all unrep stations! Prepare for underway replenishment, port side!"

Lights came on to a chorus of groans. There was a wan tone to the fluorescents, as if they weren't sure they should be on at this hour. The 1MC loudspeaker in the corner blared again. *"Now man all unrep stations. The ship will be approaching* Savannah, *port side!"*

Halloran climbed up the last ladder from deck berthing, took a right turn and stepped out onto the quarterdeck. After the air-conditioned interior of the ship, stepping out into the humid Mediterranean night was like walking into a warm, wet sponge. Around him, other sailors, chiefs, and officers stumbled over the decks in the darkness, stepping over gear laid out to precise instructions.

Halloran joined a file of men and women, indistinguishable in their baggy dungarees and the dark.

Waiting in line, he grimaced as acid churned in his stomach, his eyelids still heavy with sleep. For a moment, the world went hazy around him. A warning of extreme exhaustion. Nothing new. When his turn came at the front of the line, he took a life vest and safety helmet. He donned both, the vest still cool and damp from the last time it had been used. He reached into his life vest and broke out a chem stick, twisted it until it glowed and clipped it to his vest. Then he headed for his place for the underway replenishment, midships line #2.

Supplies and fuel are used up at sea. Port visits take time and money. A warship can only use friendly or neutral ports, though its very mission requires it to operate off hostile shores. The answer is underway replenishment, or UNREP. Any Navy ship can resupply any other Navy ship, cruising alongside each other and transferring fuel and supplies by helicopter, cable, and winch. UNREPs let Navy ships operate for months at a time without touching shore. UNREP keeps the machines functioning, fueled and maintained. Admirals and strategists love it. Halloran repeated all these facts to himself as he walked, trying not to think about how much he hated it. As did most people who actually had to do

UNREPs. UNREPs were what you got instead of port calls.

Halloran arrived at his place and sat down on the deck among the other line handlers for that station. Sea spray on the deck soaked his pants instantly. He ignored it, looked at the people around him. Some were nodding off as they sat on the wet decks, others were talking in low tones. A hundred yards away, *Savannah* matched course and speed with *Kimmel*. Work lights cast reflections on the water, shadows between the lights spotted by the firefly glow of chem lights clipped to other sailors. The crashing of the sea against the ships grew louder as they closed. An alarm echoed across the waters.

The two ships matched speeds, the massive bulk of the supply ship alongside the sleek lines of the destroyer. Halloran, his mind wandering, envied the bridge crew for a moment. While he waited in the sea spray, far above him they were dry, conning the ship, manning signal gear and carefully judging course and speed.

In the shrinking space between *Kimmel* and *Savannah*, curling waves seemed frozen into immobility by the movement of the ships. Whistles and shouted orders echoed between the ships. BM3 Mayes, boss of the line handlers for this station, clapped his hands loudly. "Get up! Everybody get under cover! Check your buddies! Make sure your boots is bloused and your vests is tight!" Mayes watched his line handlers get under cover.

Halloran and the other sailors filed back into the ship for safety while shot lines were fired from ship to ship. Gunner's mates with shot lines in their rifles stepped onto the deck. One gunner's mate was a tall, black-haired, hook-nosed first class named Shawcross. Rifle in hand, he leaned in the door and grinned at Halloran. "Halloran, you're striking gunner's mate! Do you want to fire the lead line over to *Savannah*? The Army taught you to shoot, didn't it?"

Halloran grinned and stood up. "No sweat! Is it okay if I put that line through the captain's porthole?" Cheerful now, he stepped forward.

"Negits!" Mayes stepped in front, blocked him from the door. "You ain't no gunner's mate yet, Halloran! You still in deck division! GMG1, Halloran's on my line handling detail, not yours!" Halloran's smile instantly vanished. He glared at Mayes. The BM3 glared back.

Shawcross almost said something, but was called out onto the decks to make his shot, and vanished in the darkness. Mayes snapped, "Set your old ass down, Halloran! You still on my detail!" Then he went back to looking over his detail, making sure everyone had their gear on right.

Brief images of smashing Mayes's face flashed through Halloran's head. Then he thought about having to spend the rest of his hitch in deck division if he did so. He bit back words, clenched his fists, and sat down.

Outside, whistles blew. Rifles banged and popped, firing the orange lead lines over to the other ship. "Move!" barked Mayes. "Get the line! Get out on the deck!"

Halloran scrambled out onto the decks with the other sailors, over decks slick with spray. He saw Mayes grab the lead line from Shawcross and tie a heavier line to it as the line was pulled over to the other ship. The process was repeated at each station, progressively heavier lines being passed. Soon, a web of lines was strung, bouncing and skipping over the waves churned between the two ships. Ropes fed through block and tackle, streaming water from where they had been doused.

Halloran knew phone lines were being run from ship to ship, for men who would gauge the distances between the two ships from deck level and bridge. Each phone line was backed up by a second phone line in case the first one broke. Signalmen with flags waited, in case the phones went out. But those were for other details. His detail hauled on wet, inch-thick nylon cables run through pulleys.

"Heave!" called Mayes.

"Heave!" The line handlers repeated in unison, hauling on the line. A pallet of supplies tied to the cable began sliding towards *Kimmel*, swinging back and forth on the ropes. As he hauled on the heavy rope, chanting "Heave!" with the crew, Halloran saw cranes feed over fuel lines from the tender. Every line, every pull, every signal was done according to formulae worked out over decades and laid out in dozens of manuals. Sailors on the decks grimaced through the sea spray in their eyes, cursed their work, and tried not to step off their ship in the dark.

Fuel shot through the hoses into the tanks of *Kimmel*. The first pallet came across, was pulled onto the deck and broken open, giving the line handlers a brief break. Halloran saw the pallet pulled off to one side and broken down, to be passed into the ship by a daisy chain of other sailors. He picked up the line as he saw a second pallet prepared on *Savannah*.

The process was repeated over and over. Even in the muggy night, sailors grew chilled with spray. Halloran's arms burned with exhaustion after the first dozen pallets, while he and the other line handlers listened closely to the line as it creaked and groaned.

If the ships surged forward or back, they might part the lines. The nylon cables would snap back with power that could cut clean through a man's body. So everyone listened to the ropes for the musical "pings" from the line that would be their warning that the lines were about to part.

Finally, it was done. Signals were given, flags raised and lowered. Lines were passed back in reverse order, heavier lines pulling back lighter lines until the lead lines skipped back over the waves. As dawn rose over the ocean, the two ships cut away from each other. Halloran watched *Savannah* break away and sail off, wished he was on it, or anywhere other than where he was. Then he shuffled off, first to stow away his life jacket and safety gear, then to get breakfast.

Another day had begun on USS *Kimmel.*

Commander Matt Reisling was a happy man as he picked up the microphone that would carry his voice throughout the ship. His ship. *"Good morning, straight shooters!"*

In the decks below, men and women paused to listen as his eager voice echoed over the loudspeakers.

Reisling contemplated the flaming dawn that lit the sky to starboard. *"That was an outstanding UNREP this morning. I talked with the CO of* Savannah. *He says we were one of the sharpest crews he's worked with on this deployment.*

*"We've got a busy day. I know we're all tired. We'd like to take it easy after the pickup last night. But we still have a mission to support. I can confirm some of the scuttlebutt you've been hearing—*Kimmel *is going to be the staging vessel for a hostage rescue operation into Libya!"* Reisling looked at the stunned faces of his bridge crew and enjoyed the shock.

"I know we're all excited about this, but let's not let it get to us. We have to be ready for this mission. After that, we're on our way back to the States, and we want Kimmel *looking good. We have to paint the weather decks and do a freshwater washdown. Our helo crew will be practicing touch and go landings today. We're going for a squadron record here, so I need our flight deck crew to outdo themselves on this! Some spaces are looking a little shaky. Finally, engineering will be conducting Beckies today."*

Beckies were simulated engineering failures. They involved a lot of work, added to the routine maintenance carried out by the engineers, or "snipes."

"So we have a full schedule. I need everyone out there, charging hard! Once again, great UNREP, straight shooters! Kimmel *has a great reputation on the waterfront! If you keep up this work, it'll stay that way!"* Reisling put away the microphone, smiled at the BMOW, senior enlisted man of the deck personnel who stood lookout, steered the ship, and made coffee for the bridge crew. "How's it going, Boats?"

"Just fine, sir." The BMOW smiled, wishing the CO would clear the bridge so he could lean against the bulkhead. "Looking forward to going home, sir."

Reisling smiled. "Me too, Boats. Me too." What Reisling was truly looking forward to was a message. Today, tomorrow, maybe the next day. News that Commander (SW) Matt Reisling, USN, was soon to become Captain Reisling, in rank as well as position. His previous two shots at promotion had been unsuccessful, but this one was certain. Especially after an operation like this.

He'd been busting ass for two years, driving the crew of *Kimmel* through every operation he could get them into, taking advantage of every training opportunity. In the process, he'd managed to avoid making any port calls for more than two months. Granted, he missed the down time as much as anyone, but foreign port calls were guaranteed ways to end your chances for promotion. All it took was one drunken seaman hurting one local girl, and whoever was unlucky enough to command that drunken seaman's ship might as well douse his personnel folder with gasoline and light it off. So he'd kept them at sea, going from operation to operation.

Time enough for liberty when the next captain took over.

What nagged him was that, in the old days, that would have been enough. In today's Navy, a 300-ship fleet trying to meet obligations incurred by a 500-ship navy, everybody was pushing hard. Every promotion slot was bitterly fought over. If this operation had come a few months earlier, in time to go into his promotion package . . . In the back of his mind lurked the knowledge that this was his last chance. Suddenly pensive, he left the bridge.

The BMOW relaxed and called out. "Captain off the bridge!"

Seaman Halloran savored the salty flavor of the bacon, took a sip of coffee. Bitter on bitter tastes mingled. He enjoyed his quiet moment amidst the tumult of the crew's mess, his clothes still damp from sea spray. The paint spots on his hands, normally a reminder of the day's work to come, held no frustrations for him now. He had become a crank.

He had been a soldier once. Army Airborne, in the 101st "Screaming Eagles" for three years. Then he'd gotten tired of jumping out of airplanes and sleeping in the mud and left the Army to become a National Guardsman. There, he'd driven a tank over the hills of Michigan and his native Ohio for two weeks out of the year and one weekend a month, in exchange for a college scholarship. That got him the status of sergeant and unemployed college graduate.

After three years of looking for a job that paid more than minimum wage, he decided to return to the security of the regular military. But not the Army. He was going to join the Navy! He had signed up eleven months ago for three years in the Navy, to see the world and save some money. His recruiter told him no schools were available but certainly a smart guy like him would be promoted fast.

Yeah, right.

He sipped his coffee, chewed his bacon. Bitter on bitter.

The recruiter and the ads hadn't mentioned he would not get the sea pay they talked about until he became a petty officer. They had told him he would lose his NCO status from the National Guard, which was standard. What they hadn't mentioned was deck division.

Everyone who didn't have an Advanced (A) School started out in deck division, or as a fireman in engineering, or a lucky few as airmen in aviation units. Everyone who failed A-School went to deck division. Everyone who lost their rating, the skill designation which meant you were Somebody in the Navy, went to deck division. There, you did the work no other divisions wanted to do: cleaning, steering the ship, boat detail, painting, painting, and painting.

They hadn't told him that to go from deck seaman to petty officer, you had to pass four separate tests. Studying was done on your own time, when you weren't standing watches on the bridge, lookout watches, inport watches, and working from seven-thirty in the morning to five in the evening most days. Assuming you were permitted to strike out of deck division. As deck division was perpetually undermanned, that was not always possible.

Eleven months into a three-year hitch in the Navy, Seaman David Halloran sipped his coffee and brooded over the fact that he was looking forward to three months of mess cranking because it would be easier, cleaner, and more comfortable than what he'd done for the last eight months, and what he'd be doing for twenty-two months after cranking was done.

He sipped coffee and chewed bacon.

Bitter on bitter.

GMG (Gunners Mate, Guns) 1st Class Harlan Shawcross finished assembling the last M-14 rifle, then gave it one final look to ensure he hadn't missed anything. He was a tall, long-limbed man, black hair cut short, with a jutting nose he'd inherited from a Cherokee grandmother and everything else about him screaming "Missouri farmboy.'' Around him in the armory, his kingdom, the small arms assigned to *Kimmel* were in their places. Each gleamed with a light coat of oil, ready for use. Beside him steamed a cup of coffee. In the corner, his tape player softly played Waylon Jennings. All in all, he thought to himself, he was just about in Heaven.

''Shouldn't one of the seamen be doing that?'' asked a female voice from the door.

Shawcross turned to face the woman who had spoken. Lieutenant Jimmelle Washington leaned against the doorway, an ironic grin on her face. She was also his boss. ''I cut 'em loose after the UNREP. They haven't been getting much sleep lately.''

Jimmelle grimaced. ''Nobody sleeps on the *Kimmel*. Didn't you know that? Besides, sleep's bad for you.''

''Oh yeah?''

''Sure. Think about it. Everybody who's ever slept has died. Millions of people die in their sleep every year. So the Navy is just trying to protect you from the dangers of sleep.'' Shawcross had noticed Washington never talked that way around anyone else. With everyone else, she used prim and proper English. Around the officers, she was straight business, the very picture of the ambitious, respectful young officer. Around him, she spoke in the slang of the streets she'd grown up on and was disrespectful of her superiors to a degree that would have destroyed her career if they had heard it. As he agreed with most of what she said, he kept her comments to himself and recognized them as the confidences they were. In turn, she never repeated those comments in front of the junior personnel. To Shawcross, that would have been a cardinal sin.

At first it had bothered him to be bossed by a woman—a black woman at that. Not that he was prejudiced, it just took some getting used to. Her willingness to listen to his advice, and her insubordinate humor helped in that.

Shawcross laughed and put away the rifle. ''The Navy did a study. They proved that you only need three hours of sleep a night.''

''Yeah, right. What study? What people?'' Washington stepped into the office and collapsed into the chair. ''Were they all Chinese or Jamaican or something? Those people who work three jobs at night, then go to college? It's just like that vote they keep saying they took, where they had all the bluejackets vote on whether to keep the old dress uniforms that looked really dope, or go back to those goddangit ''crackerjack'' dress uniforms. I've talked with tons of people, and nobody recalls even seeing that vote. But the Navy says everybody voted for those dang-on Popeye-lookin' polyester suits.''

Shawcross shrugged and locked up the gun cabinet. ''You have ten minutes to officer's call, ma'am.''

She nodded, crossed her arms. ''I was officer of the deck when we were closing on *Savannah*. The CO of *Savannah* called over at 0330, said they were ready to UNREP, how about we start at 0700? Reisling just sat in the captain's chair and said 'Nah, wake 'em up now. It'll be good training!' Like we ain't trained after the last seven months of chasing our tails.''

Shawcross shrugged. ''Welcome to the Navy, ma'am.''

Washington nodded, stood up, and checked out her uniform. ''So did you use that wondergun of yours?''

''Why ma'am, using Amelia for an UNREP would be like hitching a race horse to plow my fields!''

''You ain't never plowed no fields and you wouldn't know one end of a horse from another,'' Washington said, grinning. ''I read your 201 file. You grew up in the 'burbs, so don't even try that 'farmboy' act with me!'' He grinned back. She looked at Shawcross's personal rifle, locked away in its own cabinet. ''I can't believe the CO ever let you bring that onboard. You *know* what happened in New Orleans. Deck division's motto was almost changed to 'Armed and Dangerous.' "

While the ship had been in drydock at New Orleans, half a dozen of the younger and dumber sailors in deck division had decided they needed handguns. Having more money than common sense, they'd bought them, then compounded the stupidity by showing them off. The result: one dishonorable discharge and a dozen "captain's masts," the nonjudicial punishment before the CO that was one step below a court-martial. The CO had made it clear there would have been more discharges if he wasn't so short of deck personnel.

Shawcross shook his head. "I got written authorization for that baby before we went to New Orleans. One match-grade Springfield Arms M-1A with glass bedded stock, heavy barrel, ten-power scope, and all the trimmings. CO signed it himself."

"Why?"

"It was before you came on, even before the yard period. We did counter-drug ops in the Caribbean. I persuaded the skipper that we should have snipers in the rigging in case we had to stop any boats."

"But that was three years ago!" Shawcross grinned. Washington shook her head. "Don't tell me no more, I don't want to know." She went to officer's call.

RM3 Darnell "Tiny" Rogers shifted in his seat and checked the encryptor as it decoded a stream of radio messages. Navy ships kept constant radio communications going, whether they had information to send or not. Thus potential enemies could not tell the state of readiness by differences in the volume of radio traffic.

Like most men with the nickname, "Tiny" Rogers was a huge man, six feet four inches tall, two hundred and ninety pounds, so large he couldn't sleep in a normal crewman's rack, using instead one of the couches in the ship's rec room. Much of him was outsize even for his large proportions. Huge arms, powerful hands, a massive expanse of chest, and a stomach far too large. His skin was dark even for a black man's, his face normally cheerful underneath close-cropped hair. Now, he looked woeful.

He looked at the door to the radio shack. Solid steel, designed to stop any enemy long enough for the radiomen to smash the mountain of classified equipment in the room. It couldn't protect him now.

The phone rang. He ignored it. There were days he wished he'd never left Philly. "Hey RM1, who are these hostages we're rescuing, anyways?" Like most of the crew, he'd been out of touch with current events for months.

The phone rang.

"They're from an Air France 767, out of Athens airport. Terrorists hijacked it three days ago." RM1 Davis was a skinny red-haired man, reading a news report the ship had picked up off shortwave. "Two days ago they released everybody except the Americans and flew over to Libya." The phone rang. "Then Khaddaffi told them he wasn't playing that game and ordered them to leave. The news reports say the terrorists flew it out over the Med and blew it up with everybody on board. I guess word isn't out yet that they're still alive." The phone rang. "Damn it Tiny, pick up the phone!"

With the air of a man going to his execution, Tiny picked up the phone at his elbow. "Radio Room, RM3 Rogers."

"Tiny, this is HM3." The voice of doom. Hospital Man Third Class Lee Springer, the closest thing *Kimmel* had to a real doctor. "You were scheduled for weigh-in and bodyfat check this morning. I hate to say it, buddy, but you have to get down here pronto. It's your third shot at this. If you aren't under bodyfat percentage, it's a discharge."

"Okay. My watch ends at 1100 hours. Can I come down then?"

"1100 hours sharp, Tiny. I'm sorry, but you dodged this bullet as long as you can. The CO asked about you. He noticed you skipped mando commandoes all this week." Springer hung up.

"Mando commandoes" were personnel who were over Navy weight standards, or had failed physical readiness tests. By order of the CO, Mandatory Physical Training ("Mando PT") was held for them every day before lunch, on the flight deck. Tiny thought back over the past month. It just seemed there was always something he needed to do whenever Mando PT was being held. Not on purpose, but . . .

He tried his old excuses. They all seemed stupid now. He just hadn't wanted to go. He could have cut down on food too. He hadn't wanted to. He'd always been heavy for his size. It just seemed so easy to put on the pounds since he'd been assigned to this ship, after his first two years in a shore billet. Now, with two years left on a six-year enlistment, he was staring an "other-than-honorable" discharge in the face because he'd been overweight for his size on the last four weigh-ins. He thought back and tried to figure out why. No sense to it.

In sudden honesty and regret, he shook his head. He looked up, saw RM1 peering at him. "That HM3, calling about your bodyfat?" Rogers nodded. "You should have seen this coming." Trust RM1 to say something comforting. "It could be worse. You could be one of those tourists. Hell, you could be in Libya."

Every day on every Navy ship begins with Officer's Call. There the officers and chiefs—the "khakis"—gather to receive the day's orders from the captain. On *Kimmel*, Officer's Call was held aft of the bridge. Following Officer's Call, each division of the crew mustered for quarters, for the orders and instructions to be passed down to them. Supply mustered on the mess decks. Engineering mustered on the fantail, the back of the ship, and so on. Deck division, those not on watch, mustered in a narrow passageway between the bosun's locker and the deck office.

In that passageway, Seaman Recruit Mark Coltrane ticked off fingers. "That's seven night UNREPS in a row. Doesn't this guy know you can do those things in the daylight too?"

"And no portcall in ten weeks," added Seaman Apprentice Lucas Toombs, "Tombstone" to his friends. Of average height, he was so powerfully built he seemed larger than he actually was. He leaned against one of the wall stanchions, standing next to Coltrane.

Coltrane was taller, his hair just a bit longer than regulation, cheerful and smiling. The child of a western farmer and a Korean mother, he was the only six-two Asian with a cowboy accent on the ship. Coltrane's build was massive, his hands scarred from the fights that had kept him a recruit for over three years. Currently, he and Toombs were trying to figure out when they would next see the exotic ports the Navy recruiters liked to promise. "So are we going to do portcall in Rota or not? Spain was pretty cool."

Toombs shook his head. "Negits to Spain. The CO volunteering us for 'Operation Dragon Hammer' killed that. We're haze-gray and underway until we see Norfolk."

"Hey, the Navy told you it'd show you the world. It just didn't mention that three-quarters of it's covered with water!" Coltrane laughed at his own joke, looked down the passageway they waited in. "Here comes Tweedledum, Tweedledumber, and Tweedledumbest."

The senior petty officers of deck division had just stepped out of the deck office, a tiny steel-walled space wedged behind the forward rope locker, just above the sonar dome. In the lead was BM1 Ramon Magsaysay, whose perpetually worried expression was partly the result of much harassment over his thick Filipino accent.

"Don't give 'em a hard time," said Toombs. "Think how bad your Tagalog would be if you had to join the Philippine Navy."

"If I was in the Philippine Navy for thirteen years, I'd speak Filipino like I was born there. He's just a rock, like Snyder." Snyder was an amiable, gangly, white BM2. Beside him was BM3 Mayes.

"We've had worse," said Dave Andrews, a tall, crazy-eyed seaman apprentice with two months left on his hitch. "Cut 'em some slack."

"Deck Division, atten-shun!" snapped BM1 Magsaysay. The twenty-odd people in the hall went to attention. "At ease." The BM1 tossed the POD to Toombs. "First Lieutenant and Chief just got done with officer's call. They say to read off the POD and they be down here by the time we finish. Seaman Tombstone, you read the POD. The rest of you, listen up."

The Plan Of the Day, or POD, was four pages of photocopied print that announced all ship's activities, watches, and shipboard evolutions. It passed messages to the crew from various officers and divisions heads. For anyone who hadn't been paying attention for the last seven months, it also listed who was captain, second in command, and so on. While changes in it were routine, it gave the crew some idea of what to get ready for, and a baseline from which to adjust to changes. With every newspaper and magazine on the ship at least two months old, it had also become very popular as crewmembers grew more desperate for something to read.

Toombs read off the POD quickly and clearly. He'd taken speech in high school and during an aborted try at college and he was proud of his vocabulary and ability to speak clearly. He took a lot of ribbing from some crewmen he referred to as "gangsta-wannabees," who gave him a hard time for what they called "talking white" and what he called using good English. But it was only words to him. They didn't dare do more. Toombs also lifted weights, and bulged with muscles as hard as his nickname.

The schedule of the day done, Toombs read various bulletins. Notes of birthdays and children born back home. A message from the Morale, Welfare, and Recreation (MWR) officer that a softball team was being formed to compete once the ship got back to Norfolk. A note from the executive officer chewing out the crew for trash found lying in ship's passageways. CHENG's (Chief of Engineering's) notice that due to excessive use of fresh water by the crew, fresh water hours would be instituted immediately, in which the crew's showers, sinks, and water fountains would have water for only a few hours each day. Mentioned so close to the announcement of a planned fresh-water washdown of the ship, this failed to have its desired chastening effect. And so on.

By the time Toombs was done, the chief and first lieutenant had arrived, fresh from officer's call.

Bosuns Mate Chief (SW/AW) Martin Stolchak was a smiling, broken-nosed old salt with the build of a fifty-five gallon drum and a shock of hair gone white so long ago, even he denied remembering what color it had been. He'd started out piloting patrol boats in the Mekong Delta. In a thirty-plus-year career broken by a decade of civilianhood, he'd been on just about everything that floated, and gone everywhere the Navy went. He knew everything, loved the Navy, loved being a chief, and was, in short, one of the people whose hard work, can-do attitude, and self-sacrifice enabled the Navy to completely disregard the welfare of its people.

The First Lieutenant (actually an Ensign) was Dan Pullman, a tall, gangly young man out of NROTC for all of six months and, in the grand Navy tradition, thrust straight from training into the most difficult slot available.

"Okay, hold it down!" bellowed Stolchak. "BM1, has the POD been read?" Magsaysay gave a thumbs-up. Stolchak nodded, flipped open his green pocket notebook, squinted at his notes from officer's call. "Here we go. OPS is bitching about the quarterdecks again, says there's rust and geedunk wrappers and pop cans everywhere." The operations officer, or OPS, was in charge of several divisions, including deck. His pet peeve was candy or "geedunk" wrappers left lying around.

"Chief, that's bullshit!" snapped Andrews. "My section did sweepers on port side this morning! OPS is yanking your chain."

"After seven months away from Norfolk, I'm ready for somebody to yank my chain!" said Stolchak, grinning. "Even Snyder's starting to look pretty good!" Laughter. "Okay, Andrews, take, uh . . ." He checked a roster. "Take Smith and Halloran and do it over again."

"Halloran started mess cranking yesterday, Chief," said Coltrane. Stolchak was one of the few "Khakis" on *Kimmel* that he actually liked.

Stolchak nodded, checked his roster again. "Now he gets a chance to spoil my food. Is he working the chief's mess? Those pissants they have in the goat locker are trying to starve me!"

"Davis says he's got a place in deep sink picked out already." That drew a cheer from the assembled deck apes.

"Rat bastard!" snorted Stolchak. "Those ass-kissers from Administration and Signals are probably getting the good jobs. Who did we get back from mess cranking?"

Snyder gave the names. The chief nodded, wrote furiously in his notebook. "We'll be doing flight operations most of the day, so you people on the crash and salvage team, be where you're supposed to be. Not hitting the ship's store for geedunk, not getting haircuts. Do that on your own time. Toombs, go with Andrews.

Green—he's on watch, right? As soon as he's relieved, he'll take over on the quarterdeck. Coltrane, you have the paint locker."

"Cool! I get to breathe fumes!"

"Not if you turn on the damn vent fan. Villanueva, do you have the vent fan running?"

"The parts are on order, chief." The damage control petty officer (DCPO) for deck division shrugged. Every division of the crew had its DCPO, who was responsible for every assembly and light in every space that belonged to that division.

"Parts are on order, my ass!" Stolchak glared at Villaneuva. "If you ain't got the hang of being DCPO after four months, maybe we need to keep you at it for another six months? Whaddya think, Big Nuts?"

"That fan'll be running by noon, Chief."

"Out-fucking-standing, Big Nuts! Keep that up and you'll be as cool as me someday! Okay, the padeyes on the bow need work. Whoever did 'em last time gundecked everything so bad, even the CO noticed." Gundecking was doing maintenance incorrectly, usually from memory. It was a cardinal sin to the Navy. "Mayes, take Chambers—"

"Commence ship's work! Sick call!" blared the 1MC.

"Crash and smash, now commence sweat-ex," muttered Coltrane.

"Flight quarters, flight quarters! All hands man your flight quarters stations! Smoking lamp is out throughout the ship! Remove all headgear outside of the skin of the ship. Weatherdecks are secured aft of frame 41. Do not throw anything over the side. Do not hang over the side." Members of the flight deck crew started moving.

"Stand fast!" snapped Stolchak. "We finish quarters first! Especially you, Coltrane! You're not on the flight crew!" A grinning Coltrane shrugged and stepped back in place. "Bledsoe, you have the bosun's locker." Stolchak rattled off assignments for the rest of deck division.

Some were cleaning, some painting, some doing maintenance. All would have to accomplish the work regardless of whether they'd gotten any sleep the night before between watches and the oh-dark-thirty UNREP. That was life in deck division.

Work assigned, Stolchak checked the list again. A lot of BS announcements, stuff that could wait for them to give him enough time for an uninterrupted quarters. Besides, he was dying for a smoke. ''That's it. You got anything for 'em, sir?'' He turned to Ensign Pullman, who shook his head, eliciting a grin from Stolchak. ''Deck division, atten-shun!'' They snapped to attention. ''Dismissed.''

Everybody got moving.

Pullman was eager as a setter on point this morning. ''Chief, I need to get my control tower qualifications signed off. Do you need me for anything?''

''Negative, sir. It's all under control here. If something comes up, I know where to find you.'' As he rolled towards deck office and the pack of unfiltered Camels that waited there, he fished in his pocket for his battered Zippo. Smoking lamp was out throughout the ship, which meant no smoking during flight quarters. But nobody could keep him from smoking in his own office.

Chapter Four

Lieutenant Steiner signed off the last item on her checklist and handed it to her crew chief. Her eyes were currently covered by sunglasses, both for the bright Mediterranean sun, and to hide the shadows under her eyes. ‘‘That’s it, Chief. How’s the FOD walkdown going?’’

Aviation Bosuns Mate Chief Hamner smiled, pointing a thumb over his shoulder. A line of sailors walked shoulder to shoulder across the destroyer’s tiny flight deck, looking down onto the rough surface. They picked up any bits of trash or loose material that had been dropped there during the night.

FOD, or Foreign Object Damage, was a flight crew’s nightmare. Any loose material on the deck could be sucked into the helicopter’s turbines, or fly loose, the downdraft of the helicopter rotors turning it into lethal missles. So before any Navy aircraft started its engines, every available sailor walked across the flight deck in a FOD walkdown, picking up anything loose on the flight deck. "They should be done in a couple of minutes. The tower's manned. What record are we breaking anyways?"

"The squadron record for the most helicopter touch and go landings in a twenty-four-hour period this year." "Touch and go's" were landing aircraft just long enough to touch the deck, then go. Spending a day doing it seemed a tad excessive to Steiner. The lieutenant brushed a stray lock of hair out of her face, and slapped one hand against the Seasprite CH-60 helicopter she flew. The light helicopter was the most effective sub hunter *Kimmel* possessed. It was also useful for long-range patrols or ship-to-ship transport or air-sea rescue. Maybe too useful, thought Steiner. The CO was always coming up with new jobs for the ship's sole air asset. "A real live hostage rescue mission, promotion lists about to come through—the CO really has the sweat pumps going on this one."

Chief Hamner chuckled. "Sweat pumps one through twelve on line, sweat pumps thirteen and fourteen standing by. Well, there's worse ways to spend a day. What about your promotion?"

"Hell, Chief, I've got a year left on my hitch. Then I go to work for some millionaire as his pilot." She flashed a glamorous smile, the effect ruined by her baggy OD coveralls. "Or maybe I just get some sleep. I'm pretty junior to go to lieutenant commander, anyways. Making lieutenant in eight years is pretty good these days."

The FOD walkdown completed, the flight deck crew settled into their places as the hangar doors fully opened. Each member of the flight deck crew wore different colored shirts over their uniforms to show their jobs. Fueling team wore purple, "chocks and chains" wore blue. Crash and salvage team, or "crash and smash," wore red shirts and stood by with enough firefighting equipment to make most small-town fire departments envious.

Ground control wore white, stained by salt spray and jet fuel. Chief Hamner's white shirt indicated he would be the only person normally allowed on the flight deck during flight operations. His was the final word on whether the helicopter landed or took off.

The flight deck crew rolled the Seasprite out. Once it was in the open, "chocks and chains" blocked the wheels of the helicopter to keep it from moving when the ship rocked. Other flight crew unfolded the rotors. After seven months, everyone knew the drill.

Steiner climbed into the helicopter's cockpit as her copilot, Ensign Freeman, finished his checklist and spoke to the tower. Signal lights flashed as the tower crew checked them out. "Hi ma'am. Are we going to be at this all day?"

"Looks that way," answered Steiner, putting on her helmet and preparing for a communications check. "The rotorheads on *Burke* did seventy-four touch-and-go's in one day last month, and they don't even have their own helicopter."

Freeman nodded. "Still seems damn silly. We're going to burn up a lot of fuel."

"Free, I thought you liked flying this bird."

"Flying, yeah. Touch and go's? No thanks." Freeman threw a switch with a wicked smile. "Hey, why don't we have the chief throw somebody over the side so we can rescue him? Get some excitement."

Excitement. Yeah. Steiner thought of a CH-46 that suddenly decided to lose an engine and drop into twenty-foot swells in the North Atlantic. With her onboard. At two AM. Yeah, excitement. "Nah. Give me boredom any day." Water pouring into the cockpit, seat belts jamming suddenly as the helicopter sank like a stone, lit dim red by the interior lights. "Boredom, any day of the week."

* * *

Matt Reisling sat in the stillness of his quarters.

Twenty-two years. Annapolis, War College, seminars and conferences, buttering up the Admirals and taking the right courses. It all came down to this. Sitting in his quarters. They might not seem like much, just a small office and a smaller bedroom. But there was the pride of command, lordship over an entire ship. Now, there was the waiting. Waiting for the promotion. And now a rescue mission! It would have to take place too late to affect his last promotion board!

He tried to work at the papers on his desk, but gave up after a few minutes. He couldn't concentrate. He poured himself some coffee and considered getting a nap. Twenty-two years. All coming down to this.

He could go out on the bridge, watch the crew go through their drills But that would let them see how nervous he was. Couldn't have that.

The phone rang.

He lunged across his space, picked it up. "Captain's cabin."

"Sir, this is RM1. We just received the promotion list."

Voice cheerful. Good! "Outstanding, RM1! Bring it up immediately!" The next five minutes were unending torture. Twenty-two years of effort.

A knock on the door.

Reisling threw the door open. "Where's my message traffic?"

Grinning, RM1 handed him a stack of messages. "Full instructions from CINCLANT for you sir! They're already calling it 'Sudden Lightning.' "

Reisling took the priority message first. A message from Commander in Command, Atlantic Fleet, had the same priority as a direct message from the Almighty. "How did you do, RM1?"

"I'm a chief, sir! Made it my first try!" Reisling smiled as he skimmed the message. He skimmed the orders quickly, noting the time. Then he noticed RM1 was still standing there. "Thank you, RM1. And congratulations."

RM1 left. Reisling studied the orders again, picked up the phone, called the XO and OPS, and told them to meet him in his quarters.

That done, calls made, people on the way—now he could look at the list. It wasn't the huge promotion lists he'd seen as a junior officer in a much larger Navy, but it was still a long list. Until he came to the much shorter section listing promotions to Captain. He read it.

The section was too short.

By one name.

His.

Commander (Surface Warfare Qualified) Matthew Reisling, Commanding Officer USS *Kimmel*, sat in his quarters, looked at his message form, and waited for the XO and OPS to arrive.

Admiral Cliff Madison (AW/SW/UW), Chief of Naval Operations and Chairman of the Joint Chiefs of Staff, studied the situation board of the Gulf of Sidra. The men who would handle the rescue mission sat around the table in the war room beneath the Pentagon. Around him. Madison was a lean, white-haired man with hard gray eyes in a weathered face that had seen all the world's oceans. He was at the head of the table, in charge. Just where he liked to be.

Beside him sat Ken Wrangel, CIA. Wrangel was a short, stocky man with a vague accent, supposed to be an expert on operations like this. From what Madison had seen of the man so far, Wrangel's only real skill was getting on Madison's nerves.

"I can't believe *Kimmel* is your only asset in that area," said Wrangel. "Where's the rest of the fleet?"

"The available ships are moving into position to support the mission." Madison almost growled out the words. Being CNO meant he got to be Johnny-on-the-spot for this one. You didn't get to be CNO by delegating away the important jobs. "Once the operation begins, the *Thomas Jefferson* battle group will enter the Gulf to cover the withdrawal and launch diversionary airstrikes."

"Gentlemen, let's not get ahead of ourselves." The Chairman of the National Security Council was there representing the president. He might not be responsible for the plan, but he could veto it at will. "Admiral, can the briefing begin?"

Madison nodded and gave the cue to the Commander from Navy Special Warfare. The ex-SEAL stood and spoke. "The operation is codenamed "Sudden Lightning." It will begin with SEAL team six, which has been reinforced for this mission. They're getting ready to deploy to *Jeff* now. We're pulling the Marines out of 'Desert Thunder' in Kuwait, in case we need more bodies."

Unlikely, thought Madison. Since it was the Navy's turn to be Chairman of the Joint Chiefs of Staff, that meant they could run this operation the way it should be run—Navy, all the way.

"All ships except *Kimmel* are keeping away from Libya to avoid tipping the Libyans off that something is underway. At 0900 hours tomorrow, the SEAL will land on *Jeff*, then fly to *Kimmel* onboard the mail chopper, a CH-46 transport. That will also be the insertion aircraft.

"They will land on *Kimmel* at 1230 hours. At 2130 hours, the helicopter and SEAL team will enter Libyan airspace under cover of darkness, flying beneath radar. The SEALs will land three miles from the target at 2230 hours, then approach the camp on foot so that the noise of the helicopter doesn't alert the terrorists. At that time, the *Jefferson* battle group will launch all aircraft. *Kimmel* will stand by for air/sea rescue and provide forward radar observation.

"At 0030 hours, *Kimmel,* aircraft off *Jefferson*, and

Air Force planes out of Spain and Italy will take out Libyan radars and coastal defenses. At the same time, the SEALs will hit the target and rescue the hostages. At 0045, six CH-46 transport helicopters from *Jefferson*, with air cover, will arrive at the camp to fly out the hostages and the SEALs team.''

''Is one SEAL team enough to secure a perimeter and rescue the hostages?'' asked Wrangel.

The Commandant of the Marine Corps answered that. ''Each CH-46 will be carrying a squad of Marines from *Jeff*'s Marine detachment. They'll provide any additional firepower we need. There's a reinforced Marine force recon detachment standing by on the *Iwo Jima* off Kuwait, in case the SEAL team is unavailable.'' The Commandant of the Corps was not about to let the Marines be shoved aside in an operation this important.

Madison spoke up. ''This schedule is still subject to change. Specifics will be decided when the SEAL team arrives at *Kimmel* and evaluates the intelligence provided''—he nodded at Wrangel—''by your Libyan agent.''

Wrangel nodded back. ''The Director sends his thanks for your quick response.''

Madison nodded, smiled. On this operation, there would be enough glory for everyone. It was rare to have a mission as clear-cut as rescuing hostages. ''Everybody wants those people safe. That was fast work, your people getting out the word so quickly.''

''Sometimes, by sheer random chance, things work out. We had a lot of good people already working on this.''

The NSC Chairman asked, ''What opposition is expected?''

Madison answered. ''Intelligence indicates the Libyan subs are in port, along with most of their patrol boats. Any that aren't will be taken out by *Kimmel*. As to aircraft, any Libyan plane in the air near this operation gets shot down.''

''The target is one of four Sword of Islam camps in Libya,'' Wrangel said. ''None of them have more than a hundred personnel. There are no Libyan Army units larger than company strength near it. Our people will face small arms and light armor. I hope your SEALs are bringing along their LAWs this time?''

That earned Wrangel an icy stare from the ex-SEAL. In Grenada, a SEAL team assigned to seize the President had been pinned down for a day by a single ex-Soviet armored car, because not one member of the team had brought an antitank weapon along. Wrangel grinned thinly and went on. ''Your plan is good as it stands. Langley hated to lose their best indigenous Libyan asset, but they got used to that. I'm worried about your Captain Reisling.''

''You mean Commander Reisling. Why?''

''I read his file. He was just turned down for promotion. Is he the man for this job?'' That caused a tense silence around the table.

Admiral Madison drew back, arched one eyebrow. ''Commander Reisling is a fine officer with a distinguished record. He was turned down by the promotion board, but that's nothing unusual these days. There are a lot of officers who began their careers during the eighties, when the fleet was growing. It's a shrinking fleet now. There are only so many slots open for promotion. We've had to cut some good people, so everyone is stretched thin.''

''I was wondering about that. It looks as if you have one ship at every operation underway by anyone, in the entire Mediterranean.''

''Showing the flag. Those commitments were made years ago, when we had a larger fleet. If we still had an adequate fleet, our people wouldn't be scattered so widely.''

"The situation was different years ago. Now that you don't have to face off the Soviet Navy, why don't you cease a few of these commitments and concentrate your ships?"

As Madison had first thought, the man had a real talent for getting on his nerves. "Let's get back to the mission. I believe this operation proves how much this country needs a Navy. When we have a job to do, we make it happen. We drive our people hard, Mr. Wrangel, but they get the job done."

The CIA man shrugged. "Maybe you wouldn't have to drive them so hard if your planning was more realistic."

Madison frowned. He really didn't like this man.

The Mekong air was hot and wet, humid, smelling of marsh and death and cordite. The stink of the swift boat's diesel was a welcome relief. On the twin-fifties, Vasquez swung the guns slowly from left to right. Stolchak checked his engines. Low idle, ready to go. In front of him, ready to go, was an old Browning thirty-caliber he'd swapped some ARVN for, and bungee-corded to the roof of the cabin. The rest of the crew of PBR (Patrol Boat, Riverine) 472, "Hadley's Heroes," stood to their weapons, peering into the night. In flak jackets, steel helmets, and OD fatigues, none looked like sailors.

Stolchak faintly saw the two other PBRs waiting in the muddy waters of the Mekong, everybody waiting, everybody quiet. A quarter moon was all the light they had. That seemed like too much to Stolchak. No cigarettes, no talk, no light. This was deep in Indian Country, Charley's Territory, and they were here to pick up some very unwelcome guests.

Movement, the smell of Old Spice and pipe tobacco. Ensign Wade Hadley stood beside Stolchak. Ten months out of Annapolis, trying to seem older than he was, but not a bad officer for all of that. Smart enough to listen to Stolchak, brave enough to occasionally disregard his suggestions. He'd do, thought Stolchak. "How's it going, Big Nuts?"

"Not too bad, Boats. Anybody see anything?"

"A big, fat negative on that one, Skipper. Vasquez has the starlight." Their only working night vision gear, the starlight scope magnified light to the point where the Vietnamese night was bright as day to the viewer.

The sound of jets passing overhead. Humid jungle night. The crumping of artillery, off in the distance. Fetid smell of marsh water and dead bodies. None of their business. Just another night in Vietnam, the Republic of.

The sudden popping rattle of a machine gun echoing across the water. A dozen automatic rifles firing as one. That was their business. "Showtime!" muttered Stolchak.

Hadley unslung an M-79 grenade launcher as he peered into the dark. Muzzle flashes, dead ahead. "Vasquez, what do you see?"

Peering through the starlight scope, Vasquez said, "It's them, Skipper! Close to the shore." The other boats' engines raced, white wakes of foam growing at their bows.

Well, thought Stolchak, no need worrying about quiet now. He ran up the RPMs on the engine and shouted above the roar of the engines. "Look sharp! Remember, we got friendlies out there! Don't fire blind!" The twin Detroit diesels shook the tiller under his hand as their boat moved forward, brown Mekong water churning up.

"Fire only when I illume!" snapped Hadley. He held the grenade launcher steady, peering into the darkness as if his eyes could burn a hole in the night. More muzzle flashes, clearly visible now. Some orange tracers going inland. Friendly. Maybe. If Charlie wasn't using captured weapons tonight.

Green tracers coming out of the jungle now, toward

the boats! Some product of the Skoda or Putilov works, kicking out bullets that seemed to float toward them, with one in five a green commie tracer.

Rattlesnake-quick, Hadley fired a flare round back at the machine gunner, illumed half a dozen VC on the water's edge. The flare blinded them, but left the Americans hidden in the darkness.

''Fire 'em up!'' bellowed Hadley. Vasquez slewed around the twin-fifties and opened up. Bradley was already chewing up the water's edge with his M-60 firing from aft, portside. Hadley cracked open the 79, fed in a new flare round. Stolchak concentrated on where they were going and let the boys do their job. The PBRs moved by jets of water instead of propellers, so they could turn on a dime and go in where brush would have tangled normal screws. It made them perfect for operations like this. Lucky them.

Pop-flare arched into the sky. ''I got the signal Skipper!'' barked Stolchak. He firewalled the engines, felt the boat leap forward, grinned as he saw the other two boats racing forward too, machine guns pouring out fire into the jungle. Yeah, it was great to be nineteen and driving his own boat.

The boys on the beach weren't having much fun. The SEALs loved these crazy raids into Indian Country, but never seemed to consider how hard it might be to get out. They wanted out now. He could see a ring of M-16s and Stoner machine guns pouring fire into the jungle. It looked like most of the SEALs were there, on the river's edge. Enough muzzle flashes for a company of NVA regulars in the rest of the treeline. Oh goody.

Stolchak used one hand to fire the Browning 30, laying down suppressive fire as he guided the boat in. Hadley fired a second 40mm flare into the jungle, then crammed a high explosive round in and looked for a target. Men screamed, lit up by muzzle flashes, crouched behind cover. Streams of tracer everywhere. A SEAL on the water's edge held an orange flare, waving it back and forth. The PBRs closed in to pick up the raiding party.

PBR-471 took a rocket propelled grenade in the cabin, near stacked ammo and grenades. The boat blew up like a firecracker.

The shock wave knocked Stolchak off his pins. He was staggering out of the way when the bullet came in that blew off Hadley's head.

The young ensign stood for a second, the upper half of his skull spraying in the air. A dying finger twitch-fired the M-79. The 40mm shell sailed into the jungle. He fell down.

Stolchak took the helm again, just in time to see a white phosphorous grenade explode exactly in the center of the seals' perimeter. They were silhouetted as they died, streams of burning white fire spraying over them. Screams and death. Green tracers coming in from everywhere now. Another RPG explosion in the water, spraying water everywhere. Stolchak clamped down on his fear, brought the boat around, tried not to feel the wet bits of—something—that were dripping down the side of his face. "That did it!" he bellowed. "We're pulling out!"

To his right, he could see PBR-470 slewing around, every gun pouring fire into the jungle, diesels roaring as they bugged out. Mission over. No SEALs, no pickup.

"Fuckin' A right, we're pulling out!" shouted Bradley. "Them SEALs is toast!" Now he was the closest member of the crew to the shore and not liking it one bit. He crouched behind his 60, firing. Five hundred rounds belted together in one huge can and he was going to fire them all. The other gunner was firing too, spraying panic fire everywhere. That was fine with Stolchak. There were no more friendlies out there. He kept trying not to think about what he'd been splashed with. Blind panic sounded like a real good idea just now.

Then Vasquez shouted, "Flare, port side! Ten o'clock!" Stolchak looked, swore. A lone figure, downriver from the SEALs, outside the firefight. Waving a flare.

A SEAL cut off from the rest? Some smart VC trying to sucker them in?

"He's one of ours! He's got the uniform!" shouted Vasquez, looking through the starlight scope. "Let's get him!"

The flare was drawing fire now from upriver, from inland. Stolchak accelerated and headed downriver. "Hey, you fuck!" shouted Vasquez, realizing they were passing by. "That's one of our guys!"

"He's VC, trying to sucker us in!" answered Stolchak, praying he was right, pouring RPMs into the water jets, feeling Hadley's corpse tangling his feet.

"You chickenshit bastard, he's one of ours!" shouted Vasquez. He fired the twin-fifties in rage, thumb-sized bullets that punched through trees, rocks, hills. Laid down a world of hurt on the gunfire from the shore. "That's one of ours!"

Stolchak felt a hand on his shoulder. Warm and wet with blood, smell of Old Spice and pipe tobacco, as Stolchak's heart seized up and dropped into a pit. "You never leave your people behind, Boats," said a young voice, a voice he'd hear forever. He turned. Hadley was standing there, upper skull blown away, one eye still in place, blood and brains running down the side of his head. It didn't interfere with his voice, growing into a scream. "You never leave your people behind! You never leave your people behind! *You never—*"

Stolchak woke up.

He jerked awake, banging his skull on the overhead. Swore.

Slowly, it all came back.

Clean sheets. The tiny 6 x 2½ x 2½ foot metal box where he slept. His rack, exactly like every other rack on the ship. Clean sheets. Vent fans. Air conditioning.

He massaged his barrel chest, steadied his breathing. Looked into the tiny mirror in his rack. Gray hair, scar, broken nose. No more 19-year old. He settled back in his rack.

It's been—what—thirty years? Damn close. He still had nightmares. He'd been through bad experiences since. Almost drowned off the Virginia Capes. Pulling burned bodies from Turret B of the *Iowa*. Fishing three-day-drowned Haitians out of the sea on the windward passage. A sailor's life was a hard one. God made the sea, and He made that sea unforgiving. But none haunted him, except that.

Unfinished business.

But what he'd done made sense. No way someone would have split away from the raiding party that far. He was sure that guy on shore had been VC, using a captured uniform. Positive. As positive as you could be and still wonder.

Geez, he should have risked it and gone in. Better dying than wondering for the rest of your life whether you left a man to die.

He checked his watch. 1030 hours. He'd ducked into Chief's berthing for some sleep after the CO's damned oh-dark-thirty UNREP. So much for that. He felt like he'd run a marathon, heart pounding, soaked in sweat. He needed a cigarette bad.

Stolchak rolled out of his rack, pulled on his shirt, put on his boondockers. Two decks up and he'd be on the superstructure, aft of the pilothouse. One of only two places on the ship you could smoke. Someday, he thought as he headed up the narrow ship's ladders, some bright boy would decide to make the Navy caffeine free as well as smoke free, and then they would be well and truly screwed.

He was outside the skin of the ship before he remembered—flight quarters! No smoking. Then he saw the smoking area. A dozen people were standing there, wearing headgear and smoking. Flight quarters must have been secured while he was sleeping.

It was a beautiful day actually, blue sky dotted with clouds, water the grayish blue of deep ocean, breezes flecking the waters with whitecaps. The command master chief was off to one side, staring out over the ocean. Stolchak walked over. "Morning, Master Chief."

"Morning, Boats." Command Master Chief William Kandel (no one on the ship would have dared call him "Bill") stubbed out his cigarette, field-stripped it, and put the remains into his pocket by long habit. "Did you hear? The promotion lists finally came in."

"Great! I've had some people sweating bullets over that." Then he remembered. "Did the CO get his promotion?"

Master Chief shook his head. "Can-exed, for the third time."

Stolchak whistled. "Stand by for heavy rolls as the ship comes about."

Master Chief nodded sagely, sat on a flare locker, and lit a Pall Mall. "He pulled every string he had, called in all his favors, flew back to a specially convened board four months into a Med cruise. All for nothing."

"That second board was what screwed him." Stolchak tapped out an unfiltered Camel, lit it, drew deep. "The old Master Chief told the CO to wait a while before sending in his second promotion package, pick up some more seniority. But not our skipper. *He* had to try to get promoted in record time! You just can't do that in this man's Navy any more. Too many officers and not enough ships. Hell, you're only supposed to get two shots at the promotion boards anyways!"

"He had to get his nose pretty brown to get a third promotion board," agreed Master Chief Kandel. "I just wonder what happens now? I've seen this before. Most of the time, one of two things happens: Either the CO stops giving a damn about promotion, and you wind up with the happiest ship in the Navy, or the CO goes nuts trying to produce some miracle that'll get him promoted anyways.''

''I'll lay fifty bucks on going nuts, Master Chief.'' Stolchak took a deep drag on his cigarette, looked out over the sea. ''His wife left him after she caught him with that lap dancer in New Orleans. He doesn't have much left on shore. This'll mean mandatory retirement. Which will drive him bugfuck.''

The master chief nodded. ''He secured from flight quarters right after the messages went up. Oh, and congratulations, Boats.'' Master Chief suddenly grinned, put out his hand. ''Your name was on that list, Senior Chief.''

Stolchak smiled at that, put aside other people's problems, shook the master chief's hand. As he did so, *Kimmel* went into a sharp turn, setting course for the Gulf of Sidra. Momentum leaned the ship over to port as it turned to starboard. The outside decks of *Kimmel* were covered with a rough-surfaced material called Nonskid, to give the crew footing when decks were pitching and slick with spray. Yet even sure-footed people adjusted their stances as the deck tilted steeply. Stolchak kept his footing with the ease of long practice.

A tardy warning came over the 1MC. *''Stand by for heavy rolls as the ship comes about!''*

Mess Specialist First Class (MS1) Davis was a chubby black man with a receding hairline, a vigorous mustache, and a lot of nervous energy. Just now, that energy was going into collecting his mess cranks from their various jobs on the mess decks. Currently he was collecting Halloran. ''Yo, Halloran, you stack potatoes during the UNREP?''

Halloran finished mixing fruit drink in a dispenser on the beverage line and shook his head.

''Good! If you had, your ass would be in deep sink

forever! Some rocket scientist put fifty-pound sacks of potatoes on the bread pallet an' crushed the bread, then they fell off and now they all over the place. All y'all mess cranks got to clean it up.''

Halloran joined the other cranks, going down into the labyrinth of coolers and storage rooms below the mess decks, in the midsection of the ship. Beneath coolers, offices and *Kimmel*'s tiny closed-circuit TV station were the food lockers. Potatoes were everywhere, rolling along the deck as the ship rocked back and forth. Scattered everywhere were small mounds of packages that had fallen off shelves after being stacked by UNREP personnel eager to get to their breakfasts. MS1 Davis, who'd come along to make sure the less enthusiastic cranks kept moving in the right direction, rolled his eyes at the mess. ''Pod people! You supposed to keep this from happening! Where were you?''

MS3 Dan Podlogar, who looked a little like Elvis with a crewcut and a bad attempt at a mustache, shrugged, grinned. ''Can't be everywhere, MS1. You know the CO always puts us through heavy rolls when we cut away from an UNREP. This stuff just fell over!''

Davis looked at the crushed bread. ''Man, they are gonna bitch about this. This was the only pallet of bread we got, wasn't it?''

Podlogar nodded. ''Chief says to keep the night baker going on bread for the Chief's mess and wardroom. They don't like this store-bought stuff anyways.'' He turned to the mess cranks. ''Hey, fresh meat! You guys start cleaning up! Halloran, you got tagged for cranking?''

Halloran grinned. ''Tragic, ain't it? I already miss the midwatch!''

Podlogar laughed. ''Think we can do some gaming, now that you're free in the evening?'' Halloran nodded. ''Cool! Okay you guys, get to work! Restack this stuff.'' They began restowing the fallen items. The air was heavy with the earthy smell of potatoes, the tang of refrigerant as people worked. Halloran picked up loose potatoes, stowed them in a spare box. Working beside him was a yeoman named Mills.

"Man, this sucks!" groused Mills. As a yeoman, he worked as one of the ship's secretaries. "One night out of three I gotta lose sleep to feed a bunch of non-rate seamen."

Halloran chuckled. "Be glad you aren't in deck division. This is a vacation for me. I actually get to sleep two nights out of three now."

"Choose your rate, choose your fate," snapped Mills. "I became a yeoman so I wouldn't have to waste my time on this crap."

"You became a yeoman 'cause your recruiter didn't screw you over," jibed Tosado, a chubby Puerto Rican fireman. Like Halloran, he saw this as a vacation. "My recruiter lied his ass off to me. Told me once I was at sea, I wouldn't have anything to do, I'd be bored."

"Yeah, that sucks," quipped Seaman Apprentice Mitchell, a chirpy little sprite of a girl from supply division whose cheerfulness didn't get obnoxious until you spent at least five minutes with her. She made occasional efforts to pick up the dropped food. "This is okay for you guys in deck division or engineering, but we've got real jobs to do!"

"Bite me!" Halloran snapped, straining to pull a sack of potatoes from where it had wedged in between two shelves. "My recruiter lied too. You ever notice, most of the deck apes and snipes are from places that aren't near the ocean?"

"That's 'cause anybody who knew anything about the Navy wouldn't become a snipe or a deck ape," Tosado answered. "They make such a big deal about this Apprentice Training Program. Man, that ain't nothin' but starting at the bottom and having to work your way up!

I thought I was gonna be throwing grenades or shooting guns."

"No sympathy for you, guy." Mills helped Halloran pull the sack of potatoes loose and helped lift it onto the right pallet. "I've never seen a commercial for the Navy where they're firing guns or throwing grenades. You want that, you join the Army."

"Yeah, the Army deals straight with you," Halloran said as he got down on the deck and pulled spilled items from behind a shelf. "They have dirty jobs that don't give you any job training—infantryman and tanker. So they give you a bonus to take them. The Navy tricks you into the jobs nobody wants to do by calling them the Apprentice Training program."

Podlogar, who'd been listening in, spoke up. "I must have been crazy to come in! I was making fifteen dollars an hour before I came into the Navy!"

"Then you must be dumber than mud!" snapped Mills. "They have pay charts in the recruiting office. Even you can read! What happened to this fifteen-dollar-an-hour job?"

"I got fired." Podlogar grinned sheepishly.

Another new crank entered the room with a box of potatoes and started putting them in an empty sack as he spoke. "I came in on the Nuclear Program. They never told me what would happen if I failed the program."

"Man, the Navy sure loves the nuke program." Halloran shook his head. "Get lots of high-IQ guys to enlist, then wash out half of them to work in the fleet. But they got me on their best scam!"

"What's that?"

"It's best to start out as a non-rated sailor because—"

Everybody joined in the chorus "—then you get to see everything and choose what you want to do!" They laughed and went back to work.

Chapter Five

In the self-contained world that was a ship at sea, food was served in three areas—the crew's mess (mess decks), the chief's mess (goat locker) and the officer's mess (wardroom).

In the wardroom, officers dined amid traditions unchanged since the days of sail. Instead of the formica and stainless steel of the crew's mess, the wardroom had wood-paneled bulkheads, fine china, and good linen on a long, walnut-finished table which was still secured to the deck to keep it from moving when the ship pitched in heavy seas. The deck was carpeted, the room lit by indirect lighting. Every place had its own china and silverware, even if the food was cheeseburgers and french fries. The mess cranks on duty in the wardroom wore special waiter's jackets, white shirts and ties, and waited on the long table.

Lunch in the wardroom was served in two styles. If the CO was taking lunch in his quarters, it was informal. If the CO was dining in the wardroom, rigid protocol had to be followed as the two dozen officers of the ship gathered. All officers not on watch were in the wardroom when Reisling arrived. He'd considered taking lunch in his quarters, but decided that would be giving the wrong message to his people. As he entered the wardroom, everyone present snapped to attention, to a discreetly barked "Captain on deck!"

Reisling entered in silence, surveyed them, gave the best smile he could. "At ease. I'd hoped to have our guest here, but I've been told he's still sleeping off his late night. Let's have lunch, gentlemen. I'm starved."

He sat at the head of the long wardroom table and the rest of the officers seated themselves in order of precedence. Each place had its own bowl of salad. The mess room cranks would not serve lunch until the CO had finished his salad and called for the main course. Normally, Reisling plowed through his greens with the enthusiasm of a true health nut. Today he picked at the salad, pensive until he realized people were looking, then took a healthy bite of lettuce and tomatoes. Subdued conversations began.

The commanding officer of *Kimmel* decided to face this head-on. "I suppose all of you have heard of the results of my promotion board." Sympathetic noises. Reisling continued, doing his best to maintain the air of Zeus dispensing wisdom from Mount Olympus. "Well, these things happen. You junior officers, take note—promotions in today's Navy are getting harder and harder to come by. As General Grant said, the race is not always to the swift, nor the combat to the strong, but that's the way to bet."

There was nervous laughter at that. The CO might be on his way out, but he would still be writing officer evaluations for the next six months, which gave him a choke hold on their careers. Reisling ate a few more mouthfuls of salad as the atmosphere lightened slightly, somewhat approaching a normal day in the wardroom.

Finally, he gave up, pushed his plate away, and motioned to the senior wardroom crank. "Tell MS1 that the salad was delicious, and would he please send out the main course." The crank took away his salad dish, and brought back two cheeseburgers fresh from the grill, along with french fries, peas, and corn.

Reisling sipped icewater, trying to settle a raging stomach while the other officers traded their salads for the main meal. Of course, none of them would start to actually eat it until Reisling took his first bite. His mind was elsewhere.

"I'll be reading the promotion lists over the 1MC after lunch, of course, but I can tell you now, we have several promotions here. First I'd like to congratulate Lieutenant Washington. It's no surprise to me that she made Lieutenant Commander on the first try, especially in light of her being the first female gunnery officer to ever serve on a U.S. Navy destroyer." There was scattered applause from the officers.

Reisling turned to his second-in-command, Lieutenant Commander Dave Kendricks. "Dave, it seems there will be two Commanders on this ship in a little while. I will take great pleasure in pinning on your silver leaves."

Whatever Kendricks said was lost to Reisling in the babble of congratulations and the sudden churning of his stomach. Reisling clamped down control on himself. "Gentlemen, the briefing for our upcoming mission will be tonight. I've—" A surge of stomach acid. "I've got to plan that. Lieutenant Washington, please join OPS, the XO and me in my quarters at 1300. Continue with lunch, gentlemen." He stood up suddenly.

"Atten-shun!" All stood as the CO left the table. If anyone noted the green cast to Reisling's skin, they didn't say anything. They sat down to discuss promotions and the mission as they finished lunch. Reisling made it to his cabin before he threw up.

*   *   *

Lunch on the mess decks was raucous bedlam. Cheeseburgers, or "sliders," were always popular with the crew. The normally long chow line doubled in length, running down the narrow starboard passageway of the ship all the way to the administration offices forward. Sailors leaned on bulkheads or the firefighting equipment lining the passageway, and talked about the new mission. As the cruise had dragged on, smaller things seemed more important. Now the crew had a real mystery to talk about. Word had leaked of the message to the CO and the course change.

Tiny Rogers got his two sliders, entered the chow hall grinning, and cruised through the salad bar. His tray was already piled high with food. He went to work on his cheeseburgers with the intensity of a skilled craftsman. Cheese and hamburger were joined by pickles, onions, peppers, tomatoes, a sprinkling of grated cheese, ketchup ("Don't forget ketchup for the fries"), a couple of jalapeño peppers for seasoning, then the top bun rammed down on the bottom.

He'd spent the last year oscillating between two states of mind. It had always been that the present meal would be his last big one. Then he'd start on a real diet to get ready for the weigh-in. After each weigh-in, he'd slip into the state of mind that it wasn't worth worrying about, because it was too late to change. Until the next time.

He looked around for a table. He normally needed a full bench just for himself. There! A booth with all four occupants, firemen, getting up and heading down to their berthings to get a little sleep. Rogers squeezed into the booth, proud of his speed, and took his first bite. Ambrosia! Then he realized he'd forgotten his drink, picked up his empty glass, and headed for the beverage line. Which, of course, was when the ship caught a wave sideways and rolled to port.

Forty-seven people were eating in the crew's mess.

Forty-six pairs of hands grabbed their trays to keep them from sliding off the tables as they rolled with the ship. Tiny remembered his tray a second too late. He turned just in time to see it careen off the table and drop to the deck in a smooth dive. It hit the floor at a ninety-degree angle and his lunch flew off, a spray of food vaulting off the plate.

Rogers watched his lunch hit the floor. One hamburger patty had already been stepped on before it stopped rolling. Half a dozen idiots applauded. "Nice show, Tiny," quipped BM3 Bledsoe. "An outstandin' way to show you mean bidness 'bout your diet!"

Bledsoe grinned broadly, all pumped muscles and smiles. Tiny considered breaking him in half, but decided that would just make a lousy day worse. So he bent over and started picking up the mess. A minute later, Halloran joined him. It took him a minute to realize Halloran was wearing a white crank's hat and undershirt instead of a dungaree shirt.

"Ignore those dickweeds," growled Halloran, scooping up handfuls of the mess into a cardboard box. "Everybody's a fucking comedian."

Rogers nodded. "When did you start cranking?"

"Yesterday. I'm working bev line. If you get a chance, try my ice tea. I used real tea bags, not that instant junk." The two of them threw the last of the ruined meal into the box, wiped their hands on napkins. Around them, the incident was already forgotten as people got on with their meals. "You gonna make another try at the mess line?"

Rogers thought about waiting through the mess line again, but couldn't work up the will for it. "I think I'll wait a while. Guess I didn't need it anyways." The two of them left the mess decks, entered the comparative quiet of the ship's passageways. "Don't you have to mind the bev line?"

"Nah. Everything's full. I've got a minute. I'm tired

of hearing these guys bitch about the powdered milk anyways. Want a soda?''

They ambled down the passageway towards the soda machines. ''So how you like bein' a crank?''

Halloran grinned. ''It's great. We get to eat before everybody else. You know how the food smells so good when you're working in the morning, then you see what they're serving and you wonder what happened to it? That stuff actually tastes good when it's hot.''

They walked to the two perfectly normal pop machines outside the ship's store that dispensed sodas for twenty-five cents a can. Both men grimaced. Every light on both machines blinked red, for empty. To Rogers, this was the cap to a perfect morning. ''Those motherfuckers in supply got three pallets of soda in the UNREP this morning! Motherfuckers had all morning to load these machines up! This is just a fine Navy day!''

Halloran's only comment was a savagely muttered ''Jerkoffs.'' For lack of anything better to do, they stepped into the ship's small recreation room. Their conversation went on over the sound of a videotaped Schwarzenegger movie, two chess games, one particularly noisy game of dominoes ruled by the kind of idiots who have to slam their dominoes down with table-rattling force, and several discussions. A typical noon crowd for the rec room.

Coltrane was also there. He looked up as they entered, and sidled over. ''Hey, what's up? Darnell, I hear you got called in on weight. What did they say?''

Rogers sighed. ''They gonna give me an ''other than honorable'' discharge, dog. Failure to adapt. It's bull-jive! I can meet every PT requirement! I'm just over-weight!''

Halloran grimaced sympathetically. Coltrane just gave a sympathetic smile as he spoke. ''That sucks. But at least you get off the 'Kimmel-catraz.' '' That got a smile. Coltrane pulled at the collars of his blue dungaree shirt. "You get to dump these prison blues! No parole officer neither!"

Rogers chuckled and shook his head sadly. "Don't know what my problem is, dog. Didn't have any problem with my weight in A-School or basic. Just since I got here." He looked at his uniform. "These do look like prison blues, don't they?"

Halloran nodded. "Everything's painted gray here too. Now, you do get paid here, but you get more sleep in prison. But we put ourselves here."

"Don't fool y'self, Halloran. All those Gs in prison, they put themselves there too. Every one of 'em whine an' bitch about how unfair it is, how the cops had no right to stop 'em, how nobody gave 'em a chance. Not one of 'em honest enough to admit they shouldn'ta been doin' the deed in the first damn place. Thought they was so slick when they was on the streets! Anybody knows if you break the law enough, sooner or later somebody gon' catch your ass." He sighed, looked ruefully at Halloran. "Guess I ain't got no excuse either. Too late now."

Out of things to say, all three sat there a while. Then Halloran got up, clapped his friend on one massive shoulder. "Keep hopin', Tiny. Anything's possible."

Coltrane watched Halloran go, then asked, "You got some change I could borrow? I want to hit the soda machines."

That got a laugh from the big radioman.

Seaman Apprentice Lucas Toombs pulled the last coil of air hose over the bottom lining of the door, and stepped onto the quarterdeck. It was at the center of the ship, one of the few places you could cross from port to starboard of *Kimmel* on this deck.

A brass plaque on the wall told of the ship's namesake.

HUSBAND EDWARD KIMMEL

Born in Henderson, Kentucky, on February 26, 1882, Husband Edward Kimmel attended Central University in Richmond, Kentucky. Appointed to the U.S. Naval Academy in June, 1900, he graduated 13th in his class on February 1, 1904. His first ship was the battleship USS Virginia, *on which he participated in the round-the-world cruise of the Great White Fleet. Specializing in Gunnery and Ordnance, he served two CINCPACs as Gunnery Officer and was an aide to then–Secretary of the Navy Franklin D. Roosevelt. In October 1917, following America's entry into World War One, he was attached to the Royal Navy as a gunnery advisor, in which capacity he observed the Battle of Heligoland Bight. Following that, he served as Gunnery Officer on the staff of Rear Admiral Hugh Rodman in Battleship Division 9, leaving to become XO of the battleship* Arkansas *in 1919. He attended the Naval War College 1925 to 1926, excelling in the senior course on Strategy and Tactics. In 1939, as CO of Cruiser Division Seven, he led a goodwill tour around South America. On February 1, 1941, he took command of the Pearl Harbor Naval Base. There he energetically drilled the U.S. Pacific Fleet in preparation for the coming war with Japan. He retired from the Navy with the rank of Rear Admiral on March 1, 1942.*

Toombs had read it before. Now he walked past onto the outside quarterdeck. The midships section of *Kimmel*'s weatherdecks served many purposes. The two ship's boats waited on davits there, ready to be dropped into the ocean on short notice. The fixtures for fuel transfer during UNREPs were there. In port or during evolutions, the quarterdeck would be the nerve center of the ship. Now it was just another place to be cleaned.

Toombs settled into his place by the midships deck railing, and checked his equipment. Face mask, dust filter, ear protection, hat, gloves. He looked back at the air connection, the fixture that attached his sander to the low pressure air lines that ran all over the weather decks of the ship. It was solid. All right. He turned to the job at hand, started sanding the deck railing, sending a cloud of dust, particles of paint, primer, rust, and steel in a thin cloud that slowly disappeared over the waves. Gleaming steel began appearing on the railing.

"You spend too much time on that safety shit," said Andrews, untangling his air hoses. "Man, I hate these air hoses! Wish to hell we could just use electrics! They're faster too."

Toombs grinned. "You'd be faster too if you were working with some electrical gear when a wave splashed you. It's the price of doing business."

Andrews finished untangling the air hose and plugged it in. Next he plugged a deck chipper into his air hose, and took it to where the paint on a bulkhead was flaked away and crusted with sea salt. "We shouldn't even do this at sea! That metal you're sanding, it'll just get sea spray on it before you can lay down some primer. That'll rust under the paint in a week. We should wait until we get back into port to do this."

Toombs concentrated on the job at hand. More dust clouds flew. "What's the big deal? You got some other place to be? Got a hot date tonight? Think of all the overtime you're getting."

Andrews laughed at that. "Man, can you imagine how much we'd make if they paid us by the hour?"

"Or by the job. That's why I take my time with all the safety gear. It isn't like I'm in a hurry. OPS is just going to find some other dumbshit job to hassle us when we finish this."

Andrews's next comment was lost in the roar of the chipping hammer as he went to work. Toombs went back to stripping paint. The ear protectors and face mask seemed like a layer around his perceptions, as if he was somewhere else and just watching this happen over a screen. That concept gave his mind something to work on as he sanded. After a few minutes, he looked up again. Endless ocean, stretching away. A big change from where he'd started out.

Sitting there, he saw Chambers step onto the weatherdecks and walk up to Andrews to tell him something. Next he walked over to Toombs. "Hey man, BM3 says don't forget to return the air connections to the bosuns locker when you done. They almost all disappeared."

"Why hassle us? You know the GMs and the signalmen have most of those."

"Yeah, but I'd have to climb all them stairs up to oh-six level to tell them." Chambers grinned. "Man, you heard? Bledsoe gonna re-up."

"I thought he was getting out."

"He too smart for that. He's the realest cat on this ship and the Man can't touch him." Chambers gave a look up and down the weatherdecks. No khakis in sight. He leaned back against a locker.

Toombs looked up from his work. "Bledsoe is the realest cat on this ship?"

"He fucks with anybody who comes down to the bosuns locker, if they ain't down with him, especially the white boys. He been wrote up five, six times, spent three months in the brig and the Man ain't shook him up yet! He's really real!"

"That's what you call really real? Messin' with people? Does somebody got to get themselves in trouble with the Man to be down? Got to let the Man take away they stripes and they money, just to be real? Man, that's for suckers!"

Chambers grinned. "Damn! Tombstone! You talkin' just like a brother now! I thought you just be passin' from the way you talk."

Toombs grimaced. "I'm not trying to pass for anything. It isn't trying to pass just to speak good English. My aunt, she brought me up after my mom died. She beat my butt if I talked street."

"So that why you joined the Navy?"

"I joined the Navy 'cause half my friends was dead or in jail. That's the choices in South Central, my brother."

"You from South Central? That's the 'hood, man! I'm just from the 'burbs, but that don't keep me from bein' real! The way you talk, I thought you grew up around white people."

Now it was Toombs's turn to laugh. "So do a lot of white people. Folks reacts to you the way you talk. If you talk like a gangsta, everybody treat you like you be a gangsta. Me, I talk good English, so they're comfortable around me. I could still be talkin' street and dappin' wi' my friends, drinkin' a forty on some street corner back home. One of these days, I'd just wind up on a slab, probably shot by some other brother who wa'nt even aiming at me. Instead, I'm saving those bones, got me a bank account. Got four thousand dollars collecting interest back home and by the time my four years is up, I'll have fifteen thousand and my GI bill. Go to college, become a edjimicated black man and then, watch out!"

"Man, that ain't real!"

"What is real, fool? Pissin' everybody off so they fuck you?" Toombs didn't like to preach, but Chambers had hit one of his buttons, something that bothered him every time he saw it. The belief that working to better yourself meant you were trying to be white. That trying to get an education and a career meant you were selling out. "Damn, Bledsoe been busted down three times an' you wanna be like him?"

This hit Chambers pretty hard. The people he hung with all had a ready list of excuses for failing. He wasn't used to someone telling him he could control his own life. Time to change the focus of this conversation. "Reality is, you just another nigger in the white man's Navy!"

"Does that mean I couldn't be a chief, or an officer? Does that mean the white boys wouldn't have to salute me if I was? Damn, G, I know the Navy's bulljive! But I'm here for four years and bitchin' and moanin' only gonna make it worse! Wa'nt nobody put a gun to my head. I put my hand up and swore I'd give 'em four years of my life. A man keeps his word! I'll give 'em four honest years and get everything out of it I can! Then I never have to do this shit again in my life! I ain't gonna fuck up the rest of my life just 'cause I don't like where I am! That's what's really real!"

Chambers started to say something then, but looked over and saw Chief Stolchak coming out onto the weatherdecks. Quick as a flash, he ducked away. Toombs shook his head ruefully and went back to work.

Majors woke slowly, tried to remember where he was.

Oh, yeah. The ship.

He rolled out of the narrow bed and sat up. Then he went through his mental check list. Information passed on. Package organized to brief the seal team when they arrived. He'd stayed up until three AM to do that. He checked his watch—2:15 PM. He'd really been tired.

He called the captain's cabin on the ship's phone, and Reisling filled him in. He had a day to wait until the seals arrived. Plenty of time. That done, he looked around.

Jeez, this was the CO's cabin? It was so small. Well, he'd heard destroyers were the small ships of the fleet, so he guessed that made sense. Still, it had a shower. Right now he needed a shower badly. Sea salt from last night was crusting up on his skin. He went to the shower and turned the nozzle. Nothing.

He threw on some clothes, went to the door, and

opened it. A sailor was standing there. This one had a stripe on his sleeve. "Excuse me, the shower isn't working."

His guard shook his head. "Water hours. They're short on fresh water, so there's only water available between six and eight in the morning and 1900 to 2100 at night. They shut off all nonessential water the rest of the time."

He translated from military time in his head. No water until seven PM? "Everywhere?"

"The engineers always have hot water, in the engine rooms."

Majors grimaced. "Oh well. Is there any place a guy can scare up food around here?"

The guard shrugged. "All the messes are closed. You bein' a guest though, the cranks might get you something."

"Okay. Out in five." Majors shut the door, dressed in fresh underwear and khakis. He had been through worse than having to skip a few showers in his life. That problem gone from his mind, he went over the previous night in his head. Too much had been happening all at once for him to remember everything. The CO and his people seemed to be on the ball. He reminded himself to find out what this ship could do to support the mission. His stomach growled. At least he could take care of that.

Feeling vaguely human, he stepped out into the hallway and looked at his guard. "Well? How do I look?"

The sailor looked at him. "You need a haircut." Then he handed him a black plastic nametag. "The Master at Arms made this up for you. You pin it above your left pocket." Majors read the name tag: "SECRET AGENT MAN." He chuckled, looked at the blue dungaree shirt of his guard. Stenciled above one pocket was "MONK."

Majors pinned on the tag. "These things make it easy to remember other people's names?"

Monk grinned. "Yeah. It's pretty bad though, because you get used to being able to read everybody's name, so you don't remember them anymore."

Everything in place, Majors straightened up. "Okay, let's go." Once again, they threaded a maze of corridors, lit by white light this time. The passageways were busy, individuals and little groups of people shoving on past, everybody in a hurry, everybody tense. Majors noted that most had bags under their eyes. "Is something going wrong?" he asked Monk.

"Naw. Just another fine Navy day! We're doing a lot of drills to get ready for this big raid. Are you going to go on it?"

"If I can persuade the SEALs to take me."

"Man, good luck. Those are some crazy mothers. I went through three weeks of seal school before I washed out. Here we are."

The two men stepped into the crew's mess. First, Majors noticed how clean it was. Everything was clean and polished, every corner, every bit of metal, behind the machines, even the ceiling. The floors gleamed with wax, the tables were spotless.

Second, he noticed it was empty, except for one group of people. Over in the corner, four or five sailors were clustered around a table, hunched over papers and manuals and some oddly shaped dice. "Yo, cranksters!" called Monk. "We got somebody to feed here!"

"Yo, cannon cocker, why don't you feed him someplace else?" came a good-natured retort. Majors saw it came from a familiar face, the gray-haired sailor who'd brought him dinner the night before. The man looked up from the group. "Time out. Guys, meet a real, no kidding, CIA operative." The others at the table looked up, and called friendly greetings.

"Are you really a secret agent?" asked one black-haired kid with a crewcut and a stripe on his sleeve.

"I could tell you the answer to that," warned Majors in his most ominous tone, "but then I'd have to kill you."

That got some cheers from the group. The gray-haired sailor, Halloran, according to his shirt, left the table and said to one of the other people there, "Finish rolling up the characters and assign positions. I'll feed this guy and be back here in five. Pod, can I borrow the keys to the cooler?" Keys obtained, he looked at Monk and Majors. "Follow me."

They stepped into the ship's kitchen. Halloran fished through a key ring until he found what he was looking for. "Dinner is served in three hours, so how about just something to hold you over until then?"

"Sounds good. Do you have any more of that ham?"

"No sweat. Some was left over from lunch. It's a little dry." Halloran unlocked a big refrigerator, and opened it. "Here's where we keep leftovers. Take what you want, eat what you take. If you want something that's not here, you can get snacks at the ship's store."

"Negative," said Monk. "The ship's store is closed today for drill."

Halloran sighed. "Belay my last. Did they ever load the soda machines?"

"Yep. Diet soda, that weird Israeli shit again." Both the sailors made faces at that. Majors set to finding food.

Five minutes later, Majors sat down in the crew's mess with a sandwich and mug of coffee and watched the little knot of mess cranks around the table. Halloran seemed to do most of the talking. Dice started rolling, and as he ate, the CIA agent started picking up bits of comments like "Fire up that sucker" and "I throw a grenade" and other testosterone-laden phrases, along with enough numbers and percentages mentioned to delight a math major. He looked over at Monk, who was sipping a cup of coffee he'd snagged himself. "What the hell are they doing?"

"Playing that 'Dungeons and Dragons' stuff."

Halloran reared up from the table. "I'll have you know it's 'Delta Commandoes!' The finest modern combat role-playing system ever written!"

Monk grinned, nodding his head. "Yeah, that 'Dungeons and Dragons' stuff."

Halloran regally sneered. "Ignorant peasant!" Then he grinned. "Besides, we play Dungeons and Dragons on Tuesdays. Monk, I still have your ranger, if you want to try again." Halloran looked at Majors, shook his head ruefully. "I tell you, feed one guy's character to a dragon and he never forgives you!"

Everybody got a laugh out of that. Halloran went back to his game. For lack of anything else to do, Majors listened as he ate. Halloran seemed to spend most of his time describing the situation and the actions of some guys called "scavengers," interspersed with graphic descriptions of what various high-tech weapons were doing. He frequently referred to an OD-colored manual, which Majors gradually realized was a rulebook for the game. The others kept on talking about what their characters were doing, using other hi-tech weapons, scheming and planning with each other constantly.

Majors had played a little 'Dungeons and Dragons' in college himself, and done some role-playing games used for training at Langley. The players each ran a character appropriate to the situation, who responded to situations set up by the Games Master or GM. The characters were defined by statistics written down on papers called Character Sheets. It was as if readers were given control of characters in a story, with the GM as the story's author.

This game seemed complicated. Players chattered back and forth with plans and requests for fire, discussed where to attack and asked dozens of questions, most of them fielded by Halloran. Just listening, Majors gradually picked up that the characters were storming some warlord's fortress to rescue captive scientists in a radioactive wasteland. Jobs were assigned, targets chosen, and goals set by the players, with Halloran telling them the results of their actions after consulting masses of notes, flipping through the rulebooks, and rolling dice.

"Okay, I fire up the squad with my M-60."

"Check the map. You mean those guys by the building, in the middle of the compound? Look at the map. Remember, you're over by the ruins."

"Yeah. Give 'em a full belt of ammo!"

"Right. Roll your dice. Your percentage chance of hitting is . . . forty-three."

Dice rolled. "I got a seventy-two!"

"Okay, you missed your targets. Now roll again."

"Why? Do I get another chance?"

"No. If you take a look at the map, you'll notice that Podlogar's and Mills's characters are on the other side of that squad from you. You may have just shot them. Those bullets have to land somewhere."

Majors chuckled as the players squawked. Just then, a cook came in (Majors guessed he was a cook, since he was wearing a white cap and T-shirt). Whoever he was, he didn't seem happy as he shouted, "We got evening meal in thirty minutes! Put that shit away and get to work!" The game broke up in a bustle of questions, papers rapidly stuffed away, and mess cranks heading for their jobs.

Majors realized two and a half hours had passed. He had finished his sandwich and coffee without noticing. He walked over to Halloran, who was still stuffing game materials into a briefcase. "You're pretty good at this."

Halloran grinned as he worked. "Thanks. It helps pass the time and it doesn't destroy as many brain cells as beer."

"How do you manage to keep all that in your head?"

Halloran shook his head. "I don't. It's all written

down. I plan this stuff before the game starts, set up the scenario, then let the players run through it. See?'' He shoved a stack of papers at Majors. The agent leafed through them. Neatly hand-printed on a dozen pages, the text laid out situations, names, weapons and directions, all footnoted to a pair of crudely drawn diagrams. Amazed, Majors realized he could make sense of what was written.

''Why did you put the machine gun there?'' He asked, pointing to a section on the map.

''It's the high ground. It commands that whole side of the fortress. The warlord—the guy they're fighting—is pretty competent. His troops are doofs though, just cannon fodder. So everything's laid out properly, but the troops fight badly. Gotta go. Can I have that?''

Majors handed the papers back, watched Halloran leave. He noticed that, as the sailor left, his grin was replaced by a sullen expression as he returned to his day-to-day life. Interesting.

Majors put that memory among many others, and went back to his cabin.

While it was evening in the Med, it was early afternoon in Washington. Planning for Sudden Lightning was in full swing. Information was pouring in now that they knew which camp the terrorists were using. Wrangel briefed them using slides of satellite photos and a laser pen that projected a dot of red light on the screen where he pointed. ''The Sword of Islam base camp has been designated Whiskey Six. It is located near an old Italian garrison post, twenty miles east of Ras Al-Unuf, eight miles inland past the coast road. The only structures left by the previous owners are these stone barracks, which are being used to house the hostages. Note the guards posted outside each door. Second photo.''

The slide changed to one from higher up, showing tents, a helicopter, and vehicles. ''The helicopter is a

Libyan Air Force CH-47C, Italian manufacture. It's used to fly supplies between the camps. This large vehicle here is an M-48A5 main battle tank, formerly Bundeswehr, one of a batch that were sold as scrap, then diverted to third world clients. The terrorists use it for training purposes, and maybe as extra firepower."

"Is it functional?" asked the Marine commandant.

"At least partially. That would explain why this camp was used for the hostages."

The Commander from Navy Special Operations said, "Team Six will neutralize the helicopter and tank on the way in."

"Make sure you take enough to destroy that tank," said General Crawford. "I've seen tanks take multiple hits from RPGs and keep fighting. I recommend at least one Dragon Missile launcher."

"Not needed, sir," answered the Special Ops Commander. "Team Six will infiltrate the perimeter and neutralize the tank with demolitions. In addition, all team members will be carrying AT-4 light antitank weapons. A Dragon would be too heavy to carry in." The commandant refrained from comment.

Wrangel went on. "Terrorist strength is fifty to sixty fighters. Eight to ten are on guard duty at all times. The camp is fenced in by triple-strand concertina wire. Two guard towers mount RPK machine guns and overwatch the camp. Most of the Sword of Islam fighters sleep in these tents." He pointed to two neat rows of tents, next to a small vehicle park. "We believe the end of the stone building is used as a headquarters for the camp, as well as officer's quarters. There are no mines or sensor systems in place. If they have night vision gear, it's in the towers.

"The camp is commanded by Jamal Rakhman, a Palestinian Arab who lived in the U.S. for several years." A picture flashed on the screen of a chubby-faced, smiling man with a receding hairline and a bushy mustache.

"Jamal Rakhman, thirty-seven years old, one brother still living, one brother killed by Israeli riot police in Gaza, 1982. One sister, killed in IAF retaliatory raid, southern Lebanon, 1987. Association with Abu Nidal and Hamas terrorist factions, believed to be involved in the most recent assassination attempt on Arafat. Fought with radical Islamic factions of the Mujaheddin in Afghanistan, 1984 to 1986. Resided in New York City, 1987 to 1994, expelled when his green card expired."

"We're going to have to kill this guy," the Special Ops Commander announced. "In that part of the world, vengeance feuds are an old tradition. He won't give up the hostages. Team Six has authority to inflict maximum casualties on the way out?" There was nodded assent from around the table.

Wrangel flicked off his light pen. "That concludes my briefing."

Admiral Madison stood and faced everyone at the table. "The next order of business is the Libyan military. General Boswell?"

The Army Brigadier handling ground threat assessment stood up. He had started his career jumping out of a plane into North Vietnam in 1971, and had hated intelligence ever since. Perversely, that was where the Army kept assigning him. He looked at his file as a large map of Libya flashed up on the screen. "Libyan ground forces are pretty thin in that area. A few companies of mechanized infantry are training nearby. Nothing heavy. The Libyan Air Force was at a high state of alert following the shootdown of the helicopter, but has returned to normal operations. No forces will be able to intervene at that camp for at least two hours."

Special Ops grinned. "Fine. Once Team Six is in position, our operation is timed to take twenty minutes, first shot to last."

* * *

Halloran looked down the beverage line as Davis spoke to him. It was stocked with red and green bug juice, iced tea, teabags for hot tea, packets of sugar and creamer, coffee, hot water, regular milk, and chocolate milk that he'd had to haul up from supply himself. They'd been brought on board during the morning UNREP, but nobody else had wanted to haul the heavy five-gallon milk containers up three flights of stairs. The bev line looked better than it had since they left Norfolk.

"Why are you switching me to deep sink?" Halloran's voice, trained to carry orders over the sounds of automatic weapons fire, could be heard in every adjoining space. "Bormann and I have bev line rolling!"

"Chief Campbell says you got deep sink and Harris goes to bev line," snapped MS1 Davis. "Now get out of my face!"

Glowering, Halloran stepped into the passageway and began walking towards deep sink. He stopped. Looked around. Nobody was there. He was alone in a passage, standing by a fire station with two coiled hoses.

He let the rage loose.

He screamed and smashed his fists into a canvas hose coiled nearby, hammering again and again, wishing it was someone. Davis, his recruiter, Harris, anybody. Everything in him that hated his mistakes that had put him there, hated where he was, drove his fists. He kept at it, pouring out the rage, venting fury, until his rage wore itself out enough for him to stop. It didn't go away. It couldn't. It was fed every day by where he was and what he had to do. But it could dissipate enough for him to get on with things.

Besides, hoses couldn't charge you with assault.

A little calmer now, he took a deep breath. Deep sink. Cleaning dishes in the hottest, steamiest space on the ship. Normally a punishment detail. It was now all his. He grimaced.

Temper under control again, he stepped into his new

work space, the humid room where the automatic dishwashers were kept, and where the pots and pans from baking were scrubbed in huge sinks full of steaming, greasy water. Machines clanked and shook, rinsing off trays of dishes in scalding water, shoving them through. They emerged from the machines with steam pouring from them. Even wearing only a T-shirt and dungarees, Halloran could already feel himself perspiring. Strangely, the only other figure in deep sink was Seaman Recruit Mills. He and Halloran had come on the ship together, back during the yard period in New Orleans.

Halloran shouted over the noise. ''Where's Harris? I'm replacing him!''

''That whiny bitch disappears five minutes before every meal!'' answered Mills. ''Could you sort the silverware? They're always short of spoons out there. They tagged you to replace him, huh?''

''Yeah!'' Halloran went to work sorting silverware. ''What do you mean he disappears?''

''I mean five minutes before each meal that useless lazy fuck says 'I got to make a head call' and disappears for an hour. I guess Davis got tired of chasing him down. Weren't you on bev line?''

''Yeah. Me and Bormann had it sown up! So I got stuck in here and Harris got my job because he's too hard to find?''

''Yeah!'' shouted Mills, grinning. ''This way they figure they won't have to chase after Harris when he disappears They probably figure Bormann can handle bev line by himself, and I heard Davis say you were a hard worker so he wouldn't have to keep an eye on you! Welcome to the U.S. Navy! Where no good deed ever goes unpunished!'' He slammed another tray of dishes into the machine.

Halloran gingerly grabbed a tray of silverware, scorched his hands on the scalding water. His bellow of rage couldn't be heard over the hammering of the machines. Mills looked over and shook his head. "Deep sink ain't that bad, man. Hell, you sweat your ass off wherever you work in the galley. At least here, you stay clean. Aren't you the guy who runs war games?"

Halloran nodded, momentarily distracted. "Yeah. I used to play Dungeons and Dragons, but now I run this new game, Delta Commandoes. Modern combat role-playing. Grenades and M-16s instead of fireballs and swords, that kind of stuff. You're trying to rebuild civilization after a nuclear war."

"Cool! Podlogar talked about you. Are you running a game tonight?"

Halloran thought about it a minute, gingerly sorting hot silverware, all his anger gone. "Yeah, after chow. Hey, if I can get enough players, we can game during the morning breaks, between meals. We could even use the mess decks. We're cranks, aren't we?"

Mills nodded, grinning, then shoved another tray of dishes into the dishwasher.

Sally Harris woke up just after midnight. Not that she could tell the time. The bad men had taken all their watches, and the room was lit night and day by a single lightbulb hanging from the ceiling. She just knew that she had to go to the bathroom.

She went to the bucket in the corner they had been using for days. After all this time, shyness was gone. That business done, she went back to her mother's arms and snuggled into her warmth. All the women were huddled together for warmth, under a few blankets the "Mooja-heddin" had given them. Sally scratched herself. She itched from the dirt, worse than she had ever itched before. She was hungry too. She wanted to cry, but she knew not to. The bad men hit you if you cried.

She thought of home and being clean and watching Barney on TV. When she got home, she was going to take a long bath, with lots of bubbles, then dress in her nice warm flannel pajamas and watch Barney and eat five peanut butter and jelly sandwiches. She had decided this the day before, and told her mother in a very mature and adult tone. Her mother had nodded and smiled, but then her eyes had started watering like she was going to cry, but she hadn't cried.

That was when Sally knew something bad was going to happen. She might only be seven years old, but she knew about bad things. They mostly happened to grown-ups, but on the TV sometimes, she saw them happen to little kids too. She thought about her father, wondered where he was. They had led him away when they were brought here and shoved into this bad room. She almost cried, but she didn't. She couldn't. Her mother had told her to be brave. Her mother had also told her to pray, and bad things wouldn't happen, but she'd been praying and bad things had been happening for a while now. She was pretty sure they were going to keep happening too. But she prayed anyway.

Praying, she went to sleep.

Chapter Six

"Clear the flight deck! Incoming aircraft!" The roar of the 1MC echoed through the cavernous hangar bay of the USS *Thomas Jefferson.*

Airman Apprentice Tom Davies woke to the roar of the loudspeaker's commands and almost fell off the helicopter he was servicing. Reflexively, he grabbed the rotor and held on. His tool kit however, fell off as he thrashed. It slid off the sides of the CH-46 helicopter and hit the deck with a clanging of metal on metal, tools and spare parts falling out. He looked down at it. "Shit."

At 0330 hours, there was only one witness to Davies's accident. A third class who'd been working inside the helicopter came out of the cabin on the helicopter and looked up. "You drop something?" Davies, his mind now sharp from the sudden wakeup, noted the petty officer was smiling.

"Dropped my tools."

"Imagine that." The petty officer looked back into

the helo at the cleaning he'd been doing, then looked back up. "Just don't fall off there, or I'll have to fill out a ton of paperwork on how you broke your neck." He spotted the tool kit. "Stay up there. I'll pass your stuff on up. You almost finished?"

Davies thought, tried to clear a mind fogged by a few too many forty-eight hour days. "Uh, yeah, almost. Just gotta put together the rotor assembly."

Randall nodded, found most of the tools, and threw them into a bag. "Okay. Finish it right." He passed the tool bag up. "But remember: Those SEALs are going to need this helicopter as soon as the COD brings them in. So get it done quick."

Davies nodded, rubbed his eyes. The carrier had been on alert ever since the CO heard of this big secret mission they were part of. Most of the aircraft were already on the flight deck, some of them loaded for training runs, others already uploaded for the air strikes they would be making that night supporting Sudden Lightning. *Jefferson*'s CO, like every other captain in the Navy, had one response to any upcoming task: Drill the crew like fiends, round the clock, and get everything ready for action right the hell now. Those crew who could get away were trying to catch some sleep.

Not that Davies knew all this. He was doing as he had been told, as they had been telling him ever since that day in basic training when they informed him his test scores didn't qualify him for an A-School, so he was going into "Apprentice Training Division." Also known as ATD or "Another Thirty Days," it was where you went after basic training and were given thirty days training as a seaman, fireman, or airman. Which of the three you trained at was a matter of pure chance. He got airman.

Now, he had been on *Jefferson* all of two months, more tired than he'd ever been in his life and he was doing maintenance on the folding rotors of a CH-46 transport helicopter. It was made more difficult by the fact that he'd been awake for almost two days. Over the last few months, he'd grown used to that. So used to it that dozing off in a quiet moment was no big thing. All the chiefs and petty officers bragged about all the times they'd stayed awake for two or three days at a stretch. Davies tried to keep a good attitude like they told him.

He did not notice he had failed to replace the main rotor nut. It was the proper part, installed properly, but intended for only five hundred hours of service. He had checked off the item when he'd gone to work on it, just before he dozed off. Exhaustion just clouded his memory about not getting it done. Everything was in place, so he shut the access hatch, leaving in a main rotor nut that was already over its designated service life. Military procurement, wise in the ways of the world, normally compensated for accidents like this by overengineering the parts. What they could not have taken into account was a contractor supplying substandard parts. This main rotor nut was one of a batch made from a lower grade of steel than required. It was already filled with invisible, microscopic fractures from the stress it had undergone.

Jamal Rakhman folded his prayer rug as the sun rose over the mountains. He was a cheerful looking man, his jovial air often fooling those who could not see the spirit of a Mujaheddin burning within him. Around him, other Mujaheddin were folding their rugs, shaking sand loose from them and checking the weapons they kept at all times.

The beauty of the dawn filled him with a sense of wonder, amazement once again at the beauty that Allah created in the world. It sometimes made him wonder why Allah permitted it to be sullied by unbelievers. The cold night wind of the desert was still bracing as he smelled the tea brewing in the camp. Then he looked around at the camp and the moment was gone. Reality set in.

He remembered how it had been when he first came in, the movement, with thousands of Mujaheddin in camps across the Arab world, recruited from the teeming squalor of the refugee camps, armed and equipped with the oilbased largesse of their Arab brothers in Saudi Arabia and Kuwait, trained by the Soviets and their terrifying East German mercenaries. They had been young and fierce and fearless then, eager to battle the Zionists, eager to retake the homeland few had ever seen. Yes, the Satanic Americans had been allies of the Israelis, but they were weak and decadent as befitted unbelievers, unwilling to act even when their own people were being kidnapped wholesale. Then, victory had been assured.

Strangely, Allah had not seemed so important then. He had not known the truth then and the Russians had, discreetly, ridiculed those who still followed the teachings of the Koran. Its beliefs were a tool to be used to motivate others, one instructor had told him, the night he had been introduced to alcohol.

It had all changed when the American cowboy, Reagan, took power. Suddenly, borders were no longer sacred. Marines landed in Lebanon, and though one fanatic went to glory killing hundreds of them, still their ships and planes had done tremendous damage That was when PLO warriors discovered that, decadent though the Americans might be, their soldiers were fierce, and craftier than most in the skills of the warrior Jamal had fought against the American Marines in Lebanon and the Soviets in Afghanistan. Against their tricks of tactics and weapons, fanaticism could only endure. But endurance was not enough

American bombers had shattered Khaddaffi's palace. Suddenly the Colonel's courage had gone. Libya was no longer a refuge. The Russian empire had collapsed and their advisors had gone home. The Egyptians kept their peace with Israel even with Sadat murdered. The last bit of hope had been when Arafat allied the PLO with Iraq.

Those had been heady days! The dream of the Grand Jihad had seemed almost real then, a vision of the whole Islamic world rising to smash the hated Satans of the West. That dream died when the Americans, always the cursed Americans, broke Hussein's army like a cheap toy and threw it aside. That was when the Arabs whose wealth had once sustained the PLO had left, enraged over its support of their enemy, Hussein. No more petrodollars from Saudi Arabia or Kuwait. Arafat's gamble had turned allies into enemies.

Now, even Arafat had made peace with Israel. Many had gone home, giving up the struggle, joining Arafat in his betrayal. Those left had to scrape by on what was given them by the Libyans and the Iranians. The camp they lived in now was all too typical. Built three years before with materials from other, abandoned camps, it housed less than a hundred fighters.

The hostages were useless with the Libyans afraid to reveal them. What good were hostages if you could not parade them in front of the camera? Let them do that, and the unbelievers of the West would see that the Sword of Islam was still sharp. Let them see their children die on camera, as he had seen his nieces and nephews die from American bombs in Lebanon, or from the poison gas of the Russians in Afghanistan!

But no. The leadership kept telling him they were trying, kept telling him to keep alert, to move the hostages soon. He kept telling his fighters to keep training for the final struggle. In his darkest moments, he sometimes wondered whether Allah had abandoned them, whether the final struggle would ever come.

He thought of his family. So many killed, fighting the Israelis and the Americans. That kept the fire burning. He thought of the years in the Afghan mountains, fighting the same Russians who had once trained him. That was where he had returned to the Shiite faith of his youth. There had he discovered that faith was all, that life meant nothing save to serve Allah by spreading his word and slaying the infidel. Allah might test his faithful, with fire and steel and blood. What matter that they might be defeated today? Death meant only the entrance to Paradise! If unbelievers had to die, even the children, that was the will of Allah.

He heard one of the young hostages crying, a tremulous wail coming out of the stone buildings they were imprisoned in. He thought of leveling his rifle on all of them, of emptying the magazine into them. He thought of his dead nieces and nephews, brothers and sisters.

He smiled.

SEALs have special training equipment.
Like telephone poles.
SEALs are great swimmers.
They jump into the water with telephone poles.
SEALs are skilled at demolition.
They get to blow up telephone poles.
SEALs believe in teamwork.
Because you can't carry a telephone pole alone

—*Anonymous*

The Grumman C-2A Greyhound came in over *Jefferson*'s flight deck in a perfect landing, the result of intensive training and lots of practice. As a COD (Carrier Onboard Delivery) plane, its mission was to fly high-priority supplies out to the carriers. Mail had the highest priority. Until today.

In the cargo bay of the stubby, twin-engine turboprop, Lieutenant Commander Mick Havran felt the arrestor cables catch the tailhook of the plane, and made sure he was strapped in. Suddenly, the plane jerked to a halt, going from 105 mph to zero in under five seconds. The passengers took it in stride.

The eighteen men strapped into the cargo bay of the COD were graduates of one of the most difficult special warfare schools in the world. A yearlong course, with a washout rate of over 85 percent, it was at least comparable with SAS, less brutal and more efficient than Spetznatz, and head and shoulders above everything else in the world. People sometimes tried to compare them with the Army Green Berets, which Havran always pointed out, was apples and oranges. The Green Beanies were soldiers, true, but they also worked with local civilians, generated popular support, trained defense forces, inoculated kids, and all that other "Hearts and Minds" stuff that gave people warm fuzzy feelings. SEALs killed people and blew things up. End of story.

Seven men were last-minute additions to the team, beefing it up for the mission. For some problems, there was no substitute for warm bodies. Loaded with demolitions, sniper rifles, silenced weapons, night vision gear, ammunition, and whatever else each of them thought they might need, one of the older SEALs had seen them load up and jeered at them for taking too much along. Havran knew better.

After Vietnam, most of the combat veterans had left the SEALs, their place taken by career-oriented types who saw SEAL training as a ticket to punch, fanatics about physical fitness and macho-BS games they thought proved how tough you were.

Reality set in during the Grenada invasion. An entire SEAL team had drowned trying to swim to shore from the submarine that dropped them off. Various other idiocies got more good men killed, until the learning curve began to catch up. In Nicaragua, they were tasked to aid the Contras against the Sandinistas. In that environment, you did it right every time or you died. A lot of the macho games went away there, replaced by hard common sense. The Ninja stuff was all well and good, but there was no substitute for basic field tactics.

The men in the cabin behind Havran were the product of that brutal learning process, volunteers whose skills were a blend of the esoteric and the practical. The same type of men who'd terrified the Iraqi rear areas in Desert Storm and fought against the tragic betrayal that was Somalia. Each of them had seen the movie *Navy SEALs* and thought it was pretty cool. Each of them agreed they would never let a loose doorknob like the Charlie Sheen character from that movie onto their team.

The COD jerked to a stop, the twin-Allison turboshafts suddenly losing their volume, dropping from deafening to painfully loud. The SEALs had their gear ready to go before the door opened. Carrier landings were old hat. So was moving fast and carrying their gear with them. What awaited them outside the door of the COD, however, was something they were totally unprepared for.

Cameras.

Half a dozen video cameras, including one of the big pedestal-mounted studio models. At least two dozen 35mm cameras, most of them with flashes, among a mob of sailors. As he blinked into the glare, Havran could dimly make out the CO of *Jefferson* stepping forward with hand outstretched. Behind him, Havran heard his chief sniper, groan, "Aw damn, it's Somalia all over again!"

Captain Edward Callaghan stepped up to Havran, grabbed his hand, and smiled into the cameras, "Smile for the cameras, men. We're making history today! Welcome aboard USS *Jefferson*!" The SEAL team leader tried to smile into the cameras as he shook the captain's hand. Squinting through the flash images, Havran could eventually see that everyone present was Navy. Callaghan hadn't completely lost his mind. These were all Navy, probably part of the ship's crew.

"Hey Nolan!" he called back to one of his team. "You always gripe about how we don't get cruise books. We'll be in these guys' cruise book. Maybe you can get a copy!''

Callaghan laughed at that. ''It's a deal, Lieutenant Commander! Your whole team will get copies of our next cruise book. Now one more pose for the cameras, and we'll get your people some lunch.''

Havran smiled again for a last barrage of photos. Then Marine MPs from the carrier's detachment shooed away most of their audience. Havran tried to handle this diplomatically as he spoke to Callaghan. ''Sir, my people appreciate the offer, but we'll have to pass. We have to get to *Kimmel* as soon as possible. The helicopter is ready, isn't it? Sir?''

The veiled threat to anyone who threw a monkey wrench into this operation was not missed by Callaghan. ''Of course It's being brought onto the flight deck now. Are you sure you won't eat here?''

''Sorry sir, but there's photo intelligence we need on *Kimmel.* Thank you for the offer.'' Havran looked around, saw a CH-46 being brought up on an elevator even as he spoke. ''There's our ride, people. Move!'' Led by an aviation bosuns mate chief, they moved.

The space they crossed was big enough for three football fields, complete with sidelines and end zones. Perched to one side was the twelve-story-tall structure known as ''The Island,'' from which operations were directed. Parked on the flight deck were eighty fixed-wing aircraft and half a dozen helicopters. Aircraft carriers only have space to store a fraction of their aircraft within the ship. Rain or shine, a deployed carrier keeps its planes on deck. Which makes things very crowded.

The strike aircraft were already uploaded for the air-strikes that would begin in twelve hours. Planes were festooned with drop tanks of extra fuel, ''smart'' missles and cluster bombs, gun pods, flare pods, electronic counter measure equipment, and ordnance ranging from hi-tech fuel air munitions to no-tech 500-pound ‘‘iron’’ bombs.

Callaghan made a brief address to the cameras, then headed up to the flag bridge. Rear Admiral (Upper Half) Tyner was at a NATO conference in Brussels, which meant Callaghan would be calling the shots from *Jeff*. That made it an opportunity for Callaghan.

On board the helicopter, the crew chief was turning his bird over to CWO1 Lloyd Nolan, the pilot the SEALs had borrowed for this mission. Nolan was just a shade under retirement age and had flown in every American military involvement since 1972.

‘‘Here’s your checklist. We had to put on drop tanks to give you range to reach *Kimmel*, so with your team, you’ll be flying pretty heavy. My people have been doing preventive maintenance on it ever since we heard you were coming. Do you want to do a full check yourself, or just a walk around?’’

Nolan looked over the checklist and the preventive maintenance system (PMS) sheets. Everything looked solid. The crew chief didn’t appear to be hiding anything. Plus, he’d get a taste of how the bird flew while they were going to *Kimmel*, and do any fine-tuning there while Havran and his team did final preps for their mission. ‘‘That’s okay, Chief. Let’s just do a quick walk around. We’re burning daylight.’’

The two men walked around the helicopter, doing a thorough visual inspection, Nolan checking for any signs of sloppy maintenance. He found none, went into the cabin, and started the checklist with his copilot and the crew chief. Meanwhile, the SEALs stowed their gear, strapping everything down for the long flight to come. All of them were a little tired from the long flight, but excitement overrode exhaustion. By the time everything was strapped in, Nolan had completed his checklist. The crew chief gave him a thumbs-up and left. An electric cart towed the CH-46 out onto the flight deck as Nolan started the engines.

On the flag bridge, Captain Callaghan watched the helicopter start up, and looked out over the aircraft he commanded. The helicopters and jets on his flight deck were more than a match for most of the world's air forces, easily capable of neutralizing the Libyan Air Force by themselves. Flight operations had ceased while the seal team was on board, but Callaghan could see two F-18s waiting on the catapults, ready to launch as soon as the helicopter was clear. To one side, he saw the firefighting teams, standing by as they always were during flight operations. Around them was enough ordnance to wipe out an armored division. Callaghan smiled. He loved his job. "Commo!"

"Here, sir."

"Send a message in clear to *Kimmel*. The mail helicopter is on the way."

The CH-46 is a transport helicopter, a flying boxcar with rotors at both ends. Like its larger cousin the CH-47, it has both engines at the rear. If the CH-46 loses engine power, the centrifugal force of the rotation will keep the rotor blades spinning fast enough to slowly lower the helicopter, a technique known as autorotation. This makes for a big helicopter that needs lots of room.

Nolan increased the RPMs, watched his ground controller, and listened to the chatter from the tower. Some buffeting, more winds from the huge bulk of *Jefferson* shoving through the air. The crew chief had been correct. With the drop tanks that gave them the range to reach *Kimmel*, the team and all its gear, plus (he chuckled) a dozen bags of mail, the CH-46 was riding very heavy.

There it went. Green light!

Nolan stepped up RPM on the rotors, and increased the pitch of the blades. They bit deep into the air, grabbing huge chunks of the atmosphere and ramming it downwards, slowly lifting the helicopter off the deck. All signals were good. Nolan increased power, stepping up RPMs even more. The GE Turboshaft engines poured out 3000 shaft horsepower, lifting the helicopter steadily. Updrafts started catching the helicopter, above the relatively calm zone immediately over the deck, and Nolan really opened up the throttle, giving the rotors even more pitch to tear the helicopter free of the turbulence, using the blades to lift them into the sky.

Which was when the main rotor nut shattered.

It happened on the rear rotor, eighty feet above the flight deck. The loss of the rotor nut instantly unbalanced the rear shaft. Nolan felt it the second the nut snapped, and knew he was about to lose his rear rotor. He killed power to the rotors immediately, began to autorotate in. It would be a rough landing, he knew, but better a rough landing than a crash.

The terrific centrifugal force of the rotor, its lift versus the dragging weight of the helicopter, stressed the rotor assembly beyond endurance. It began to disintegrate. Then a chance crosswind caught the helicopter, blowing it sideways. Towards the Island.

Callaghan saw it happen from the flag bridge. One seaman on the bridge saw it too, and muttered the most common last words before violent death. "Oh shit."

The rotors tore into the bridge like a chainsaw. Callaghan saw one broken rotor fly out over the sea. The other rotors punched through the window glass of the bridge, decapitated one lookout, hit a steel bulkhead, and shattered. Shrapnel from graphite-titanium composite killed half the people on the bridge.

One deck above, on the flag bridge, Callaghan heard the collision and screams, and grabbed the 1MC ship's microphone on the wall. If the word hadn't been passed already, he knew it wasn't going to be from the bridge. *"Prepare for emergency landing on the flight deck!"* His voice was still echoing over the ship when he turned to the yeoman standing next to him. The boy looked blankly at him. "Go to the bridge! Give me a damage report!"

In the helicopter, the pilot was too busy to think, operating on pure reflex and barking commands into the radio. "Mayday, mayday, clear the deck for emergency landing!" His voice was rock steady as he reminded himself he'd been in worse spots than this one. He and the copilot wrestled with the stick as the rear rotor assembly wiped out the bridge, throwing the rear of the helicopter back and forth even as the copilot cut shaft power. Too late. Before the rotors could slow, what was left of the rotor assembly tore itself loose. The heavily laden rear of the CH-46 dropped like a stone.

On the CH-46, Nolan felt the rotor assembly give way and knew he was going to die. With his bird still too high to drop safely, he had one option. He poured more power into his front rotors and tried to pull the helicopter out over the water. It did no good. The weight of the two engines and the extra fuel were too much. The back of the helicopter dropped while the forward rotors kept elevating the front of the helicopter.

Those who survived and saw it would forever after talk of the picture. One kid with nerves of steel and a video camera actually caught it on film. A CH-46, with seal team aboard, upside-down as, from seventy feet in the air, it dropped onto four uploaded F-18 Hornets.

The front rotors chewed into the planes like a threshing machine before they disintegrated. As the weight smashed down, drop tanks shattered. The still running jet engines ingested wreckage and exploded like small bombs, spraying fragments of white-hot metal through the mass of smashed metal and jet fuel.

Fire Fighting Team One was already moving, filling the lines with seawater under pressure as they ran. Team Two was deploying a second later, charging their own hoses, preparing to lay down a screen of cooling water over team one, the "Attack" team, so that they could get close enough to fight the fire.

They'd been under the sun since daybreak, been on duty since before dawn. Adrenaline was pumping as they moved forward. They were mostly junior seamen, non-rated snipes and deck apes, kids out of high school, led by NCOs and officers who were just as tired as they were. They knew exactly what they were marching into. They went anyway, because that was their job.

From the flag bridge, Callaghan saw them close in on the fires already raging, knew they were in a race against the fire.

They lost the race.

Hot fragments of metal had already sliced open the casings of solid-fuel rocket motors on the missles. More casings had been crushed open. Flame set them off. Suddenly, missiles were flying out of the wreckage on wild, unguided courses. The next thing to go was a coil of detonation cord on one of the seals. Fire burned through its plastic casing. Detonation cord is sensitive, used to detonate more stable explosives like C4. Fifty feet of it exploded next to four one-pound blocks of C4. Sympathetic detonations started among the ordnance on the helicopter, blew burning fuel and fragments of men and metal everywhere, and set off the ordnance that had been on the jets. Six 500-pound iron bombs popped off like firecrackers, throwing flaming wreckage into the other parked jets, wiping out Fire Fighting Team One, then Team Two.

Every alarm the ship had was ringing. One of the survivors on the bridge was calling out orders over the ship's loudspeaker. Reserve fire fighting teams were grabbing gear and rushing to their stations. Throughout the massive carrier, watertight doors were being sealed, emergency equipment was being broken out. From deep in the heart of the ship, engineers in Damage Control Central were already responding from long practice, following the fires on charts and coordinating fire fighting efforts against them.

Callaghan turned from the horror outside the window, and ran to the ladderwell that went down into the bridge. He knew what to do. They had to bring *Jefferson* across the wind, blow the smoke and heat away from the Island so fire fighting teams could get in there before the flame spread. If they were fast enough, they might even be able to still support the mission. But first he had to save his ship.

That was when half of a semicrushed Maverick missle, flying unguided from the ignition of its propellant, sailed into the window of the flag bridge on sheer bad luck and blew up.

"Fire, fire, fire! Class bravo fire in main machinery room two!" the 1MC loudspeakers roared. The ringing of the alarm bell had not yet faded. *"Damage control parties, provide from repair locker two! Set condition zebra throughout the ship! All personnel move up and forward on starboard side, down and aft on port! This is a drill!"*

Toombs grinned, dropped the mop he'd been using (excuse me, he thought to himself, the swab) and ran down the passageway towards the repair locker. He was on the port side and the repair locker was aft of him, so he headed to the rear of the ship. The directions for movement were to avoid jams of people moving both ways on the narrow ship's ladderwells and passageways. They worked, mostly. As Toombs moved, the word was passed. *"Halon deployed, time: 1324. Halon ineffective."*

As he ran, Toombs rolled down his sleeves and buttoned his shirt up to the neck. Repair Locker Two was mass confusion, everybody grabbing gear. Two chiefs with stopwatches and red baseball caps observed the chaotic training exercise around them.

"Hose man number one, here!" yelled Toombs. "Toss me out some flash gear!" A rolled-up bundle of flash hood and gloves were tossed at him. He threw them on, pulled open an OBA locker. Inside were the harnesses and gear for OBA—Oxygen Breathing Apparatus—rigs that generated oxygen from chemicals, so fire fighters could operate where fire had consumed the air. He strapped one on, then put on asbestos gloves and a fire fighter's helmet with face mask, and tucked an unopened breathing canister into the OBA.

Coltrane shoved past him, and yelled into the repair locker, "Hose man number two, here!" Coltrane began suiting up.

Toombs grinned underneath his face mask. "Yo, Dog, you stop for a drink on the way?"

"Had to get my long-sleeved shirt!" Coltrane strapped on his OBA as he spoke. "Not my fault the 1MC in the paint locker doesn't work."

"Yeah, especially when you switch it off and dog the door shut!"

Coltrane gave a sideways grin. "Yo, G-Money, you know I need my beauty rest! Not as much as you do, though!"

Damage Controlman 1st Class Corbin, in charge of the damage control locker, tapped them both on the shoulder. "We've got two inches of burning fuel on the floor of MMR Two! Move!" The two men, fully suited up, joined the file of sailors running for the simulated fire. When they got there, the hoses were already laid out and the rest of the hose teams were ready. They took their places, the lead two men on the hose.

Snyder, the team leader, called forward, "Charge hoses!"

Toombs picked up the nozzle, turned on the voice amplifier mounted on his OBA, and asked Chief Stolchak, who was wearing an evaluator's hat for this,

"Chief, do we charge the hoses or just simulate charging 'em?"

"Simulate!" Stolchak checked his clipboard. "Team Leader, are you manned and ready?"

"Manned and ready, Chief!" called Snyder.

"Then why don't you tell DC Central?"

Snyder jumped at that, turned to the sound-powered phone talker near him who maintained communications with damage control central. "Tell DC Central we're manned and ready. Request permission to enter the space! Woodall, secure power to MMR2!"

At the breaker panel, Woodall, the team's electrician, opened the panel, and tapped the breakers she would hit in the event of a real fire to cut off electricity to the affected room, to kill any electrical fire or shock risk.

"Power secured to main machinery room two!" Woodall's contralto was a sharp contrast to the male voices, but at least she could really make herself heard.

Merris repeated the message, then called back, "Permission is given to enter the space!"

Standing by the door, Toombs saw Snyder give him the "go" signal to open the door, reached for it, then stopped. He looked at Stolchak, who had an eager grin on his face. "What are you waiting for, Tombstone?"

Toombs grinned, pulled off one glove, and put the back of his hand against the steel of the door. "How does it feel, Chief?"

Stolchak smiled, checked off an item. "Nice going, Big Nuts. The metal is hot to the touch but has not scorched your hand."

"The metal is hot to the touch!" called Toombs.

"Metal hot to touch, aye!" answered Snyder. "Smoke curtains are up! Fight that fire!"

"Charge hose! Simulated!" barked Toombs, his voice turned to a mechanical roar by the amplifier built into the OBA.

"Charge hose, simulated, aye!" came the reply from

back in the line. That signified the hose was being filled with seawater under pressure.

The team's entrance man threw open the door, and stood back. Toombs entered the cavernous space deep within *Kimmel*. Two of the four General Electric jet turbines that drove the ship half filled the space. Four stories below was the bottom of main machinery room two. They were simulating a massive fuel leak, with burning fuel puddled on the decks, consuming all oxygen and filling the space with smoke.

"It flared up as you opened the door!" called Stolchak. "What now?"

"I set the nozzle to high-density fog and move forward." Toombs looked at Stolchak, who nodded.

"Secure from drill!" blared the 1MC. *"Restow all gear!"*

Stolchak looked up at the 1MC at that. "What the hell is going on up there? I decide when this drill is over!"

"Chief Stolchak, please dial 101."

Coltrane looked at Stolchak. "Something's up. That's the CO's cabin!"

Stolchak nodded and went to the nearest ship's phone. "Go teach your grandma to suck eggs, Coltrane. If the CO wanted this cut short, he better have a good reason!"

Most of the other fire fighters were already hauling gear back to the DC locker. Toombs and Coltrane stuck around. Something was up and they wanted to know what. Curiosity didn't keep them from shedding their fire fighting gear, however.

Stolchak stood at the phone talking, at first angrily, then with a shocked expression on his face. He listened for a while, spoke, his words lost over the roar of the engines. Then he hung up the phone and looked at Toombs and Coltrane. "*Jefferson* has a fire on the flight deck. It sounds like *Forrestal* all over again. Our commo is talking to *Ticonderoga*. They can't reach anybody on

Jeff.'' Stolchak looked at Coltrane and Toombs. ''Keep this quiet. We don't know anything yet. And restow your gear.'' He headed up to the captain's office. Coltrane and Toombs looked at each other.

Coltrane spoke first. ''Minor change of plans, G-Money?''

''Minor change of plans, Dog.''

Woodall finished restowing her gear, folded up her OBA rig, and tucked it into the locker. That done, she tried to figure out what she could do other than go back up to the EM shop and get her tool kit. Chief Morgan was in the EM shop. Every time she went in there, he was watching her. Saying nothing, doing nothing, strictly formal. Just looking at her.

It had all started out so simply, Seaman Woodall told herself. On their first liberty when they ''in-chopped''—entered—the Mediterranean, beginning the Med cruise, she'd gone ashore with EMC (Electrician's Mate, Chief) Lance Morgan on the buddy system. The crew of *Kimmel* had enjoyed three days of liberty in Marseilles, during the Bastille Day weekend. Chief Morgan was fun to be with. She'd spent a lot of time with him.

She'd done the same at the other liberty ports the ship had visited—not that there'd been many. The last couple of liberty ports, Morgan had seemed to be around all the time. He'd started mentioning his recent divorce, talking about how bad his wife was—not like Seaman Monica Woodall, he hastened to say. He'd begun hanging around Woodall at sea, more and more often as the cruise went on.

It was the kind of thing Woodall had been through before. She was, by her own description, a ''babe.'' Five foot seven, short blond hair (Morgan was always advising her to let it grow long), 119 pounds, trim and in shape, with cornflower blue eyes and everything right where it should be. She had been told, with various degrees of tact, that she could be the Playboy centerfold for any month she chose. That had boosted her ego a little. Before this all started.

She knew there were women in the Navy who tried to get by on the "Oh, poor little me, I'm just a girl" routine. But she took pride in the fact that she could pass the male physical training requirements, not just the easier female requirements. She took pride in how she looked, though it was sometimes a hassle from overgrown adolescents trying to score on every available female. She'd always been able to handle it before.

Chief Morgan was a different case. At first she'd tried to be friendly, one of the guys. He'd taken it as an invitation. She'd tried to distance herself. He'd accused her of playing hard to get. The final straw had been in a club on their last liberty at Haifa. He'd cornered her off the dance floor, a few too many drinks making him cruder than usual. When he'd put his hand on her breast, she'd slapped him. He'd accused her of leading him on. She'd told him to go to hell, then fled the club.

The next day, she was made damage control petty officer (DCPO) for the electrician's mates. Responsible for their division's maintenance, DCPOs did much of the work themselves, along with their normal jobs. Extra work went out to people in the division and all work was signed off by the division officer. Suddenly her work was never good enough for Morgan. Whenever anyone in the division didn't like their assignment, Morgan could always find a reason why they were right and why Woodall had to do it.

Her normal work suffered. Chief Morgan scrutinized that too, assigning her extra training. Maybe she had led him on earlier, maybe she— She drove that thought from her mind. She had *not* led him on, or taken any favors from him. She would not think that way just because he accused her! She'd read about the psychology of sexual harassment, knew it backwards and forwards. She'd just never had it happen to her before.

But, oh, going in to the shop again . . .

She was standing there, her mind turning that over and over, when Coltrane and Toombs, a couple of the non-rates from deck division, came around the corner. Like most of the males on the ship, they had hit on her at one time or another. Like most of the males, when she had said no, they had accepted that and gone on. She'd had second thoughts about Toombs. He was cute and soft-spoken, a rare trait among most of the crew. Somebody had taught him manners. She thought of what her grandmother would say if she said a black man was cute. She grinned at the thought.

Walking by, Coltrane saw her expression. "Whoa, Woodall's smiling! Somebody get a camera, it's a first for this cruise!"

She laughed, letting out tension. "You stop that! I am not that grim!"

"Oh yes you are!" Coltrane answered. They stopped to talk, in no hurry to get back to their work. It would be there tomorrow, and the day after that. "You're scary, Woodall! Always going around with this mean expression like you're going to bite people's heads off!"

"Yeah, well it keeps me from getting hit on all the time." Her smile was fading. "Too many guys on this ship won't take no for an answer."

Toombs raised an eyebrow at that, balled massive hands into massive fists. "Somebody been hasslin' you?"

"It's no big deal. I can handle it."

Coltrane grinned, went into a martial arts stance. "Yeah, well if you need a hand, you tell us! They don't call my man here 'Tombstone' for nothing! Me, I'll kick their ass just for the fun of it!" Coltrane mimed punches and kicks, narrowly missing the others in the passageway. "I'm a bouncer at this club back in Virginia Beach, some guy gets out of line, *Boom*! His buddy comes up, Oh! You want some too! *Pa-pow*! Down he goes!''

Toombs ground one fist into a palm, and said in a low, grim voice, ''You just let this guy know you got some friends can whip his ass. It don't have to be on the ship. We can wait 'til they off on they own in the street, no uniforms around.''

Woodall smiled again, shook her head. She'd never take them up on their offer, but it was good to know they were there. ''Thanks. I know y'all mean it. But I have to go.'' Chief Morgan had started showing up whenever she did maintenance on the division's fan rooms, sitting in to ''observe her work.'' Desperation hatched a plan.

They went off to their jobs.

Chapter Seven

In the CO's cabin, Commander Matt Reisling knew two things had just come to a crashing end—Operation Sudden Lightning, and his career. Not that anything was his fault, but it was an unsuccessful operation. That kind of thing followed a man around forever. That poisonous association meant he'd be lucky to get command of a reserve frigate after this.

Over the radio in his quarters, the voice of the damage control assistant of *Ticonderoga* spoke. "*Jeff* is doing about ten knots. The last detonations ended twenty minutes ago. We're picking up flashing lights from the bridge. They say they are steering from engineering, but the island has lost all power. Fire got into at least one of the hangar bays. There are still flames on half the flight deck—a couple of tankers got caught in the detonation. We pulled in to use our hoses on the fire, but once they got underway again we had to back off to avoid collision. They're laying down fire fighting foam now, and they've brought her across the wind. They should have the fire under control in about ten minutes.''

The officers gathered around the radio listened in shocked silence. Reisling asked, ''What do the aircraft look like? Are any of the helicopters still intact?''

''Negative. All aircraft on deck are destroyed. They were shoving planes over the side to make a firebreak. The combat air patrol broke off about ten minutes ago and headed to Galleta.''

Whistles of shock and surprise around the table as that set in. Hundreds of millions of dollars worth of aircraft, no telling how many sailors. Gone. Reisling picked up the microphone. ''All right Tim, thanks. Let us know if we can help. At Flank 2, we could be there in eight hours.''

''The show'll be over by then, Matt. *Ticonderoga* out.''

Reisling looked at his assembled officers and NCOs. In the back, the CIA agent, Majors, looked as if his world was coming to an end. ''I want options. Do we have any?''

The XO spoke up. ''With *Iwo Jima* off Kuwait, there are no decks in this area big enough to support the hostage rescue.''

Reisling nodded. ''What about the relief carrier?''

''*Nimitz* just cleared the Virgin Islands,'' explained Washington. ''She won't be here in time either.''

''How about staging it out of Israel?''

Kendricks answered that. ''They'd have to cross Egypt. I don't think the Egyptians would permit it.''

CHENG, or Chief of Engineering, was a heavyset lieutenant commander who was concerned only with his people, his engines, and his upcoming retirement, in that order. He stood up and shook his head. ''Folks, this operation is as dead in the water as the *Jefferson*. But it isn't because of us, and the solution, if any, is not our responsibility. Our job is to await further orders.'' He turned to the CO. ''Captain, this is a waste of time. We have a lot of work to do. I suggest we get on with it, and wait to see what the boys uptown figure out.''

Reisling looked sour at that. ''CHENG, I didn't think there'd be any harm in discussing options. But you are correct. Right now we're very small fish in a mighty big pond. Let's keep the crew training, however. Guns, I want you to continue missile drills and gun drills. If they figure out something higher up, we might still have a job to do. Dismissed.'' The officers and chiefs filed out. Eventually, only Majors was standing there.

The CIA agent looked at the captain. ''It doesn't look good, does it?''

Reisling shook his head, looking at a chart of the Med on the wall. ''Twenty-two years of service down the drain, Mr. Majors. Twenty-two years!'' His voice turning savage, he hurled his pen against a bulkhead. It shattered. That seemed to let some of the tension out of him. ''It was a long shot anyways. We're a minor ship in a major operation. It only would have amounted to one last good evaluation in my record.''

''I meant for the hostages.''

Reisling jumped at that. ''Oh, yes! Yes, that's a tragedy. But don't give up on the hostages yet. Some of the best brains in Washington are working on this right now.''

The best brains in Washington were watching *Jefferson* burn from a live satellite feed. The CNO glared at the ship furiously, as if by sheer force of will he could put the fires out.

Wrangel was working his way down a checklist of their options. ''State Department says no way with either Italy or Israel. Staging an antiterrorist operation out of Italy requires notifying their government, which guarantees the Libyans find out. U.S. helicopters staging out of Israel would be would be spotted crossing Egypt.''

''Parachute insertion is out,'' said the Air Force representative. "Any plane big enough to carry the assault team is too big to slip through Libyan radar. Also, we still wouldn't have a way to get the hostages out."

Special Operations said, "The backup seal team is loading into a second C-130 now. They can be in Galleta before dawn. There, they can get another helicopter and jump from *Ticonderoga* to *Kimmel* to stage for the rescue."

The CNO shook his head. "No good. The only transport helicopters left at Galleta are CH-53's. Those things are fast, they carry fifty troops at a shot, and they're too damn big to land on the deck of a destroyer. Hell, to land CH-46s on *Kimmel* they have to fly sideways onto the flight deck, and then it's a damn tight fit. Also, to get into position, *Tico* would have to cease assisting *Jeff* and shift east. If they do that, we may still lose *Jeff*."

The National Security Advisor put down his phone. "Gentlemen, I just spoke with the President. The State Department says they can negotiate for the hostages." Sudden quiet.

Wrangel shook his head. "No go. Khaddaffi has already given the word to 'disappear' them if their presence is revealed. At the first mention of these people by us, they are dead, buried, and deniable."

The National Security Advisor nodded. "The President has seen the evaluations, but he doesn't believe we have anything else solid to go with. Unless we can give him an alternative in ten hours, we'll try diplomacy."

An unlucky yeoman chose that moment to deliver another item of news. "Sir, preliminary report from the damage control assistant on *Jefferson*." The CNO's glare briefly silenced the younger sailor.

"Well?" snapped Admiral Madison, finally. "What did he say?"

"Sir, DCA *Jefferson* reports heavy structural damage to the flight deck due to the bomb detonations. He says it'll be at least twenty-four hours before any sections of the flight deck can be cleared for use by loaded helicopters.''

The CNO went back to glaring at the screens as plans were discussed.

The rest of the day on *Kimmel* was relatively quiet, as quiet as things ever got. Word percolated through the crew that *Jefferson* was burning and that their mission had been canceled. Drills continued at a more moderate pace, but the pressure was off.

Majors prowled the ship, deep in thought, his escort following along. Out of idle curiosity, he asked his escort to give him a tour. He was shown the machine shops, the ship's armory, the bridge, and even a quick peek at CIC before Chief Carter chased them out. They made a brief stop at the ship's library, a tiny, hot, noisy space crammed with well-thumbed paperbacks, an astounding variety of odds and ends, a career counselor trying to catch up on his paperwork, and several dozen hardcover books ranging from *Jane's Fighting Ships* to the collected works of Gilbert and Sullivan. Majors took the copy of *Jane's* and retired to his quarters.

Seaman Woodall entered the fan room with her DCPO tool kit, took off her hat, opened the kit. The fan rooms had dust filters which had to be removed and cleaned, a dirty, difficult process. In the Mediterranean heat, the fan rooms were dusty ovens. Her blue dungaree shirt was quickly soaked with sweat, sticking to her skin as she worked. Then, over the whirring of the fans, she heard the door to the space open, close, and latch shut.

She'd mentioned to Morgan, out of everyone else's hearing, that she was working on the fan room today.

Okay, she thought to herself, and checked her equipment.

Morgan was wearing his most pleasant smile. Perspiration was already staining his khakis. "Good morning, Seaman Woodall. How goes it?"

"Just a fine Navy day, Chief," she said, loosening a stubborn screw.

Morgan mopped one sweaty brow. "Man, it's hotter than a two-dollar pistol in here. Mind if I take my shirt off?"

"Whatever, Chief."

He took his shirt off, flexed his muscles. The funny thing was, she thought, the man was attractive. A blond beach bum in his youth, he was still in shape. He was just the particular kind of idiot who couldn't understand that No meant No. Or was turned on by the fact. "Shame you can't do this, Seaman Woodall." He winked. "Tell you what, you can take your shirt off if you want to. I won't tell anybody."

"No thanks, Chief. Actually, I don't consider that funny."

He grimaced. "Loosen up. You could make things a lot easier for yourself in this division." He was getting less attractive by the second, she noticed, more and more like a hungry animal. That made it easier.

"I just want to do my job, Chief." She concentrated on her work, even as he stood up and stepped over to her.

His voice was almost pleading. "That's what I respect about you, Woodall. You don't ask for favors. You aren't like these bitches who whine about everything. You really are something." He put his hand on her shoulder. "I know I've gotten carried away a couple of times, but, hey, it's a long way from Norfolk, you know? It could be different."

She faced him, his face inches away from hers, her voice neutral. "Chief, please let go of me and back away."

His answer was to put his arm around her waist and smile, holding their bodies together. She felt his body, hot and damp next to her. She wanted to be sick. She wanted to die. She felt helpless. She felt dirty. "I'm chief of this division, Woodall. The division officer does what I say. There aren't any witnesses. It's your word against mine." His voice grew rougher, savage. "What can you do about it, bitch?"

With a supreme effort, she controlled her voice. "You're being videotaped right now, Chief." His eyes widened. "I bought a camcorder at the ship's store. Look to your right and you can see it in my tool kit. I set it to record when you came in here." He turned, looked. The glass eye of the little 8mm video camera looked back. "Even if you smash it, that tape is intact."

He jumped back as if he'd been stung, gouged his head on a bolt, and swore furiously. The dominant element in his curses was "fucking bitch," uttered no less than seven times in one minute. Slowly, the stream of obscenities stopped. He glared at her. "So what do you want from me?"

"Nothing, Chief. Just let me do my job. I don't want anything from you at all. But if you ever touch me again, the CO gets a copy of that tape."

He threw on his shirt, shot her a furious glance, and left.

She sat down, utterly drained. A sob tried to force its way out her throat. She choked it back. A couple of minutes later, the door to the fan room opened again. EM3 Leggett came in, gave her a curious look. He was a bible-thumping Baptist from Arkansas, and he didn't always approve of Monica Woodall, but he was her friend.

"How'd it go? I wish you'd let me hide in here as a witness."

She slammed a fist against a bulkhead. "I shouldn't have to do this garbage! I shouldn't have to blackmail someone just to be let alone!" Her face was twisted with suppressed tears.

Leggett stood there, embarrassed, knowing it was an evil world, and hating what it did to people. He didn't really see why she was so upset, though. If he'd pulled off something as slick as what she'd done, he'd have been puffed up like a pouter pigeon over his own cleverness. "This world is the devil's and the next world is God's and that's all there is to it. God don't need to put any suffering in the world. We do it all ourselves," he said, finally. "You tell the chaplain about this, next time we see him. He'll make sure this stops."

She stepped closer to Leggett and hugged him. "Oh shut up," she said.

"Knock off ship's work!" Pause. *"Clear the mess decks."*

The roar of the 1MC took Majors out of his thoughts. He had been sitting at the desk in his cabin, poring through his borrowed book, reading up on the abilities of *Kimmel*, which it referred to as a KIDD-Class Guided Missile Destroyer. What he'd seen amazed him. It had also planted the seed of an idea.

The 1MC roared again. *"Sweepers, sweepers, man your brooms! Give the ship a clean sweepdown! Sweep the ship down fore and aft! Sweep down all ladderwells and passageways! Now, sweepers!"*

He went to the door of his cabin, and opened it. His escort was out there—a different sailor than he'd had this morning, a heavyset, red-haired kid with one stripe. "Excuse me, do you know where Halloran is?"

"He's in deck division, isn't he?" The escort, who had "REYNOLDS" stenciled on his shirt, thought a minute. "I think he's cranking. Why? You want to hear him gripe about the Navy?"

That took Majors a moment to figure out. "He complains about the Navy a lot?"

"To anybody who'll listen. Man, he hates the Navy! Doesn't make any secret of it. Always talking about how he was Airborne and a tanker and all that shit.''

''Yeah, that's the guy. Doesn't he get in trouble for it?''

That stopped Reynolds. ''No,'' he finally admitted in a mystified voice. ''He's even striking gunners mate. He's okay as long as he's talking about guns and weapons and stuff. Why do you want to know?''

''Where does he sleep?''

''Deck berthing, up at the front of the ship. Why don't you have him paged over the 1MC?''

Majors considered that for a moment, but decided against it. ''No, not yet. Let's see if we can catch him in deck berthing.''

Deck division poured into its berthing in a tidal wave of dungarees, paint stains and coveralls. ''Fire drill, man overboard drill, missle drill! Next thing you know we'll be doing sweepers drill!'' Coltrane yelled to be heard over the babble. He went back to his rack—a 6 x 2½ x 2½ foot metal box with a mattress, a locker, and a fold-up drawer. He stripped off his paint-stained coveralls and hung them up. Then he reached past his curtains to turn on his boombox, felt around—nothing. ''Hey, what happened to my tape player?''

''Ask the master at arms!'' BM3 Bledsoe spoke without looking up from the magazine he was reading at one of the tables in the berthing. His dungarees were spotless as always, pressed and starched. ''I told you enough times about leaving your shit on your rack. Hale, your walkman is with the master at arms too.''

''You all don't be messing with the berthing master!'' shouted Chambers, at his rack, laughing. ''G-Money gonna nail your ass! You mess up our inspection, he'll make you pay!''

''That's bullshit, man!'' Coltrane slammed his locker shut. ''You couldn't see it with the curtains shut!''

''Don't you think the XO can look past the curtains?''

snapped Bledsoe. He folded his magazine and headed up to chow.

Coltrane muttered various comments about Bledsoe as he stowed away his coveralls and put on a clean undershirt. As he did so, BM1 Magsaysay came into the berthing and shouted, "Everybody, listen up!" Sudden quiet. "OPS just called down to the office. He says the nonskid on the foc'sle is chipping and breaking off. He wants everybody in deck division out there tonight after chow with chipping hammers to clean it off. Tomorrow we lay down fresh Nonskid."

"Tonight after chow?" Chambers squawked. "That's fucked up! Give me a chipping hammer, I'll use it on OPS's head!"

"Do we have any Nonskid left to put on?" asked Toombs. "I thought we used it up last week on the missile decks."

"Just be out on the foc'sle after chow!" snapped Magsaysay. He left to a chorus of angry voices.

Coltrane shook his head as he went back to his rack. It got quiet again as he stowed his gear and got ready for chow. When he turned around, some guy in khakis, without rank badges, was standing behind him. It took Coltrane a second to realize this guy was the CIA agent they'd rescued.

"Is Halloran around here?" The man's voice was quiet, but it carried.

"No. He's mess-cranking. I think he's in deep sink."

"Does he sleep in here?"

"Sure. That's his rack there." Coltrane pointed it out.

Majors looked at the metal boxes the sailors slept in. The racks were stacked three high, with the top rack open to the pipe-studded ceiling. They were about the size of a Pullman bed, with a small bookshelf and reading lamp at one end. Halloran's was typical, neatly made, the shelf crammed with a stationary pad and books. Coltrane watched as the CIA agent read off the titles of several well-thumbed volumes.

"*How to Make War. Enemy at the Gates* by Craig, Catton's *Grant Moves South.*" The CIA agent muttered the titles as he read them, nodded his head. "Nothing like a little light reading."

Coltrane, whose reading tastes ran to westerns, watched carefully, made sure the CIA agent put back each book. "Halloran's always reading that heavy shit. If you're looking for a book, we've got a library."

Majors gave a funny smile. "No, I think I'm going to be busy." He turned to his escort. "Where's deep sink?"

Looking into the hot, steaming space a few minutes later, Majors almost gave up the idea in the back of his head. Halloran was shoving trays of dishes and silverware through the machines, occasionally scorching his hands and cursing furiously, his face a sour, angry mask. But Majors noted that the man was also working steadily at the job, which had to be pretty unpleasant.

Majors shouted in over the noise of the dishwashers. "Halloran! Could I talk to you?"

Halloran looked up at the sound of the voice and suddenly smiled. It changed his face completely, Majors noted. "We're pretty busy now. Maybe after chow—"

The other man in deep sink said, "Go ahead, Halloran. I got this covered." Halloran thanked the other sailor and came out into the passageway.

"What can I do you for?"

Majors decided. "Follow me." They went to Majors's cabin and left the escort at the door. Once in the cabin, Majors invited Halloran to fix himself some coffee, which he did. No sugar, lots of cream, noted Majors. Halloran commented that he couldn't leave Townsend hanging too long, he had to get back soon. Which brought a smile to Majors's face. "Had you heard *Kim-*

mel was going to be part of a hostage rescue mission?''

''Yeah. Scuttlebutt says that *Jeff* had an accident, and the operation's been canceled.'' Majors nodded. Halloran raised his eyebrows in surprise, sipped his coffee thoughtfully. ''So *Jefferson* is out of the equation?''

''The Navy's most powerful combat vessel in the Mediterranean is currently a twelve-alarm fire north of Malta.''

Halloran grimaced. ''Shit.'' His eyes narrowed in thought. ''Man, for once, I thought I was actually going to be involved in something important! Can't they fly in Marines from *Iwo Jima*?''

''Without the *Jefferson* to stage from, those Marines would have to swim to get to Libya. The same goes for flying in another SEAL team.''

''What about the SEAL team they were going to use?''

''It was their helicopter crashing that caused the fire. They're pretty comprehensively toasted.''

Halloran pursed his lips at that. ''Jeez, the whole team wiped out.''

Majors said, ''It'll be three days before *Jefferson* can launch anything. We have less than thirty-six hours before they execute the hostages.'' Halloran sat there, lost in his own internal frustrations. Time to pop the question, thought Majors. He pulled a map of the terrorist camp from his gym bag, tossed it on the table in front of Halloran. ''Take a look at that. You were a grunt before you joined the Navy. What do you think?''

Halloran looked the map over. It was a tactical map, one square to every fifty meters, showing every terrain feature around the camp as well as the camp's layout. He shook his head. ''These dipwads don't know squat from tactics. There are hills overlooking both sides of the camp. Two dry streambeds run just past the perimeter. A company of troops could infiltrate right up to the wire and nobody would know they were there. How many terrorists are in the camp?''

"Fifty or sixty."

The deck seaman shook his head, sat back, and sipped his coffee, never taking his eyes from the map. "It's a shame. The SEALs would have had these guys for breakfast. Hell, my old platoon from the 101st could bust this place open."

"You don't have your old platoon."

Halloran looked up from the map, confused. "What?"

"You don't have your old platoon. You have the crew of this ship, whatever equipment she carries, and twenty-four hours. I have the captain's ear." Majors leaned forward now, all irony gone, his gaze intense, focused. "So, Mr. ex-Airborne, malcontent Navy deck ape, could you put together a landing party to go ashore, assault a terrorist camp, free those hostages, and get them out?"

Halloran looked at the CIA agent as if the man had lost his mind.

Halloran looked at the map.

Then he looked up again.

And he grinned.

Halloran had been poring over the maps for thirty minutes, jumping back and forth between a large-scale map of Libya and the map of the terrorist camp. The change in the man, Majors noted, was amazing. His whole body was animated, his body language completely changed. Even his eyes were a lighter color. His hands moved very little as he spoke, except to support him as he leaned or to point out a feature on the maps. "We start by having *Kimmel* drop us off at the coast. It's only a ten-mile hike to the camp. Not much fun, but we should be able to do it in under three hours. The camp itself's a piece of cake."

Majors nodded, watching. It was interesting watching how the man's mind worked. "How will you crack it?"

"Two teams, a cover team and an insertion team. The cover team sets up on this hill overlooking the camp." He pointed to a hill outside the camp. "From there they can cover the doors of the stone buildings, so nobody gets in or out. They can also watch the road into the camp. The insertion team approaches through this ravine, under cover of the first team, cuts the wire, and enters the camp, here." He pointed.

Majors looked at the map. The print was hard to make out in the light of the cabin lamp. He moved it closer, smoothed a wrinkle. "That hill is at least two hundred yards away from the camp."

"Closer to three. Which makes it perfect for us. See, all the rifles in the armory are M-14s. They fire a real rifle bullet, 7.62 NATO, effective out to twelve hundred yards. Those terrorists are carrying AK-47s. Maximum combat range for an AK is two hundred fifty yards. Once the fight starts, our cover team will be able to pick off those terrorists in complete safety. Plus, if those terrorists act like everybody else I've ever seen with a full-auto rifle, when they start taking fire they'll start firing from the hip, just spraying bullets out. That chops effective range down to about fifty yards."

"The cover team acts as snipers. What about the insertion team?"

The seaman paced back and forth, one arm hugging his side, one hand cupping his chin in thought. As he paced, he stepped from light to shadow, to light again. "They'll be doing close-quarters fighting. The M-14 is all wrong for that. But we've got shotguns and .45 automatics in the armory too. The insertion team goes in with those. We'll saw off the barrels of the shotguns and see if the machinists mates can rig up silencers for the .45s. That gives us close-quarters weapons." He snatched a pad of paper, jotted down notes.

When he was done, he leaned on the table and closely examined the map. "The insertion team goes in silent.

Nobody starts shooting until we're in position, or we're being fired upon. We hit the camp about two AM, when everybody is either sleeping or wishing they were asleep. If the insertion team runs into lone sentries, they kill them with the silenced pistols. That should put us inside the camp without the terrorists even knowing they have infidels in the wire. Once we're inside, we check out the tank, see if it works. If it does, we use it. If not, we give the signal and everybody opens fire at once. We'll take along C4 to blow the doors. The cover team will pin the terrorists down and we'll free the hostages . . ." He suddenly froze in place. "Oh shit."

"What's the problem?"

Halloran's face began to screw up with a familiar feeling. Failure. "What do we do with the hostages once we've rescued them?"

Majors smiled, and pointed to the helicopter on the map. "You load them into that helicopter and fly them out."

Halloran closed his eyes, grimaced. "If it was a snake, it would've bit me." Then he opened his eyes. "Okay, so I'm a little slow today. Fly them out in the Libyans' own bird, huh?" Majors nodded smugly. Halloran smiled back. "I like it. We'll have to take in our own pilot, though. We should take in two pilots, in case one gets killed. There are only two helicopter pilots on *Kimmel.*"

"We'll get both. How large a group are you talking about?"

"Keep it small, to avoid attracting attention. Plus, any group moving on foot can only move as fast as the slowest member. The bigger the group, the slower they move. The real choke point is the helicopter. Everybody we bring will have to fit on that CH-47."

"We aren't going to have to take everybody out. We're going to lose some people."

"Belay that!" said Halloran. The seaman turned to

Majors, his face the casual look of someone who knew all the rules for this sort of thing, but had never experienced it. "Do not write off anybody on a job like this. That's telling people they're going to die. It tends to be bad for morale. Let's maintain the illusion we're bulletproof as long as we can."

His voice had the chilling innocence of someone who had never seen the consequences of violence, but what he said sounded right to the CIA agent. Majors forced a smile. "Okay. But intelligence says three companies of Libyan mechanized infantry are training near that camp. What do we do if one of them intervenes?"

Halloran breezed through the objections without a second thought. "We can call in airstrikes. We have to make sure our radioman can talk with our air support. But they shouldn't be any problem."

"How so?"

Halloran laughed. "They're well inside the country, on training missions. That means no live ammo. They'd have to get ammunition. By then we'll be long gone." He grinned and sat on the desk.

Major looked at Halloran, then looked at the map. "Okay, you've killed the terrorists, you've rescued the hostages, and you've loaded them on board the helicopter. What then?"

Halloran grinned. "Then we go to Wally World!"

Bosuns Mate Third Class Carlton Bledsoe gave his best Eddie Murphy smile to *Kimmel*'s career counselor. NC1 Samms was the man who handled reenlistments, rate changes, and promotions testing for the entire crew. The NC1's office, wedged into the tiny ship's library, was a chaotic jumble of rating manuals, test forms, filing cabinets, and bookshelves. Bledsoe ignored the clutter around them. He hated clutter. "NC1, I've finished my sea tour and I've got two months until my hitch is up. Where do I go next?"

Samms looked at Bledsoe's 201 file for a minute, then set it down. The brown folder was Bledsoe's military biography. Every sailor had one. Bledsoe's was thicker than most. "You're supposed to begin reenlistment procedures six months before ending time in service."

Bledsoe nodded in agreement, and put on his best rueful smile. "You're absolutely right, NC1. I know I put this off longer than I should. But you're the best. You can adjust for that."

"Actually, no." NC1 shook his head slowly. "Bledsoe, you're a petty officer third class with eleven years of service. You are maxed out for time in grade. You didn't even take the last promotion exam. The real nail in your coffin is your record. Four separate racial incidents in the last five years. This last one—"

The smile vanished off Bledsoe's face. "Am I supposed to let some punk-ass boot call me a spearchucker?"

Okay, thought NC1, the gloves are off. "He didn't call you a spearchucker. For the record, you were quoted as having said, "Oh, nigger, please!" and Seaman Apprentice Johnson, who is black, said—"

"Johnson ain't black! He's half-white, paler than you!"

Samms grimaced, but read on. "Seaman Apprentice Johnson, who seems to believe that he is black, then said, "Now, now, none of that, we're all spearchuckers here." Which was when you tried to report him. I'm the equal opportunity counselor too, remember? I was at the hearing."

"So because I don't put up with that shit, I can't reenlist?"

"You can't reenlist because you have too much time in rate. The reason we're not jumping through hoops to get you an exemption is because you never miss a chance to start a racial incident. I'm not even going to mention the complaints we've kept off your record."

Bledsoe's fist slammed down. "That's bullshit! I'm going to the XO!"

Samms just kept his seat, leaned back. From his casual appearance, you wouldn't have been able to guess that he was positioning himself to plant a boot in Bledsoe's face if the man came across the desk at him. "I took your file to the XO already. Your last two evaluations recommend against letting you reenlist. He signed them."

"That motherfucker! I'll—"

"Give it a rest, BM3. I don't know what your problem is, but it sure appears as if you don't like white people. Understandable, there are a lot of white people I don't like myself. Along with brown people, red people, and black people. But you let it interfere with your job. Instead of dealing with it, you cause incidents. Then you make sure each incident raises as big a stink as possible." Samms opened his hands in front of him and shrugged. "Bledsoe, you do not play well with the other children, so we're going to let you go." He sat there, waiting for the next outburst.

Bledsoe surprised him. He left, slamming the door to the small compartment as he went.

The bosuns locker was six decks down and at the other end of the ship. It took Bledsoe five minutes to get there. By the time he did, he had progressed from mere anger to blazing fury. Which didn't help when he came into his space and saw Seaman Apprentice Lavarre Chambers reading his latest issue of *Jet* folded back so it would break the spine, with his feet up on Bledsoe's desk. "Nigger, get your non-rated, funky-ass, goat-smellin' feet off my desk!"

Chambers jumped in surprise, and fell back flailing. The chair flew out from under his gangly body and he hit the deck with a clatter, banging his head against a shelving unit. That, at least, got Bledsoe to smile a little.

Chambers looked up from the deck. "Yo, G! You done cahootin' with NC1 already? W'zup?"

Bledsoe looked out the door into the passageway. Nobody in sight. When he spoke next, his voice was quiet and angry. "The white man has fucked us over again, my brother. I wouldn't take their shit, so they gettin' rid of me."

"Damn! That's cold!" Chambers got up, put the magazine back on the desk, and rubbed his aching head. "Ain't no reason to yell though, G! I'm hangin' wit' you, you know that. You the realest brother on this ship!"

Bledsoe nodded, sat down, and thought, ignoring the younger man. He'd come into the Navy right out of high school. He might bitch about it, but he'd learned early that the Navy was a system a smart man could play like a piano. Even when he'd boasted of how he was leaving the Navy this time, a voice in the back of his head had kept saying "And do what?" The Navy was all he knew. Now time had run out. All he had to show for eleven years in the Navy was a collection of really good suits, a suspended driver's license, and memories of getting drunk and trying to pick up girls in half the ports of the Atlantic.

What would he do now?

Damn white man couldn't leave a brother alone.

Those two thoughts bounced back and forth in his mind.

Reisling looked at his cadet picture. Had he ever been so young? Shaven-headed, eager to graduate from Annapolis so that he could start the long climb, the one that ended with the stars of an admiral on his shoulders, command of destroyer squadrons and carriers and task forces.

He shut his yearbook, reshelved it. All done with now. In six or eight months he would have to leave the Navy, take some reserve position or go straight into civilian life. All because, he was sure, some idiot seaman had done bad maintenance somewhere on *Jefferson* and caused an accident at the worst possible time. Sudden Lightning was a failure now. With it went his last chance for the salvation of his career. He opened a small lacquered case he'd had made in the Philippines, back when he was a boot ensign on his first WestPac. Inside it, on a board covered with black velvet, gleamed symbols of brass and chrome and gold. Complete rank insignia for the U.S. Navy, from ensign to admiral of the fleet. He had bought them the day he graduated from Annapolis, sworn to himself he would wear every one.

Only holes remained of the insignia from Ensign to Commander. Now, the twin silvered eagles of a Captain glinted at him. The eagles he had dreamt of wearing for so long.

For a moment, he felt an urge to throw the box against a steel bulkhead, to smash it and everything it contained into scrap, then throw the whole mess over the side. His hands trembled for a second, as he burned with suppressed fury at his fate.

Then he calmed himself. Sighed. Shut the box. Put it away. He sat for a moment in the quiet, paneled room that had been his goal for so long, only to turn into a dead end.

There was a knock at the door. "Captain?" It was the voice of that CIA agent, Majors.

"Come in!" Why not? Perhaps this would take his mind off things. The CIA agent, entered, followed by one of the deck seamen, an older-than-normal deck seaman, Reisling noted, one with gray hair and a perpetually sullen look, who he had seen around before. Halloran, that was his name. Reisling prided himself on knowing his full crew by name. Interestingly, Halloran seemed like a changed man just now, smiling, eager, as if he could barely contain himself. Reisling found himself smiling faintly just from Halloran's presence. ''Agent Majors, what can I do for you?''

Majors seemed curiously buoyant too, Reisling noted. His appearance was jarring. His hair and bushy mustache, well beyond regulation length, were a wild contrast with his khakis.

Majors took a deep breath. ''Captain, I believe we can still do the hostage rescue.''

Reisling shook his head. ''I'm sorry, Agent Majors. The seal team was a total loss. They have us standing by, but it's probably just for form. If they were sending in another team, they would have informed us by now.''

''No, Captain. I didn't say they would do the hostage rescue. I've been talking with Seaman Halloran here. You might not know it, but he was in the 101st Airborne Division, U.S. Army, for three years. He says that using the personnel and weapons you have on this ship, you can land a small raiding party to get into the camp and free the hostages, then fly them out on the Libyans' own helicopter.''

Reisling's head spun for a second. Hope returned is a heady wine. He focused his best glare on Halloran, who smiled back at him. ''Seaman Halloran, I have better things to do than listen to someone shoot his mouth off. I can call the personnel officer right now and check your record. Were you in the 101st Airborne Division?''

''Yes sir! Third Platoon, Alfa Company, First Battalion.''

Not a second's hesitation. No doubt in it at all. ''Very well. Show me how you intend to do this rescue.''

Halloran stepped forward, laid out the map, and quickly explained his plan. Majors sat down and watched. Reisling listened, skeptical at first, then shocked. Where had this man been all this time? Halloran's scheme actually seemed possible. What would it mean to the man who commanded something like this? A destroyer captain, assembling his own landing party to take on a mission normally reserved for the elite of the elite? Dangerous, yes, but if they pulled it off . . .

Wait. Slow down. Halloran finished his presentation, started rambling about various weapons and tactics. Reisling cut him off with a wave of his hand. "I'm convinced, Seaman Halloran, thank you. Agent Majors, this makes sense to you?"

Majors nodded eagerly. He spoke, bouncing on his feet. "But the clock is ticking. They'll execute the hostages at dawn, the day after tomorrow. We have to begin preparing now. We cannot wait for permission from Washington to start getting ready. Should we go ahead with it?"

For the first time since he'd heard of the fire on *Jeff*, Reisling smiled. He leaned back in his chair. "We'll go ahead. I'll put Lieutenant Commander Kendricks in charge of the landing party. Lieutenant Washington, Gunners Mate Chief Robertson, Ensign Jeffries, and Senior Chief Marlowe will be leading the squads. . . ."

Listening, Halloran suddenly felt cold reality hit him. He had been thinking as if he would lead this mission in. Worse, he knew the people that Reisling was putting in charge of the mission. In growing horror, he realized Reisling intended to land fifty people on this landing party, led by fleet line officers and chief petty officers. The more he heard, the more his heart sank. It only took a moment to realize how hopeless his position was. When Reisling slowed with his planning for a moment, Halloran went to attention and stepped forward. Bitterly, he reminded himself this was the Navy. He knew what he had to do.

"Sir," Halloran said, interrupting Reisling as he paused for breath. The sailor stepped forward, back straight, looking like a man walking to the firing squad. His next words staggered Reisling. "The people you are putting in charge of this mission are all highly trained experts in their own fields. But none of their fields of expertise include light infantry tactics. If they are in charge of the landing party, this mission will fail.''

That stopped Reisling cold. Commanders of U.S. Navy vessels are not used to being spoken to in that way by junior enlisted. He looked at the gray-haired seaman. ''That's why we need you to go on this landing party, Seaman Halloran. Lieutenant Commander Kendricks will need your expertise.''

Halloran shook his head, his face set in bitter disappointment. ''Sir, no line officer ever born will listen to advice from a deck seaman.'' Reisling glared at the sailor in fury. Halloran went on. ''I am unvolunteering for this mission.''

Reisling's voice was deepening now. Anger was overcoming shock. Beneath his own anger, Reisling was amazed. This non-rated deck ape was standing there and defying him! Far from his anger, something whispered in Reisling's mind that the man might just be right, that no matter how skilled an officer was at stellar navigation and engineering and gunnery, he might be lost in a battle on land. But he could not admit that to this sailor. He snapped out savagely, ''This mission was your idea, Seaman Halloran. I can order you to go!''

''I will refuse to follow that order, sir. Court-martialed is better than dead. If these people are in charge, the landing party will die, the mission will fail, and the hostages will be executed.''

For a moment, Reisling was speechless. Whatever skills Halloran might have, that was no way to talk to an officer! Yet at the back of his head, a nagging thought persisted that the arrogant pup might actually be right.

Majors spoke up, his voice calm, smoothly persuasive. ''Excuse me, Captain, uh, wouldn't the absence of so many senior officers from your crew seriously degrade your combat capabilities?''

Reisling switched his glare from Halloran to Majors.

After a moment's thought came a quiet, grudging, "Possibly."

"You may have to fight your way in and out, correct? And the rescue team will need your fire support for the extraction, at least to eliminate Libyan aircraft. Won't they?"

Reisling saw a way out too, but still kept his manner withering. "Yes," he said finally, through clenched teeth.

The CIA agent nodded sagely. He kept speaking, sounding like a used car salesman. "Now, I have had extensive training in covert operations. Perhaps it would be better if I chose the landing party and led it myself? I would take mostly junior personnel, so as to leave the combat ability of the ship intact. Volunteers would be best. We would need both of your helicopter pilots, however."

For a long minute, Reisling said nothing. Neither did Halloran, a fact for which Reisling was infinitely grateful. The CO of *Kimmel* shot a venomous look at Halloran. Halloran adopted an innocent "Who, me?" expression. Then, as intellect overcame anger, Reisling nodded. "Very well, Agent Majors. You may ask for volunteers from the crew. Assemble your team in the crew's recreation room. Do your briefings there. Draw whatever weapons and supplies you need from the ship's armory. Our quartermaster will get with you to chart a course in and out."

Reisling's voice was neutral now, expressionless, quiet, and purposeful. "We will drop you off tomorrow night. You can have both of my helicopter pilots. I will also," another glare at Halloran, "be sending along one of my officers to supervise the men on the landing party. Is that acceptable?"

Majors nodded. "Yes it is, Captain. Thank you for your help. I'll get right on it."

"Just one more thing," said Reisling, quietly. His

voice was icy calm, a pronouncement of sure and certain doom on anyone who angered him. ‘‘No word of what went on in this office will be discussed with anyone else. Seaman Halloran, you are going on that landing party. If you ever speak to me or any of your superiors in that fashion ever again, I will see to it you remain in Leavenworth until you are much older and grayer than you are now. Do you understand?’’

Halloran’s face remained neutral. ‘‘Yes sir.’’

Reisling leaned back in his chair. ‘‘Dismissed.’’

Chapter Eight

Once the two men were out in the hall, Majors turned to face Halloran. "What in the hell was that about?"

"Just what you saw."

"I saw bullshit! We can't do this with your ego on the line!"

"It wasn't ego! He was going to try a commando mission with fifty people! We'd have been spotted before we went half a mile!" Halloran took a deep breath, shook his head. "Look—a Navy officer is conditioned to take charge. It is pounded into them from the get-go, wherever they are, whether they know the situation or not, they take charge! Too many people have accepted incompetent leaders to avoid rocking the boat, and died because of it! I am not going to die to be a good sport!"

"If these officers are such idiots, why are they commanding you?"

Halloran shook his head. "I never said they were idiots. Hell, most of them *are* smarter than me! But I know ground tactics! That's what counts here! I've *forgotten* more about tactics than any khaki on this ship will ever know!''

Majors looked at the man and saw, beneath everything else, an angry, unyielding will, a flinty, stubborn certainty that in this at least, he was right. ''So why did you accept me being placed in charge?''

''You aren't a Navy officer.''

Majors thought for a moment. Win, lose, or draw, he had his team, and he needed this man to deliver the goods. He pulled out the Polaroid, looked at it for a second. Looked at Halloran. He gave the picture to him. ''Look at this.''

Halloran looked. ''Somebody you know?''

Majors scowled. ''No. Just some kid. Right now she is scared and she is cold, and if we don't save her, she is going to die!'' Fury burned out of his face. It was the kind of fury Halloran knew well. ''This is *not* one of your fucking games! We're using real bullets! Real people will die! So the next time you want to torpedo this mission because you don't like how it's being run, you think about that girl!''

A still, small corner of his mind whispered that he'd said enough. Halloran wasn't arguing, he was just looking at the picture. Pushing him further risked a reflexive argument they didn't have time for. Halloran was the available asset. He'd just have to use him. Drive on. ''Where is this crew's recreation room?''

''Down by the soda machines. Follow me.'' Halloran headed down a ladderwell. As the man went, he began speaking. Majors followed, and the two men wound their way through the passageways of the ship. ''We'll need night vision goggles. They have a few of those on board. We'll also have to fix up some kind of uniforms. Dungarees are going to be worse than useless in the desert. We need to talk to GMG1 Shawcross. He's in charge of the ship's armory. That's where we head first. They have most of the toys we need.''

Nerves and frustration finally got to Majors as he snapped, "Stop being so fucking playful!"

Halloran started to say something, but stopped. When he spoke next, he sounded embarrassed. "Sorry. Guess I'm still wound up. It isn't every day I get to tell the CO to go pound sand."

"Yeah, well, will this GMG1 Shawcross want to run the mission too? Will you refuse to go on the mission if he wants to take charge?" Shocked, Majors saw Halloran actually thinking about it.

Halloran shrugged. "No, I'd go. Shawcross knows tactics and weapons. And I can talk to him. If he insists on being in charge, I'll go along."

"Well gee, thanks a lot! Man, I hate working in a union shop!" Majors opened the door to the armory, wondering if his sarcasm had been lost on the sailor. "Hello! Anybody here?"

"Come on in!" called a voice. Majors looked in and saw a lanky, dark-haired man with a jutting nose sitting at one desk watching a TV, one of those little jobs that had a VCR built into it. On the screen, a bearded man dressed as a native god stood defiantly in the middle of a bridge over a chasm as natives destroyed that bridge from both ends. The man who'd been watching the TV had a coffee mug and a soda can near to hand, and a wad of chewing tobacco in one cheek. In racks around the space were rifles, machine guns, flak vests, stacks of steel helmets, and dozens of boxes.

Shawcross, who had three stripes on the sleeve of his blue dungaree shirt, smiled as Majors and Halloran entered. "Sorry Halloran, I'm beat. I'm not signing off any training tonight. Do you want to watch a video? It's *The Man Who Would Be King*, with Sean Connery and Michael Caine. It's good stuff."

Halloran cut off Majors. "Oh, I got something better than that, GMG1. How would you like to land in Libya and go rescue some hostages?"

Shawcross stared blankly at him for a second, then shook his head. "Sorry, Halloran, I don't play that 'Delta Commandoes' game of yours. Thanks anyways."

"It's no game, GMG1. We're really going to do it. We just got permission from the CO to assemble a landing party. He's on the horn to get us permission, but we have to get to work now. We need your help."

Shawcross looked hard at Halloran, then at Majors. Majors nodded. Shawcross thought a moment. "How are we going to do this?"

Once again, Halloran broke out the maps and explained the plan. This time, he stopped frequently as Shawcross cut in with suggestions. It took about five minutes. Shawcross changed his chewing tobacco once, put in a fresh wad, offered some to them. They refused. When the briefing was done, Shawcross looked up from the map. There was a rueful look on his face. "Halloran, it looks like we can do it. But there's, uh, one problem. You used to do this grunt shit for a living. Now me, I know guns, but what I know about tactics, I've just read about. How about I boss the shooters on the cover team, and you call the shots overall? For tactics and such."

Halloran gaped. Majors nodded and gave a silent prayer of thanks. Trying to keep his voice casual, he said, "I think he's up to that. We'll assemble in the rec room. Can you get the gear together and talk with the machinists about making up silencers for the .45s?"

"Sure. How many people are going on the party?"

Halloran had recovered enough to start speaking. "We checked in *Jane's*. It said there a CH-47 in Nam carried 147 people. But a lot of those were probably civilians and kids, and none of them had field gear. Let's divide that by a factor of three. Plan for forty-nine people. With thirty-two hostages, that gives us a seventeen-man landing party. That'll have to do."

Shawcross nodded. "With us three, two pilots, uh, we should take the medic—you still need eleven people."

The CIA agent had been looking at one of the massive .50 caliber Brownings in its rack. He turned to them. "Will getting volunteers be difficult?" Shawcross and Halloran both chuckled at that.

Halloran answered, laughing. Majors noticed again that, when the man laughed it took years off his weathered appearance. "After seven months on this tub, we could announce liberty on the outer circle of Hell and we'd have people waiting on the quarterdeck. We're going to have to beat the volunteers off with a stick on this one."

Shawcross nodded. "Somebody in the ship's office should be checking records too, make sure people have the skills they claim they do." He searched through his files, produced several sheets of names. "This list is everybody I qualified on the M-14 rifle before we left Norfolk. This list"—another sheet of paper—"is everybody who went through ship self defense force school in Little Creek before the deployment." SSDF was a concentrated course in close quarters combat and security, for crew members assigned to armed security while in port. Shawcross next produced a spare clipboard, handed it to Halloran. "Keep the clipboard. You'll need it to get things organized. I'll handle things with the machinists about the silencers and getting the barrels on the shotguns sawed off. Now you two better get moving. We all have a lot to do."

They nodded and left.

Shawcross went to a locker and opened it. He pulled out his personal M-14, sighted down the barrel. Glass bedded, walnut stock, heavy barrel—three hundred yards? This baby could just about drive nails at that range. "Amelia," he muttered to the rifle, "we're going to war."

Their next stop was the rec room. Every night underway, unless training was going on, movies were shown over the ship's closed-circuit TV system. The small recreation room was packed with crew watching the movie. There were other televisions in the berthings and on the mess decks, but the rec room was the first place most people went to.

Halloran looked at Majors. "Here's your first job as leader of this group. You have to tell these people the CO gave us this room tonight and they have to leave. They won't believe me, but you . . ." Halloran smiled, held out his hands palms up. "You're the secret agent." Halloran walked up to the TV, switched it off. A chorus of angry questions and comments started.

The CIA agent stepped in front of Halloran, raised his hands for silence. "Gentlemen, ladies, your attention please! You all have to leave this room! We are assembling volunteers for an extremely dangerous mission. The captain has given us this room to assemble the volunteers in! Please leave immediately!" That silenced the room for a few seconds. Then everybody started asking questions. At that moment, the 1MC blared, drowning out their words.

"Attention, straight shooters! This is the captain speaking!" All bouncy and full of cheer again, Halloran noted, judging from his voice. *"As you know, earlier today we were tasked to support a mission to rescue hostages being held in Libya. A SEAL team was to have landed on* Kimmel *this afternoon, then flown into Libya tonight. That plan was canceled when the fire broke out on the* Jefferson. *I recently spoke with the CIA agent we picked up yesterday. He believes we can assemble a landing party of volunteers from the crew to go ashore and rescue the hostages. In a few minutes, he will begin accepting volunteers for this mission in the crew's rec room. The recreation room is secured until further notice to everyone except the landing party. All crew are to cooperate fully with Agent Majors, under my orders. Officers and CPO's may only volunteer after receiving*

my permission. Keep in mind that we have not yet received final approval for this mission. Washington may have plans we do not know about.

For the rest of the crew: Stand by for more drills and training. This ship will have to be in sight of the Libyan coast to land our people. We need to clear the decks for combat. We've come a long way in the last few months, straight shooters! This is our final challenge of the cruise, a mission that will show how good the Kimmel *really is! I know you won't let me down! Captain out.''*

For a moment, the recreation room was silent. Then Majors spoke up. Halloran noticed that when he spoke this time, he sounded like a game show host. ''Okay, everybody who wants an all expenses paid trip to Libya, stay in this room! If you stay in this room you are going to Libya! If you do not want to go to Libya and get shot at, get the hell out!'' That finally started people moving out the door. In a few minutes, the room contained only Halloran, Majors . . . and Coltrane.

Coltrane just sat there, sipping one of the vile Israeli diet sodas, chewing on a piece of beef jerky and looking at them both. ''Where do I sign up, Hallor-addin? You always say I should go with the tour groups.''

In the ship's medical office, HM3 Lee Springer got up from the cot. Kept in there for casualties, it gave him a place to sleep that was much more peaceful than berthing. But he had a feeling he would not be getting much sleep for a while. On a mission like this, they were sure to want a medic. He opened one of the lockers in the room and pulled out his desert camouflage fatigues. They were souvenirs from his first tour as a combat medic with the Marines. He began changing uniforms.

The second volunteer was Toombs. Wearing workout gear, still sweaty from the ship's tiny weight room, he literally bounced into the room, muscles bulging, excited. He spoke to Majors at the door. "I'm volunteering! I went through SSDF school before we went on deployment, and I got my marksmanship medal on the M-14 a month before that."

Majors checked his lists, nodded. "Great! Glad to have you on board. Why don't you go talk with Halloran? He's in charge of the tactics for this mission. Do you have any problems with that?"

"Naw, he was in the Army. I was afraid one of the khakis might be running things. Halloran loves this shit."

The next person at the door was an enormous, overweight young black man with "ROGERS" stenciled on his shirt. "RM3 Darnell Rogers. I'm here to volunteer for the mission. I shot expert on the M-14 at Little Creek. Y'all gonna need a radioman."

Majors looked at all the extra weight this guy was carrying around and looked doubtfully back at Halloran. Halloran grinned, gave him a thumbs-up. Reluctantly, Majors shook the man's hand. "Welcome aboard. Seaman Halloran will brief you."

Rogers squeezed past the CIA agent and sat at one of the tables behind him. Halloran came over, leaving Coltrane and Toombs at the map. "Hey, Tiny, I didn't expect to see you here! I would have thought you were too smart to get involved in something like this."

Rogers gave a shy grin. "Yo, Dog, what you doin' here then?"

Halloran grinned back and punched him in the arm. "Tiny, you know I'm a crazy fuck. I'm glad to have you here."

The radioman nodded. "I figure, you know they're washing me out on account of my weight. If I do this, maybe I can get out with an honorable or something. Maybe even get a second chance. Y'know?" Halloran nodded. Then he heard a familiar whine and looked towards the door. Sure enough, Seaman Apprentice Mitchell was standing there, the tiny girl's head bobbing up and down as she stridently insisted she be included in the landing party. Behind her, Halloran could see Woodhall waiting.

"Hang on, Tiny. I've got a disaster to avoid." As he went to the door, he could hear Mitchell's voice.

"I went to SSDF! You can't keep me off this team because I'm a woman! That's discrimination! You have to accept me as a volunteer!" Majors looked at Halloran. Halloran stepped forward.

"Seaman Apprentice Mitchell, we will be glad to have you on the landing party. As soon as you do twenty push-ups."

"Oh, this is such macho bullshit!" she chirped, then got on the deck and started doing women's push-ups—her lower body on the deck, only the upper body moving.

"Nope! Negative!" snapped Halloran. "Twenty full push-ups! Back straight, arms fully extended, no rests!"

"These push-ups are accepted for women!"

Halloran inhaled quickly, built up the back pressure in his lungs, and yelled—a wall of sound, focussed on Mitchell. *"No! We are going to have to cover ten miles of rough terrain with full field packs in three hours! That is reality, and it does not give a shit whether you can carry your own pack and rifle or not! I am not going to carry you, your rifle, or your pack, and neither is anyone else! So if you cannot fucking carry them, you are not going on the fucking mission! Is that clear? Now get on that deck and give me twenty honest push-ups, or get the hell out of my face!"*

Mitchell fled, crying.

Halloran coughed, his throat suddenly raw. It had been a while since he'd had to use his Sergeant's Voice.

Woodall stepped up, looked at both of them defiantly.

"Yes?" asked Majors, still a little deafened.

Without saying a word, Woodall dropped to the deck

and banged out forty push-ups, her back ramrod-straight, her breathing controlled and even. Then she bounced up to her feet. "I am Seaman Monica Woodall. I've shot expert on the .45 and qualified on shotgun for Ship's Self Defense Force. I am going on this mission." Then she pointed at Rogers. "Now I want to see *him* do twenty push-ups!"

Everyone present looked at Rogers.

Halloran went back to the seat, sat down, and spoke to the huge radioman out of the side of his mouth. "Tiny, you *better* be able to do twenty push-ups." Rogers got up and, with a look of resignation on his face, dropped to the deck.

Admiral Madison looked at the charts again, then looked at his cup of coffee. It had grown cold over the last hour, ignored as he saw plan after plan, each one fatally flawed. This whole affair would, he thought, make a good argument the next time the Navy's appropriations went before Congress. It was a concrete demonstration that the fleet was spread too thin. But here and now, it was monumental frustration.

The mood around the conference table varied from glum to furiously angry. All day, options had been tested and discarded. The Italians would not loan the U.S. CH-47s on such short notice without being told what it was for. The Egyptians, already under pressure from their own Islamic radicals, would not permit U.S. aircraft to operate from their bases without an explanation, which would have blown security. Two CH-46s had been dispatched from the *Iwo Jima* Marine Amphibious Ready Group. Both had experienced mechanical difficulties from the long flight by the time they hit Turkish airspace. Then the Greeks had put up a fuss over U.S. aircraft there, and stalled them further. The only option left was the diplomatic route, which everyone agreed would simply get the Libyans to "disappear" the hostages sooner. But now it was their only option.

A yeoman handed a message to the CNO. Madison sipped his cold coffee and glanced through it. Put his coffee down. Read through it again. Read it a third time, minutely examining it. Then he handed it to the Special Ops Commander and shook his head. "I'll say this for Reisling, he's no quitter. That shows initiative, at least."

"What's that?" asked Wrangel. The CIA agent sat back and stretched, bones popping as he did so.

Madison smiled thinly. "That was a message from Commander Reisling, on *Kimmel*. He has requested permission to put ashore a landing party of volunteers from his crew. They will then hike inland, free the hostages, steal that Libyan Air Force CH-47, load the hostages aboard it, and fly out." He grinned, looking at the charts. "He's got nerve, I'll give him that. He says he already has his volunteers."

Wrangel and the Commandant of the Corps both made the mistake of laughing at that. Wrangel really got a laugh out of it. "A bunch of sailors do a mission like this? That is one for my memoirs. We really needed some humor about now!"

That rankled the CNO. "Just what the hell do you mean by that?"

Wrangel calmed down. "Admiral, you know and I know, they're a bunch of junior sailors out there. All your senior people get shore billets. Those guys are a bunch of deck sweepers and paint chippers! They can't pull off an operation like this!"

Special Ops spoke as he examined the message form. "One of your agents proposed it. One member of the landing party is ex–Army Airborne. It isn't as if this job is physically demanding. They only have to cross ten miles. No vertical cliffs to scale, no rivers to cross. Tactically, it's a snap."

Admiral Madison leaned in closer to Special Ops. "Commander, no bull here. Could they do it?"

Special Ops took one last look at the message. Reisling had repeated Halloran's plan, chapter and verse, simply not mentioning who had come up with it. Then Special Ops looked up, his expression that of a wolf who, having lost sight of his prey for a moment, suddenly smells fresh blood. "They aren't who I would choose, but our first string is dead. The second string can't even get onto the field. No bull, Admiral, these guys should be able to pull it off."

"Now hold on!" Wrangel didn't like the way this was going. "We were going to have elite troops do this! Now you're telling me a bunch of swabbies off a destroyer can do it?"

"They are destroyermen, Mr. Wrangel," said the CNO. "They are used to getting the dirty jobs dumped on them. They are also our only option right now, unless the situation has changed radically in the last five minutes. Has it?" Silence. "Very well then. Mr. Barton," he said to the National Security Advisor, "inform the President we have a plan. I will be getting the final details to him in an hour." The CNO leaned over and hit a buzzer at his seat. "Yeoman, I want a real-time, scrambled link to USS *Kimmel*, and I want it ten minutes ago. From the CNO straight to the CO of *Kimmel*. Is that clear?"

"Roger that, sir. We're on it."

Then the CNO looked at the officers and officials sitting around the table. The craggy old man remembered his younger days, shipping out on the graceful *Adam*'s class destroyers, storms and cruises and ports of call, so long ago. "Gentlemen, these men have volunteered to do the job. We will support them every way we can. They are at the end of a very long supply line, so we may not be able to do much, but by damn we will do whatever we can. Get on it!"

* * *

"Hey, c'mon, c'mon, G-money, if we go along on this, no way can they diss you!" Seaman Apprentice Chambers was hyped, almost dancing around BM3 Bledsoe. "We can do this! They need us, G! We'll show 'em how they do it in the 'hood! Get a shotgun, Bang! How you do that thang? They need somebody who's bad for real!"

Chambers had been on the foc'sle, chipping away at Nonskid with the rest of deck division when the word was passed. Coltrane should have been up there too, but had slipped away while BM1's back was turned. That was when Chambers stood up and told BM1 Magsaysay that they were volunteering for the mission. They were almost at the rec room, Bledsoe wondering how he had ever let Chambers talk him into this. It had seemed like a chance to get his reenlistment. Now he was getting a bad dose of second thoughts.

A dozen sailors were waiting outside the room, talking and watching who went in. Before he could duck away, one of them saw Bledsoe and Chambers, and called out. "W'zup? You goin' to volunteer?"

"Damn skippy we are!" said Chambers. "Me an' Bledsoe gonna go in there an' regulate thangs! Niggah with a AK, gonna blow them away! Regulay-*tors*!" He rattled on, rapping and jiving with a couple of the other brothers outside the rec room. Bledsoe wished Chambers would shut the hell up, but smiled as if he were having the time of his life. Then they stepped into the room.

It was crowded, people gathered around tables talking and going over maps and charts. "Where can a couple of bad brothers sign up?" shouted Chambers. "We ready to be mah'fucking hee-roes!"

"I'm taking names," said the long-haired white dude with the shaggy mustache and clipboard. He must be the CIA agent, thought Bledsoe.

"BM3 Marcus Bledsoe. Qualified SSDF, pistol marksman's medal."

The dude with the clipboard looked at his lists and smiled. "Good to have you. They're having a bull session back there. Once we get our last couple of people, we'll begin formal briefing and training." Then he looked at Chambers. "You?"

"Seaman Apprentice Chambers, bad-ass motherfucker and NWFA!"

It took a second for the white guy to figure out what NWFA meant, but he chuckled at it as he checked the lists. Then he checked them again. "You aren't qualified on any weapons, or on SSDF. Do you have any weapons training?"

"Do drive-bys count?"

"Not if they didn't make it into your 201 file." Bledsoe could see Majors already had the skinny black kid typed. Lots of enthusiasm, zilch on common sense or training. At that moment, Bledsoe's own enthusiasm dropped from zero to negative percentages. Then he thought about going back out into the passageway and having to admit he'd backed out. No way he could explain it. They'd seen him coming in. He mentally cursed Chambers again.

The white guy said, "Sorry. Thanks for trying, Chambers, but it's a no go."

Chambers almost squawked at that. Then he looked at Bledsoe. "Sorry, G-Money, looks like you got to carry the show! Let 'em know what the baddest cat on this boat can do!" Then he left. Bledsoe knew Chambers was still happy with the situation. Always alert to any chance to get out of work, Chambers would know that with sundown so close, no way would they put him back on deck chipping. Bledsoe grimaced and sat down.

At the table, Lieutenant Steiner was going over the plan. "I can fly the CH-47, if it's working. It's just a bigger CH-46. But it has a larger rotor diameter than the CH-46. We can't land it on the flight deck."

Halloran nodded. "How about hovering above the flight deck, dropping lines, and letting people lower themselves on the lines?"

Steiner didn't seem happy as she nodded her head. "It won't be easy, but I can do it. But what about Freeman and me? We're stuck on the helicopter."

Halloran smiled at that. "Once all the passengers are off, you ditch the helicopter in the sea and the ship's boat picks you up."

Steiner's skin went grey at that, a tremble creeping into her hands. Her voice became tinny, afraid. "Ditch the CH-47? In the sea?"

Mystified, Halloran answered, "Yeah, ditch it in the sea. Would that be a problem?"

"No. It happens all the time." She closed her eyes, rubbed her eyebrows. "Okay, brief Freeman on the codes and the mission. I've got to lie down for a minute." She left.

At the door, Majors was confronted by a big, rawboned kid wearing an affable smile, desert camouflage fatigues, and full web gear. Majors looked him over for a second before he spoke. "Who are you? A Marine?"

"Naw, but I hung around with 'em on the beach for a couple of years." The kid smiled and shook Majors's hand. He had the air of a good ol' boy looking forward to a day of hunting. "I'm HM3 Lee Springer, the pecker checker. The Medic, you know? I fired the M-14 and the M-60. Y'all need to take a medic along."

"Welcome to the party, Springer." Majors wrote down his name. "Glad to have you. You wouldn't happen to have a spare set of those desert cammies, would you?"

"Sorry, I only packed the one pair. Y'all are gonna need something. Those blue dungarees really stand out on the beach."

Sitting nearby, the big black kid they all called Tombstone spoke up. "We got a handle on that. The chiefs are donating a bunch of used khakis for us. They'll blend with the sand better.'' The phone rang. Tombstone, who had been fielding calls ever since he was briefed, picked it up. ''Wrecked room!'' Listened. ''Just a second.'' He put his hand over the mouthpiece. ''Halloran, GMG1 wants a list of the weapons we're taking. He says only three of the M-60s are still good, number four's got a broken firing pin. Both the grenade launchers are good, but all he's got for them is flare and HE. Does that stand for high explosive?''

''Yeah. I wish we had some antitank weapons.'' Halloran checked his own list. ''Okay, we'll need two M-60s, seven rifles, both M-79 grenade launchers, eighteen .45 pistols and seven shotguns. If he has enough barrels, I want to take one full-length barrel and one sawed-off barrel for each shotgun.''

Toombs repeated the requests, listened for a moment, then relayed the comments. ''Good on everything but the shotgun barrels. He can only give you three spare barrels.''

''Okay, leave the spare barrels at full length, saw off the regular barrels. It's his call on how much ammo goes with each weapon. We'll need hand grenades too. I also want eight quarter-pound blocks of C4 with six-second fuses for blowing the prison doors. Seventeen flak vests and steel helmets, night vision goggles and whatever web gear he has.''

An angry BM3 Mayes came into the room and spotted Coltrane sitting over in the corner watching the fun. ''C-C-Coltrane!'' he snapped. ''You supposed to be on the bridge! This is section two watch! G-G-Get up there!''

''D-D-D-Don't have to!'' mimicked Coltrane. ''I'm going on the hostage rescue, Skater. I ain't got time for watch!''

''Negits!'' Bledsoe stood up and faced Coltrane.

"Nobody said you were off the watch schedule. Get on up to the bridge, Coltrane!"

"Halloran, Majors, help me out!" Coltrane looked at the two men. "How can we get ready if we're standing watches?"

Halloran and Majors looked at each other. Majors said, "I'll talk to the Captain, but it'll take time. Just go stand this watch. We'll clear it up tonight."

Halloran nodded. "Sounds like a plan. Does anybody else in this room have watches tonight?"

Fireman Tosado, who had come in and volunteered a few minutes before, raised his hand, shrugging. "I have to serve mid-rats tonight."

Halloran smiled and shook his head. "Sorry, guy. I should have thought of this sooner. Look, Majors will talk to the Captain. Everybody whose name is on that list will be excused from all other duties, starting at 0600. All of you come back here after breakfast, so we can get the equipment ready and finish the briefing. In the meantime, unless you have a reason to be here, hit your racks and get some sleep. Everybody's tired, and tomorrow is going to be a busy day."

Halloran stepped out on the midships quarterdeck to get some fresh air. All exterior lights on *Kimmel* were off, except for running lights. It was dark, as dark as it gets at sea. The stars were a vast bowl around them, bright gleaming diamonds this far from any city light. The sea dimly reflected the quarter moon. The rushing of water past the ship was a constant noise. Behind him, the ship was a darkness against the stars.

He was tired, but it was a different type of tired than he was used to. He had been trying to put a finger on it. He felt as if a tightly coiled spring inside him had been let loose.

Everyone had gone to get some sleep except for Shawcross, who was in the machine shop trying to iron out some problems with the silencers. Halloran hoped they could make them work. Taking out sentries with knives was a risky, difficult business for experts. He wasn't sure he was up to it. He was positive most of his volunteers weren't. He checked his watch. 0215. Damn.

The glow from his watch dial drew a comment from the shadows. "I could report you to the CO for breaking 'darken ship,' you know." A cigarette was lit. In the brief light, Halloran could see Lieutenant Steiner. She drew deep, exhaled, and looked at him, with the cigarette dangling negligently from one hand, hips cocked.

"Well, I could report you for smoking on the quarterdeck. We're tied, ma'am."

A brief flash of smile in the darkness, another draw on the cigarette. The darkness was kind to her face. Halloran suddenly realized she was probably his age, the lines in her face those of worry. "Well, as long as we're both in trouble, d'you want a cigarette?"

It was Halloran's turn to smile. "No thanks. That's just about the only bad habit I never started." He sat on a coil of rope and looked out over the waves. After a minute, she did too. They remained that way for a few minutes in companionable silence. Halloran, never one to leave well enough alone, was the first to speak. "So what was it there when we talked about ditching the helicopter? You looked like I'd just said you were going to be juggling chainsaws."

"I'd rather juggle chainsaws, if I could juggle." Another puff, face dreamy, neutral, looking at the moon. "I flew CH-46s off *America* for a couple of years. One night in the North Sea, my engines decided to blow up. Don't ask me why. Anyways, we hit the water hard, in rough seas. The flotation gear kept us on the surface for, oh, a good three or four seconds. I don't know why they bother with that crap. It never works." Her eyes were unfocused as she spoke, far away from where they were.

Another puff. A try at blowing smoke rings, which

were instantly destroyed by the sea breeze. "I was knocked out for a second when we hit. I woke up when the seawater hit me. My harness latch had jammed. I worked on it. The pilot was dead, a broken neck from the crash. Water was pouring in. It turned out later, enough air was trapped at the tail section to keep us on the surface for a while. I didn't know that though." Another puff.

"In case you ever had any doubts, drowning is bad. I had seawater in my eyes, had my lungs full of air. It hurts at first, then your body kind of adjusts for a few seconds. It's almost comfortable. Then you start to need to breathe, and it's cold, and you can't breathe, but reflex starts making you want to and your lungs are burning so bad . . ." Her voice trailed off. She took one final puff on the cigarette and ground it out against the deck. "So I breathed, and my lungs filled up with water. It was so cold, like knives of ice. Finally, I died."

Halloran listened, trying to figure it out. Was she making a sick joke?

She half chuckled, half sobbed. "Not that I stayed dead, mind you. One of the SAR swimmers off *America* got into the wreck, cut me loose from my harness with his knife, and got me to the rescue chopper. They did CPR, reinflated my lungs, the whole nine yards. I woke up with pneumonia in sick bay on the *America*. I carry my own knife now, you know?" She pulled out a diver's knife from a boot sheath, waved it before her eyes. Its surface was dark, nonreflective. It looked sharp. "Never bothered with them before the crash. I always took off my survival rig because it got in my way."

Halloran suddenly realized he had stopped breathing. He took a deep breath and shook his head. "Damn. Will you have to back out?"

"I'll get the job done." She put away her knife and sighed. "I'll deal with it. Women internalize their problems. We hold them all inside and let them eat us up until we can deal with them. Men are lucky. You get to externalize your problems. Like this raid. You get to externalize your problems all over those terrorists, and the poor bastards aren't even going to know what hit them."

Halloran laughed at that and stretched catlike. Bones popped and crackled. "I guess that explains why I feel so good. This is the best time I've had since I joined the Navy."

She tossed brown curls, stuck her head out in the sea breeze for a minute, and closed her eyes. "So tell me, Halloran. Why aren't you an officer? You're running this operation, which is fine with me. But you went to college. You're not some kid just off the block. Why didn't you ever get a commission?"

Halloran shrugged. He didn't like where this was going. "Never willing to put up with the BS, I guess."

"So you get angry with what the people who are in charge do, but you aren't willing to do what it takes to get their job. Is that it?"

Halloran looked at her, almost shouted out a denial. Her eyes were still closed, her voice only slightly mocking. With her face calm, Halloran suddenly realized she was beautiful. Then he considered what she had said. Much as he hated to admit it, he said, "Yeah, you're right. So did you get a psychology degree?"

"Theater, bachelor's. But I took some psych courses. So what do you do after this is over and you go back to being plain old Dave Halloran, non-rated seaman?" She turned and looked back at him, eyes to eyes, expression slightly mocking, slightly . . . something else?

"Beats me. It'll be hard to go back to just being a deck ape, though." She smiled again. She had a nice smile, kind of a sideways grin. "Think about it. You're really good in there, you know. I could see you coming up with your own ideas, then holding back sometimes when you wanted to shout someone down. You really do listen. That's a rare thing."

"About half the time, their ideas are better than mine." He looked at her, really looked at her for the first time. Officers were so completely in their own world aboard ship, he hadn't wasted any thought on her before. Now, he noticed that her dark eyes glimmered in the moonlight. "But I won't know that unless I listen to them. Listening to other people isn't easy for me." He'd curled up back into himself now, legs pulled back against his body, back against the wall. "I'm really doing good in there?"

She looked back at him, nodded her head, smiled. "Yes, you're good. It's been a long time since anybody told you that, hasn't it?" He nodded, sat up straighter. "Well, you are the man with the plan, the guy who knows what to do, in command. That wouldn't work if you weren't sure of yourself. Some women find that very attractive."

Halloran suddenly realized their faces were slowly moving closer together. "They do?" His voice had become a low whisper, barely audible over the waves.

"Uh-huh. Especially when the guy doesn't realize it." Her answer was almost inaudible, her lips parted, their faces inches apart. She could see the stars reflected in his eyes.

"This is a drill, this is a drill! General quarters, general quarters, all hands man your battle stations! Move up and forward on starboard side, down and aft on port! Set condition zebra throughout the ship! Reason for general quarters—impending air attack! This is a drill!"

Both of them sat upright as the alarm bells rang. "What the hell is this idiot doing?" Halloran's voice was incredulous. "A GQ drill at two AM?"

"The ship can be attacked after midnight, you know." Steiner got up, brushed sea salt from her flight suit.

"Yeah, but you don't drill people at two AM the

night before you're going to do a night operation!'' Halloran was tucking his slacks into his boots and rolling down his sleeves. ''How the hell does he expect people to stay awake tomorrow night?'' Cursing his commanders, Halloran ran off to his GQ station.

Steiner flicked her cigarette into the ocean, shook her head, looked the way Halloran had left. ''Get yourself some rank, Halloran, or this place is going to drive you nuts.'' She started walking to the flight deck.

Chapter Nine

Throughout *Kimmel*, crewmembers staggered out of their racks, threw on uniforms and footgear, and groped their way through the red-lit passageways. Many had difficulty waking up, the cumulative effect of seven months of this schedule. Others tried to ignore the wake-up until rousted out of their racks by petty officers. Most of the crew did as they had been conditioned to, stumbling through their jobs half-awake, running on reflex.

The bridge was chaos as the mid-watch section was replaced by still-drowsy GQ personnel, many of them tucking in shirts or missing uniform items. Gas mask bags, life preservers, and steel helmets were passed out in the darkness, men and women tripping over the tangle of gear on the deck.

In the captain's chair, Reisling shook his head and looked at his watch. Fifteen minutes, and people were only now getting to their stations? This was unsatisfactory. The ship could be sunk by now. Finally, after a quarter of an hour, the general quarters stations around *Kimmel* were reporting in.

"CIC, manned and ready!"

"Damage Control Central, manned and ready!"

"Mount Five-One, manned and ready!"

A presence stood beside him in the darkness. Kendricks. He could already sense the man's disapproval. "Sir, the crew are tired enough already," Kendricks said in a low voice no one else could hear. "They're going to need rest for tomorrow night."

"Have some faith in our people, Davey." Reisling spun his seat to face his XO. "Train them hard and you get results. Besides, remember, we're the old men around here. Most of the crew are just kids. Missing a night or two of sleep is nothing to them. If we get tired, we can rest back in Norfolk." Kendricks was silent, unconvinced. Reisling shrugged, turned his seat back to look out over the sea. He sipped his coffee, feeling the warmth enter his body. Idly, he wondered how many hundreds of gallons of the stuff he had drunk on this deployment alone.

Another presence behind him. "Good morning, sir. CIC is ready." A reedy voice. Lieutenant Commander Scott.

"Good to hear that, Wendell. How are you holding up?"

A chuckle at that. "Not bad at all. Sir, I know now might not be the best time, but . . . I would like to volunteer to lead the landing party. I believe I am the natural choice."

This was a surprise. Reisling had been considering which officer to send on the landing party. Four of his junior officers had already requested to lead it, an admirable display of enthusiasm. Of course, all of them knew that the officer who led a mission like this could expect to receive a Navy Cross at the very least. Reisling remembered the thrill he had felt talking to the CNO over the scrambled radio link, knowing that a call like that as good as pinned the eagles on his collars. If he carried out this mission successfully, he would have guaranteed his next several promotions. For a moment, he had considered leading the party himself, but then reality had set in. Besides, his promotion was set. Let someone else have a little glory. But who?

"Wendell, I appreciate the enthusiasm, but I had been planning on sending Ensign Jeffries. He did a summer with the Marines while he was at Annapolis. He'd be right at home on the beach."

Scott—or the shadow that Reisling could see of him in the dark—seemed to tense at that. "Sir, there's already a Lieutenant going along on the mission. Lieutenant Steiner. Do we want to send an officer who will be outranked by an aviation officer?"

Interesting point. "That's true, but Jeffries is a line officer. Steiner is an aviation officer. She can't take command while he is present." Navy line officers were expected to be able to do everything, and were always superior to specialist officers.

OPS nodded eagerly. "With all due respect, it still might create some confusion among the enlisted men. Whereas, I do rank Lieutenant Steiner. Further, I spent a summer with the Marines myself, back in my Annapolis days. It's like riding a bicycle. You never forget how to do it."

Reisling thought of that, thought of the arrogant little whelp, Halloran, standing there and defying him. Would a junior officer have the salt to slap him down, keep him in line? Further, Scott was right about the confusion among the men over ranks. He had considered sending Kendricks, but his XO, while capable, had a tendency to be soft on the crew. OPS was a hard driver, someone who would get the most out of them.

"OPS, I think you have a point." Reisling turned his seat around and shook Scott's hand. "The landing party is yours. I'll advise you to listen to the CIA agent for advice. He seems to know what he's doing. And watch Seaman Halloran. He has a lot of knowledge, but he's disrespectful and insubordinate. Use what he knows but let him know who is in charge."

"Yes sir!"

Around them, the mid-watch general quarters continued.

Majors cursed as he worked his way up to the bridge. His escort had mentioned in passing that when GQ was called away, every watertight door on the ship was dogged shut to prevent the spread of fire and flooding.

They also made it a royal pain to get anywhere on the ship.

He had not been able to go twenty feet without having to open and reshut a steel door. He had lost count of how many by the second deck. His escort had taken the job of opening the doors, which Majors then resealed once they passed. By doing so, the two men were finally on the bridge level. "I'll stand by out here, sir."

"Thanks. Hopefully, this shouldn't take long. If it does"—Majors looked around—"paint this hallway. Something cheerful, you know, bright colors or pastel. All this white and gray paint, it's just so military!"

The sailor laughed at that. "Anything you say, sir."

The CIA agent stepped out of the red-lit hallway into darkness.

"Shut the damn door!" hissed a voice.

Majors shut the damn door, and stood there for a moment to let his eyes adjust. Gradually, his eyes picked up enough light to see from the dimly illuminated controls scattered around the bridge. "Where's the Captain?"

"Over to your right, at the front of the bridge," answered a familiar voice. Majors looked over.

"Tombstone, is that you?"

"Seaman Toombs, messenger of the watch, standing by. You going to talk to the CO, let him know we can't stand GQ if we're on the landing party?"

"You're a perceptive man, Tombstone. Any hints as to how to approach him?"

"Just let him know we can't be in two places at once. He's no dummy." As his night vision adjusted, Majors noticed the flash gear everyone was wearing, everyone except him and an individual wearing a baseball cap who was walking around the bridge quizzing people. The CIA agent moved towards the captain in the darkness.

As Toombs had said, Reisling quickly understood. The landing party would need to be exempted from all ship's evolutions after 0600 hours the next day. Reisling assured Majors they would be left alone to train in the rec room. Lieutenant Commander Scott introduced himself as the man who would be leading the landing party. He immediately set Majors's internal alarm bells ringing when he tried to enlist Majors's support in keeping the enlisted sailors in line. Majors knew from experience the kind of snafu that typically developed when peacetime officers tried to impose order on irregular warfare. By the time he left the bridge, he was already feeling trepidation over what would happen when this man and Halloran butted heads over who was in charge. Majors had no doubt that they would.

The drill finally ended at 0345 hours. At that time, over the 1MC loudspeakers, Reisling both congratulated the crew on a job well done, and chewed them out for not doing it better. After that fifteen-minute speech, everyone who could staggered off to their racks. Majors had already collapsed on his rack with his clothes still on. Just as he was dozing off, someone knocked on his door.

"Agent Majors?" A reedy voice. OPS. Damn.

"Agent Majors, are you in there? I'd like to go over the plan."

"Scott, come back tomorrow. I'll brief you then. I need sleep."

Laughing, the lieutenant commander opened the door and stepped into the room, shaking his head. "Majors, if you're going to do operations like this, you are going to lose sleep. I remember one time during Desert Storm, I went seventy-two hours straight without seeing my rack. Now I need to see the plan. Just give me a few minutes to familiarize myself with it, will you?"

Contemplating how much fun it would be to crush this guy's windpipe and explain the error of his ways to him while he suffocated, Majors opted instead to talk. For now. He got up, broke out the maps, and explained the plan. Scott listened, nodding.

When Majors had finished, the lieutenant commander shook his head. "No, this won't work at all. You never split your forces in the face of the enemy. We should go through the fence as a group, hit them hard. Perhaps a few people to one side, to cause a distraction. We'll need more people in the landing party too. Do you think that—"

Majors sighed as Scott went on, changing every portion of the plan from beginning to end. He'd had supervisors in the same mold, the kind of control freaks who had to make changes in everything they reviewed, to show their power over it. He went to the toilet kit which had been left for him when he'd come on board, looking for aspirin.

Which was when he came up with a bright idea. Among the toilet items he'd been given when he came aboard, some helpful person had included several Dramamine tablets—seasickness pills—with instructions. Majors, the son of a New England fisherman, had no trouble with seasickness, but he had hung on to them in case they might come in handy. "Scott—uh, Wendell," asked Majors, looking over at a pot of coffee that had been brought to his quarters earlier that night. "You don't mind if I call you Wendell, do you? Wendell, would you like some coffee?"

Scott nodded without looking up from the maps and photos. "Yes, thank you. Three sugars please. You know, I think we should standardize the weapons for this operation, have everyone carrying rifles. Pistols for the NCOs and officers, of course, and that silencer idea is a good one, but shotguns are all wrong for—" As he rambled on, Majors prepared his coffee.

Gordon Richmond shivered, huddled against the cold, and looked out the small stone window of his prison. No one had ever told him that the desert was cold at night. He had given away his suit jacket three days ago to one of the women, and had been freezing every night since. He hoped she still had it, that the terrorists hadn't taken it from her. Then he mentally pictured one of the terrorists wearing a single-breasted Armani suit jacket over one of their uniforms. That gave him his first chuckle in a few days.

He couldn't know whether the woman still had his jacket, because the terrorists had strictly segregated the male and female hostages since they captured them. Their leader, a chubby little guy who Richmond swore had been his cab driver once in Brooklyn, had lectured them on how Islam would not let them sin by coming into contact with each other.

Oh, they'd massacre them for the cause, but they were worried about them sinning. Gee whiz, thanks.

One of the guards—the hostages had nicknamed him "Stinky" because he exercised a truly appalling lack of personal hygiene—was standing at the gate, AK-47 slung over his shoulder, warmly wrapped against the night chill. A fire burned in a coffee can on the ground near him. Whenever the terrorists wanted hot tea, they apparently just dumped some diesel fuel in a can of sand and lit it. The fuel would burn off from the sand gradually and they heated their water over the fire. One of the other hostages—some history nut, a college professor who'd been returning from Turkey—had called the thing a "Tommy Cooker," and said that soldiers in the desert had been using that trick since World War Two.

Funny, he thought to himself. This whole world out here, it had always been out here and he'd never known a thing about it. He was the kind of guy who always threw away the news sections of the papers, always flipped past CNN when he was channel-surfing, unless the financial reports were on. He traded his stocks, he paid his taxes, he griped about how much of those taxes was wasted. That was it. He'd never thought about going into the military. That was for idiots. He'd gotten his business degree instead, done something useful with his time. Until this world reached out, and grabbed him away from his own.

It made a man think.

"Stinky" had unlimbered his rifle and pulled the clip from it. Checking for sand, Richmond supposed. Then Richmond started paying attention. He watched how the man worked a crank on the side of the rifle, ejected a bullet, and fed it back into his magazine. Then the terrorist put the magazine back into his rifle and worked the crank again. In the still night air, the sound of a bolt slamming home was a clear, metallic noise. Richmond observed everything.

Yeah, he thought to himself, just go out there and grab that gun. Gordon Richmond, financial advisor turned commando. But then, if they didn't rescue themselves, who would? This wasn't the eighties, when Ronnie the Ray Gun sent in troops every time Americans got in trouble. Did they still do that stuff at all? He hadn't even known that the PLO was still hijacking people. He'd thought Arafat had made some kind of deal with the

Israelis. In the endless days since their capture, talking with the other hostages, he'd learned that the situation was more complicated than that. Would they have a rescue? Did anybody do that anymore?

The terrorists didn't seem to think time had passed them by. They spent hours haranguing the hostages about the decadent West, Israel, and the Great Satan, America. They'd beaten the hostages a few times and played sadistic little mind games like putting them in the empty room, holding a gun to their heads, and announcing they were going to execute them. Then they'd pull the trigger—and the hammer would drop on an empty chamber.

A member of Handgun Control Incorporated, Richmond had started observing how the terrorist's gun worked after that particular bit of sadism. A couple of the other hostages, sleeping in a heap over in the corner, knew about guns. He'd been grilling them about how guns worked too. You never knew. So much for pacifism. Right now, he'd kill for half a pack of cigarettes, a good meal, or a nice long, hot shower. Or, for that matter, for enough water to stop being thirsty.

He considered returning to the heap of guys sleeping in the corner. All of them were equally filthy, so none of them noticed the smell. They roasted during the day, froze at night, discussed meaningless theories about what was going on, and slept in a heap of bodies to conserve heat.

His train of thoughts was interrupted by the sound of a girl crying. That was quickly silenced. The hostages had learned early on, for all their talk about protecting women, these terrorists sure seemed to enjoy beating them. Well, at least he knew they were still alive.

Some of his cellmates were actually outraged that this could happen to them. Not Gordon Richmond. Outrage didn't pay the bills. All his illusions about this part of the world had been blown away. He knew negotiations.

He could tell something was going wrong with these guys' negotiations. That meant they were probably going to die. But he had vowed one thing, the last time he had been tied in a chair with these filthy murderers hitting him.

If he died, he was taking some of them with him.

Leftenant-Colonel Mohammad Faisal sipped his tea and looked over the encampment at a dozen BTR-50 armored personnel carriers, eight-wheeled lightly armored vehicles topped by a small turret with a 12.7mm heavy machine gun; four BRDMs, four-wheeled armored command cars, each carrying six laser-guided antitank missiles; 112 Libyan soldiers under his command. The Great Leader himself had spoken to him two days ago, explaining the gravity of the situation. The freedom fighters might refuse to eliminate their hostages, from misguided fanaticism. His company of troops was one of three units keeping an eye on the camp. For the good of the revolution, the Libyan troops would ensure the hostages were quietly eliminated.

Tonight, at two AM, Major Aboussys's company would surround the camp to overawe the Mujaheddin with the presence of their armored vehicles, while Faisal's company and one other company stood by. Personally, Faisal thought it a tad excessive to have three full companies of troops standing by, but the Great Leader had spoken.

He sipped his tea and watched the sun rise over the mountains.

Endless as the night had seemed, eventually it ended. After an early breakfast, Shawcross went over to the machine shop to check out the progress of the silencers. There, he found Machinists Mate 1st Class Doug Flanders at work welding threaded extensions to the barrels of the .45s. Shawcross sat back and waited for him to get done with the one he was working on. As he did so, Halloran came into the room, shoving some black material into his mouth. He sat next to Shawcross silently, chewing it and working it back and forth in his cheeks. Shawcross grinned. "Finally started chewing, huh?"

"Oh, I always chewed. How are the silencers going?"

Shawcross used his spittoon—a pop can with the lid peeled back—then offered it to Halloran, who shook his head. "The silencers were easy. The bitch was finding some way to attach them. Normal silencers are threaded on the end of the barrel. Your standard .45, well, the barrel doesn't go much past the detent pin, so there's no place to screw it on. You can't thread the inside of the barrel because it's too thin, once you put in threads deep enough to hold the silencer." Shawcross used his spittoon again, shoved a fresh wad of tobacco into his mouth, offered the spittoon for Halloran to use. Halloran refused.

Shawcross shrugged, picked up the first .45 that Flanders had modified, and showed it to Halloran. "What Doug had to do was weld a threaded fitting to the end of the barrel, strong enough to hold it on over the muzzle pressure. Then we screw the silencer on." Halloran examined the weapon. The silencer was made from a length of steel tubing, lengthening the pistol overall by about five inches. With the mounting welded on, the pistol couldn't be disassembled because the fitting jammed the barrel bushing and covered the detent pin. But for a one-time mission, it was more than adequate.

Flanders finished his welding, pulled the safety mask from his face, and looked over at them. He was a tall man with a closely trimmed mustache and a voice that could abrade steel plate. "The welds will hold. You're damn lucky I'm a good TIG welder. That's Tungsten Inert Gas, for you ignorant types. The only way we can really test 'em is by shooting them. I should be able to whip up six of them." Then he noticed that his audience was chewing. ''Damn it, how many times do I have to tell you, you stupid cannoncocker, no chewing in my shop! That's a disgusting habit! That goes for you too, deck ape!''

''Sorry, Doug,'' said Shawcross. He spit out his tobacco into the spittoon. Halloran just swallowed his chaw.

Shawcross gaped at him. ''If that was tobacco, you're about to be sicker'n a dog eating roadkill.'' Halloran just grinned back at him.

Curiosity got the better of Flanders. He walked forward, looking at them, removing his welder's gloves. ''What the hell were you chewing?''

Halloran produced a small red box. ''Raisins. They're better for you than tobacco, and just as disgusting when you spit.''

''Okay, that's it! Out of here now!'' Flanders yelled as he threw the door open. ''Get the hell out and take your tobacco and raisins and whatever else with you and let me work!'' The two offenders left, Shawcross still laughing. Flanders slammed the door behind them.

''Tell me, Halloran, d'you stay up late to think those things up?''

''What things?'' Halloran put on his innocent face again. ''Anyhoo, I need you to bring some weapons to the rec room so I can familiarize the troops. We're not going to turn anybody into experts, but they need to know the basics.''

''Good idea.'' He frowned as he thought, going over his mental lists as they navigated their way deeper into the ship, towards the armory. ''Let me see, y'all need one weapon of each type, right?''

''That sounds like it. Want some help carrying them up?''

''Sure. Let's move before the CO calls away another drill.''

* * *

As it was, they got the weapons into the crew's rec room just before another general quarters drill was held—flooding, this time. The noise of the alarms didn't disturb the class because Coltrane had wrapped several deck jackets around the 1MC loudspeaker to muffle the noise. Sitting in the room were all his volunteers from the previous day—including Bledsoe, which was a surprise for Halloran. He didn't think Bledsoe could do anything, other than hide out in the bosuns locker and harass the non-rates. And sing. Halloran had once heard the man singing to himself in the bosuns locker, with a voice that could make the angels weep. Once he'd found out Halloran was listening, though, Bledsoe hassled Halloran so obnoxiously that he'd left.

Steiner, Ensign Freeman, and Tiny Rogers were going over maps and books of radio frequencies. Coltrane and Tosado were comparing a remarkable number of knives they'd produced overnight. Halloran had carried a Swiss army knife since he'd come to the fleet, and intended to borrow a bayonet before he went ashore. Any more cutlery seemed excessive. Toombs and Woodall were talking. Majors and Springer were absent, along with whatever officer the CO decided to saddle them with. Maybe, thought Halloran, hoping against hope, whoever had the job wouldn't show up until they were heading to the beach. Or maybe Majors would keep him at a distance and let Halloran handle his end.

Five new people waited: Seaman Wade MacKenzie, the SAR swimmer who'd pulled Majors out of the water; GMG3 Don Monk, one of the gunners mates; BM3 Raul Villanueva; MS3 Podlogar; and BM1 Magsaysay, who'd shown up wearing his own desert camouflage fatigues and had on full web gear, including a pair of machetes in a nifty little over-the-shoulder rig. Halloran did a little quick math. With the officer that the CO had promised, that made eighteen people. Well, the helicopter could probably take one extra person.

Halloran and Shawcross laid out the weapons on a table in front of the room. Tension in the room increased noticeably as they did so. They'd been thinking of this mission in abstract terms before. With the weapons in front of them, gleaming blued metal and harsh angles, it became real. The smell of gun oil and steel and the faint tang of cordite was in the air. The polished wood stocks of the shotgun and the rifle at least gave the touch of life to the display, the sight of something that had once been living. All else was metal, dead, and deadly serious.

Shawcross said as he pulled the seaman to one side, "You give them the mission brief. I'll run them through the weapons. If you have anything to add, raise your hand. Any problem?"

"No sweat." Halloran stepped forward, choked down a sudden nervous feeling. "Good morning, campers! I assume everyone present in the room is a volunteer for the landing party. Is there anyone here who does not intend to be standing on Libyan soil by 2300 hours tonight?"

"Who put you in charge, Halloran?" burst out Podlogar. "I thought that spy was running things."

"I do not know where Agent Majors is. I'm doing the tactical briefing. Then GMG1 Shawcross will be doing the weapons familiarization. Majors is in charge of the mission. The CO will also be sending along an officer."

"So why are we bothering with you?" Podlogar grinned broadly, sat back, and folded his hands behind his head. "We go in, we rescue the hostages, we all get guest shots on the TV news!"

Halloran's temper was beginning to show. He flushed red at being interrupted, spoke in a lower, almost growling tone. "Podlogar, we don't have time for a lot of arguing. Now—"

"That's MS3 Podlogar to you, seaman." Podlogar

was having a terrific time. "You may have been some big-shit airborne dude, but—"

"Podlogar, that's enough!" Shawcross snapped. His dark, Indian eyes gazed at the mess specialist for a moment, coldly calculating. "Get out of here."

Podlogar hadn't expected this. He had only intended to jerk Halloran's chain a little. "What? Wait a minute, I was just messing with—"

"Get out of here now, Podlogar, or your ass goes to captain's mast." Muttering under his breath, Podlogar left.

Shawcross faced the room full of sailors. "Listen up. We're going on this mission. Halloran knows tactics, so the minute we hit the beach, he's calling the shots. Nobody else. If y'all have a problem with that, quit now. Because if you come ashore with us and play this happy horseshit, you will be a casualty." The room was filled with tense silence. Shawcross looked at Halloran after a moment. "Okay, Davey, they're all yours."

Halloran went to a map of Libya that had been pinned to a wall and indicated their position with a pen. He was still a little wound up from the exchange with Podlogar as he spoke. "We are currently a hundred miles north of Libya. At 1900 hours tonight, an hour before sunset, *Kimmel* will begin a flank speed run into the Gulf of Sidra, putting us off the Libyan coast at about 2200 hours. We'll be dropped off by ship's boat. We have one hour to get on shore and get organized.

"*Kimmel* will stand by until we head inland, then stand off at thirty miles. We will hike inland, starting at around 2300 hours. We have three hours to cross ten miles to where the terrorist camp is. That should be plenty of time. Once there, we check to make sure that the helicopter is there, whether or not the motor pool has vehicles in it, and if the hostages are on the site."

"Why check the motor pool?" asked Coltrane. "We've got a helicopter."

''Which is real useful, if the helicopter is there.'' Halloran thought for a second how to put this. These people were all volunteers, and he needed everybody he could get. But he, of all people, knew how easy it was to unvolunteer, and he didn't have the captain's rank to intimidate people with. ''If the helicopter is not there, we will have to capture the vehicles in the motor pool, load the hostages into the trucks, and drive them to the coast, to get taken off the beach by *Kimmel*.'' His audience stared at him in shock.

Time to give them a little dose of reality. ''People, things will go wrong on this mission, *guaranteed.* In every military operation ever run, only one thing is consistent—something *always* goes wrong. We just don't know what it is yet. That chopper may not be there. It may not be running. The hostages may not be there. We may get lost. We have to be ready for things to go wrong.''

Halloran paused a moment to let that sink in. ''Okay, does anybody want out? Speak up, shipmate, because I tell you now, it's too late to back out when we're getting into the motor whaleboat.''

Bledsoe asked, ''Why the hell do all this planning then?''

Rogers answered, glad to be able to slap down Bledsoe. ''He already said, this is what we do when things go wrong, Dog. This is just GP, that's all. Let the man talk.''

Halloran smiled. ''Thanks, Tiny. Anything else?''

Coltrane spoke. ''What if the trucks in the motor pool don't work?''

''Then this operation gets really hairy.'' Halloran paused. ''If the trucks don't run, we arm the rescued hostages with any weapons we take from the terrorists, stake out a perimeter, and call for help.'' That got a storm of questions and comments from the people assembled in the room. It took Magsaysay and Shawcross a minute or two to restore order. Halloran went on, switching from warning to persuasion. "It isn't that bad. That tank the terrorists have will be mighty useful for that, if we capture it intact. Tiny will have a radio, which means he can call in airstrikes to support us. It won't be easy, but we should be able to hold until they can get choppers to us."

"Choppers from where?" burst out Coltrane. He hadn't thought a lot of this through. The sudden admission that things could go wrong had shaken his normal good nature. "I thought half the reason we were doing this is because they lost *Jefferson* and they couldn't send the choppers!"

Steiner had looked into this herself, coordinating flight plans and radio frequencies. Her voice in a calming tone, but pitched to carry, she said, "That's only because this operation needs to be covert, to protect the hostages. Once we're out in the open, they can do a lot more. I checked the charts—they're bringing *Savannah* in from Gibraltar again. The CH-53s flying out of Galleta can stop on her to refuel and reach us. The only reason they haven't done it already is that *Savannah* won't be in position for another day." This produced another storm of comments.

"People!" barked Halloran. The room grew quiet. "Look, I made a mistake. I started talking about worst-case scenarios before I laid out the plan. Now if you'll work with me, we will run through the basic plan. Then we will go over the contingency plans. While I am giving the basic plan, please don't interrupt me or we'll never get through this."

There was a wary silence.

Halloran knew that was the best he was going to get. He plunged ahead. "Okay. So we arrive at the camp at roughly 0200 hours. When we get there, we confirm with *Kimmel* that the helicopter and the hostages are on site. Once *Kimmel* gets that confirmation, they head back out to sea. From then on, their missiles are our air cover. Other than us, if it flies, it dies. *Kimmel* will control any air support they can fly in for us. With air-to-air refueling, we'll probably have planes from Europe and maybe *Nimitz*. Tiny, that means you have to sign out a backpack radio and batteries from the radio shack."

"Signed one out this morning, along with those three wif-coms you asked for and spare batteries. We solid." Rogers sat back, smug, and sipped from a glass of water. He hadn't realized it yet, but since he had volunteered for this mission, he hadn't eaten, or drunk anything except water.

"Outstanding. Because once we confirm the helicopter and the hostages, we split into three teams." Halloran unrolled their map, now much spotted from planning they had done on it. The people in the room rolled forward in a wave to look at it. "On the radio, *Kimmel* is Alpha, we are Bravo. Bravo Knight is GMG1 Shawcross and four other people with M-14s. Only people with marksmanship medals need apply. We leave one grenade launcher and one machine gun with them. They will cover the camp and the doors to the rooms where the hostages are kept. They will also cover the road into the camp.

"Bravo Queen will be Lieutenant Steiner, Ensign Freeman, and one other person. Bravo King is everybody else. We will approach through this ravine." He pointed as the people in front crowded around the map. "It should take us up to the wire, where we will cut the wire and go through. If we run into any sentries, we use the silenced pistols. No shooting with anything else until I give the order, or until they fire on us. Once we're through the wire, Bravo Queen goes to the helicopter to make sure it flies."

Steiner spoke, her voice calm, her nightmares dealt with. "Seaman Halloran, it takes thirty minutes to do any kind of preflight."

For a moment, Halloran thought of what had—almost—happened the night before. Then he recovered. ''Uh—yes ma'am. I'm sorry, but we can only give you ten minutes. Just check it enough to let us know you can fly it out.'' She nodded, mercifully silent. Halloran concentrated on his job. ''While you're doing that, Bravo King will go through the wire and head for the tank. We'll use the bolt cutters to open it, then I go inside to check out the tank. I'll need two people to help me. Next, four people rush the end of the stone building. Bravo Knight can hit every section of the camp from their hill, except for the area directly behind the stone building. We cover the rear from our area.

''By this time, with most of us inside the wire, it's likely somebody will see us and the shooting will start. If no shooting has started by then, we wait for Bravo Queen to report on whether the helicopter can be flown. Once we know that, four people from Bravo King will rush the end of the stone building and start firing down both sides. Bravo Knight will open fire on the camp. GMG1, please use the M-60 to take out the tents first, then the vehicles. I want the grenade launchers to fire two flare rounds apiece, directly over the camp.''

''Hold up.'' Monk looked up from his notebook. ''Flare rounds will light up the camp. I thought we were trying to sneak in.''

''We are. But once we're inside that camp we want light, for two reasons. One, the shooters in Bravo Knight will be able to see everything that goes on in the camp, which will help them find their targets and hopefully prevent them from shooting us by accident. Second, it lets us see what we're doing while the terrorists are still trying to wake up. Three, with the camp lit up, the terrorists won't be able to see our shooters, who are out in the darkness.''

Coltrane said, ''That's three reasons. You said you had two.''

The gray-haired seaman shrugged. "Hey, I flunked math. Anyways, once the shooting starts, the rest of us in Bravo King leapfrog the guys at the end of the stone building and work our way up the front of the building. We blow the doors as we go. According to Majors, the hostages are behind these doors." He pointed, his hands moving in smooth sweeps to illustrate the plans.

"We'll use the bolt cutters and the C4 charges if we have to. The important thing is to get the doors open, let the hostages know they're being rescued, guard them, and sit tight. The guys going up the rear will be Bravo King Two. Kill anybody who's not a hostage. Also, cover the end of the building. Their leaders are probably in a room at the end."

Toombs asked, "What if they have the hostages wired? Explosives planted in their cells?"

Shawcross fielded that. "If they have explosives planted, they need to have wires running to the charges. When you people get near the stone building, watch for wires. Cut every wire you see." He held a pair of wire cutters aloft, clicked them shut a few time. "All the explosives in the world don't do any good if you can't detonate them."

He nodded to Halloran, who took up the briefing again. "Thanks, GMG1. So we've freed the hostages and killed the terrorists. GMG1 and Bravo Knight have shot up the vehicle park and the tents where the terrorists are sleeping. The camp should then be secure, and Bravo Queen should be warming up the helicopter. That's when we move the hostages to the helicopter and fly them out. We will fly the helicopter to *Kimmmel*, where Lieutenant Steiner will hover just aft of the flight deck and unload us. Then she will ditch the helicopter in the water and be picked up by the ship's boats. Any questions?"

Tosado raised his hand. "You ain't got us using the tank for anything. What do we use the tank for?"

"We're grabbing the tank to keep it away from the terrorists. We have enough firepower to do the job already. We don't need the tank, and none of you know how to use it. In the time it would take me to show someone how to use the tank, we should be out of there. On the other hand, if those terrorists get to the tank first, nothing we have can stop it. So, we grab the tank, we use it as cover, and we free the hostages on foot. Next question?"

"Yeah." Coltrane looked over the map. "When do we get our Medal of Honor and the date with Heather Locklear?" The laughter that followed broke up the tension a bit.

Halloran waited for the chuckles to subside. "Okay, now comes the fun part. What. We. Do. If. Things. Go. Wrong. Listen up, boys and girls. First, if Landing Party Bravo gets to the camp and the hostages are not there . . ."

At the operations officer's stateroom, Majors and Springer were looking at OPS, who was still in his rack, groggy and sick-looking. Springer said, "Sir, the CO said you'd missed officers call this morning. What's the problem?"

"Don't know what's wrong wi' me." Lieutenant Commander Scott's voice was slurred and reedier than usual. "Jus' tired."

"Let me look at you, sir." Springer examined OPS, wondering why Majors was here. He checked out the eyes, the pulse. Funny how there was no fever. Majors tapped him on the shoulder.

"Springer, can I talk with you for a minute?"

"I'm in the middle of an examination here, sir. Can it wait?"

"This is pretty important."

Cursing all the senior people who always thought their concerns were more important, Springer patted OPS on the shoulder. "I'll be right back, sir." They stepped out into the passageway. Regardless of rank, or anything else, Springer was a medic with his patient, and woe unto anyone who interfered with him doing his job. His voice conveyed all of that when he spoke. "Sir, please make it quick. I have a sick man in there."

"He's not sick. He's overdosed on Dramamine."

That stopped Springer cold. "And who overdosed him?"

"I did. Look, Springer, he's the man the captain put in charge of the landing party. He wanted to take over, change everything—"

Springer held up his hands, palms out. "Whoa. I know OPS, and you're right, he is a real gold-plated carbuncle. I can imagine the kind of goat rope he'd turn the landing party into."

"So you see why I dosed him with Dramamine?"

"Yeah. When did you do it?"

"Last night at three AM when he came to my room for a briefing after the drill. Three tablets, stirred into his coffee."

Springer grinned, shaking his head. "Now I know why you're the secret agent. But you can't keep dosing him with the stuff. I'm not the only person on this ship who can tell somebody's on seasickness pills."

The CIA agent reached into his pocket and produced a small brown flask. "That's why I want you to dose him with this."

Springer eyes took on a hard look. "I ain't poisoning anybody. Now—"

Majors grinned. "It isn't poison. It's syrup of ipecac. I carry it to deal with poisons. Just give him a little in some medicine."

Springer restrained a sudden laugh and hid the flask away in his bag. "Okay. Yeah, I can give it to him. When he throws up, I'll say he has the stomach flu.

That'll knock him off the mission for sure. But why didn't you give it to him last night?''

''Hell, I didn't want him puking all over *my* stateroom!''

Chapter Ten

Once the mission briefing was done, Shawcross started the weapons briefing. He made sure each member of the landing party knew how to load, use, and clear the M-14 rifle, the .45 pistol, the grenade launchers, machine guns, grenade, and shotguns. Shawcross finished his class with a few quick tactical lessons.

He started by opening a small cardboard box encased in green cloth. He peeled back a small strip of cardboard, and pulled out a long, gleaming belt of linked 7.62 ammunition, draping the belt Pancho Villa–style around his shoulders. The linked bullets hung there, deadly brass jewelry gleaming in the light. "Anybody ever seen someone do this?"

His audience applauded and shouted out names. "Yeah, John Wayne!" "Rambo!" "Chuck Norris!"

Shawcross slammed the belt to the ground. A ringing of metal. Sudden silence. "If I see anybody do that, I will whup you like a red-headed stepchild! If you do that, your ammo will get tangled. Then dust and twigs and all kinds of garbage will stick to it. When you feed it into your weapon, all that crap feeds right in with it. Your gun jams. You die of terminal stupidity!"

Coltrane asked, "So how do we carry it?"

"Leave it in the box and peel a strip of cardboard off the top. It's marked." Shawcross showed them the marks on the ammo box. "This cloth bag the box comes in hooks onto the weapon. Then you feed the belt straight from the box into the weapon. No tangles, no dirt, no jams."

Next, Shawcross picked up the shotgun. The 12-gauge riot guns from the armory had five-round magazines. The barrel of the one he held had already been sawed off even with the end of the tubular magazine, turning it into a compact, savage-looking weapon. "I've already shown you how to load this. Sawed-off, it has an effective range of thirty yards, it kicks like a mule, and it hits everything in front of you. Watch where you point it.

"You have to load your shells in this one at a time." He loaded five shells into the tube under the barrel, working quickly, in eight seconds. "That takes time. Whereas with a pistol it takes about two seconds to load seven rounds of ammo. That's why magazines are nice to have. Everybody with shotguns is going in with a pistol too. For close-quarters fighting, that .45 is darn near as wicked as a shotgun."

"Excuse me." Halloran faced the others. "If you're using a shotgun, whenever you get a quiet second or two, slam a couple of shells into the weapon to reload it. Never fire yourself dry."

Shawcross put down the shotgun and picked up an inoffensive green cylinder with a grenade spoon and pin on one end. "This is your Mark 3A2 demolition grenade. It's a charge of TNT in a cardboard casing, so it's all explosion, no fragmentation. We're taking it because it's the only type of grenade we have in the armory. Remember, grenades are safe." He banged the grenade three times, hard, against a table. "It won't go off from shock or fire. It can only go off if you pull the pin."

He pulled the pin, still gripping the grenade and its spoon.

"This grenade is still safe. Until I let go the spoon." Every eye in the room was now on the spoon of the grenade, held firmly in Shawcross's hand. "Once I let go of the spoon, this baby goes kaboom in four seconds and nothing on earth can stop it. You cannot stop it by putting the spoon back on, because when that spoon came off, the fuse started burning. Any questions?"

"Could you put the pin back in the grenade, please?" asked Halloran.

Shawcross grinned, looking at his decidedly nervous audience. "Sure. If you haven't let the spoon fly off, you can just lock it back in place with the pin, no harm done." He reinserted the pin. The people in the room started breathing again. "Oh, by the way, this is a dummy grenade." He grinned even wider at the outraged looks directed at him.

Toombs held his hand out, palm up, to Coltrane. "You lose the bet. Pay up."

"Talk to me on payday. I'm a little short right now."

Shawcross began tossing the grenade from hand to hand. "Now, grenades only go as far as you throw them. The good part is, they can be thrown over walls or around corners. Bullets are strictly line of sight weapons. Throw grenades through windows to clear out rooms, or onto the other sides of walls or buildings. Grenades don't have any muzzle flash to give away your position, so throw them from cover. You can give your enemies a world of hurt without them knowing where you are.

"We'll each have two grenades when we go ashore. Every person with a rifle will carry two hundred rounds of ammunition in twenty-round clips. If you're carrying a shotgun, you'll have fifty rounds for it. Each pistol will be issued with four loaded magazines, seven rounds each. The people carrying the M-79s will each carry two bandoliers of 40mm high explosive, plus four flare rounds. The people with the M-60s will each carry one box of ammunition in the weapon, plus three more boxes. Every person in the landing party will carry one box of ammunition for the machine guns. Once you're loaded up, I'll open cases of 12-gauge, 7.62, and .45 ACP. If you think you can carry more than I've issued you, knock yourself out. But remember, you have to drag it all ten miles.

"Another thing. Uh, Halloran, lean against the door, willya?" Mystified, Halloran did so. "Okay, Halloran is one of the terrorists at the door. Bang! Halloran, you just been shot. Die." Halloran slumped to the floor. Shawcross went to the door and took out a small stick of what looked like modeling clay. "This is a quarter-pound block of C4. High explosive. It'll have a six-second fuse and a blasting cap in it. Now I go to the door with the hostages"—he stepped over Halloran—"and try to open it. It's locked, and the lock is part of the door, so I can't take it off with the bolt cutters. Whatever will I do?

"Every block of C4 has one side covered with stickum-glue, covered by wax paper. I take my block of C4, peel off the paper, and stick it to the door, right near the lock." He peeled off the paper and stuck the C4 to the steel door. The people in the room gradually began to realize—that was a real block of high explosive on the door.

Shawcross had their absolute attention.

"The bad part about explosives, if you place them in the open like this, is that the force of the explosion just sprays away from the door. You may only jam the door in place. So you take your dead sentry, who is lying in front of the door, and lay him over the C4. That uses their body like a sandbag, to force the blast into the door." He lifted Halloran from the floor, grunting from the weight. ''Damn, Halloran, I hope them terrorists ain't been eating as well as you!'' That got a decidedly nervous giggle from some of the people in the room. Halloran, who'd played with C4 a few times himself and had taken pains to observe there was no blasting cap in Shawcross's block of explosive, grinned and played along.

''You prop them in place with their own rifle.'' Shawcross picked up an M-14 to demonstrate. ''Don't be gentle with the bastard, he's dead already. Next, you warn the hostages you're going to blow the door, so stand back. Light the fuse and head for cover, because in six seconds, there's gonna be itsy-bitsy pieces of terrorist flying everywhere. It'll be a hell of a mess.''

Propped against the explosive, Halloran spoke up his nervous audience. ''Any questions?''

''The hell with this!'' burst out Bledsoe. He shot to his feet. ''You people are out of your minds! Playing with explosives and grenades and shit! Keep your damn landing party! I'm out of here!'' He shoved his way towards the door.

As he approached the door, Halloran stepped aside. Shawcross called out, ''Hey Halloran, didn't I say he'd quit on us? Go ahead, Bledsoe, chicken out.''

Bledsoe glared at Shawcross, then Halloran. ''Fuck you. Seaman Halloran, I will deal with your ass later!''

Halloran smirked as Bledsoe glared at him, letting his temper get the better of him. ''You're pretty brave when you can hide behind your crow, BM3. It's funny—you act like a badass so much down in the bosuns locker, I always knew you'd wuss out when the crunch came.''

Furious, Bledsoe took a step towards Halloran, fists balled up—then stopped when Shawcross said, ''Uh-uh, BM3. People are watching. Why don't you just run along. It isn't like everybody will say you chickened out or anything.'' Bledsoe froze in place. ''I mean, nobody saw you come in here, did they?'' Bledsoe stood there, a bundle of suppressed anger. "Besides, I'm sure they'll let you reenlist even if you quit this mission."

Bledsoe glared at Shawcross, who leaned against one table. "So stay or go, BM3. Makes no difference to me." The man still stood there, glaring at everybody. The room was silent for a minute.

Toombs broke the silence. "Hey brother-man, you gonna stay? We sure could use you."

Bledsoe sat down, glaring. Halloran cursed himself. If he'd kept his temper and been silent, Bledsoe would probably have quit the group, which seemed like a good thing to him.

Shawcross, on the other hand, was pleased with himself for precisely the reasons Halloran was angry. He'd thought that if he stung Bledsoe's pride the man would stay. He wanted someone with a little mean in them. Most of his volunteers were just too damn happy. "Glad you reconsidered, BM3. Because we do need you."

"Yeah, just get on with the training." Bledsoe glowered, and sat alone.

Halloran looked at his watch. Everybody in the room was tired, the edginess of the last few minutes some very real evidence of that. "Okay, people, it's about time for the noon meal. Be back here at 1300 hours for the final briefing. Does anybody have anything else to say before we go?"

Shawcross put in his final word of the morning. "I've got web belts, canteens, and ammo pouches, but not enough. I want you all to find backpacks, those small overnight packs a lot of people on the ship have to carry books and such. If you don't have one of your own, borrow one from somebody who does. Belly bags are good too, anything you can use to carry ammunition and gear."

That caught Halloran by surprise, mostly because he knew he should have thought of it himself. He tossed in his own addendum. "People, we'll be leaving for the mission from this room. When you come back, bring everything you think you'll need. If you think you'll need a knife or snacks, a cigarette lighter, matches, anything, bring it with you. Bring your raincoats too, with liners—the desert gets really cold at night, and you'll need those coats. Woodall, could you get me a couple of rolls of electrical tape from the EM shop?'' She nodded. ''Okay, that's it. See you at 1300.'' They all went to chow.

Stolchak was back in the Mekong. It was night again. He stumbled through the swampy water, fetid, warm liquid splashing on him as he struggled forward through the night. Trees hung over the banks, mangrove roots a tangle of darkness that green eyes looked out of. ''Unfinished business, Boats.'' Ensign Hadley's voice. ''You never leave unfinished business behind.''

There was a splashing behind him, the dim red glow of a flare. It was the man he'd left behind, he knew it. He ran through the water, waded through mud, his feet heavier and heavier, the glow of the flare closer, the splashing behind him ever louder. The man he'd left behind was chasing him, was coming for him, and when he caught him he'd make him look into his eyes and Stolchak would die. Panic gripped his heart, his arms flailing, the splashing closer and closer—

He woke.

''Chief? Are you in there?'' Somebody was banging on the door to the deck office. Crammed into this space were three desks, two computers, masses of files, several hundred manuals and handbooks of various kinds, two seabags of personal gear, half a dozen dress uniforms still in the dry cleaning bags from Haifa, heaps of papers, a rapidly diminishing hoard of pens, and Snyder's personal stash—the last two cartons of Marlboros on the ship.

Stolchak shook his head, rubbing bleary eyes. ''Hold

your damn horses! Just a minute!'' He got up and opened the door. Ensign Pullman was standing there. He stepped quickly into the small office and went to his desk.

''Chief, have you seen the boat reports?''

''Yeah, uh, third drawer to the right, filed under B. Why?''

Pullman opened the drawer, fished through it. ''OPS is confined to quarters with stomach flu. He may have to skip the mission, so he's getting even with us by going over all the boat reports. Are the ship's boats ready for tonight?''

''As ready as they can be, with the CO calling away drills every fifteen minutes. I'll go up and check them now.'' He headed for the boat decks.

As he walked, he thought back to the nightmares. He'd had them before, when he was cruising the ragged edge of exhaustion. Now, so was nearly everybody on the ship, thanks to that damn midwatch GQ. But these last few nightmares had been especially bad. Maybe it was time to get out of the Navy, get that bait and tackle shop in Florida he'd been promising his wife for so long. He could retire any time. Maybe after this deployment. Then again, maybe not. On *Kimmel*, he was lord and master of deck division. Out of the Navy, he'd just be another ex-Navy chief. That would be hard to face.

With such thoughts occupying his mind, he arrived on the boat deck. Hale and Andrews were slapping deck gray paint all over the ship's motor whaleboat, to make it less visible. ''How much longer, big nuts?''

''Not much longer, Chief!'' answered Andrews. ''What do we do with the brightwork?'' He referred to the gleaming chromed and brass fittings on the boat. Their gleam was the result of much polishing, ordered by OPS, and as such, was a matter of pride to the CO and to himself. But that was peacetime thinking. They were going to war.

"Paint over those too, and the windows!" answered Stolchak. "Anything that might reflect light. Don't worry about being pretty, just get it done!" Andrews nodded and went back to work. Stolchak knew Andrews hated his job but was good at it. A common trait in deck division, thought Stolchak. So common he didn't think about it much.

He crossed the quarterdeck to check out *Kimmel*'s other boat. The captain's gig was a small motorboat, brightly painted. As its name implied, it was used for short trips by the CO. Stolchak would use both boats to put the landing party ashore fast and get out of there. He'd had enough of hanging around hostile shores in 'Nam. He tried to see the bright side of everything, but small boat operations were one thing he had no good memories of.

The noon meal that day was sparsely attended, most of the crew ducking into their berthings to grab sleep instead of a meal. During the meal, Shawcross broke out and prepped the night vision gear they would be using for the mission. Halloran hunted up Majors to find out what was going on with OPS. Majors had persuaded the CO to give OPS a chance to recover, freeing the landing party of interference from officers for the afternoon.

After lunch, the landing party reconvened in the rec room, now joined by Majors and Springer. Small groups of the volunteers fetched field gear, flak vests, and helmets from the armory, or went to the chief's mess and the wardroom to collect the used khakis donated for the landing party. There was a merry hour of confusion as people sorted out the clothes, finding what would fit, and tried to make a usable combination of field gear for each person. All of landing party Bravo had some kind of backpack, ranging from military issue "Alice" packs to a bright purple Power Rangers backpack that Monk normally used to carry his manuals and stationary. Then the taping started.

"People, listen up." Halloran shook off a sudden feeling of drowsiness. The adrenaline high of last night and this morning was wearing off. "A little demonstration. Tombstone, come on down!"

Toombs stepped forward. He was wearing baggy khakis that were a little tight around his massive chest and arms. Over the khakis, he wore a black military raincoat. On top of that was his flak vest from the armory. Belted around his waist and shoulders was a web belt and harness, with two ammo pouches, two canteens, his own flashlight, a bayonet in its scabbard, pistol holster, pistol magazine pouch, and first aid pouch. His backpack was a green nylon one designed for schoolkids but very military-looking—other than the GI Joe logo and pictures on it.

"Okay Tombstone, jump up and down." Toombs did so. Straps and metal ends and clips and buttons bounced as he jumped, rattling and ringing off him. "At night, you see with your ears. Anything that makes noise when you move can give you away. To stop this, you tape down anything on you that rattles or makes noise, so that you can move silently. GMG1, can you help me please?" The two men went to work, taping down any loose gear with the electrical tape Woodall had brought back. When they were done, they stepped back. "Okay, jump up and down again."

Toombs grinned. "I feel damn silly doing this." He hopped again. Only a few items rattled. He stopped, and Shawcross and Halloran went to work again. The third time he jumped up and down, the only noise he made was of his own movement.

"There you go." Halloran stood up. He was wearing the same kind of improvised field rig Toombs had worn, with a battered green canvas knapsack on his back. He held his arms out. "Now, tape everything on me that makes noise."

Toombs walked up to him and slapped a big piece of electrical tape over his mouth.

Once the laughter was done, the volunteers went to work taping down gear. Halloran watched them closely. Exhausted as they had been, he'd seen how the excitement of the upcoming mission had kept the volunteers alert all morning. After lunch however, with full stomachs, everyone was becoming drowsy. After the gear was taped, Monk began a demonstration of night vision gear, but while he did his best, Halloran could see everyone in the room except Majors beginning to nod off. It was time.

Since he had joined the Navy, Halloran had really missed one thing the Army had that the Navy had never heard of—a sleep plan. He moved next to Majors and spoke quietly. "These guys are beat. Everybody's been run into the ground."

Majors nodded. "What should we do about it?"

Halloran looked to both sides in a conspiratorial gesture. He'd been impressed by how the CIA agent handled himself, but this might seem a little crazy. "Look, we've got a few hours until we issue weapons. You're in charge of the mission. Could you guard the door, and let these people grab a few hours of sleep? It could make the difference tonight."

To Halloran, after being in the Navy, it seemed like the wildest sort of rebellion. To Majors, it was common sense. "Sure. I'll say you're using night vision gear in here for training." He stood up and spoke. "People!" Monk stopped his presentation. "Here is what we're going to do . . ."

Outside the rec room, the afternoon went on pretty much as the morning had, with the sole exception of Majors standing out in the passageway. Shawcross ducked out for about an hour to check on the silencers and the weapons, then came back. Majors hung out in the hallway, nursing a soda. He watched the constant flow of people passing him, staying unobtrusive, but making sure no one disturbed the rec room.

At three PM the executive officer, Kendricks, came walking towards him with a folder of papers in his hand. Majors noted that while the man seemed as tired as everyone else on the ship, he also seemed alert and intelligent. This might be tough. Kendricks shook hands. "Hello, Agent Majors. I thought I'd brief the landing party on the intelligence we have. Why are you out here?"

Majors shook his hand, thinking fast. "Thank you, Lieutenant Commander. I'll pass those on to the group myself." He reached for the papers.

Kendricks held on to the papers adroitly, his eyes taking on a steely glint. "Thank you, Agent Majors, but I'll do the briefing myself. The CO has said that if OPS can't command the landing party, I will take it over. I want to meet my people. Why are you out here?"

"They're training on the night vision gear. Any light might damage the gear. I'm making sure the door isn't accidentally opened. Let me warn them someone is coming in." He knocked hard on the door, three times, and said loudly. "Take off the night vision gear! Let me know when it's off!"

There was no reply.

Majors knocked and spoke again, louder. Kendricks looked more suspicious. "Agent Majors, I heard you were training them on night vision gear earlier this afternoon too. How long does that take?" Majors stuttered. Kendricks shoved past him. "I've used night vision gear. Normal lights won't damage it."

Kendricks threw the door open. The rec room was dark, the benches and decks in it covered with sleeping men and women, oblivious to the world. Every member of landing party Bravo had slept through Majors's attempted wakeup. With the light from the passage shining on their faces, they still slept the sleep of the just. The just exhausted.

Kendricks gave them a long cold look. Then he shut the door. His voice was thick with controlled fury. "Agent Majors, you had better have a good explanation for why your people are sleeping while this crew is running its ass off!"

Majors nodded. With the secret blown, he might as well speak plainly. His voice was low, but intense. "Those people are sleeping because they are exhausted. Exhausted people make mistakes. They are going to be awake all night on a difficult mission. They were awake all last night doing some drill. This is the only chance I have to give them some rest."

The CIA agent noted that Kendricks seemed to lose some wind from his sails when he mentioned the drill of the night before. He also noted that the fury in his voice was quickly fading. "The rest of the personnel on this ship aren't getting a chance to sleep, Majors."

"That's not my problem. These people are my problem, and they need some sleep. Good lord, they didn't wake up when I pounded on the door! They didn't wake up when you opened the door, not one of them! Doesn't that give you some idea of how tired they are? How close they are to breaking?" Kendricks held up one hand. Majors stopped speaking.

"You're right. I've seen what happens when people are too tired to do their jobs correctly. Here are the reports." He handed his file to Majors. "Study them. I'll be back here at 1800 hours to brief them, and to prepare for the mission with them." He faced Majors, looking at him with burning, tired eyes. "I am trusting you, Majors! Don't screw me on this." He walked off, his steps a quick, angry stride.

The CIA agent started breathing again.

* * *

Around the Mediterranean, the elements of Sudden Lightning began to come together as night approached. Aboard the crippled *Jefferson*, the fires were out. The escorting cruisers and destroyers prepared to head south at flank speed to aid *Kimmel*. U.S. submarines, silent and lethal, were already sliding into place outside Libyan naval bases. If the Libyan missile boats sortied, they would die.

Targets which had been assigned to the Navy were switched to Air Force planes based in Europe. Air-to-air refueling would be the order of the day for the A-10s and F-15s assigned to the mission. West of Gibraltar, USS *Nimitz* went to flank speed, leaving behind the cruisers and destroyers of her escort, launching the F-14s and FA-18s that would be the Navy's contribution to air strikes supporting Sudden Lightning. Their numbers were limited by the number of KA-6 intruders that were available. These were A-6 Intruders modified as fuel tankers for air-to-air refueling. *Nimitz* could send no more planes than could be supported by the available tankers. The KA-6s off *Nimitz* were augmented by additional KA-6s flown in off *Carl Vinson*, from the Indian Ocean.

Everywhere, units ran into one unalterable fact. The titanic U.S. military establishment that had once been the centerpiece of NATO was no more. Too many bases had been shut down, too many units disbanded. Planning hit one limitation after another, of available bases or available planes or available range. But within those limitations, when the operation began, Libyan radars had to be knocked out. Libyan aircraft, if they sortied, had to be shot down. With *Jefferson* out of the equation, the numbers were decreased, but there were still enough to do the job. Barely.

Majors looked at the photograph. The girl's face looked back at him, lost, afraid, alone. As the afternoon wound down towards the evening meal, he had found himself glancing more and more often at the picture. He could tell himself that he was getting obsessed, that in the scheme of things one small girl didn't mean much. Horrible things were done to little girls like this all over the world, all the time. He could remind himself that nothing he did could help that girl in Leningrad. He could tell himself his worry for a civilian was unprofessional.

But he had seen this girl. He needed absolution. That made the difference. He could look at the picture and see the fear in her eyes, and remember another face, equally fearful, because of him. That made all the difference in the world.

Fuck professionalism.

The 1MC roared. *''Knock off ship's work. Early chow for watchstanders and chow reliefs.''*

He checked his watch. 4:15 PM. He debated whether or not to wake up the landing party. Eventually he decided that, whether or not the rest had done them any good, they had to start final preparations. He took one more look at the picture and put it away. Then, Majors threw open the door to the rec room, switched on the lights, and shouted. ''Up and at 'em! Time to go rescue some hostages! Wake up!''

The volunteers in the room woke without a struggle, having slept enough to get back over the line from being exhausted to being merely tired. The sleep had left them a little groggy, but they pepped up fast as memory of what they were about to do came back to them. Majors saw second thoughts on the faces of a lot of them, including Halloran. That worried him. But after a second, Halloran was circulating around the room, shouting, clapping people on the shoulder, a constant stream of chatter that woke people through sheer ability to annoy.

''Come on, people, let's roll!'' Halloran worked himself up to a cheerful state. ''It's chow time! Grab one more meal! You can't tell where your next one is coming from! Stack your gear and leave it against the wall before you go to eat! After chow, we'll draw weapons."

The volunteers got moving, Toombs and Coltrane racing to get to the mess decks, Rogers moving more slowly, Monk and Magsaysay muttering something about getting a cigarette and heading topside. Both pilots had left when the sleep break was called. Shawcross stopped to talk to Majors before he left the room. "Vince, I'm going down to the armory. I ain't hungry. I'll have everything ready for issue by 1715 hours." Majors stared blankly at him. "A quarter after five, civilian time. If y'all are a Marine, Mickey's big hand will be on the—"

Majors's laughter cut him off. Shawcross grinned briefly at his own joke. Both of them were too nervous to laugh much. Shawcross looked to both sides almost sheepishly, spoke to the CIA agent in a low tone. "Vince, no bullshit. You ever done anything like this?"

Majors shook his head. There had been that time in Guadalajara, when—"No. Intelligence work is pretty boring, most of the time. I've pulled a couple of pretty hairy ops, but nothing like this. How about you?"

Shawcross shook his head.

The gunners mate looked over to where Halloran and Tosado were high-fiving each other, ready to go, eager to go. "Man, right now, wouldn't it be great to be young and stupid again?" Majors nodded emphatic agreement.

Shawcross left without another word.

At the mess decks, the chow line was its average length, running down a third the length of the ship, when the first khaki-clad volunteers appeared. Toombs and Coltrane worked their way to the end of the line, shaking hands, being clapped on the back, hearing words of encouragement. As, one by one, the other people from Bravo came into the line, the atmosphere in the passageway grew more raucous, part high school football game, part parade. Old feuds were forgotten as the crewmen of *Kimmel* shared in the glory, cheering the volunteers, releasing months of tension in the excitement of the moment.

MS1 Davis stepped into the passageway in the middle of the raucous celebration and shouted, "Shut the hell up!" The noise dropped to a low roar. "All the condemned dummies is getting a hearty meal! All y'all in the landing party, get on to the head of the chow line! Move fast, before I get mad!"

They came forward, buoyed by the reception. Fear and doubt would come later. Now, they were heroes. They enjoyed it for all it was worth.

On the bridge of *Kimmel*, Reisling checked the time. Forty minutes to sundown. It was time. He sat in the captain's chair for a few more seconds, looking over the bridge. The men and women on the bridge looked back at him, standing to their stations. Ensign Pullman, serving as officer of the deck, was in command of the bridge even while Reisling was on the bridge. The captain could take over the bridge if he wished, but he had to announce that fact. The formalities had to be observed. Reisling put down his cup of coffee, cleared his throat, and looked to the horizon. "Officer of the Deck, I have the bridge."

Pullman grinned. Normally, the CO taking the bridge was a criticism, a clear statement that the OOD was incapable of doing his job. Here and now, everyone knew it had a different meaning. "Captain has the bridge, aye. Ship is bearing 275 degrees true—"

"Belay all reports." Reisling smiled as the bridge grew silent. Call away GQ? No, not yet. Savor the moment. He felt a sudden thrill and realized: This was what he had become a Naval officer for. This moment, this place, this mission. Commanding his ship as it went into enemy waters.

He was not a man given to introspection, especially not on the bridge with the entire watch section waiting for his next word. But the thought did occur to him that sometime in the long climb towards admiral's rank, somehow he'd forgotten all that. Until now.

Now, all he had to do was speak the words and it would begin. The words of command that he had practiced for twenty-two years, in fair weather and foul, on this and other ships. He knew what to say. He said it.

"Helm, right ten degrees rudder, set course 178. Lee helm, all engines ahead flank two, set pitch and RPMs for thirty knots."

The helmsman spun the wheel to bring the ship to the ordered bearing, eyes shifting between the control that told him the attitude of his rudder and the LED indicators that told him the ship's bearing. "Right ten degrees rudder, come to course 178, aye sir!"

The lee helmsman signaled the engine room to increase rotations on the propeller shafts and change the pitch of the twin screws that drove the ship. The bronze variable-pitch propellers increased their angle, biting deep into the water. "Set pitch for thirty knots, aye sir!" The lee helmsman watched the readouts, compared RPMs and pitch to the chart at his station. "Ninety-five RPMs and 100 percent pitch for thirty knots, sir!"

The engines increased their power in a noise heard throughout the ship as it shuddered and increased speed. The smooth Mediterranean waters *Kimmel* was passing through grew into sheets of white water spraying up both sides of the bow. The destroyer cut through the waves, wind whistling through her rigging, beginning to slowly rock back and forth as speed built up.

Lt. Jimmelle Washington was in CIC, supervising the harpoon missle controls as they loaded the computerized target packages, directions for what the cruise missles would be destroying. That done, she checked in with the fire controlmen operating the standard missle launchers.

"FC1 Wisher, any further problems with the standards?"

"Not a problem, ma'am. If it flies, it dies!" Hunched over the instrument panels, Fire Controlman 1st Class Jacob Wisher was in heaven. Tonight he would supervise firing more missles than most FCs fired in their entire careers.

OS1 Ingalls stepped up behind Washington. "Ma'am, we have a call from the ship's armory. It's Shawcross. He wants to talk to you."

Washington patted Wisher on the shoulder. "Keep up the good work, FC1." They headed for the phone. The black woman looked at Ingalls questioningly. "OS1, you *are* keeping Harrison off the Spa-48, aren't you?"

Ingalls shook his head. "He's been counseled, ma'am. You have to give people a chance to learn from their mistakes." At Washington's shocked look, he grinned sheepishly. "Don't worry, ma'am. I'll be keeping an eye on him myself."

She thought a moment. Countermand a decision by a First Class? You had to trust your subordinates, she told herself. Even, a small voice asked her, if you think they're just trying to ignore a major problem? She was still thinking as, in the darkness of CIC, they arrived at the cluttered watch officer's desk. Washington picked up the phone. "Guns here. What can I do for you, GMG1?"

"Ma'am, I'm down in the armory, about to do ammo issue. I've, uh, I've written a letter home, to be given to my wife. It's in the top left-hand drawer of my desk, in a small manila envelope. If I . . . if something happens, you'll make sure she gets it?"

The words, made tinny and flat by the ship's phone, still shook Jimmelle to the core. She did her best to laugh it off, but when she spoke, some of her control had slipped. "Ain't nothin' gonna happen to you, farmboy. Y'all just get to steppin' with that."

Shawcross tried to laugh it off. "Yeah, I know." A silence heavy with thought followed. "I know. But, if, well . . ." He couldn't say it. Neither of them could. That was the funny thing about the people you worked with on a ship. You actually did become like family. Not in a lovely-dovey "I love you, man!" type of way, but like feuding brothers and sisters. Stuck with each other, you learned to get along even as you fought, and woe betide any outsider who picked on one while the other was around.

She'd been terrified of this tall, hook-nosed man when they put her in charge of the division. She'd covered that fear with humor, and humor had worked. Besides, she'd long ago found out you either learned to deal with people or you gave up. One thing Jimmelle Washington had never been was a quitter.

She'd never expected to be friends with a gunner's mate from Missouri either, but life was funny that way. She nodded unconsciously, as if Shawcross could see her, and thought how strange it was to want to give one of your first classes a hug. "Don't worry, GMG1. If something should happen, I'll take care of it."

Six decks below, in the armory, Shawcross thought remarkably similar thoughts as he spoke into the phone. "Thank you, ma'am. It's been a pleasure." He hung up the phone and began breaking out the ammunition.

In the tiny first class mess, they had gathered to send off their own. Shawcross had ducked through the mess line, grabbed a sandwich, and split, but BM1 Ramon Magsaysay was the hero of the hour and he was sticking around to enjoy it. He'd had to put up with a lot of ribbing about his accent. On this day it mattered not at all.

He stood against a bulkhead, glass held aloft in one hand, machete in the other. Behind him, the bulkhead was covered with awards and plaques, pictures of the ship and crew and ports of call. The rest of the tiny room was crammed with first class petty officers, sitting and standing. ''Gentlemen, we are gathered here to give a sendoff to an fellow first class and a good shipmate!'' SK1 Martins, six foot four and 245 pounds, chairman of the first class mess, towered over the tiny Filipino he stood next to. ''Let's give a toast to Ramon: Fair wind and following seas!''

Magsaysay grinned and spoke up. ''Confusion to our enemies!'' They drank together as the first classes cheered. Then the cheering petty officers drank to them. Magsaysay's grin turned to surprise as he drained his glass. ''What's going on?''

Martins refilled his glass with what Magsaysay had thought was red bug juice. ''Our master at arms did an inventory of the wine locker this afternoon. It turns out that a couple of bottles of red wine I picked up in Marseilles got broken in storage! Darn shame, huh?''

Magsaysay went back to smiling, and drained his glass. ''That is a darn shame, SK1. More bug juice please!''

Martins poured the last of the red fluid into his glass and said, ''Gentlemen, when I heard we had a Filipino coming onto *Kimmel* who wasn't a cook, I figured that the paperwork had to be wrong, or he wasn't Filipino.'' Filipino cooks had a long tradition in the U.S. Navy, dating from the Spanish-American war. ''But the first words I heard him say, I knew he was a Filipino. And the first time I saw him get near food, I knew he wasn't a cook! I think that dumpster in Naples is still burning!'' There was laughter at that, and embarrassment on Magsaysay's face. At a dockside barbecue in Naples, Magsaysay had managed to burn or drop more hamburgers and hot dogs than any three other people working the grills, then had climaxed the event by accidentally dumping hot coals into a dumpster and starting a fire.

''That is enough of that!'' Magsaysay declared loudly,

grinning from ear to ear, and waved the machete he held. They cleared a space in front of him even in that crowded room. "When I was a boy in Olongapo, I would see the sailors every day and I shined their shoes and I knew I want to be one of them. Then, when I was older, my family move to the country and I chop pineapples and sugarcane with one of these!" He dexterously waved the blade in his hand. "But when I was in the fields, I see the planes fly overhead, and I know they are Navy too. I never stop dreaming of being in the U.S. Navy. When I get old enough, I study English more and I take the test, and for fifteen years, I have been a sailor. I work hard to come here. I work hard to be American."

He stopped speaking for a moment, in the suddenly silent room. He was a simple man, who knew small boats and ship handling, sea and anchor detail and splicing lines. Now he had to try to put into words thoughts he had never told anyone else. And for the first time, they were listening to him. "You are all born American, so you do not know what that can mean. To want to become American. I know. Just like I know some of you laugh at me because my English still not so good. But many of you help me too, many other shipmates help me since I join the Navy. Now, other Americans need to be rescued, and I will show that my machetes can chop more than pineapples, and that I can help my fellow Americans!"

The first class mess shook with their cheers.

High over Libya, a reconnaissance satellite slid through its trajectory. It was not the newest or most powerful recon satellite in service. But it could give visuals in real time, beaming pictures to a ground receiver, and it was in the right position to scan the target. Its lenses and sensors shifted silently in the vacuum of space, responding to telemetry beamed from ground control, beaming telemetry back. Encoded in the signals was an overhead view of the target. At ground control, the signal was computer-enhanced, electronically augmented until the Photo Intel crew at NSA could confirm it.

The signal flashed to the Pentagon over secure, scrambled lines, and the signal was good. At dusk, the CH-47 was at Base Whiskey Six, the target. Thermal scans indicated that the stone building was occupied by several large heat masses, presumably hostages. From the planning group at the Pentagon, communications flashed to the White House and back. Finally, the message was sent to the units converging on Libya, from the A-10s and F-15s launching from Germany, to the F-14s and F-18s just passing Gibraltar, to the ships still aiding the crippled *Jefferson*, to a lone destroyer near the Gulf of Sidra, headed south on the darkening seas.

Sudden Lightning was a go.

Chapter Eleven

One by one, the members of the landing party entered the cramped ship's armory to draw weapons and ammunition. First went the four silenced .45s that hadn't blown up or made noise when test-fired. Shawcross, Halloran, Magsaysay, and Steiner each took one. Each person collected their load of magazines, ammunition, grenades, flares, and weapons, with Shawcross making sure everything was correctly worn or stowed away. When that was done, he pointed each person to several open cases of ammo. With each person, his words were the same. "Take what you want, eat what you take."

Halloran, with a shotgun and an M-79 grenade launcher, loaded up with 12-gauge, pop flares, and an extra bandolier of 40mm ammunition. Coltrane, with a shotgun, tried to grab two more bayonets, was refused, settled for more 12-gauge ammunition. Toombs asked for a second .45, loaded up on pistol ammunition, and took three extra grenades. Rogers got extra pop flares, Bledsoe stuffed his pockets with extra shotgun shells,

Magsaysay took two extra boxes of belted 7.62 for the M-60s and four extra grenades for himself. Steiner signed out one of the ship's .38 revolvers, tucked it into the small of her back, and took an extra box of ammo for it. Mackenzie had shown up with a roman *Gladius Iberius* short sword he'd picked up in Barcelona swinging at his hip. Now he drew extra grenades. He explained to Shawcross, "I intend to be either real quiet, or real loud."

Shawcross grinned, handed him a stainless steel hatchet, a match for one that the one-quarter Cherokee gunners mate had on his own rig. "Take one of these babies too. I figure they always show us Injuns with tomahawks, we might as well carry 'em when they're going to be useful."

"I'm a MacKenzie. They're who raised me, not any Indians." The young man looked grim. "If I have to be one or the other, I'll be a MacKenzie."

Shawcross nodded. "It doesn't have to divide you. You can be both. Let it make you stronger."

MacKenzie thought about that for a moment. He took the hatchet.

Loaded up, each person exited the armory and climbed the stairs to the boat deck. There, they sat on stacked life jackets while Halloran worked his way up and down the line, checking gear to make sure it was properly worn. They were all there when the general quarters alarm went off. There was chaos around them as people headed to their battle stations. Led by Stolchak, the boat crew ducked below to draw pistols, flak vests, and the last M-60 for their own use in putting the party ashore. Then Shawcross and Stolchak inspected the landing party and the boat crews.

On the bridge, Reisling looked with satisfaction at the bridge crew. General quarters stations had been manned in record time. Everyone waited, greyhound-tense, for the next order. Reisling ordered the junior OS who was keeping the bridge in touch with CIC, "OS3, tell CIC to set Emcon Four throughout the ship." Emcon Four was electronic silent running, the shutdown of every electronic emitter on the ship, from the radars and radios to the closed-circuit TV station in the ship. Radars enabled the ship to see for miles in every direction, but their emissions could pinpoint the ship for miles beyond their effective range. Reports came in quickly.

"Emcon Four set in communications."

"Emcon Four set on the flight deck."

"Emcon Four set in CIC." Now, *Kimmel* was almost blind. The only detection gear still being used was passive gear, scanning for radio sources or radars that might sweep the ship. The only other detectors the ship had still working were the lookouts at their stations and the signalmen on the "Big Eyes." As their grandfathers had done before them, the lookouts, junior sailors with binoculars, scanned the horizon unaided by any technology other than finely ground optics. Personnel waited by the controls of every emitter, however, ready to light off the systems the moment the ship was threatened.

"Activate Prairie Masker."

"Activating Prairie Masker, aye." Prairie Masker was a counter-sonar device that sprayed a steady stream of tiny air bubbles from the keel of the ship up to its sides. Making a 563-foot destroyer silent in the water at thirty knots was impossible, but with Prairie Masker running, passive systems would pick up the sound of a rainstorm dappling the water, not a warship plunging through the seas.

A message from CIC. "Sir, Guns requests we shut off running lights and IFF beacon."

"Tell Guns to make it so, OS3. Good work." Reisling smiled. He'd had doubts about a female gunnery officer, but Washington was working out just fine. *Kimmel* was now an electronic black hole gliding over the seas. That image was still in his mind when his XO stepped up behind him. "Sir, I've left my personal papers in my stateroom. I'll go down to take over the landing party now."

Reisling turned to face his XO. Some things you had to say face to face. "Dave, that won't be necessary. I've made a change in plans. Well, actually, it's just a return to our original plans. . . ."

On the quarterdeck, the landing party and boat crew made final checks of their gear. They had seen the lights go out, seen the radars cease their rotation. As full darkness fell, they tested the night vision gear Shawcross brought up from the armory, stepping out from the red-lit quarterdeck into the stygian blackness of the decks. They had the ship's only two AN-PVS 5s, bug-eyed night vision goggles that turned the night world into green-lit daylight. Shawcross also brought up two AN-PVS 7 "Starlight" scopes, which magnified any light source as bright as day for the user. They were mounted on rifles for the cover team.

A familiar figure walked across the deck towards them. As he checked the batteries on his radio, Rogers's reaction was typical. When he saw who it was, he muttered under his breath. "Aw shit."

Coltrane saw the man approach, and whispered to Halloran. "Ooh, look, he's got a pistol belt! And a canteen! I'm so impressed!"

Lieutenant Commander Wendell Scott, looking a little pale but fine other than that, stepped into the middle of the group. He was dressed in starched khakis, with the pants bloused into his gleaming, polished flight deck boots, and a web belt with canteen and pistol holster around his waist. Ignoring the sailors, he walked up to Majors and shook his hand. "Here I am! Agent Majors, I'll be commanding the Navy personnel on this mission.

I'm sorry I'm late, but I look forward to working with you."

Majors thought frantically. "You have the stomach flu, don't you?"

Scott grinned, slapped his stomach in hearty good health. "I hate to contradict HM3 Springer, but it must have just been something I ate. I feel just fine now." He turned to the rest of the landing party. "People, I'll be taking command of the landing party once we hit the beach. Once you have all your gear stowed, I will inspect everyone's gear, so make sure everything is in place." Then he turned back to GMG1 Shawcross. "GMG1, load me up!"

Shawcross had just come in from helping the boat crew rig an M-60 on the whaleboat. He looked at OPS, then Majors. Majors shrugged. "Okay, sir, if you'll follow me to the armory . . ." They left.

Majors crooked a finger at HM3 Springer. "Could you come into my quarters please?"

Once they were in the privacy of the stateroom, just off the quarterdeck, Majors shut the door. "I thought he was out of it for the day! I saw you order him to get twenty-four hours of bed rest."

Springer shook his head. "Sorry, Vince, but I'm just a little ol' Third Class pecker-checker. He's a big ol' lieutenant commander. What I say is just advice, really. If they want to ignore me, ain't much I can do about it. That stuff we gave him wore off, and now he's full of beans and ready to win himself a medal."

They rejoined the landing party on the quarterdeck. In the darkness, few of them were talking to each other. Alone with their own thoughts, many of the volunteers were only now truly realizing what they'd gotten themselves into. The idea of OPS taking over the landing party didn't fill any of them with glee either. Halloran was working his way down the line of volunteers with plastic sandwich bags, rubber bands, and brown paper lunch bags he'd gotten from the mess decks. "Okay folks, put the lunch bag over the muzzle of your weapon, then wrap a rubber band around it. That'll keep water from getting in the barrel. Then put all your personal gear except your watches into these bags. Money, rings, jewelry, keys, especially wallets. Take only your Navy ID card and your watch. Put everything else into the bags and write your name on them."

Rogers tossed his wallet and change into the bag, and handed it to Halloran. "What happens then, G?"

BMC Stolchak explained, "I'll take care of them, Big Nuts. When you get back, pick them up at the master at arms office. That change jingling in your pocket can give you away. That or jewelry. And don't take anything you won't want to leave behind."

Bledsoe rolled his bag up tightly and tossed it to Stolchak. "Heads up, Chief!" Stolchak made a one-handed catch and began collecting the bags while Halloran helped people waterproof their weapons. Tosado put all his personal gear into a bag, then pulled out a small, gleaming St. Christopher's medal on a chain. It was his souvenir from a trip to the Vatican during their Naples port call. He looked at it for a moment, kissed it, then put it back on around his neck.

Toombs stood up, a worn bible in his hands, and announced, "Everybody, I got something to say." The area, already quiet, grew silent. Only the sounds of the ship, and waves crashing outside on the boat deck disturbed the quiet. "I've never been one for praying to kill people, but what we're doin' here ain't because we want to kill someone. We're going in to rescue those hostages. I think that's something you can pray for. Now, my aunt, whenever she had a tough decision to make, she'd take this bible and flip it open and whatever page it opened to, she'd read that and try to see what God was telling her as advice. I'm going to take this bible with me when we go ashore. So, if everybody could bow their head, just say a little prayer, I'm going to do what my aunt did.'' Everyone bowed their head. Toombs opened the bible, read the first words his eyes came across.

''And Moses said unto Joshua: Choose us out men and go out, fight with Amalek. Tomorrow I will stand on the top of the hill with the rod of God in mine hand.''

Exodus, after Israel had departed Egypt.

''So Joshua did as Moses had said to him, and fought with Amalek, and Moses, Aaron, and Hur went up to the top of the hill. And it came to pass, when Moses held up his hand, that Israel prevailed, and when he let down his hand, Amalek prevailed.''

The quarterdeck was silent as Toombs read in his clear, deep voice. As he read, the XO came onto the quarterdeck, then OPS and Shawcross. They all listened silently. Through steel walls came the muffled crashing of the waves.

''But Moses' hands were heavy, and they took a stone and put it under him, and he sat thereon, and Aaron and Hur stayed up his hands, the one on the one side, the other on the other side, and his hands were steady until the going down of the sun. And Joshua discomfited Amalek and his people with the edge of his sword.'' Toombs shut the book and closed his eyes, looking down. ''Amen.''

''Amen'' came the answer from a dozen mouths.

The XO stepped forward and spoke, an olive-drab bag over one shoulder. ''As most of you know, I have been designated by the squadron's Catholic chaplain to perform services when he cannot be here. If any members of the landing party wish to receive communion, I will hold a brief service in the CO's in-port cabin. If Agent Majors doesn't mind?'' The tall black man looked at Majors with an expression that said anybody who minded had better have a good reason.

Majors smiled. ''No problem, sir.''

The XO went into the stateroom, followed by Halloran, Tosado, Stolchak, Freeman, and several others. After a moment's thought, Bledsoe got up and went in. MacKenzie gave him an odd look. He shrugged as he passed and whispered, "Gotta cover all the bases."

That done, attention focused on OPS. Lieutenant Commander Wendell Scott had strapped on every weapon he could find. He wore a .45 at each hip, another .45 in a shoulder holster, an M-14 slung over his shoulder, and bayonets taped to each boot. Hung on his flak vest were half a dozen grenades and a gas mask. He had ashes smeared on his face as camouflage, bandoliers of ammunition, and one of the ship's few kevlar "coal scuttle" helmets at his belt.

The last item drew considerable envy because the kevlar supposedly gave better protection than the steel helmets the rest of the people had. Looking at him, Steiner thought to herself that if she wished to personify six feet two inches of balding, deranged military fantasy, she couldn't do much better that what was standing in front of her.

Shawcross set down four heavy packages. Each was about the size and shape of a bread pan wrapped in duct tape and had a pair of wires sticking out of it. Shawcross pulled a coil of wire and an electric detonator machine out of his pack. "Okay people, pass 'em around."

"What are those?" asked Freeman.

Shawcross sat down, exhausted. "Claymore mines, the homemade version. You take a bread pan, then you mold a block of C4 plastic explosive onto the bottom and lay a bunch of nuts and bolts on top of that. Stick in a blasting cap, wrap that sucker up in duct tape, and you have yourself a claymore mine. Sumbitches are heavy, though."

Toombs looked at the things nervously. "How do they go off?"

Shawcross held up the electric detonator. "This thing.

You run a wire to 'em, then detonate them from a distance. The blast sprays out all that scrap metal as shrapnel. Hell of an antipersonnel weapon. Halloran asked me if I could whip up a few."

OPS noticed that the volunteers in the landing party seemed to accept things more easily when Halloran's name was mentioned. That told him something. "So Halloran is skilled at this?"

"Halloran is ex-Army. He knows all this shit." Coltrane stepped forward to examine the things. The wires protruding from each one were covered by electrical tape.

OPS nodded. "I'll remember that. But everyone here, listen!" The volunteers still in the room looked at OPS. "There will be one commander when we hit the beach. Me. We won't have time for debates. When I give the word, I want people to move! No questions! We have to move as one! There is no room for individual showing off on this mission! Remember, we are from the USS *Kimmel*, the finest ship on the waterfront! Let's show these terrorists what that means!" He paused for cheers. There weren't any.

He went on. "This mission means a lot, to this crew and to all of you. I think I can safely say, when we return from this mission, all of us will be looking at promotions and decorations. But most of all, we will have shown the world what the U.S. Navy is capable of!"

The underwhelming response continued as the volunteers who'd gone off to receive communion returned. OPS went on, mixing a lecture on military discipline with a history lesson on the U.S. Navy and an attempt at a pep talk. After five minutes without a response, the XO saw the way the wind was blowing, stepped forward, and clapped OPS on the shoulder. "Lieutenant Commander Scott, thank you. People, time is running out. If any of you have something to say, say it now. If you have nothing to say, do us all a favor: Don't say it."

That got a few nervous chuckles from the group.

It was an uncomfortable quiet for a few minutes, no one quite knowing what to say. Most of what they had to say to each other, they had already said in the last day and a half.

Finally, Halloran stepped forward and raised his hand, for all the world like a kid in his first day at school. "I'd like to say something, sir."

Kendricks nodded. "Go ahead, Seaman Halloran."

Halloran cleared his throat. Two years of high school speech and NCO academy hadn't quite prepared him for this moment. He spoke anyway. "We are all here for our own reasons. They're different for each of us. For me, I'm here because, well, this is what I've always wanted to do." He gave an embarrassed grin. "I left the Army before Desert Storm. The closest I got to it as a National Guardsman was filling in for guys in Europe who'd been sent to Kuwait. Afterwards, well, I just never seemed to be where stuff was happening. For me, it's been a lot like playing Army, with all the toys provided by someone else. Until now. Now, we do this for real."

The room was silent again, but this time it was because they were all listening. Halloran's voice stopped at times as he reached into himself, searching for the words. Reaching through the frustrations and the anger and the disappointments, for once in his life in the right place at the right time, David Halloran knew what he wanted to say. "There's people who need us very badly. Our enemies are people who'd look women and children in the face, and kill them. Not by accident, but purposefully. For that, they're going to die. We're going to kill evil men. I know, it isn't cool anymore to talk about evil. But that's the only word to describe someone who'd look innocent people in the face and kill them. But it's more than that.

"We're going to be heroes. All of you must have dreamed of being a hero sometime in your life, or you wouldn't be here. Most people spend their lives just getting by from day to day. They may dream of being heroes, but there's always fuzzy lines and excuses and compromises, and each day that dream dies a little. Except here. We know what's going on. We could have backed out, but we didn't. This is a terrible thing to have happen. But if it has to happen, I'm glad I'm here to stop it. There's no other place I'd rather be. There's no other people in the world I'd rather be with. Whatever happens, I'm proud to be here with every one of you."

Coltrane leaped to his feet and shouted, "Landing party Bravo rules!"

That got a cheer.

They were still cheering and slapping each other on the back when the phone on the quarterdeck rang. The XO answered it and listened for a moment. He spoke for a few seconds and hung up the phone. "Man your boats! Landing party Bravo, prepare to go ashore!"

The people on the quarterdeck split up under the direction of Stolchak, a third of them climbing on board the captain's gig, the rest getting into the motor whaleboat. Each boat rested in a cradle, lifted into and out of it by a davit—a curved crane which was used to put the boat into the water and hoist it out. High above the water in their cradles, the boats were difficult to get into. Typically, the boats were dropped into the water with the boat crews, then passengers went over the side on rope ladders to board them. After brief consideration of what it would be like to board a small boat in pitching seas carrying a full combat load, Stolchak had decided to load the boats while they were still on the davits.

Once on board the boats, each member of the landing party took a place assigned by the boat crew, shucked off their packs and equipment, put on life jackets, and hung on to safety ropes hanging from the davit above each boat. Deck seamen and bosuns mates laid out belaying lines and guide lines to keep the boats from swinging when they were hoisted into the air, then keep them even with the ship as they were lowered to the water. Within a few minutes, everyone had their gear stowed. The boat crews were standing by. The boat decks were ready.

Then they waited, in the darkness, in the boats, in the wind of the ship going thirty knots, with a fair distance still to go. They waited in the darkness, trying to keep warm, checking their gear, trying to stay calm.

After nearly an hour, the order was given. "Away all boats!"

Kimmel slowed to five knots, no lights showing on her weather decks, only a thin moon and the stars providing illumination. Ahead of them, beneath the stars, a band of darkness covered the horizon. Libya.

Like every other shipboard evolution, putting a boat in the water was a carefully drilled procedure. The boat crew, both on the boats and on the boat deck, had their jobs. Everyone had lines to pull on to steady the boats, controls to man, spacing to watch. The davits whined and hummed as their electric motors worked. They lifted the boats by a hook mechanism which released the boat only when its weight no longer bore on the mechanism.

With a whining of hydraulics and electric motors, the davits smoothly lifted the boats over the side. Once the boats were in the water, safety lines became important. Tied to the bow of each boat, they ran up to where they had been wrapped in figure eights around cleats fastened to the deck. As the water dragged at the boats, the lines grew taut holding the boats even with *Kimmel*. Once the boats hit the water, their buoyancy took the weight off the hooks, instantly releasing the hooks to the cable hanging from the davit. The davits raised their hooks back quickly as the boat pilots started their engines, picking up speed. Within a minute, they were moving faster than the destroyer, which had slowed for the operation. As the boats picked up speed, the safety lines lashing them to the ship went slack. Deck seamen quickly unlashed the lines and tossed them to the boats.

Within five minutes, both boats were in the water and heading to shore.

From the starboard bridge wing, Reisling watched the dark form of the motor whaleboat head for shore, the waves glinting silver from the crescent moon. The seas were perfect for this, smooth with only a small chop. The waters they were in were just barely deep enough for safe operation, a mile from shore.

Reisling looked at the shore. No lights at all. Good. A desolate section of coast. Beside him on one side, the starboard lookout watched the shore with his binoculars. On his other side, an alert gunners mate watched the shore also, behind the deadly, sharp-angled mass of a .50 caliber machine gun, locked and loaded, a belt of ammunition fed into the weapon. Looking below, he could see the forward 5-inch gun mount traversing also, its gunner obviously using the optical sights to scan for targets. Everything had been done. Once the ship's boats were back on board, they could head back out to sea. Now, all they could do was wait. And listen.

Halloran huddled inside his life jacket and tried to dodge the occasional spray of water that came up over the side of the boat. It seemed to take forever to get to shore. Every minute he was in the boat, he could feel gun barrels taking aim at them, feel the Libyans watching. Any minute now, they would open fire.

Slowly, that conviction grew. Suddenly he realized how insane this all was. Sailors and one ex-soldier who'd never heard a shot fired in anger, landing to fight terrorists? Unwelcome realization came to him, of how far they were from home. Of what could happen if they were captured. Of how easily they could be killed. The fear had been nagging at him all day, suppressed by action. Now, it struck full force.

Next to him, Coltrane had conquered his own attack of nerves, and he grinned and whispered to Halloran, just loudly enough to be heard over the engine noise, "All hands stand by for Libyan port call! The tour bus for terrorist training camps is departing in fifteen minutes!" He grinned at his own joke, turned to see Halloran smile at his humor

Halloran's face was frozen in fear.

Coltrane felt new fear himself looking at that face. Sullen anger or a sudden smile he was used to. Halloran could even surprise him sometimes with some dry wit, usually at the expense of the Navy. But this kind of terror? "Hey, Hallor-addin, snap out of it! Nothing's that scary, except that chick in Virginia Beach who says I married her!"

That face, the terrified face that, itself, terrified Coltrane, stared back at him. "We've got to turn back! What the hell are we doing here? We're out in the open!" His voice was little more than a squeak.

Coltrane looked back at the rest of the passengers and the boat crew. Everyone was lost in their own thoughts. OPS was standing up in the center of the boat, trying to look inspiring and catching facefuls of water every time they crested a wave. The big Asian from the American West moved to block anyone else's view of Halloran. Then, covering his movements with his body, he slapped Halloran across the face, twice. Not hard. Just enough to get his attention. Then he said in a savage whisper, "Listen, you loudmouthed sonofabitch! Don't you *dare* get scared now! I only went on this dumbshit operation because you said you knew what you were doing! Halloran, if you go chickenshit on me now, I will fucking kill you!"

The pain of the slaps took Halloran out of his funk a little. The harsh words did so too. Some of the Halloran that Coltrane knew came back into that face. ‘‘Do you realize what’s going on? Coltrane, do you have any idea what can happen?’’

‘‘No! I’m too fucking stupid to know what’s going on, and I don’t want you to tell me!’’ Coltrane hissed, and gave a savage grin. ‘‘C’mon, you dumb fuck, I want you to reach down, grab your balls, and give ’em a yank! ’Cause if you don’t suck it up, OPS is going to take over and he’ll wind up having us chip paint in a Libyan jail!’’

That got a sudden, nervous chuckle out of the gray-haired seaman. ‘‘He’d probably make us do fire fighting drills in prison too!’’

Coltrane gave a relieved smile. ‘‘That’s the Halloran I can always borrow ten bucks from! C’mon man, all they can do is kill us! We’re here now, let’s just do it, okay? Port call in Libya, you know? I hear those terrorist chicks are really hot!’’ As Coltrane kept babbling nonsense, Halloran couldn’t help but laugh. As suddenly as it had come, the fear left. After all, Coltrane was right. He had things to do.

There was the grinding of beach gravel beneath the keel. They were there. ‘‘All ashore that’s going ashore!’’ Stolchak said in a hoarse whisper. ‘‘Hit the beach!’’

They got out of the boats as fast as they could, the boat crews tossing their gear to them in the darkness. Working without lights, stumbling in the waves, all of them managed to get soaked in the process until, finally, everyone was ashore and grabbing their weapons. The boats headed back out to *Kimmel*, eager to get away from the hostile shores.

On the beach, not really believing he was finally there, Halloran pulled his bundle of gear onto dry land. The beach gravel and sand crunched beneath his boots. The air was chill, the dry cold of the desert night. The sky above was a desert sky, stars diamond bright, incredibly numerous.

He'd wrapped up most of his field gear in his raincoat. Now he grabbed the bundle and barked, in a low voice, "Move! Get off the beach! Run for those rocks! Go, go, go!" He took off himself once people began moving, headed to the cover of some boulders on the edge of the beach. The rest of the landing party followed. Once off the beach and under cover, he unrolled his coat and put the gear on. Around him, others did the same.

As he threw on his gear, Halloran spoke as quietly as he could and still be heard. "Lock and load, people! BM1 Magsaysay, please go up to that hill." He pointed to a low hill overlooking the area, about a hundred yards away. Then he handed his silenced .45 to Coltrane. "Coltrane, here's my pistol. Go with BM1, if you see anybody coming, warn us. Kill 'em silently with the pistols if you have to."

"Belay that!" OPS was speaking in a normal tone of voice as he strapped on his gear. Unfamiliar with much of it and overburdened with too many separate pieces, he was having a rough time. "Those pistols don't have the range. Seaman Toombs, GMG1, take an M-60 and a rifle and set up an overwatch position there." He pointed to a different hill.

Hoo boy, thought Toombs.

Halloran had finished putting on his gear. He was already watching the surrounding hills, crouching behind a boulder on the gravel beach. He spoke without looking at OPS. "Sir, one shot from those weapons and every Libyan in twenty miles will know we're here. Sound carries pretty far in the desert."

OPS stopped trying to put on his gear and looked at Halloran coldly. "Seaman, your advice is not needed. GMG1, Toombs, get going!" With a questioning look at Halloran, they got going. As they went Halloran took back his silenced pistol from Coltrane and gave it to

Toombs. Everyone else continued the frenzied process of getting their gear on. On Halloran's advice, most wore their black military raincoats over the borrowed khakis, then strapped on their gear over that.

"Okay folks, spread out!" Halloran got up from behind cover, his eyes never ceasing their scan of the hills as he went from one person to another, tapping them on the shoulder. "Stay at least ten yards apart! Get behind cover and watch the hills." He worked his way through the group, sawed-off shotgun in one hand, M-79 grenade launcher in the other, forming a loose perimeter with the landing party as they finished putting on their gear. Then he stopped, looking at the one person on the beach still wearing Navy dungarees.

"S'up, Halloran?" Seaman Apprentice Chambers, dripping wet, looked at him and smiled. He had been one of the boat crew and slipped over the side in the confusion of unloading. As one of the boat crew, he had been issued a .45 and a flak vest. "C'Mon, G-Money, I got to hang with my homey! Bledsoe can't do this job alone! You need some bad mah'fuckahs to regulate this! Regulay-*tors*!" He was grinning from ear to ear.

Halloran choked back his first real laugh of the night. "Chambers, shut up! Somebody might hear us!"

OPS didn't take it nearly that well. By then, he had put on all his gear. He strode angrily over to the noise. "Who is talking? Who are you? Seaman Chambers, is that you?"

"Sir! Seaman Apprentice Chambers ready to move out!" Chambers hadn't taken Halloran's advice to heart, his voice rising nearly to a shout. Half a dozen of the sailors on the beach hissed at him to keep quiet, several inserting comments on his general intelligence and his relationship with his mother.

"Seaman Chambers, shut up immediately!" snapped OPS. He stood there, looking at him and Halloran. "Seaman Halloran, is this your idea?"

Halloran shook his head. Chambers, having finally gotten the message, whispered his next words standing at rigid attention. "Sir, I took my own initiative!"

OPS glowered, took off his helmet, and scratched his head. He hadn't bothered to camouflage the bald spot on his head. With his helmet off, it shone like a beacon. "We do not have time for this, Chambers. When we return from this mission, you can expect a court-martial. Back on *Kimmel*, someone is going to have to take your place during GQ, because you are not where you are supposed to be!"

"Uh, sir?" Halloran said. OPS glared at him.

Lieutenant Commander Wendell Scott did not like the way this was turning out, not one bit. He recalled seeing Halloran sulking around the ship before now. Whatever the seaman might or might not know, he had no time for listening to the man's complaints. "Make it quick, Seaman Halloran."

"Sir, let's get off the beach and get our bearings. Everybody has their gear ready."

"I was about to call for that, Seaman Halloran." He turned to the landing party, and noted a disapproving look on the CIA agent's face. Well, the man was a civilian. Of course he wouldn't understand how the Navy did things. "Everyone, head to where the sentries are. Move!" They left the beach at a jog, arriving at the cover of the hills a few minutes later.

Majors dug into his backpack, and broke out the map. "Lieutenant Commander Scott, let's try to get a fix on where we are. Halloran, why don't you get everyone ready to move out."

"Agent Majors, I'm in command of this landing party," said OPS. "If you have instructions, put them out through me." Now OPS could see the problem. Too many of these people thought they were in command, a typical civilian fault. There was one way to solve that problem. Hammer them hard and let them know he was in command. Still, he supposed he should give Halloran a chance to prove himself. "Halloran, go ahead and lay out a tactical formation. We'll move out in ten minutes. Seaman Rogers, I want you to do a communications check with *Kimmel* now, and every thirty minutes from now on."

Rogers, a vast, dark bulk in the night, had just finished checking his backpack radio in the illumination of a blue-filtered miniature flashlight. He said hesitantly, "Sir, the plan is to maintain radio silence until we hit the camp. The radio shack won't be expecting it."

"They'll be listening, won't they? I'm telling you to do radio checks every thirty minutes! How else will they know our status?"

Halloran, already tired of these exchanges, tried again. "Sir, all it takes is one radio interception and everybody in Libya will know we're here. If we're unlucky, they may even be able to triangulate and find our position." He was doing his best to control his voice, but anger was already coloring his tones.

"Seaman Halloran, I am in command, and I say we are doing radio checks! Now do the job I just assigned to you! There will be no further discussion!"

Majors thought about speaking further, but decided not to. As OPS concentrated on the map, the stars, and a compass, he looked over at Rogers. The radioman pointed at his radio, held out his hands palms up in a questioning gesture. Majors made a throat-cutting gesture. Rogers smiled, nodded. The CIA agent turned his attention to Lieutenant Commander Scott's land navigation.

Doing a slow burn, Halloran reined in his temper with a struggle. It was easier once he saw the signals exchanged between Rogers and Majors. He spoke to the assembled landing party in a tone pitched to carry only a short distance. "We'll be moving in an Indian file formation, just like I briefed you. Tiny, stay in the middle with the radio. Springer and the pilots stay in the middle too. We can't afford to lose any of them. The first person, the point man, has a silenced .45 and the night vision goggles. He watches to the front of the formation. The point man is our only warning of ambush. If we get hit, point man buys it first. If we spot them before they spot us, it'll be because our point man is doing his job. We rotate point every thirty minutes. Who volunteers to take point first?"

Woodall raised her hand first, followed half a second later by Toombs. She spoke quickly, her southern accent stronger under stress. "I shot expert on the .45, and I used to go huntin' with my daddy and my brothers."

Halloran thought about it a second. "Okay, point man is a woman. Woodall, just remember—"

"Don't make any noise and give the signal to stop if I see anything." Woodall gave a quick grin. "Y'all told us, Halloran."

Halloran nodded. "Okay. Number two man has the M-60. Whoever it is, stay thirty yards behind point. You watch towards the right and remember, once you pull the trigger on that ugly mother, we're in for a fight. Now—" Halloran went from person to person, establishing a definite order of march. He already knew he'd spend the next hour telling people not to bunch up. People always bunched up in the field, just by natural herd instinct. Losing himself in the job, he tried not to think about OPS.

Majors, working with the Lieutenant Commander, had just pulled out and unfolded the map when Scott, looking at the sky, said "We're going that way." He pointed in what looked like the right direction.

Majors gave him a skeptical look. "How can you tell?"

OPS smiled, his smugness coming across even in the darkness. "Stellar navigation. Give me a good night sky, a watch, and five minutes and I can tell you where you are in the world, and where everything else is. Let's check with the compass to make sure, but I promise you, the camp is that direction." He pointed.

A few minutes later, after they'd double-checked the map and compass bearings, Majors had to admit the man was right. Now if he could only trust him about other things. Then he thought to himself, the man was intelligent. Perhaps the dirty tricks had been the wrong approach. It was time to talk. "Lieutenant Commander Scott, could we talk?"

"Certainly, Agent Majors. Call me Wendell." Pleased with his work, Scott was putting away his map.

"Okay, uh, Wendell. Don't you think you were a little hard on Halloran?" Amazingly, that elicited an amiable grin from the man.

"Oh, perhaps. But a bitching sailor is a happy sailor, Agent Majors. It's when they stop bitching that you worry. Halloran, well, I'm sure he means well, and the other men seem to trust him. But he has to be reminded that he's not in command of this mission. I'm just disappointed that the other officers and the first classes haven't come down harder on him. It's a shame I've had to." There seemed to be real regret in the man's voice. "Don't worry, Agent Majors. You noticed I had him lay out the tactical formation. I realize he has experience at this sort of thing. I promise you, I'll use it. We will pull off this mission successfully and I will win my Navy Cross. Trust me." The map folded, he strode off to the group.

Majors checked the load in his pistol, considered what to do. He had advised the man. Perhaps . . .

OPS didn't give him time for further thoughts. He strode up to Halloran and looked over the assembled landing party. "Well, Seaman Halloran, is everyone ready?"

"Yes sir. Point the direction you want us to go and we'll move out." Halloran spoke crisply, firmly, still happy at getting the chance to use skills he thought he'd never get a chance to. OPS pointed. Halloran said, "Okay, point man, move out. Number two, wait for her to get thirty yards out. Wait!" Woodall got up, moved out. A minute later, Toombs rose from cover and followed her, his M-60 a sinister black shape in the darkness. One by one, the others broke cover and followed. Halloran turned to OPS. "Sir, I've got them moving in an Indian file formation, Woodall on point. The M-60s are with the number two man and drag." A questioning look from OPS. "Uh, the last person in line."

Half a dozen people watched what happened next.

It started simply enough. "Very good, Seaman Halloran. I want you to put out flankers to both sides, two people on each flank, forty yards out."

Too late, Majors realized what was going on. OPS had made changes in every step of the plan since they started, to show he was in command. There was no way he would pass on an opportunity to change this.

Halloran suddenly felt all the previous frustrations of this night return, sharpened by fear. The radio check. The sentries and their armament. Now this. It began to go around in his head. Gamely, he tried to explain. "Sir, you put out flankers when you're trying to *make* contact with the enemy. We want to *avoid* contact. We need to go single file."

OPS had listened to just about enough from Halloran. He'd tried to be courteous to the man, but he had to let him know, once and for all, who was in charge. "Thank you for your advice, Seaman Halloran, but I am in command. GMG1 Shawcross, designate four people to go out as flankers, two to each side."

Shawcross, squatting nearby, had said difficult things in his life before, but crossing a lieutenant commander in a disagreement with a seaman passed them all. "Sir, I think Halloran has a point. Maybe—"

That did it for OPS. This had gone far enough. This

seaman actually had petty officers bucking lawful orders! "GMG1 Shawcross, you will do as instructed! Seaman Halloran, from this point on, if I want your suggestions I will ask for them!"

Majors made one last effort to save the situation. He noticed one thing, looking at the fury on Halloran's face. The sailor wasn't bitching. "Lieutenant Commander, could we talk in private for a—"

"That is enough!" OPS snapped out the words in tones heard by the entire group, as well as anyone else within a hundred yards of them. He stood up from cover and glared at all of them, anger overriding what little training he'd ever had in infantry tactics. "I am in command of this landing party! We are on a combat mission! I will tolerate no more insubordination!"

There was the sound of the slide on a .45 automatic being pulled back.

All the weapons they had were locked and loaded, but the noise still got everyone's attention. That was the point.

OPS turned to the noise.

Halloran's .45 was leveled at Lieutenant Commander Wendell Scott's face, at a distance of roughly four feet. The muzzle of the silencer wavered not at all, held firmly in place by two hands, clenching and unclenching but never loosening their grip on the weapon.

It suddenly got very, very quiet.

"Sir," Halloran said in a soothing, sure tone. Infuriated he might be, but there was no place here for testosterone and he knew it. Oddly, he felt at peace. "You are attempting to take command of a mission for which you have neither the training nor the experience. In so doing, you are threatening the survival of this landing party, the hostages, and myself. If you attempt to interfere with the conduct of this landing party one more time, I will kill you. Do you understand, sir?"

OPS just looked at the muzzle for a moment, his own

rifle still slung over his shoulder, pistols still in their holsters. His eyes got very big. After a few false starts, he got some words out, the stutter he had lost at age fifteen returning with a vengeance. "Seaman Halloran, you c-c-c-can't shoot me. There are witnesses."

"They'll give you a hero's funeral," said Majors. "We'll tell everyone you died during the mission. You might want to remember, Lieutenant Commander, most of these volunteers are friends of Halloran's." His voice remained calm too. Perhaps this wasn't the best way to go about it, but the step had been taken. All he could do was back Halloran's play.

OPS looked at GMG1 Shawcross. "Petty Officer—"

Unhappily, Shawcross shook his head. "Sir, don't say it. Why don't y'all just let Halloran do what he's good at. You'll get your medal, sir. This don't have to go no further."

"Just shoot the stupid motherfucker and let's go!" said a voice from the darkness. Chambers. He stood there grinning, with a shotgun that Halloran had loaned him. Behind Chambers stood Bledsoe, silent, his face filled with a savage anticipation. BM1 Magsaysay and the officers had already left, and waited somewhere out in the darkness, with the file halted.

Whatever else might be said about Lieutenant Commander Wendell Scott, he could not be called suicidal. He looked around, nodded. "Very well. This can be resolved another time. For the good of the mission . . ." He clenched his teeth, and glared at Halloran past the barrel of the man's .45. "Seaman Halloran, you have the bridge."

The use of the seafaring term almost got a smile from Halloran. Almost. He holstered his pistol, and unslung his grenade launcher. "Okay, let's move out. Keep it quiet." His shoulders tensed slightly as he turned his back on OPS. OPS, for his part, unslung his rifle, noticing that both Majors and Shawcross were keeping an eye on him.

They moved out over the coastal desert in a long file, Halloran going up and down the line reminding people to maintain their spacing and checking with Lieutenant Commander Scott to make sure they were on the right heading. The night remained cold, the last remnants of the sun's heat long faded from rocks and sand. Their exertions warmed them somewhat, but most of them were still partly damp from getting onto shore. As they marched, moving quietly with their gear taped, each person in the long file got used to watching their assigned area. Crossing the coastal road was a brief, nerve-wracking experience. Then they headed deeper into the Sirte.

Chapter Twelve

Jamal Rakhman sipped his tea, looking down the road that led into the camp. Death waited out there. Death in the form of their "allies," the Libyans. He knew three companies of Libyan troops waited out there, to ensure he and his men obeyed their instructions. Those instructions had been brought by the man standing beside him.

Mohammad Khamal had fought with him in Afghanistan, and so he was the man that the leaders of the Sword of Islam had sent with his final orders. He had arrived an hour before sunset with three truckloads of fighters from the camp near Tripoli. Then he had shared polite tea with Rakhman before giving him the news. "It is sad, my brother, but those dogs of Sudan refuse our request. The hostages cannot be moved there."

That had been hours ago. The fighters in the camp and their guests had celebrated the upcoming event that night, talking and exchanging stories, staying up far past midnight in the Libyan fashion. They were not idiot Europeans who killed themselves working in the heat of noon. In that heat they slept, then stayed up far into the cool of the evening. Now the celebrations were over, the celebrators going to their night's rest. Khamal walked up to Rakhman, dour and grim as always. They stood together silently. Rakhman spoke first. "Your men are bedded down?"

"They are sleeping in the trucks. A few of the fools complained. They have had too many nights in Tripoli to soften them. They need the stones of the Peshawar for their pillows." He allowed himself a grim laugh at that.

Rakhman nodded. "Well, we kill the infidels anyways. It bothers me to kill the children, sometimes."

His companion nodded sagely, remembering his own children, dead in Syria at the hands of other Arabs. "It is not to be helped. It is a shame we cannot do as the Sudanese do against their infidels in the south. After they have killed the parents, they take the infidel children from the south and convert them to Islam, using them as house servants, or adopting them."

"Could we do that?"

Khamal glared at him for even suggesting they disobey their commands. "You know they all must die and be lost. Do not worry. They are only infidels. You spent too much time living in the Great Satan, my brother."

Rakhman could only agree. He yawned. Another heritage from his time in America. He had become used to American sleeping patterns. "Then we must sleep, and pray to Allah. We have important work tomorrow."

The coastal desert of North Africa is not a sea of sand, but dry, rocky desolation, cut through by erosion from rare rainstorms. Moving across country, sidestepping cactus and the thorny desert bushes, Landing Party Bravo slowly moved inland. Most wore their black Navy-issue raincoats, with flak vests over the raincoats and their web gear hung on the outside of that. Most wore steel helmets, the same helmets worn five decades before on this same land by soldiers fighting men led by Hitler and Mussolini. Heavily burdened, climbing into and out of the dry creekbeds called wadis, keeping their direction and pace was a struggle. As they marched, their gear began to become disordered. Halloran stopped them after fifteen minutes of marching to give everyone a chance to resling their gear more comfortably. Then he drove them hard for forty-five minutes, Toombs switching to point after half an hour, taking the silenced pistol and night vision goggles from Woodall, passing the M-60 back to Monk. After checking his watch, Halloran began looking for a place with good cover, to stop and take a rest. Eventually, they marched past such a spot and Halloran called a ten-minute halt.

Shawcross sat down on a convenient rock, broke out his chew, and put another wad of tobacco in his cheek. Next to him, Coltrane was pulling out a pack of cigarettes. Lieutenant Steiner sat down beside them to take off a boot. She looked up as she did so, and grinned. Her voice was an eager whisper. "Would you believe it? I picked up a rock in my boot. Hurt like hell the last ten minutes." She looked over as Coltrane put a Newport into his mouth, pulled out a lighter. "Hey, sailor, cup that flame. A cigarette can be seen for two miles at night."

Shawcross spoke up before Coltrane could argue. "She's right, Coltrane. If you have to smoke, do it under a raincoat, something that'll hide the flame." Coltrane grimaced, but did so. Shawcross looked over at the pilot. "Let me guess. Survival, Evasion, and Escape School?"

Steiner nodded as she took a swig from her canteen. "Hated the damn course. Which I guess means I did it right. Slept in trees, drank from leaves, ate snakes, the whole nine yards. I couldn't stand to eat the bugs, though."

The gunners mate shuddered at that, and looked

around at the people of the landing party. No two people were dressed or equipped exactly alike. Several had slung their helmets at their belts and wore sweatbands on their heads. Shawcross had taken off his helmet the minute they got off the beach. Now he wore his ship's baseball cap reversed, the bill going over the back of his head. Some of the others had copied him. The numerous items of civilian gear doing military duty completed the impression. "Man, these people do look like Joe Shit, the ragman."

That got a chuckle from the pilot. She caught a whiff from Coltrane's cigarette and controlled a sudden, savage craving for a smoke. Mentally putting that aside for a moment, she focused on more important matters. "I hear Halloran pulled a gun on OPS?"

Shawcross grimaced. "That doesn't bear talking about. The LTC was just being a dog, whizzing on everything to show it was his. That's fine back in the ship's office, but out here that bullshit gets you killed."

Steiner was skeptical. She'd been impressed with the way the gray-haired seaman had organized the group, but this sounded a little too insane. Then again, what she'd been thinking of doing last night was insane. What had she been thinking of doing? She looked at Halloran, going from person to person to see how they were doing. Then she looked over at OPS, sitting by himself. She put her boot back on, laced it on tight. "Halloran's got an axe to grind. OPS isn't stupid."

"Ma'am, begging your pardon, but nobody said OPS was stupid." The gunners mate tried to figure out how to explain this. "He's just on turf he doesn't know. But every line officer has it hammered into them that they have to take charge. OPS figures that means whatever is proposed to him, he has to make some change in it, just to show he's in charge. I tried to pull him to one side, talk some sense into him, but he wasn't having it."

Steiner thought about that. As she thought, she pulled

out her own pack of cigarettes, and looked at it. She'd only started smoking since the accident. "Okay, I can see that happening. I'm just surprised everybody else backed him so easily."

"Well, for me, I did it because he's right. Halloran has his problems, but he lives, eats, and breathes this GI Joe crap. Most of the other bluejackets backed him 'cause, well, they hate OPS's guts. Hell, your average seaman schmuckatelli, he hates most officers. It's officers who give him bullshit jobs that keep him on the ship until eight at night, then walk off the quarterdeck at four in the afternoon. You officers may not realize it, but those junior sailors see it, every time." Shawcross worked his cheeks, spit brown liquid at a nearby rock. "Hell, a lot of 'em were probably wishing Halloran'd shoot OPS."

Steiner thought about that a moment. She'd never thought much about the enlisted men around her, other than her crew chief. Other than Halloran, none of them had seemed particularly unhappy. She mentioned that to Shawcross. He grinned. "Ma'am, you do realize, people get punished for complaining to you?"

"That's ridiculous."

The gunners mate shook his head. "It's true, ma'am. A sailor who complains too much gets stuck with the worst jobs, gets denied leave and liberty, or gets hammered on their evaluations. Mostly by officers. People get punished in the Navy for being unhappy, if they say anything about it. So around you and the other officers, most of 'em keep smiling. Halloran's just too dumb, or stubborn, to do that."

She thought about that, too. This was an odd conversation to be having when they'd be assaulting a terrorist camp in a few hours. Then she gave into temptation, threw her raincoat over her head, and lit a cigarette.

The break was over too quickly for all concerned. Shawcross took point next, then Monk, then Villanueva.

The desert was dark and quiet. Even in the cold night air, everyone perspired as they pushed on over the rough terrain. They gave any points of light a wide berth, but there weren't many. Navigating cross-country, they finally came to the road leading to the terrorist camp. They marched a hundred yards to the left of it, sticking to cover. No vehicles were in sight.

Halloran came up behind Rogers. The overweight radioman was staggering as he walked, panting, gasping for air as he pushed himself to keep up. Villanueva had already taken the heavy backpack radio for the man. Others in the party carried other items for him. Halloran mentally swore at himself for having brought Tiny on this mission. He'd known the man was way too out of shape for it, but he'd also known how Rogers needed something like this, and he had been weak. "Tiny, you going to make it?"

Rogers wiped perspiration from his forehead. "I'll make it, dog," he gasped as he nodded his head. "I'll make it if it kills me."

Halloran checked his watch. Fifteen minutes until the next break. "Is your chest hurting yet?"

"It started hurting an hour ago." Grimly, Rogers kept moving.

Unhappy, Halloran checked his map in the light of a blue-filtered flashlight. Two more miles to go. He checked his watch. It was nearly two AM already. They would be late. Grimly, he reminded himself that these things never went according to plan. Then he debated whether to keep on pushing a friend who was having it rough, or to halt when further delay might mean death.

It was time for a gamble. The overweight radioman was essential to the party. Leaving him out here collapsed from exhaustion would do nobody any good. He ordered in a hoarse whisper, "Okay everybody, halt!" No one complained about the rest. Halloran sat down himself and drank from his canteen. Majors walked up to him, disgustingly chipper-looking when the rest of them were feeling the effort.

"Why the early break?"

"Slowest man sets the pace. Tiny would kill himself before he asked me to stop, but he has to haul a lot of extra beef around. He's also our only radioman. We can't drag him, and we can't afford to lose him."

Majors nodded, sat down. Halloran was holding up pretty well, considering the circumstances. Time to check the mental part of the situation. "It's not just worry for a friend?"

Halloran nodded, then drained his canteen. "That too. I guess we could push these guys without a break and get there. But when we did, these people would be falling down exhausted. We need to get to that camp in condition to fight." Sitting down, Halloran was recovering fast. He noticed something about the CIA agent. While most of them were getting more tense as they approached the camp, Majors seemed to be calming down. "You still worried about that girl?" Majors nodded. "I just can't figure out, why the personal side? She's not somebody you know."

"It doesn't matter whether I know her or not." Majors voice grew more intense. A-ha, thought Halloran, once again, something that got beneath that calm exterior. "It isn't that things like this shouldn't happen to my family. Things like this shouldn't happen to any family. Maybe I have to accept that things like this happen. But here and now, I can stop it." He grew silent, his flash of fanaticism gradually sinking beneath the surface. Then he stood up. "I'll go check the other people. You get some rest."

Majors left. Halloran went back to running over tactics and positions in his mind, as he had been for the last day. There was a noise behind him. Lieutenant Steiner came up from behind. She sat down in front of him, crossed her arms, and looked at him. He looked back. Where he thought of her in his mind was a jumble of emotions. What had almost happened on the previous night, her being an officer, her being their best pilot, was something he had to think about. That jumble of thoughts kept him silent even as he observed that she also seemed disgustingly rested, even after the previous eight miles. He recalled seeing her run laps on the flight deck while he'd been working on the deck or standing watch. She spoke first, her expression cold, clinical. "You really ought to work out more. A ten-mile hike shouldn't take this much out of you."

He chuckled. "Well, between standing watch all night and working all day, I can't seem to find time to work out, ma'am. But I'll keep that in mind."

Her tone was skeptical. "Toombs is in deck division. He works out."

The seaman chuckled, shook his head. "Man, you motivated people annoy the hell out of me." Steiner's expression didn't change. Halloran wondered what had gotten into her. "Okay, you're mad at me. Give me a clue, ma'am, is it something I did, or didn't do?"

"Why did you pull a gun on OPS?"

That stopped Halloran. It took him a second to come up with an answer he was satisfied with. "He didn't give me any choice. He remembered just enough about straight leg infantry tactics to make him dangerous. Then he pulled rank and tried to play his little games, and if I let him, we all would have died. The real world doesn't care how many 4.0 evaluations he has, it'll just kill him if he screws up. The same for us. Maybe the way I did it was wrong. But what I did, I had to do." He crossed his arms and matched her, neutral stare for neutral stare.

Steiner looked away first. "You know he won't forget it."

Halloran nodded. "If I'm still alive this time tomorrow, I'll worry about that. And speaking of tomorrow, or whenever we get to port call, would, uh, would you care to go to dinner with me?''

That got a smile from her. ''That's fraternization. Aren't you in enough trouble?''

''Hey, I pulled a gun on a Lieutenant Commander. If everything goes according to plan, when we hit that camp we'll be outnumbered three to one. I'm in the middle of Libya and if anyone sees us, they'll shoot us. How much worse can I make it for myself?'' He smiled at her, all common sense tossed away in a situation that defied common sense. ''So how about it? Will you be free for dinner at the next port call?''

She shook her head. ''Ask me if we're still alive. Speaking of which, we'd better move out.'' She slung her shotgun and stood up.

For the last two miles, exhaustion seemed to disappear. Adrenaline hit all their systems, the final rush of adrenaline as they all sensed the impending danger. Gradually they saw the lights of the camp shining over the hills as they got closer. Finally, not really believing it, they were there. Leaving the rest of the group hidden behind the hill, OPS, Halloran, Majors, and Shawcross climbed to the top of the hill.

Halloran scanned the camp with binoculars, as did OPS and Majors. Shawcross did the same, using his starlight scope. The camp was surrounded by a thin fence of concertina wire, strung in a vaguely oblong shape. At either end of the camp were watch towers, one of which did double duty as a radio tower. The watch towers were sheet metal boxes at the tops of three telephone poles, big enough for two men each. Just within the perimeter was the CH-47, a huge, twin-rotored dragonfly, next to the hulking shape of the tank. Eight trucks, Mercedes or Russian-made GAZ 2 ½-tonners, plus a pair of Jeeps, were in the motor pool. Twelve square military tents were pitched in neat rows behind the stone building. In front of the building, one guard was posted in front of each of the four doors, slouching with an AK-47. Two more guards were at the gate to the camp. Shawcross could only spot a guard in one tower. In the other tower, the one that overlooked the gully through which they'd be approaching the camp, there was no one visible.

"Only one tower is manned." OPS seemed happy enough. "These people are sloppy."

"Most likely the man assigned to the other tower is goofing off," said Halloran. "Which still means they're sloppy."

All four of them slithered down off the hilltop from which they'd been watching the camp. They gathered among the stones, everyone silent, still. For some of them, it hadn't seemed quite real. What illusions anyone had held onto until now faded in proximity to the camp. Halloran looked from face to face. Majors, Steiner, Woodall, Toombs, and Springer had faces set in grim determination. Coltrane, Magsaysay, Tosado, Freeman, Chambers, and Monk seemed almost eager. Rogers, MacKenzie, Villanueva, Scott, Bledsoe, and, oddly, Shawcross seemed resigned, almost afraid, almost sad. Each of them had dealt with their personal demons on the march. Each was just too tired to panic. And if Halloran could have seen his own face, he would have surprised himself. His expression was eager. The freshman quarterback, about to play his first game.

"Okay, final brief. Cover team will be OPS, Shawcross, Rogers, Monk, and Villanueva. All of you have M-14s, right?" They nodded. "Okay, it's my plan, I'll take point once we get into the gully. Who has the bolt cutters and the wire cutters?" The people who had them held them up. Halloran made sure they were with people going into the camp. "Does anyone have any question about where they are?"

Bledsoe asked, "How come the white guys stay up here while all the brothers go down and get shot at?"

''What the hell you callin' me, dog?'' snapped Rogers.

''Shut up, you fat ass-kisser!''

Voices were rising. Halloran knew exactly what it was. Nerves, and a last try by Bledsoe not to go through the wire. Shawcross spoke up first. ''Shut up, the both of you! Bledsoe, what are you thinking? Besides, Rogers is black and—''

''Might as well be white, the way he's always sucking up to—''

That was all he got out before 290 pounds of enraged Tiny Rogers bowled him over, massive hands clamped around his throat. A lot of Tiny was flab. A lot of Tiny was muscle too. Moving incredibly fast, letting out months of pent-up frustration and anger, Rogers was on top of Bledsoe before the man could react. With a savage grin on his face, he set to strangling his tormenter. The others piled on, throwing all their weight against the massive radioman. Slowly, they pried him off Bledsoe as his anger faded. Shawcross faced off Bledsoe as he got up, eyes wide in anger. ''Bledsoe, one more word out of your ass and I'll shoot you dead.''

Halloran and Toombs worked together to calm Rogers, both of them speaking with their voices low, calming. Eventually, he sat back. In an odd way the brief, quiet struggle had been a release for pent-up nerves. The anger passed as fast as it had come, except for Bledsoe, who glared cold hatred at the group. Chambers went over to him, cajoling, joking, trying to bring his hero around.

Halloran took a deep breath as everyone calmed down. ''Okay, remember, we do not start shooting until we have to. Let's get as far into that camp as we can. Stay quiet, and if we have to kill anyone, let's do it with the silencers. Villanueva, I need the night vision goggles. Let's go.'' Wearing the goggles, Halloran led the insertion team down towards the gully that led to the camp.

Shawcross watched the last of them go, then turned to Rogers. "Okay, Tiny, get the radio set up, do the commo check with *Kimmel*. Then use the wif-com to stay in touch with the insertion group." Rogers went to work as Shawcross faced OPS. "Sir, why don't you and Monk stay up here and overwatch the camp? Villanueva and I will go down to the road and set up the claymores." OPS maintained his silence, and nodded. They moved out.

Rogers's radio message was received by *Kimmel* as it waited thirty miles from the coast. From the ship, final orders were relayed. The planes which had been loitering over the Mediterranean turned and headed into Libyan airspace. Northeast of *Kimmel, Ticonderoga* and the other escorts that had left the crippled *Thomas Jefferson* headed south to the Gulf of Sidra. Outside the harbors of Benghazi and Tripoli waited Los Angeles–class attack submarines, unseen, ready to destroy any Libyan ships that put to sea.

On the boat deck of *Kimmel*, a grizzled bosuns mate chief said a prayer for his people as he waited. At their general quarters stations, the crew of *Kimmel* began dozing off. They had been up most of the previous night. What little reserves they'd had left after seven months of deployment had been nearly used up by the last few days of training. Going in and getting out of Libyan waters had used up the last of them. Now, sleep seduced them, wherever they were.

With night vision goggles on, it seemed to Halloran as if he moved in a green world, working his way down the gully on his knees. The wif-com was in one hand, the silenced pistol in the other. With the squelch on and volume turned low, he spoke into the radio. "Bravo

Knight, this is Bravo King. We are near the fence. Is anyone moving in the tower yet? Over.''

''Negits, Bravo King. Will tell you if anyone moves. Over.'' Halloran smiled and leaned his head back from the gully to look at the tower. His goggles, showing the world in green-lit ultraviolet, showed heat in the tower, a vaguely man-shaped heat source on its floor. He ducked back into cover, and said to Coltrane, who was following him, ''We're lucky. One guy in the tower, and he's asleep. Let's go.''

Moving as quietly as over a dozen heavily armed people on foot can in the darkness, they worked their way down the gully. Eventually they approached the bend where it turned away from the fence, barely ten yards from the wire. Halloran poked his head up cautiously and looked. The tank and the helicopter seemed abandoned. Only a few electric lights burned in the camp, powered by a small generator he could hear chugging away. None of the lights was near enough to light the area well. To make everything perfect, the fence dipped at a low spot in the ground.

With hand motions, Halloran directed everyone to distribute themselves in the gully. He whispered, ''If shooting starts, use this gully like a trench. We've got good cover. Stay under cover until shooting starts. Don't worry about watching, that's Bravo Knight's job. Our job is not to be seen. Now, who wants to cut the wire?''

That led to a quiet moment, even in the still of this night. Eventually Coltrane moved forward with a pair of wire cutters. ''I strung barbed wire with my dad a few times. I guess I can figure it out.''

After a final check with Rogers and a few quick tips from Halloran, Rogers went over the lip of the gully, crawling forward on his belly. As he did so, Toombs came up beside him and whispered in his ear, ''What if they got mines in the perimeter?''

Halloran grimaced. He hadn't thought of that. Still—

"Don't worry. If they had mines, goats or sheep would have stepped on them and set them off. There aren't any craters nearby."

"There ain't no goats or sheep nearby either," observed Toombs.

Halloran shrugged. "Then I don't get back the fifty bucks Coltrane owes me." Grim humor masked fear for a friend, with the knowledge he had sent him in. He reminded himself, you did what you could, then . . . It was a long, long three minutes as Coltrane crept forward. He reached the concertina wire in one piece, and gripped the bottom strand with a leather glove he'd borrowed for the occasion. He held it as he cut it so the twanging of it recoiling when cut would not be heard. Two swift cuts later, there was a hole in the fence.

Halloran passed one last message over the wif-com. "We're going in. Over."

"Move fast. Alpha says fast movers are coming in, ETA in fifteen minutes. Over."

Fast movers. Jets, loaded for ground support. This was a good thing, even if Halloran did have doubts about the ability of a Mach 2 jet to accurately do close air support. Halloran turned to the landing party. "Okay, follow me on your bellies. Remember your spacing. As long as you're in the trench, be ready to provide cover fire. Our first stop through the wire is the tank, then the helicopter, so Bravo Queen, you follow me first. Let's move." He rolled over the lip of the gully, crawled towards the gap in the fence. Moments later, Steiner followed, then Woodall, then Toombs.

The crawl through the ravine was cold darkness, the feel of grit and stones beneath him, every tiny sound seeming like an avalanche. Halloran stopped for a moment. A scorpion, creeping across the path, stopped in front of him. Halloran watched, staying still. Eventually, the deadly little bug went on. He bowed his head, the old prayer in his mind, closed his eyes. "Yea, tho I go into the valley of the shadow of death, I shall fear no evil.'' He looked up, and death was in his eyes. ''For I am the meanest sonofabitch in this damn valley.'' Halloran resumed crawling, the taste of fear and grit in his mouth.

By the time Halloran reached him, Coltrane had taped up the ends of the wire. ''What now, Haddle-oran?''

''Hold the fence open, follow when I signal. Don't send anybody through until I call for them. You're my traffic light, big guy.''

''Gotcha.''

Halloran slithered through the gap in the wire, into the perimeter. Then he tensed, raised his head, and looked around. He said over the wif-com, ''Bravo King to Knight, I'm rushing the tank. Anybody looking? Over.''

''Negits, Bravo King. Coast is clear.''

Halloran bunched up. He sprang from the depression, running towards the tank as a rabbit might flee to its hole. He felt crosshairs centering on his back, until he was behind the angular steel hulk of the tank. He murmured a heartfelt prayer, unslung the M-79, checked the load. One high-explosive 40mm round, ready to go. Then he rose up, using the tank for cover, and looked. All the hatches were shut. A large padlock secured the loader's hatch shut. The turret was rotated over the back deck of the tank, and the 105mm main gun was secured in the ''travel lock'' bracket. All quiet. Good. He turned to the gully and motioned. Steiner rushed next, followed by Woodall, followed by Toombs and Freeman. There was cover for all of them behind the tank. Once there, everyone set themselves up to cover the camp as more people came in. MacKenzie took the M-60, set himself up beneath the hulk of the tank. When the cover behind the tank grew crowded, the next move became necessary. Halloran turned to Steiner. ''Ma'am, you can go for that helicopter any time you want to.''

Lieutenant Steiner tapped Toombs, Freeman, and

Woodall. "Let's go." Before she could establish an order, Toombs sprinted for the helicopter, followed by Woodall. Freeman and Steiner looked at each other, then ran.

Darkness, moonlight, angular shapes. The huge dragonfly form of the CH-47 beside him, Toombs ran around the back of the helicopter, the silenced .45 a comforting weight in his hand. The back loading ramp was down, opening into the yawning darkness of the cargo bay. Woodall came up behind him, sawed-off shotgun in her hands.

Toombs let his mind drift for a moment, looking at Woodall. Perhaps, when they got out of here . . . Then intelligence reasserted itself. "Woodall, stay back. I'll check this out."

"Y'all go ahead, Tombstone. I'll back you up." She looked tense, nervous, but not really afraid.

Toombs didn't like the idea of her getting shot. "Woodall, you can't use that shotgun. You use that, everybody in this camp knows we here."

Woodall looked at the weapon for a moment, then slung it, and pulled out a bayonet. "Okay, let's go."

Before she could jump ahead of him again, Toombs went up the loading ramp, pistol ready. He drove all thoughts from his mind except one. Clear this helicopter. Avoid doing damage. He ignored Woodall, ignored everything except what he could hear, what he could see, and what was in front of the sights of his pistol. Once inside, he switched on his flashlight. The blue filter cast an odd light over the cargo bay—and the figure of a man rising from a heap of blankets. The man said something in Arabic that sounded confused.

Toombs shot him three times. Then he moved on.

Woodall watched the man die. The pistol hadn't sounded like silencers did in the movie, she thought distractedly.

She'd never seen a man die before.

The blood smelled just like a deer's.

Then Toombs moved farther into the darkness. For her, he was a reassuring darkness within the darkness of night, and so she followed, covering his back, listening. One man had been in the helicopter. There might be two. Or three. Her knife was ready.

As Toombs and Woodall reached the front of the chopper, Freeman and Steiner came in the rear. Steiner checked the body. The corpse wore flight crew coveralls. His boots and gear were nearby. "You chose a lousy night to camp out, pal," said Freeman.

Steiner grabbed the man's pistol. "Let's go." They moved towards the pilot's cabin.

Above them, where he had improvised a hammock in the equipment racks, Sergeant Mouammar Hamideh looked down at the Americans. He had been awakened by their entrance, had seen them kill the leftenant in cold blood. The Captain was with the freedom fighters in their camp, and only the two officers had weapons. These Americans were armed and he was not. He watched from the darkness, trying to figure out what to do.

The gully was almost empty, most of the landing party having gone into the camp. Bledsoe watched them go, suddenly realizing what was up. OPS was up on the hill, sending them all in to die. Well, Mama Bledsoe's little boy wasn't about to get killed in some camp full of angry camel jockeys with guns, particularly to save a bunch of rich white people who shouldn't have been traveling here anyway.

"C'mon, G-Money, we next!" Chambers was eager, hyperactive as always, ready to go. "Time to get some!"

"Fuck that." Bledsoe dropped back into the gully. "Fuck them motherfuckers! I ain't gettin' my ass shot off in there."

"This is a hell of a time to decide that!" Coltrane's hoarse whisper carried to them. "Okay, Chambers, BM3 Chickenshit's staying here. Who are you going with?"

"Don't go, my brother." Bledsoe stared angry menace at Coltrane. "They all just goin' to die."

Chambers looked back and forth between the two men. Coltrane said, "Last train for Dodge City, pardners. You going?"

Chambers decided. "Yeah, fuck you motherfuckers! Me an' G-Money, we ain't havin' it! Not for no cowboy-gook bastard, neither!"

Coltrane shot them the finger and went through.

Chambers looked at Bledsoe. "What we do now, G-Money?"

Bledsoe looked around, thought hard.

Halloran crept up to the top of the tank with a pair of bolt cutters and went to work on the padlock. It was a cheap lock, quick work for the cutters. Then Halloran opened the hatch and slipped inside. Once inside, he dogged the hatch shut, turned on his flashlight.

For him, it was old home week. Communications helmets hung at the turret stations. Everything was angular steel, gun sights, controls, hatches, latches, and racks. The breech block of the massive 105mm cannon was closed. With a shock, Halloran suddenly noticed half the ammunition racks were full. A gleaming belt of 7.62 linked ammunition fed into the coaxial machine gun, a German-made MG3. He checked the main gun rounds. Bullet-shaped high explosive, mostly, half a dozen blunt-nosed high explosive, antitank, or HEAT, rounds. He switched on the interior lights. The rounds were service green, not training blue. Live ammo.

And he didn't need any of it.

He heaved a sigh at the thought of leaving so much destructive power unused, switched off the lights, and squirmed out of the tank. As he did so, the wif-com at his belt squawked. "Bravo King, this is Bravo Queen. The helicopter checks out. The only way we can check her out further is to start her up. Over."

Halloran loved the sound of Steiner's voice. "Bravo Queen, wait one. We're almost in position. Break. Bravo Knight, is—"

"Movement in the tower!" The radio burst over his message. "Bravo King, the tower is awake!"

Halloran turned to the tower, just as the man in it rose over the side and looked down into the gully. The man called something in Arabic. A sawed-off shotgun and a rifle boomed from within the gully. Bledsoe and Chambers, trying to figure out where to go from there, had seen the sentry up close. They fired over and over, the noises echoing hollowly over the camp, the muzzle flashes from the shotgun an erupting volcano.

"It's showtime!" called Halloran. He aimed, fired the M-79 into the massed tents. As the 40mm round exploded, he threw himself off the tank, shouting excitedly into the radio, "Crank up the helicopter, open fire! Let's rock and roll!"

Chapter Thirteen

Up on the hill, the cover team opened fire as one. The three M-14s fired steadily, like deadly metronomes. Behind the crest of the hill, Monk started firing flare rounds from the grenade launcher to arc over the camp, lighting up the area and leaving them in darkness. On one flank, RM3 Tiny Rogers snugged the M-60 against his shoulder, the machine gun seeming like a toy in his arms. He took aim at the tents and opened fire, long, ripping ten- and twenty-round bursts, walking them all over the tents. The recoil was nothing against his massive frame.

Built by TRW in the 1960s as a replacement for the M-1 Garand, the M-14 fires a bullet more appropriate for taking down medium game than human beings. Against humans, it is horrendously overpowered. That fact was just fine with Shawcross. Firing as quickly as he could aim, Shawcross picked off the four sentries in front of the stone building, noting as he did so that the center on his sight had been thrown off a bit during the march. His bullets center-punched the chests of the guards as they stood there, hydrostatic shock collapsing their lungs, shredding internal organs.

The other riflemen, OPS and Villanueva, fired their issue M-14s with somewhat less accuracy. Compared to the glass-bedded stock and match frame on Shawcross's rifle, their weapons had loose tolerances and wide shot groups. At under five hundred yards, it was still virtually point-blank range for them. They fired steadily at the towers, at any light in the camp, at anyone running around with a banana clip in their weapon, at the guards at the gates. The bullets easily passed through the sheet metal sides of the tower. Once they heard the helicopter start up, they started a steady rain of fire into the motor pool to disable the trucks. They were surprised when muzzle flashes erupted from the trucks, but almost all the shots went wild. Villanueva crammed one special magazine into his rifle. He'd loaded it with tracer rounds while they waited on the ship. Now he fired twenty tracer rounds into the motor pool, the red phosphorous tracers igniting as they passed through gas tanks, fuel drums, and truck bodies. By luck, one tracer round passed through an empty fuel tank filled with fumes. The tank made a satisfactory explosion.

Behind them, Monk decided he'd fired enough flares, picked up an M-14, and joined the firing line.

OPS spotted someone running from the tents to the helicopter, and cut the man down. Faintly, he heard one wild shot whistle overhead. This was almost like the rifle range, he told himself. Just stick to cover, keep shooting, choose your targets. As he looked for more targets, he saw Halloran leap off the tank, shouting directions behind the armored hulk. For a moment, he contemplated shooting the man. Then he disregarded the thought as unworthy of himself. Let Halloran handle the job. Afterwards, if the man survived, there could always be a court-martial.

He spotted half a dozen men running from the motor

pool, all of them firing AK-47s wildly from the hip. OPS fed a fresh clip into his rifle, and began knocking them down. Just like the rifle range.

In the camp, all was confusion, all was insanity. The terrorists awoke under attack, confused. Some shouted they were being attacked by the Israelis or the Libyans. Only a few could conceive that they were being attacked by the Americans. Jamal watched from the door of his headquarters, the last of four rooms in the stone building. His men ran from their tents, firing wildly into the darkness, their vision spoiled by the flares overhead or the muzzle flashes of their own weapons. Bullets came in from the darkness, cut them down as they ran. Tracer fire, dimly visible from a distant hill, swept through the tents again. Rakhman aimed at the distant hills with his own AK-47, then stopped himself. The range was too great for the Russian rifle. For a moment, he longed for the deadly accurate Enfield rifle he had carried into Afghanistan. He needed a machine gun. He looked around.

His assistant, young Alhwazi, had rolled off his cot and grabbed the RPK machine gun he kept beneath it. Now the boy crammed a seventy-five-round drum into the weapon, and looked at Rakhman. "What do I do?" His eyes rolled with panic, a brave child shaken by the sudden awakening. Rakhman had seen it before.

"The hill in that direction!" barked Rakhman, pointing. "Fire from the window!" Alhwazi leapt to the small window in the stone wall, the bars that had once been in it long ago stolen. The young Palestinian began firing—short, controlled bursts, green tracers guiding his aim. Rakhman peeked out the doorway, watching where the fire went, calling directions. He had heard no bullets hit the walls for the last few minutes. The attackers were no longer shooting at the stone buildings.

The young Palestinian got off five bursts before there was the sound of a pumpkin dropped from a roof. Rakhman turned to look, knowing what he would see. Alhwazi was dead, a single bullet, right between the eyes. Their enemies had snipers on the hill. Rakhman closed the boy's staring eyes, and fed a new drum into the machine gun. He had to keep up the firing, and hold off their attackers until aid could arrive. Their attackers were obviously Israelis, or maybe Americans, here for the hostages. No Libyan could shoot like that.

Then orange tracers cut across the camp from a new direction, from the direction of the helicopter and the tank. The helicopter and the tank! The enemies of Islam were closer than he thought! He had to stop them from rescuing the hostages! He dropped the machine gun and looked for grenades.

Halloran fired another 40mm HE round into the motor pool. He'd been amazed at how many men had come charging out of there. Now Mackenzie, under the truck, was salting down the burning trucks with long bursts from the M-60, driving any survivors to cover. "Bravo King One, get set to rush the building! Mackenzie, Magsaysay, Springer, Tosado, that's you!" He heard affirmative shouts over the gunfire. And one negative.

"Magsaysay bought it!" barked Majors. Halloran looked at the little Filipino, stretched out with a massive red stain on his chest, soaking his flak vest. At this range, the ballistic nylon and kevlar were useless against rifle bullets. It had just been a wild shot, random and senseless as war itself, killing Magsaysay simply because he'd been standing in the wrong spot.

Halloran tore his eyes away from the first corpse he'd ever seen close up, cursed Bledsoe for both chickening out and taking Chambers with him, and called into the radio, "Bravo Queen, this is King! Send out Tombstone! Over!"

"Roger that. On the way." Tombstone's voice.

In the helicopter, Toombs picked up his shotgun,

started to move out, looked back for one last glimpse of Woodall and was surprised to see her looking back. They exchanged glances for a moment. Then Toombs ran out the back. Behind them, from his hiding place, Sergeant Hamideh watched the black American go, realized only three Americans remained in the helicopter, up forward. Quietly, his noise masked by the sound of gunfire, he lowered himself from his hiding place up on the roof.

Outside, everyone was set up to cover the men rushing the building. Shouting over the roar of gunfire and the building whine of the helicopter's engines, Halloran called out, "Bravo King One, go up the rear of the building! Look for wires! Everyone else, cover them! Move!" The four men of Bravo King One ran, firing shotguns and pistols from the hip, those left behind firing whatever they had to cover them. Blazing away with his M-60, Mackenzie was the first to make it to the end of the stone building. He fed a new belt into his weapon and began firing down the rear of the building while the others fired down the front.

The radio at Halloran's belt squawked. "Bravo King, this is Knight! One of the terrorists made it into the hostage areas! Move out now!"

Cursing furiously, Halloran ran forward, his grenade launcher slung, a .45 in each hand. Trapped in their rooms, the hostages were actually the safest people in the camp. But if one terrorist with an AK-47 got among them . . .

Majors and Coltrane followed Halloran, firing as they ran, spraying bullets to keep the terrorists' heads down. It was madness all around them, the swaying flares overhead casting wild shadows everywhere, the echoes of gunfire washing over the camp from distant hills as fresh gunfire assaulted their ears. Screams of pain, fear, battle cries, the banshee whine of the helicopter starting up, all mixed in a haze of insanity, confusion, and death, the fog of war.

Expecting to be cut down at any moment, Halloran made it to the end of the stone building. He put a fresh clip into each pistol, and looked at the assembled men around him. "One up the rear, two up the front! Move it!"

They ran from cover, firing wildly as they ran. Halloran spotted the first door. It was still padlocked, the terrified cries of women and children coming from inside. Majors pulled out the bolt cutters, cut the lock, kicked the door in.

The CIA agent stepped into the darkness of the room and looked at the huddled shapes around him. They had all been frightened into silence. He gripped his rifle grimly and turned on a flashlight to see a child's grimy face, terrified in the light. The girl in the picture.

"We're Americans!" He shined the light up into his face. "We're here to rescue you!"

Weeping, laughing, they came forward to touch him, to prove to themselves he was real. Tears running from his own eyes, Majors dropped his rifle, and swept the crying child into his arms. "You're safe now, honey. It's all safc now." Outside, gunfire erupted again, and a shout of pain came from Coltrane. Cursing himself for losing control, Majors dropped the little girl and grabbed for his rifle.

Outside, Halloran and Coltrane had continued running forward, Halloran dropping his empty pistol, saving his loaded one as he neared the last two doors in the stone building, both of which yawned open. Coltrane fired his shotgun dry, grabbed an AK-47 from a dead guard, tried to fire it. Couldn't. The safety was on. As he diverted his attention to look at his new toy, Coltrane stood there. A wild shot hit the rifle, disintegrating it, the bullet careening into his flak vest. Coltrane had played high school football, so he recognized the pain as his ribs shattered from the ricochet. Then a second bullet caught his thigh and flipped him backwards. He screamed in pain.

Halloran stopped his headlong rush and dragged Coltrane to cover. Wincing from pain, Coltrane muttered thanks to Halloran, and motioned for him to go on. Halloran halted long enough to bellow, "medic!" then rushed forward. The last two doors beckoned. He leaped in the second door from the end, pistol ready.

The room was red-lit, from a road flare tossed onto the floor. All around the room, men and boys were huddled against the wall. In the center of the room stood an Arab, a chubby, cheerful-looking man with a green Russian fragmentation grenade in one hand and the pin to the grenade dangling from the other. "Go ahead and shoot me, American." The spoon was still on the grenade. His English was excellent, in a jeering, nasty sort of way.

Halloran had to admit the man had guts. He stared right back down the barrel of Halloran's gun without batting an eyelash, holding a grenade they both knew would kill everyone in this confined space when it went off. "If you shoot me, I drop the grenade and everyone in this room dies. So drop your weapon, American, and shut that door!"

Halloran shot him. Twice, through the chest.

The hostages looked, aghast, terrified.

The terrorist looked shocked, even as he died. Fired from close range, the bullets passed clean through his chest, impacting in the wall behind him. His hand opened and the grenade dropped, the spoon flying off as the terrorist fell.

Mackenzie and Toombs led a wild charge up the rear of the stone building, firing as they went. Neither of them saw any wires. Both fired as rapidly as they could, followed by Tosado and Springer. As they ran, they heard

Halloran call for a medic. Springer ran back, shoving his pistol into a holster. Unfazed, running on a massive adrenaline high, the three other sailors kept going with that feeling of invulnerability you get when advancing behind a belt-fed machine gun fired from the hip.

Which made it real depressing when they got to the end of the stone building, the machine gun clicked empty, and they were face-to-face with four terrorists who'd been hiding less than ten feet from them.

Mackenzie and Toombs leaped howling among them before they could start firing. Toombs dropped his empty shotgun, whipped out his .45, and began firing at ranges so close the muzzle flash scorched his clothes. Mackenzie jammed the red-hot muzzle of his machine gun into one terrorist's face with all the strength of his thick-boned arms, then dropped it and whipped out the short sword and the hatchet Shawcross had loaned him. Tosado had clipped his bayonet onto his rifle before they came through the wire, and made his charge behind a foot of sharp steel. The sailors rolled forward like a milling machine, driven by the insanity around them, the smell of blood, fear, and adrenaline.

It ended with them covered in blood, the hatchet buried in one skull, Toombs beating a terrorist's head in with his empty pistol, the bayonet snapped off in a terrorist's chest and Mackenzie pulling his sword from a terrorist's stomach. For a moment, it seemed almost quiet around them. Somewhere nearby, they heard the muffled noise of a grenade. At their feet, the mutilated bodies began to steam in the cold night air. They stared at each other, laughing like madmen. Then sanity took over and they jumped back behind the building, and cover.

Halloran leaped forward, dropping his pistol, watching life leave the terrorist's eyes as he gripped the man's arms, close enough to hear his death rattle. He had three seconds.

Savagely, he yanked the body around, looking at the floor, moving faster than he ever had in his life, forcing his body to move faster, and faster again. He spotted the green oblong shape on the floor, giving off a thin stream of smoke. He had two seconds.

He threw himself and the corpse to the floor, towards the grenade. Between the two of them, one of them should land on top of the grenade. He earnestly hoped it would be the terrorist in his arms. They hit the stone floor with bone-rattling force. He had one second.

Halloran felt no oblong shape beneath him, closed his eyes, ducked his head, rolled on top of the dead terrorist.

Whoomp!

The corpse flew up from the floor, thrashing as if attempting to regain life. Feeling as if he'd been kicked in the gut, Halloran held on for the ride. A second later it was over. The terrorist's body had absorbed the force of the grenade.

The hostages in the room cheered, whooped, and came forward, clapping him on the back, congratulating him. Sore, surprised, only now realizing the insanity of the stunt he'd pulled, Halloran was higher than a kite just to be alive.

"That was the most incredible thing I've ever seen!" some guy in the remnants of a good shirt and vest, with a New York accent said. He seemed happy. "Thanks, you crazy son of a bitch! You ever get to Manhattan, you just ask around and—"

The wif-com beeped. Tuning out the hostages, Halloran picked up the radio. "Bravo King Two, over."

"Bravo King Two, this is Bravo Knight, we got problems. Over." Rogers. He sounded worried.

Chambers and Bledsoe waited in the gully, heard the roaring of gunfire and explosions reach its peak, then begin to die down. Bledsoe kept his head down. Chambers kept looking over the top, still too keyed up from blowing away the guy in the tower to be calm. "Man, those cats are kicking ass! They are crushin' them terrorists!"

"Calm the fuck down." Bledsoe kept trying to figure out what to do.

"Man, we gotta get in there. They gon' think we punks or somethin'!"

"It ain't our fight! And you *are* a punk! So shut the fuck up!"

That was enough for Chambers. He looked at Bledsoe, shaking his head. "I don't know what you got in your mental Barney Bag, motherfucker, but I never thought you'd punk out, bitch! Fuck you! I'm going!" He scrambled out of the gully, and ran for the fence.

Shocked at this desertion, Bledsoe waited a full five seconds before he went after Chambers. "Hey, wait up! Chambers you stupid motherfucker, come on back!"

Chambers's gangly frame was already through the fence and running to the helicopter. Bledsoe went through after him. Which was when he came face to face with three armed men who'd been sleeping in the trucks. One of the three had fought in Lebanon and knew tactics. He'd led them away from the trucks, around the perimeter of the camp to come at the helicopter from behind. One was the Libyan pilot of the helicopter, eager to escape this madness. Two carried AK-47s. The pilot had his sidearm out, a Czech Skorpion machine pistol.

Chambers saw them, dived for cover. Bledsoe saw the black face of the Libyan pilot, the Arab faces of the terrorists. He suddenly knew what he had to do. Which side he was on. He dropped his shotgun, and raised his hands. "Salaam Alaikum, my brothers! I—"

They fired at point-blank range. A storm of bullets hit Bledsoe, blowing him away like a leaf in a whirlwind.

Chambers saw it all.

Screaming "motherfuckers!" he bounced up from behind a rock, less than thirty yards from them, and squeezed the trigger on his shotgun. It blasted out a spray of .32 caliber pellets, then another, then another as Chambers worked the shotgun, screaming as he walked forward, firing. All three of the terrorists were hit, screaming in pain, firing back wildly.

It ended with them sprawled on the ground, less than ten yards from Chambers. Chambers stood, swaying for a moment, then felt a sudden burning in his stomach. He looked down, shocked to see the stitching of four .32 ACP bullets from the Skorpion in a neat line across his stomach. Then he fell over and saw no more.

In the CH-47, the roar of the twin turbines was deafening now, the rotors slowly spinning. Woodall couldn't hear gunfire anymore, but she noticed that there weren't many muzzle flashes out there either. That was good, she supposed. Steiner looked back at her, as the two pilots tried to figure out the controls lettered in Arabic. "Woodall, check the cargo ramp, tell me if it's coming up!"

She ran to the rear of the cargo bay. Sure enough, the cargo ramp was slowly rising as hydraulics whined. She turned to go back to the cabin.

A thick arm fastened around her throat, a second hand grabbing at the shotgun in her hands, at her, trying to get a grip. Pulling her into the darkness. Choking her, pawing at her. One arm came across her chest, squeezing. For a moment, a hand cupped her breast.

Woodall exploded.

Screaming with fury unleashed, fear and anger and hatred and outrage, she threw herself back against the wall again and again, slamming the man on her back against the wall as hard as she could, thrashing and biting, weapon forgotten, everything forgotten except elemental fury. The grip around her loosened. She whirled in the man's arms, brought both her fists together on the man's head, tried to knee him in the groin. He fell back, arms raised to protect himself, stunned from the blows to his head. She pulled a fire extinguisher from the wall and slammed it down on the man's head, screaming fury, pouring it out, hitting him again and again.

When she came out of it, she was squatting on the bloody corpse, sobbing with release and horror. Silently she looked at Freeman, who had come running with a gun in one hand, a flashlight in the other. The ensign looked at the corpse, whistled in amazement. For the moment, neither of them could think of anything else to do.

On the hill overlooking the camp, Shawcross watched the approaching headlights on the road. At least twenty vehicles, thought the gunners mate, the ones in back silhouetting the angular shapes of troop carriers Beside him, watching the oncoming lights as well, OPS was actually asking questions for once. ''With the claymores on the road, can we stop them?''

Shawcross shook his head. ''Negative. Those are armored. We'd only scratch their paint job. Tiny, you got our air support?''

At the radio, Rogers spoke intently for a second. ''ETA is five minutes. We got that long?'' Shawcross shook his head.

OPS picked up his rifle, his face set. ''Very well. GMG1, we have to buy those hostages time to escape. That column will halt if they take fire, right?'' Wondering what he was getting at, Shawcross nodded. OPS looked at him.

Wendell, OPS thought to himself, you have been hanging around these lunatics too long, and it's catching. ''Very well, GMG1. When that column reaches the claymores, we will set those off and hit the column with everything we have. They will stop and deploy troops, buying time for the hostages to board the helicopter and escape.''

Shawcross looked at the officer in amazement. Say what you would about the man, he had sand. ''Sir, you realize that leaves us in a mighty tight spot?'' OPS nodded.

Radio mike in one hand, wif-com in the other, Rogers said, ''Halloran says he has an idea!''

Halloran, Majors, and Toombs ran for the tank, followed by a swarm of released hostages, some of whom carried Coltrane on an improvised stretcher. Many hostages had picked up weapons from dead terrorists. One had actually stopped to pick up spare magazines, the ammunition pouches an odd contrast with the remnants of his Italian suit.

Halloran climbed on the back deck of the tank and began unlatching the heavy metal travel lock that held the main gun in place. He spoke as he worked. ''Tombstone, I've seen you play video games. You'll be the gunner. Majors, you'll be our driver.''

The CIA agent squirmed through the loaders hatch and said, ''I never drove a tank before.''

''This baby has automatic shift. It's a piece of cake.'' Halloran finished taking the gun out of travel lock and looked at Toombs, who was still halfway out of the loaders hatch. ''Well, get in the tank! I'll load! Just follow my directions!''

They swarmed into the tank as the hostages ran onto the helicopter. Halloran shouted into the wif-com, ''Bravo Queen, stand by. Do not take off! They'd shoot you down in a minute!''

''We're not leaving without you, Bravo King! You owe me a dinner date and you're going to deliver! Over!'' Steiner's voice. Halloran could see her in the window of the helicopter. He waved, smiling, gave her a thumbs-up, then ducked into the tank. Once inside, he latched the hatch shut from the inside, unlocked the turret ring, and put on the green crewman's helmet. Below him, Majors squirmed into the driver's compartment, a tiny, control-studded space in the main body of the tank, separate from the turret. Toombs wedged his massive shoulders into the gunner's seat, and looked at the bewildering array of controls. Central to it all was a pair of handgrips with various trigger buttons on them. Danged if it didn't look like a video game after all, he thought.

Halloran looked around for a second, at the interior of the tank, lit red by the battle lights. It all came back to him. The sense of being trapped in an angular steel world, the night firing he'd trained on, the feel of the engine vibrating up through the floor plates. Unbidden, a quote came to him, from where he couldn't remember. "I am in the heart of the machine," he muttered to himself. "I am in the belly of the beast."

Then he snapped out of his reverie, and began shouting orders. "Put on the helmets! They have built-in microphones. The switch is on the left side. Push it to the rear and leave it there." With the loader's helmet on, Halloran reached down into the driver's compartment. Majors was looking at a bewildering array of switches, totally lost. Halloran reached in and flipped on battery power. The hydraulic drive for the turret screamed in sudden pressurization, while the microphones in their helmets came alive. That done, Halloran stood up, reached over to where Toombs was settling in, and switched on the turret power, causing its red lights to come on.

"Okay, Tombstone, the controls are exactly like a video game. Don't touch them yet. The triggers are the switches at the top of the handgrips. You see them? Don't hit them yet! Grip the bottom of the handgrips and use them to maneuver the turret around!" Toombs gripped the controls, began to work them cautiously.

Halloran had a sudden, horrific vision of the rotating turret decapitating Majors.

"Majors, get your head inside the driver's compartment or the turret will take it off!" He looked down at the CIA agent, and realized his advice was unnecessary. The second the turret whined, the agent had huddled inside the driver's compartment.

The turret spun, the main gun elevating and depressing as Toombs learned the controls. Next, the engine. "Okay, Toombs, stop. Majors, see the little red button to your right? Give her some gas and hit that button The pedals arc exactly like a car!" There was a sudden whine, then another heart-stopping whine. On the third try, the massive diesel engine roared to life, shaking the earth with titanic power. "Okay, look through the vision blocks, mash down real hard on the brake pedal, and take her out of park! The shift bar is to your right!"

As he spoke from long memory, Halloran made sure the main gun safety was on, cranked open the breech, restowed the crank handle, and pulled one of the flat-nosed HEAT rounds from the ammo rack. He fed it into the breech of the gun, pulling back his hands nimbly as the massive breech block snapped shut. Chattering out instructions, he loaded the coaxial machine gun.

Loader was typically the junior position of a tank crew, but for this situation, it was the trickiest. It also controlled the safety on the main gun, which Halloran never forgot. Whatever Toombs might do to the controls, the cannon couldn't fire until Halloran took off the safety. Firing would recoil five tons of gun barrel the full length of the turret, with enough strength to cut a man in half. Halloran wanted to make sure whoever was the loader didn't make a typical mistake and step into the recoil path when the main gun fired. The only way to do that was to *be* the loader. The gun would fire when he was good and ready, and no sooner.

Two minutes later the tank was grinding out of the

main gate of the camp. Majors was getting the hang of driving, Toombs had figured out where the controls and triggers were, Halloran had nearly talked himself hoarse, and the tank had a main gun round ready to go. Halloran's final step was to reach over and flip the arming switch to the coaxial machine gun. Of course, the second he did that, the coaxial machine gun fired. "Hands off the triggers, damn it!" snapped Halloran. Toombs gave a sheepish grin, and lifted his trigger fingers. Halloran stepped clear of the main gun, and flipped the arming switch for the massive cannon.

"Okay, Tombstone, it's live! Look through those sights and shoot whatever you see. Do it just like a video game! Each time I load the main gun, I'll call 'loaded!' Let's rock and roll!"

Majors hit the gas pedal, urging the lumbering tank forward. Ahead, through the grimy vision blocks, he could see the headlights of the approaching column.

On the hilltop, the cover team was shifting their weapons to cover the road. The column was almost below them now, entering the kill zone of the improvised claymores. Glancing to his right, Shawcross saw the tank thundering out of the main gate. Its machine gun fired an abbreviated burst, then shut off. The lead APC caught the tank in its headlights from two hundred yards Shawcross asked, "How are we set for ammo?"

The responses varied. "Good." "Three clips left." "Down to my last four belts!" Monk fed a 40mm HE round into his grenade launcher and gave a thumbs-up.

Toombs centered the crosshairs of his sights between the oncoming headlights and hit the trigger.

The main gun roared. The noise was deafening, sudden, and total. The muzzle flash was the size of a house. The tank rocked back as a 105mm round blasted out. The lead troop carrier exploded as a 105mm shaped charge hit it, vaporizing the vehicle's thin armor, blasting fragments of the shattered engine into the crew compartment.

The cover team, half-stunned from the roar of the tank gun, watched amazed as the front half of the lead APC came apart, an erupting volcano of explosion and flame.

In the turret of the tank, Halloran stamped on the shell casing kicked out by the gun, hit the vent fans to clear the fumes, and rammed another HEAT round into the breech. The coaxial machine gun rattled steadily. "Toombs, get your hands off the trigger and aim!" The machine gun stopped firing. Halloran stood clear of the gun, flipped off the safety. "Loaded!"

The main gun roared again. Another APC died.

The APCs broke to the right and left of the road, hatches swinging open, the Libyan infantry jumping out, bringing up their rifles. They had been told the Palestinians might resist them, but they had expected nothing like this! On top of the eight-wheeled BTRs, the turrets with their .50 caliber machine guns swung, opened fire. The thumb-sized bullets, capable of punching through a foot of stone or an inch of plate steel, bounced harmlessly off the sloped armor of the tank.

Shawcross saw his chance and grabbed the electrical blasting machine. "Fire in the hole!" He cranked the handle.

The four improvised claymores, placed to enfilade the road, exploded, spraying steel fragments in deadly arcs. Some unlucky Libyans were so close to the claymores that the explosions simply vaporized them. One BRDM armored car, in the process of deploying its SAGGER antitank missles, was flipped over by the explosion, crushing its missle racks. The cover team opened fire, pouring fire down the hill as the tank waded into the melee.

Majors looked through the vision blocks of the tiny driver's compartment, wincing as a flaming shape shot past the tank. Jets of flame were erupting from a little four-wheeled armored car to their left. "Somebody's firing missiles at us!"

"Kill it, Tombstone!" barked Halloran, slamming another round into the breech and throwing the safety, which automatically switched back on each time the gun fired. "Loaded!"

Toombs took aim, fired. The HEAT round, designed to defeat the armor of tanks, shredded the thin steel of the BRDM armored car. Its explosion detonated the SAGGER missiles in their racks, adding to the explosions. Around them, more explosions sprayed shrapnel through panicking men.

Majors, not knowing any better, drove them right into the middle of the Libyan troops, sideswiping APCs, running over anyone in their path. Through the periscopes he saw muzzle flashes, bigger flashes of heavy weapons, the flames of burning vehicles. Feeling the invulnerability that being wrapped in fifty-two tons of steel can give a man, he spotted a running Libyan with a small knapsack in one hand, and ran him over. Unknown to Majors, the man had been carrying a fused satchel charge. There was a muffled explosion. The right side of the tank jumped up a few inches, then crashed down. Seconds later, that side of the tank lost traction and slewed the tank around.

The satchel charge's explosion had broken the links holding the flexible sections of the track together. As the tank had rolled forward, it left its right track behind and the narrow roadwheels cut into the earth like knives. Majors wrestled with the controls, trying to pull them to the left. By trying to turn, Majors accidentally tore off their remaining track. All he knew was that he felt a sudden, violent release on the left too. The tank shook violently, but ceased moving.

"What the hell was that?" came Halloran's voice over the microphone.

"Beats me. I ran over a guy, and there was this explosion and I lost traction on one side, then the other." Majors tried to give the tank more power, which only succeeded in shaking them more violently.

"Shit!" Halloran said. "They must have knocked off our right track. I heard you give it the gas, so I'll bet we threw our left track too." The clank of a round going into the breech, the click of a safety being thrown. "Loaded!" The main gun roared.

"So what do we do?"

"Imitate a pillbox. This baby ain't goin' nowhere." Clank. "Loaded! Tombstone, rotate the turret all the way around while you fire the coax! Majors, put her back into park!" They followed their instructions, Toombs whirling the turret, firing the coaxial machine gun wildly, aiming only when he saw movement. He was having the time of his life. Halloran, too busy loading to wonder where they were, kept feeding rounds into the breech. Majors, feeling more and more trapped in the driver's compartment, could only sit there and wait.

On top of the hill, the cover team supported the tank. The last two APCs had broken and run, followed by whatever Libyan infantry had survived the claymores. Some of them had actually assaulted the hill once they saw where the fire was coming from. That had cost the cover team GMG3 Monk, killed as he fired the grenade launcher down the hill. Now, Rogers held onto the grenade launcher with one hand, the radio microphone with the other, calling out to their air support. Villanueva was firing their last belt of 7.62 down the hill while OPS and Shawcross picked off individuals.

The gunners mate had started by nailing vehicle commanders who were riding with their heads out of the hatches. Then he'd concentrated on picking off anyone carrying an RPG. That had been easy, if nerve-wracking. Now it was tough. He was picking off the few Libyans left at the bottom of the hill, men stubborn and brave enough to stand their ground when faced by a charging tank, and canny enough to take cover in the wreckage.

Of course there was no substitute for knowing how to shoot straight, he thought as he heard a wild shot whine past, the closest the Libyans had gotten to him all night. He centered his cross hairs on one man hiding behind a rock, waited for him to rise up to shoot. He fired. Another Libyan died.

Steiner inspected the controls of the helicopter one more time. Everything looked good. Beside her, Freeman was practically vibrating with eagerness in the copilot's seat. Steiner looked out the windscreen of the helicopter at the burning remains of the camp, intermittently lit by the muzzle flashes of the tank's gun. A minute earlier, a wild shot from some missile launcher had sailed across the camp, and impacted in the hill. Since that last blaze of gunfire behind them, towards the fence, it had been quiet. Freeman had already gotten the radios running, one set to the landing party's frequency, the other for their air support.

Somewhere out there, she thought. He's out there fighting for our lives and probably having a great time. She shrugged and pulled out a pack of cigarettes. "Those things will kill you," quipped Freeman.

Steiner just barely saw the muzzle flash out in the ruins of the camp. Seconds later, a spray of 7.62x39mm steel-cored bullets hit the windscreen, tearing it apart. Steiner dived for cover, then looked to one side Freeman was thrashing in his seat, blood pouring from two wounds.

Behind them, hostages and sailors screamed. As a dying Freeman sprayed her with blood, Steiner recognized another scream. Her own. "Who's standing guard outside?" she called. No answer. She realized what had happened. Everyone in the camp had run onto the helicopter, leaving no one outside to guard. She grabbed the radio microphone, set it to the cabin speaker, and cranked the volume. "Everyone who has a weapon, get outside and set up a perimeter around this helicopter! We need you to guard us while we're on the ground!"

Mackenzie was the first to act. He shouted, "Follow me!" and ran down the ramp, M-60 ready to fire. Others, sailors or rescued hostages with their scavenged weapons, ran out. Woodall, hauling an M-14 that seemed bigger than life in her arms, came into the pilot's cabin.

"Howdy, ma'am! Guess it's the girls' night out up here, huh?"

That earned her an odd look from Steiner. Staying below cover, she'd finally managed to unfasten Freeman's seat harness, and pull him out. Blood was everywhere, from half a dozen wounds. It took Steiner a second or two to realize Freeman was dead. His eyes were still open, staring into nothingness with that horrible certainty of death.

As for Woodall, killing her attacker had felt strangely liberating. She felt no remorse, just a tremendous release, as if all the fear, all the pain she'd felt had been vented on this man who had attacked her. Now, not knowing she had a cheerful grin on her face, her only thought was that the elevated cabin of the helicopter might make a good sniper post for the rifle she'd picked up.

As Woodall jumped up and started firing carefully aimed shots out the broken windscreen, Steiner closed Freeman's eyes. "Sorry I brought you to this, Free." She took a second more to strap him against one wall. Then she went back to the control panel and tried to figure out what damage the wild spray of fire had done.

Gordon Richmond, investment analyst and now rescued hostage, ran down the ramp, cursing himself, his AK-47 aimed at the sky. He'd been thinking about this for three days, and now, when his chance had finally come, his brain had shut off and he'd just run with the rest of the fleeing hostages. Once he hit the ground, the AK-47 came up to his shoulder He moved, looking for muzzle flashes in the camp.

He spotted one, held down the trigger on the AK.

Set to full automatic, the rifle blasted out twenty rounds before his finger was dislodged from the trigger The heavy wooden stock slammed into his shoulder and threw him back, most of the bullets sailing harmlessly into the sky as he fell. He landed in a sitting position, with a shock that hurt all the way up to his shoulder blades.

Around him, other weapons fired. One of the other hostages, some eager young kid, fired his full magazine from the hip then realized he hadn't grabbed spare magazines. A moment later, Richmond heard bullets crack overhead. The kid gave a brief cry of pain and fell, staring at his empty weapon as he died.

Richmond rolled over, staying on the ground. Thirty yards away, the big, Indian-looking kid with the M-60 had settled behind a rocky outcropping. Now he fired the machine gun in long bursts, sending random death out into the night.

"Damn it! I'm out of ammo!" Hansen, the male steward, huddled by the landing gear of the helicopter. His AK was smoking. He'd blasted a clip off into the desert as he came down the ramp.

The Navy medic who'd been with them came down the ramp now, his own captured AK in his hands He checked Hansen's weapon. "Yeah, you're empty. Here, change the dial to this." He adjusted a switch on the weapon. "That sets it to semiautomatic. One bullet at a time. It's easier to control that way, assuming we can get you more ammo."

Richmond watched what the man did, set his own weapon the same way, pulled out his half-empty clip, and slammed in a new one. Then he tossed the half clip to Hansen "Here, use that!" Richmond low-crawled forward to position himself beside the sailor with the machine gun. Behind him, he heard one of the other tourists, an athletic-looking woman whom the Arabs seemed to enjoy slapping around, call out, "I've got three bodies back here with weapons! Who wants them? I got dibs on the machine gun!"

Chapter Fourteen

Outside the camp, the road had become two hundred yards of dead bodies, burning armored vehicles, smoking craters, and flame. One crippled tank squatted in the center of it all, firing seemingly random bursts of machine gun fire. All this was watched over by the shrinking group of men at a hill overlooking the road. At the radio, 'Tiny' Rogers had become the deadliest man on the battlefield. Above them, a dozen heavily loaded aircraft waited to unload ordnance on somebody. Rogers looked over at the camp and saw the loose perimeter of hostages and sailors around the helicopter. Steiner had told him over the wif-com that everybody was on the chopper, before that machine gun had fired on the chopper. Now, he could see more muzzle flashes from the wreckage of the camp, scattered survivors of the terrorist force who still had some fight in them. "Tango Kilo Two, the north side of the camp is clear of friendlies! Drop no ordnance within a hundred meters of the helicopter! Over!"

"Roger, Bravo King. Shake 'em and bake 'em. Out." As Rogers was wondering what in the hell that meant, he saw. Five A-6 Intruders swept in at treetop level, if there had been any trees, flying at a 90-degree angle to the helicopter to avoid overshoots hitting the hostages. They let go a mix of napalm, 500-pounders, and cluster bombs that wiped half the terrorist camp from the face of the earth.

In the distance, Air Force A-10 Warthogs blasted a second Libyan mechanized column they'd spotted two kilometers south of the camp. Another interrogatory came from the F-15 Strike Eagles loitering ten thousand feet above the camp, looking for somebody to happen to. "Bravo King, this is Alpha Foxtrot One, are the friendlies still on the road, over?"

"Roger, Alpha Foxtrot One. I will inform you when friendlies are clear. Over." Rogers grinned at that. It wasn't often that a Navy petty officer got to give orders to some Air Force officer. Had he known that Alpha Foxtrot One was a full Air Force brigadier general, it would have tickled him pink. As always, for the rare occasions in peacetime when a mission like this was run, the senior officers had bumped aside the junior pilots, their eyes focused squarely on their chances for promotion.

Inside the tank, the floor was piled high with empty shell casings, the air was thick with fumes, and claustrophobia was setting in. They were out of main gun rounds, so Toombs had rotated the turret around to where Majors could climb back into the turret out of the driver's compartment. Now Toombs just rotated the turret, sending blasts of machine gun fire at any movement he saw on the road. Halloran searched through the equipment lockers on the tank, while Majors jammed the antenna of his wif-com out a space where a periscope should have been mounted. "Bravo Knight, this is Bravo King One, over."

After a few tries, Shawcross's voice came on. "Bravo King, I hope you know you'll have to clean up this mess!"

"Yeah, well, the test drive was kind of rough, but I think we're still under warranty." Majors gave a tense grin. "Okay, we're bailing this vehicle. Give us cover fire." Halloran came up with four smoke grenades, and handed two to Majors. Majors shut off the wif-com, and asked, "Halloran, what good are those?"

"Cover. Without 'em, we'd be real exposed coming out of the hatches. Normally, we'd use the escape hatch under the drivers seat, but with both tracks thrown, we're probably half-buried in the dirt already." He turned to Toombs, who still sprayed out machine gun fire as he rotated the turret. "Okay, Tombstone, we're getting out of here. Stop shooting."

Toombs stopped rotating the turret, and began squirming out of the cramped gunners position. Halloran climbed into the commanders seat, located above and behind the gunners seat, and unlocked the commanders hatch. He looked at the CIA agent, his eyes red from the main gun's propellant fumes. "Vince, I'll throw my smokers out of this hatch, you throw yours out of the loaders hatch. Use both of them." With that, he opened the hatch with one hand, picked up one of the grenades, pulled the pin with his teeth, and pitched the first grenade out. He repeated the procedure with the second, then shut the hatch and spit out the grenade pins. "I always wanted to do that," he confided to Toombs. "Sure hurts like hell though."

Majors pitched out his two grenades, then left the hatch open until clouds of smoke surrounded the tank.

On the hill, Shawcross waited with the wif-com held to one ear as the tank was wreathed in smoke. Then the loader's hatch popped open with a loud clang.

To one side, a machine gun among the wreckage chattered, spraying bullets through the smoke. Green tracers bounced off the steel hide. The hatch slammed shut with comical speed. Halloran's voice came over the wif-com. "Bravo King to Knight, get that shooter. Over."

Shawcross took aim, emptied a clip of twenty rounds at the muzzle flash he'd seen. "Knight to King, think I got him. Over."

The hatch opened again.

The machine gun fired again.

The hatch slammed shut again. "King to Knight. Take out that machine gun. Over."

This time, OPS, Rogers, and Shawcross each fired a twenty-round magazine at the muzzle flash. "Target suppressed, Bravo King. Over."

The hatch popped open a third time, more cautiously.

The Libyan machine gunner, whose flash was now visible from beneath a wrecked APC, fired a third time, the smoke now beginning to thin. The hatch slammed shut again.

The wif-com spoke again, now distorted because the speaker was screaming in fury. "Will *somebody* take out that *fucking* machine gun?"

This time they peppered the machine gun with two magazines each, plus their last two rounds of 40mm HE. The turret of the tank rotated toward the machine gun, its coaxial machine gun firing an unending stream of 7.62mm, hosing the area down in one long, continuous burst. The tank's machine gun fire stopped briefly, then started up again. As it did so, both the hatches on the turret of the tank flew open and the three men leapt out, over the side of the tank, and ran up the hill, crossing the intervening space in time that would have made a high school track coach proud. A few more wild shots came their way, but the cover of the smoke threw those off. The muzzle flashes only gave Shawcross more targets to pick off.

The three men collapsed at the top of the hill, gasping for breath. Behind them, the tank continued to fire. Shawcross looked at Halloran. "How'd you make it do that?"

Gasping, Halloran held up a small roll of electrical tape. "Taped down the triggers. Let's get the hell out of here!" As they staggered to their feet, Shawcross noticed that Toombs had three belts of 7.62 ammunition hanging across his chest, Pancho Villa style.

"Tombstone, what did I tell you about that damn ammo?"

"It ain't ours, GMG1. I pulled it out of the ammo bin on the tank, figured we could use it." Just short of staggering as he moved, Toombs picked up the M-60 and put one of the belts into it as they started to get off the hill.

Shawcross smiled, nodding. "Good thinking, Tombstone. You ever think of striking gunners mate?"

Halloran, who'd been the first man off the hill, looked back at them. "If career counseling is over, could you please un-ass this damn hill?"

"Belay that!" OPS shouted. He was manning the radio. "I'm calling the helicopter. They'll pick us up here."

Halloran looked down the hill, at all the open space they'd have to cross to get to the helicopter. Then he swore at himself for not having thought of that sooner. He returned to the top of the hill and looked around. One thing he knew, the classic American military mistake in situations like this was to sit on your duff, congratulate yourself on a job well done, and get zapped by the last survivor of the enemy force as you walked off the landing zone. "Aye aye, sir. Folks, we better stake out a perimeter up here. There are a lot of stragglers out there, and we don't want to give them any free shots at us or the helicopter."

Shawcross nodded assent. The two men posted the seven survivors in a loose ring, with Monk's body lying in the center. Halloran fished a pair of pop-flares out of his bag, while Toombs and Shawcross stuffed the loose belts of ammunition back into discarded ammo boxes. Majors watched the wreckage around them with the night vision goggles, occasionally firing a shot from the AK he'd taken off a dead body as they ran up the hill. Below them, the machine gun in the tank finally ran out of ammunition, or jammed.

At the helicopter, Steiner heard the call, and shouted into the loudspeaker, "Everyone get aboard! We're leaving!" The loose perimeter guard of freed hostages and sailors ran up the ramp as she gave the engines full power. So far, she hadn't found any damage done to the controls by the gunfire. The twin rotors of the transport helicopter whirled faster and faster. She'd found a pair of dust goggles hanging on the cabin wall and wore them now, a touch of the First World War that was absolutely needed, what with all the dust the rotors kicked up coming in the broken window. She spared a second wishing for a leather jacket and a white silk scarf to complete the look, then peered back into the cargo compartment. "Is everybody on board?"

Springer, covered with blood and acting as loadmaster for this flight, answered, "That's the last of 'em. Raise the ramp!"

The helicopter left the ground and headed for the hill, leaving behind devastation. In an open doorway on the helicopter, Woodall sat with an M-14, peering out at the burning wreckage.

During the airstrike, she'd watched half the camp blow up and burn. It had seemed like the world was coming to an end for a second. That had shaken her off the high she'd felt after the fight, even as the sheer destructive might of it had taken her breath away. Now, she still felt freed, in control. But she worried about Toombs. Word had been passed that one man on the hill was dead.

Someone moved in the camp below. She aimed and squeezed off a few shots.

Thirty miles out to sea, *Kimmel* was a very busy ship.

Communications was busy coordinating with Rogers on shore, and with the fighters and strike aircraft being vectored in. It was turning out to be a brisk little air battle. The last time U.S. planes had hit Libya, they had been in and out so quickly, Libyan unit commanders had been able to stall long enough to avoid getting into the air and mixing it up with the American planes. Tonight, with the American planes tasked to support the hostage rescue, they had to stick around for a while. Which meant Libyan Air Force leaders had to come out and play.

Those who had never tangled with U.S. aircraft were noticeably more eager to do so than those who had.

In CIC, Lieutenant Jimmelle Washington was not only seeing it all happen, she was about to command part of it. The twin-rail standard missle launchers mounted fore and aft on *Kimmel* were locked on targets and ready to fire. Washington had not released the direct line to the captain's chair in ten minutes, keeping up a running stream of reports as they came to her. "Sir, we are tracking twenty vampires in the area of operations. They are engaging our aircraft. We have lock on for six targets. Missile decks are clear. Request missile batteries free."

"Batteries free, this is the CO, I say again, batteries free."

There was a cheer in CIC at that, but not from the missile control consoles. There, fire controlmen launched their missiles, checked telemetry, and kept their deadly weapons on track. The ship rumbled as the standard missiles launched, bathing the missile decks in searing fire, accelerating to twice the speed of sound as solid fuel engines roared to life. Once their twin rails were empty, the newly scorched missile launchers elevated to point straight up and rotated until they were over the armored hatches to the magazines. The hatches swung open, fresh pairs of missiles slid up from the magazines onto the launcher rails, and the hatches swung shut. The launchers swiveled again as fire controlmen fed them new target data.

Jimmelle watched it all, saw her CIC general quarters watch come together like a well-oiled machine, running through weapons drills they'd done hundreds of times before, except that this was live. In the excitement of combat, she forgot that she'd had to shake four people awake at their stations when the order came. Most of her chiefs and first classes were fine. They didn't routinely stand mid-watches.

"Target hit! Hit two!" announced the FC at the aft missile mount.

"Hit Vampire X-Ray, Vampire Yankee!" This came from the forward missile mount. "Vampire Mike and November, acquired!" Then he stared blankly at the screen.

"Launch!" snapped Washington. "All weapons are free! Launch as targets are acquired!" The FC shook his head, hit the controls.

"Launching." Missiles roared, leaving their rails. Data came in as the missile acquired and accelerated. "Running hot and true."

Washington went over to OS1 Ingalls, and said in a low voice, "These people are asleep on their feet, OS1. Keep an eye on them."

"Not a problem, ma'am." Ingalls was grinning, caught up in the moment. "Shoot, ma'am, most of these kids aren't much more than teenagers. They'll be all keyed up over this, have no fear."

"I'm not afraid, OS1. We're thirty miles away from the trouble. But in a few minutes, we'll have a helicopter coming towards us squawking Libyan Air Force, loaded with a bunch of rescued hostages. We don't want an accidental shootdown." OS1 pursed his lips when he realized how easily that particular mistake could be made. He went to the controls. Washington spoke to the head fire controlman in CIC next, keeping an eye on the tally of aircraft. *Kimmel* had four kills so far. The score would climb soon.

On the hilltop it was quiet. Only the noise of flames disturbed the night. In the distance, more fires lit the sky from where the Air Force had worked over a second Libyan mechanized column. As he listened to the radio, Rogers gave a running commentary on the air battle overhead. The ground support planes, out of ordnance and low on fuel, had headed home. The F-15s overhead, without any ground targets to hit, had been called away to deal with some Libyan jets. Given the radioman's color commentary, it was kind of like listening to a football game.

The only other sound was the metallic popping of small arms ammunition cooking off in the burning vehicles below. Far away in the darkness, the helicopter thudded through the air towards them.

Halloran was starting to feel the letdown of the battle's ending when he heard boots crunch in the gravel behind him. He turned. It was OPS.

Majors saw the tall lieutenant commander go over to the seaman, and winced in anticipation.

Lieutenant Commander Wendell Scott, USN, looked down at Halloran, then squatted, looking out over the desert. Halloran went back to watching his section of the perimeter, too tired to do much else. OPS said, "Seaman

Halloran, you've done an outstanding job out here.''

That was Halloran's greatest surprise of the night, so great he actually turned away from his area to look at OPS. In the darkness, the man's face seemed sincere.

OPS went on. ''I know we had our differences. We've both made our mistakes tonight, but the mission was successful. Your contributions to that success were substantial. I don't think . . . everything . . . that happened tonight has to be recorded, or will do either of us any good if it is brought up once we're back at the ship. Do you follow me, Seaman Halloran?''

Halloran was too tired to argue about it. After bossing this affair, going back to being nobody sounded peachy-keen to him. ''I hear and I understand, sir.'' He turned back to watch his section of the perimeter. ''Have a nice night, sir.''

''You too, Seaman Halloran.'' OPS stood and returned to his section of the perimeter.

With a steady thudding of rotors, the helicopter approached. Halloran fired off a pop flare to mark their position. The huge green chopper came closer as random fire spat from the windows at its sides, people firing at movement or shadows. Steiner touched down briefly, the cargo ramp already lowering as they came down, and the men on the hill scrambled aboard, taking Monk's body with them. That done, Steiner gave the engines full power, the rotors full pitch. They blasted off the hilltop in a spray of sand and dust, cutting through columns of greasy smoke from the burning vehicles.

On board the helicopter, Toombs walked up to Woodall. They looked at each other for a minute, before Toombs sat down. Woodall went back to watching the desert below them. ''How was it here after I left?'' Toombs had to shout to be heard over the roar of the engines.

''I had to kill somebody.'' Woodall seemed a little stunned. ''They killed Ensign Freeman too. Infiltrators.''

At the thought of someone attacking Woodall, Toombs had leaped to his feet. Now he looked at her, saw the bruises for the first time. ‘‘How'd you kill him?’’

Her face couldn't seem to decide on an emotion. She looked at him, her voice trembling. Adrenaline rush gone now, it was finally hitting her. ‘‘I beat him to death with a fire extinguisher.’’ Horror came across her face, then calm. Her voice steadied. ‘‘I ain't, uh, quite sure what I should think of that, you know?’’

Toombs nodded. He wasn't quite sure what to think of it either.

On a stretcher in the back of the helicopter, with three cracked ribs, a bullet in his thigh, and morphine in his veins, Coltrane was trying to pick up a girl, one of the women who'd been rescued, who'd been by his side since they brought him on board. ‘‘So this terrorist, he gets in front of me and *pow!* Down he goes! Then this other terrorist—’’

At the rear of the helicopter, Richmond, Majors, and Halloran sat, all three of them coming down off an adrenaline high. Richmond hadn't recognized Halloran at first. When he did, he grinned. ‘‘Hey, it's the grenade guy! Hey Captain or Admiral or whatever you are, that stunt with the grenade was great! I was sure we were back to being hostages!’’

Halloran smiled at that. ‘‘I'm just glad it worked. But I'm not a captain, just a plain ol' Seaman Schmuckatelli.’’ He shook Richmond's hand. ‘‘Hi. Seaman Dave Halloran. Damn glad to meet you. This guy next to me is our resident Secret Agent Dude, Vince Majors.’’ Majors waved.

‘‘Gordon Richmond, of Strathmeyer, Weissfeld, and Richmond.’’ He smiled expectantly, then seemed disappointed there was no response. He mentally shook himself. What would these guys know of investment banking? ‘‘If you guys are ever in Manhattan, you gotta look me up. You ever been to New York?'' Halloran shook his head. ''Greatest town on earth, you'll love it!''

A quarter of a mile away, Corporal Mohammad Tarak saw the helicopter leaving the camp as he ran over the desert. He'd fled his column when the Palestinians—it had to be Palestinians, or Israelis—had attacked. That had to be them in the helicopter.

MacKenzie sat in the open doorway of the helicopter, his M-60 across his lap, and looked at the bloody hatchet he'd brought back with him. He'd lost the short sword somewhere back in the camp. He would have picked up a Scottish broadsword, a Claymore, but his dad already had one.

Shawcross squatted next to him. ''So, you got to use that thing, huh?'' MacKenzie nodded. ''Told you it was a wicked little weapon.''

''I'm still a MacKenzie. They're who raised me.''

''No problem. Just remember you're an Injun too.''

That was when Tosado marched up to them, a sad expression on his face as he presented his bayonet, its blade snapped off. ''GMG1, I broke my bayonet. I'm not going to be billed for it, am I?''

MacKenzie and Shawcross laughed. A moment later, Tosado realized what he'd said and started laughing too.

Corporal Tarak stopped running, and thought for a moment. It was his first rational thought since the tank had come down the road, blasting apart everything in sight. After a moment, he unslung the weapon he had been carrying when he jumped from his APC. It was a SAM-7 missile launcher, already loaded. Codenamed ''Grail'' by NATO, it was a man-portable, shoulder-fired, heat-seeking antiaircraft missile.

Watching the helicopter, Tarak armed the missle and removed the caps on the launcher tube. He had to move fast. The helicopter would only be in sight for a few more minutes.

In the pilot's cabin of the CH-47, wind whistled in through the shattered windshield, pushed harder by the hammering of the rotors. The two occupants of the cabin both wore crew helmets, which at least enabled them to hear and talk to each other. The air was almost calm, so long as the door to the cabin was shut so that air couldn't move through. Rogers had come forward, wedging his massive frame into the radio operator's position and establishing contact with *Kimmel*. Steiner was pushing the engines, squeezing every bit of horsepower she could out of the jet turbines. For once, she longed for the sight of open sea beneath her.

OPS came into the cabin beaming, promptly caught some flying debris in the eye, and sat down in the copilot's chair. Once the door to the cabin was shut, he put on the copilot's helmet and said, ''RM3 Rogers, inform *Kimmel* we are inbound with thirty-two passengers, and to stand by to receive casualties. We have six dead and four wounded.''

''Aye aye, sir.'' Rogers sent the message. He thought of Monk, dying back on the hill. Then he reminded himself of the thirty-one hostages they'd saved.

Next OPS turned to Steiner. ''Well, Lieutenant, it looks like we did it. You'll probably get a Navy Cross out of this, you know.''

Steiner watched the controls. Number two engine was showing a tendency to run hot at high RPMs. ''We're not out yet, sir.''

''Close enough for government work.'' OPS sat back in the seat for a moment, then leaned forward, looking at the chair. He couldn't tell what it was in the dim cabin. ''Why is this seat wet?''

''That's where Ensign Freeman was killed, sir. Most

likely, that's his blood.'' OPS jumped to his feet with a terrified yelp.

Steiner didn't laugh.

Corporal Tarak took aim at the fleeing helicopter, depressed the trigger on the Grail to its first position. A red light came on in the sights, accompanied by a loud warbling. Jets flew overhead. For a moment he considered aiming at them instead. But he knew his chances of hitting the helicopter were much better.

The red light changed to green, the warbling to a steady tone. Lock on. He squeezed the trigger to its second position.

The first stage of the rocket motor burst, blasting the missile from its tube to a safe distance, at which time the second-stage rocket motor ignited. The missile accelerated to Mach 1.5. Its heat-seeker warhead aimed at the jet exhausts of the helicopter's engines. Flight time was four seconds.

The missile hit the white-hot exhaust pipes on the starboard engine. Its contact fuse detonated four pounds of high explosive in a fragmentation casing, sending bits of steel flying into the engine housing, into the rotor, through the hole blasted in the exhaust cowling.

In the pilot's cabin, Steiner felt the hit, small but ominous. Lights all over her control panels went red as fuel lines were cut, engines were thrown out of alignment. A shuddering started in the helicopter and engine temperatures began to climb. She knew exactly what had happened.

``Shit!'' She wrestled with the controls, barked orders, ignoring OPS's shouted questions.

``Rogers, inform the ship we have taken a missile hit. My number one engine is overheating. I'll have to autorotate in! Tell them we will not, I say again, not be able to reach *Kimmel* at sea! I will have to ditch on land! We will need extraction from the sea, ASAP! Send it!''

Rogers spoke to *Kimmel* quickly while Steiner wrestled with the controls, nursing every foot of flight she could from her suddenly crippled aircraft. OPS went back to inform the passengers.

On board *Kimmel*, Reisling had Rogers's desperate message patched straight through to his seat. Once he realized what had happened, he wasted no time. Only one ship in the area could do the extraction, and their air support was already leaving with empty fuel tanks. *Savannah* was still two hours from launch point at flank speed, and the *Ticonderoga* surface action group wasn't much closer, though it was closing at a higher speed than the lumbering supply ship. For the next few hours, *Kimmel* was on her own.

Reisling checked the time. 0255 hours. Dawn in three hours.

The calculations were merciless. An hour at flank two to get to shore. At least an hour to locate the landing party and pull them off the beach with the boats. If all went well, they could be back where they were now by dawn, with the rescued hostages on board. If anything, anything at all, went wrong . . .

Reisling spun his chair to face his bridge crew. He could feel their exhaustion through the darkness. He wished for coffee, but during general quarters all food and drinks were stowed away. Anything loose that might fly around the bridge—like coffee cups—was strictly forbidden.

Well, no time for that now. This was an opportunity to excel. "Helm, right ten degrees rudder, set course 187. Quartermaster, plot a course to where we can pick up the landing party. Coordinate through CIC. CIC, track that helicopter and give the quartermaster reports on its position every ten minutes. Lee helm, all engines ahead, flank two, set pitch and RPMs for thirty knots."

As the ship heeled over in a sharp turn, he picked up the phone to CIC. "Guns?"

Lieutenant Washington's reply was quick. "Here, sir."

"Are the target packages loaded for our harpoons?" The eight cruise missiles in their box launchers amidships could be used against ship or shore targets. Tonight their targets were communications centers and coastal radars.

"Standing by, sir."

"Fire 'em. I want those coastal radars gone, ASAP." That done, he left the Captain's chair and walked over to the 1MC. This would take some explaining to the crew.

"Attention, straight shooters, this is the captain speaking." Throughout the ship, exhausted men and women watched each other, and tried to keep each other awake. Or didn't. After seven months of mid-watches and night operations, they simply had no more to give. The aft 5-inch gun crew had been told to sleep by the grizzled gunners mate chief who bossed them. Risking court-martial if anyone found out what he was doing, he was the only man of the gun crew to hear the message.

"I know the last few days have been hard on you. I've got to ask one last job of you, to complete this mission. Then it's home to a hero's welcome!"

In most places, watchful chiefs and officers circulated, making sure their personnel didn't drop off. On the mess decks, cleared to act as an emergency hospital, every mess specialist on the ship was fast asleep. *"The helicopter carrying the hostages has been damaged by ground fire. They are going to land on shore, where we can pull them off the beach with the ship's boats. This will be hardest on the boat crews and the lookouts. Personnel manning surface weapons need to be alert, in case there are hostile forces on the shore."*

On the boat decks, Stolchak had told his boat crews

to climb into their boats and sleep an hour before. He knew they would be invisible from the deck. Ensign Pullman might have countermanded his orders, except that he was sacked out too, having fallen asleep in the captain's gig awaiting further orders. *"So stay alert. Your shipmates are counting on you. Remember, you are the crew of the USS* Kimmel, *the finest ship in the fleet!"*

The alarms rang amidships, an abbreviated warning to everyone topside. Less than a minute later, the ship shook with the thundering of harpoon missiles launching. On tails of blinding flame they leaped out over the sea, then dropped to wavetop level and headed for their targets.

Kimmel gathered speed, cutting through the seas at thirty knots as it went back into Libyan waters.

In the pilot's seat of the CH-47, Lieutenant Mary Steiner was faced with a dilemma. Her number one engine was out, her number two engine was overheating, and her copilot was dead. Every minute she kept them in the air put them closer to the sea. It also risked a crash with half-empty fuel tanks that were bombs waiting to go off. If everything went well, even without an engine, she should be able to autorotate in.

If everything went well. With no copilot to back her up.

Her number two engine seized up. That settled it.

She cut off its drive to the shaft with one quick movement, flooding the engine compartment with CO_2. Both rotors swung freely, slowing the descent of the big helicopter with their downdraft.

She scanned the desert below, saw a relatively flat area, and headed for it. Behind her, Rogers kept up a running chatter with *Kimmel.*

They came in hard, hitting a small gully she hadn't seen until the last minute, almost tipping over. The front landing gear crumpled as it hit a boulder, the rear tires blew out on jagged stones. It ended with the crippled helicopter, smoking, tilted partway into a ravine with the twin rotors still turning. By her best guess, it was a mile to the beach.

Rogers turned to her and rolled his eyes. "Ma'am, I am never, *ever* going to loan you my car!"

They laughed until they cried, feeling good just to be alive. Then they picked up their gear and got moving. Steiner snagged the first aid kit as she left the chopper. Everyone else was already out, milling around in confusion. Halloran was shouting orders, trying to get the people with guns on the outside of the group to protect it, making sure everyone was out of the helicopter. OPS occupied himself organizing the civilians. Majors put down a little blond girl, picked up his rifle, and walked over. "Lieutenant, I went through the chopper before we crashed. I found some flares, and stretchers for the wounded. Is there any other gear we can strip out of the chopper in a hurry?"

Steiner shook her head. "No. We could set it on fire, use it as a flare to mark our position."

The CIA agent smiled thinly, looking around. "It might bring the wrong kind of people. If you could help us get people moving then, we have to get out of here. There could be survivors of those Libyan units that got hit by the airstrikes."

"Halloran said they were on training missions, that they wouldn't have live ammunition."

Majors nodded. "They had plenty of live ammo when we fought them back on the road. Kind of reassuring to know even Halloran can be wrong, isn't it?" With that, he joined the others in getting everyone moving towards the ocean. Steiner gradually realized that Halloran and Majors must have done some planning during the flight. OPS was leading the pack with a compass in his hands. Halloran sent out pairs of men to both flanks this time.

Those must be the flankers that Halloran and OPS had argued about before.

She checked herself. She still had her sawed-off shotgun, unfired, her .45, and the .38 she'd tucked into the back of her emergency harness. In her olive drab flight suit, she looked considerably more military than the somewhat ragged-looking sailors of the landing party. As the group started moving, she gravitated towards the back. There, Halloran, Majors, and Shawcross were a decidedly anxious rear guard, along with a civilian carrying an AK-47 who looked like he was eager to shoot somebody. Anybody.

Seeing Halloran nervous made her nervous. She covered it with a smile. "Hello GMG1, Agent Majors. Hello Dave." Halloran looked confused for a moment, then realized she was addressing him by his first name.

"Uh, evening, ma'am."

Okay, she told herself. Basic psych, 101. Halloran was a little shaken by the crash, but he'd done well so far. They needed his skills at ground combat a while longer, and that meant he needed to keep his confidence up.

Besides, she *wanted* him to be sure. Like he had been when he was organizing the party, or like he'd looked in the camp, hair shining in the firelight, giving her a grin and a thumbs-up as he'd ridden his tank off to battle. It made her feel safer, somehow, even here.

She came in close to him, lowered her voice. "Dave, if it's all the same to you, call me Mary." She looked at Shawcross and Majors. "Just between us, guys?" They nodded. Halloran smiled.

"Okay . . . Mary. Just between us."

"So what's the plan from here?"

Halloran pulled a box of raisins out of one pocket of his borrowed khakis. His M-79 was slung now, his .45 having been given to one of the rescued hostages. "Now we head to the beach, find some defensible ground, and hope *Kimmel* finds us before the Libyans do. We don't have the ammo or weapons for a stand-up fight, not anymore. Hell, I only have four more rounds for this thing.'' He patted the stubby grenade launcher affectionately. ''Uh, Mary, if you could let some of the hostages have your extra weapons, it might help if we do get into a fight. If we run into someone, with everybody shooting we can make a lot of noise, maybe scare them off.''

She nodded. ''Point out a few likely candidates. Can you help?'' She looked at the civilian carrying the AK.

He grinned. ''The guys who are willing to fight already have guns. You better hang on to yours. I don't want to think of some of these people with loaded guns. Remember, I lived with 'em for five days.''

Leftenant-Colonel Mohammad Faisal turned to his radioman, his face lit devilishly red in the subdued lights of his command APC. ''Excellent work, Sergeant. Your translation was a great assistance also.'' Though Faisal was reasonably fluent in English himself, the radio sergeant's radio interceptions of the American transmissions had been most fortuitous. He deserved recognition for his actions.

For a moment, the Libyan Leftenant-Colonel thanked Allah that he had chosen to hide the armored personnel carries under his command in wadis west of the Palestinian camp. There, maintaining radio silence, they had been unmolested by the Yankee aircraft flying overhead. He also gave thanks that his company of troops had not been the one assigned to actually enter the camp, or the one assigned to watch it from a distance.

Now the American planes were gone. His sentries had heard the stolen helicopter lose power and crash. His radio sergeant's interceptions of communications between the Yankee ship and their invading troops ashore had confirmed what he suspected. This invasion could still be avenged! With the Yankee aircraft gone, he could move freely. With the American ship coming in close to shore, his armored vehicles could destroy both the invading Americans and the ship that had brought them!

"Sergeant, put me in touch with command at Benghazi."

"I am sorry, sir. Benghazi just went off the air. So did Tripoli. There is no jamming. Perhaps they were attacked by Yankee bombers." It was a good guess. Harpoon cruise missles had sailed into the broadcast arrays and blown them to metallic scrap.

Faisal suspected something like that had happened. No matter. He had sixteen armored vehicles, every one mounting a .50 caliber machine gun, or missile launchers that could kill a tank from four kilometers. He commanded over a hundred soldiers, all well armed and eager to avenge the insult to their nation. If they could catch the American ship as it lifted their people off the beach . . .

"It is no matter, Sergeant. Switch to the company frequency and notify all vehicle commanders. We move immediately." He leaned forward, and slapped his driver on the shoulder. As commander, he rode in one of the BRDM scout cars. Just behind his position in the BRDM were six KORNET missles in a retractable mount. "Driver, start the engine."

Chapter Fifteen

The stones of the Sirte desert waited, as they always had, as impassive in the chill of the desert night as they were in the blazing heat of the day. If they could have spoken of all that had passed them by, they would have told of the small desert creatures that crawled over them. They would have spoken of the flocks and their shepherds that gazed near them after the brief rains, when the barren desert exploded into life. They would have told of the armies that had passed over them through the brief centuries, Roman and Berber, Italian and French, British and German. Now, in the dark cold of the desert night, they waited as yet another group of strangers passed over them, cursing the stones as they tripped them.

These strangers were dressed in a wild mix of clothes, carrying a motley assortment of weapons. Women and children and men, mixed together. Some were staggering with exhaustion or wounds.

Fleeing the helicopter, the hostages and sailors originally made good time. After the first quarter of a mile, everyone started slowing down. The hostages had not been well fed in the last five days. The sailors were already tired from the night's march and the fight. Halloran and Majors found themselves acting as combination sheepdogs and cheerleaders, keeping their straggling flock together and moving. Steiner held the rear guard, took the back pack radio from Rogers and, under the radioman's direction, stayed in touch with *Kimmel*. OPS navigated, with Shawcross scouting ahead for the group.

Among the refugees, some children started crying. The sailors had shared out all the water in their canteens and most had given up their raincoats, but when that was done, there was very little else they could do. Coltrane kept one group of hostages cheerful with a course-by-course description of the meal they'd be fed once they arrived on the ship. Toombs had packed half a dozen granola bars in his kit. He shared those out. Springer went from one member of the landing party to another. Finally he walked up to Halloran and held out his hand. "Here Halloran, take this."

It was a small white pill. Halloran took it, looked at it critically. "What is it?"

The medic shrugged casually. "An amphetamine. An 'upper.' Take that little fella and you'll feel on top of the world for the next couple of hours." Halloran looked even more critically at the pill. Springer smiled. "Buddy, I ain't tryin' to get you hooked. But if you're tired and you need to get over the next couple of hours, that'll do it. I don't hand these things out to just anybody, you know. That is a prescription drug, and I am prescribing it to you so you don't die of terminal lead poisoning. Take it."

Halloran nodded and dry-swallowed it, wishing he hadn't given away all his water. Cordite was already an acrid taste at the back of his throat. "Did you give these to the others?"

"Everybody who'd have 'em. Coltrane was asking for seconds. I told him no."

Halloran chuckled at that. As he did so, he realized the pill was already taking effect. He was moving faster feeling better already. "How long should this last for?"

"Oh, three or four hours. Then you'll probably crash, hard."

"Good enough. Whatever gets the bills paid."

Nearly an hour had passed on the march when Shawcross came running back to the group, signaling for everyone to take cover. People hit the dirt, hiding behind rocks in a ragged cluster as Shawcross ran up to Halloran. "The coast road is ahead. Follow me."

They headed back for the road, joined by OPS and Steiner. Between the group and the road was one last rocky hill, jagged rocks providing plenty of cover. Looking down from it, they could see the road fifty yards away, the beach three hundred yards beyond that. A mile down the road to the west, they could see tiny pairs of lights moving down the coast road away from them. Halloran took a good look with borrowed binoculars. In the starlight he couldn't make out much.

"Looks like they're leaving." OPS was annoyingly chipper. "Let's start a signal fire up here, so the ship can find us."

"Negative, sir." Halloran braced himself. "A fire up here will spot us for the Libyans too."

OPS looked at Halloran for a moment. The seaman looked back, ready for the argument. OPS nodded. "Very well. What about a fire down on the shore, where it'll be masked by the hills but still visible from the sea?"

Halloran almost said no to that, then stopped himself. He thought about it for a moment. "Uh, yes sir, that'd work." Then he thought about it for a moment more, and nodded. "Sir, why don't you and the landing party go down there. I'll keep an overwatch position up here with the radio and maintain communications with *Kimmel.*''

"Good idea, Seaman Halloran. Do you have any of those flares left?'' Halloran gave OPS his last pop flare. Steiner and Shawcross were sweeping the area with the night vision goggles and the starlight scope.

Shawcross finished his sweep, and announced, "We're clear. Skip starting a fire. Just take the filters off a couple of flashlights and shine them out to sea on white light. With no other lights around here, *Kimmel* should pick that up easy. I'll stay up here with Halloran.''

OPS went off to get the rest of the people moving. Steiner almost joined him, then turned back to Halloran. Her expression was indecipherable in the darkness. "Dave, you aren't planning on missing the boat, are you?''

Halloran chuckled. "How do you feel about Chinese food? If we can find a good Chinese restaurant, that is.''

"Just make sure you're there. I hate being stood up.'' She went back to the group to help OPS get people moving.

Shawcross looked at Halloran and grinned. "I do not believe you. 'Dave'? Trying to pick up a lieutenant? On a mission?''

Halloran shrugged. "Hey, when I'm good, I'm good.'' He looked out over the sea for a second. "Is that a ship?''

Shawcross looked through the starlight scope. "Bingo. The USS *Kimmel*-catraz at ten o'clock. Give 'em a holler.''

As Halloran spoke into the radio, he figured out a rough bearing in his head. The ship navigated by a 360-degree arc of bearings, with dead ahead being 0 degrees, 180 degrees being dead astern. He was looking at the port bow of the ship, at roughly 300 degrees relative bearing. Not that he could guide them in exactly, but he could give the lookouts a good idea of where to watch. As he passed on information, he noticed that the people in the radio room all seemed kind of dopey. Lack of sleep, he supposed. Now under the full effect of the amphetamine, he felt fine.

Hostages and sailors trooped past, eager to get to the beach. Rogers made it to the top of the hill and collapsed, looking up at the sky, panting heavily. "Just leave me here," he gasped between breaths. "Can't make it."

Springer, in passing, checked him, winked at Halloran and kept moving. He took a parting shot as he left. "Tiny, you gotta start that diet."

"First thing tomorrow, dog." Gasping, Rogers lay there.

Halloran saw Toombs hiking by with his M-60, and whistled. "Yo, Tombstone, loan me the machine gun, willya? This thump gun has no range." He brandished his grenade launcher.

Toombs shook his head as he walked over, followed by Woodall. "No way, G. Where my machine gun goes, I go. Just point me out a good spot."

Woodall spoke up as she unslung her M-14. "Me too. I think you can borrow MacKenzie's M-60 though." Halloran pointed out spots with good cover for the two, then waited.

The next three people to stop on the hilltop were Tosado, MacKenzie, and the civilian, Richmond. They didn't seem eager to give up their weapons either. Tosado said, "Hey, if anybody needs loose 7.62 or shotgun ammo, I threw a couple boxes into my backpack. Who's taking?" Halloran placed them for all-around shooting as the ammunition was shared out.

Once everyone was past, Springer came back to the top of the hill and looked around. "Now, I just want you all to know, y'all are doin' a bang-up job, and we all really appreciate y'all being up her to cover us."

Then he unslung his rifle and ammo pouches. "Anybody here need an M-14? 'Cause I ain't stickin' around on this here hill."

Halloran gratefully took the rifle, glad to have a weapon with some range again. The M-79 grenade launcher was a superb weapon, hard to beat in urban combat or wooded terrain. But out in the open desert, its range was simply not enough.

That done, Springer headed for the beach. Down on the beach, Halloran could see the flashlights being used to signal. Rogers had recovered enough to take over the radio. He kept in touch with the ship, guiding it in. *Kimmel*'s running lights were off, so the ship was just a dark spot on the sea dimly visible where the quarter moon reflected off the waves. But maneuvering this close in to shore was tricky and took time. Time they didn't have.

Through borrowed binoculars, Halloran could just barely make out the boats being lowered over the side of the ship. Rogers announced, "Boats are in the water. They should be on the beach in fifteen minutes."

Leftenant-Colonel Faisal watched through his binoculars as the American ship came closer. Excellent! They were barely a mile from his position because of the curve of the beach, perfect range for his heavy machine guns and missles. He had also seen the subdued flashes of light from the beach, though only because he had been expecting them. So the hostages were there! Even more perfect.

He put down his binoculars and went down to where his vehicle commanders and squad leaders waited. The BTR and BRDM armored personnel carriers were tucked away behind a hill, hidden from the sea. Once he knew he was on his own, he had looked at the map and driven his column hard to the narrowest point on the shore between the helicopter crash and the sea. Then he had shut down his vehicles and radios and begun to listen. The radios were useless anyway, now. With the communications centers taken out, every unit with communications gear was jamming the frequencies with panicked calls for aid, information, or reinforcements.

His plan had paid off. The fleeing Americans had come in from his left flank, almost half a mile away. That was no surprise. Navigating in the desert at night, it was easy to get lost. He smiled as he looked into the faces of his men.

"Soldiers of Libya, we are about to win a glorious victory. Here, we have two missions. First, we must destroy the American ship that has crossed the Line of Death. Second, we must kill the Yankee invaders who have murdered our fellow Libyans. To do this, I shall keep command of the vehicles here. Three men shall remain behind with each vehicle. Leave the portable missle launchers here with them. The remainder of you, under Captain Haddad, shall proceed on foot to where the American invaders are waiting. Kill them if they resist. No one is to fire until I give the signal, a red star flare. Does anyone have any questions?"

There were no questions. Here, surrounded by their comrades and their armored vehicles, they felt invincible. Faisal, who had tasted combat in Chad, knew that might change once they were hiking on foot through the desert, but by then it would be too late. "Then go. Captain Haddad, move out immediately."

Reisling had left the bridge to go down to the boat deck. After watching the boats go over the side he had made a quick walk by the .50 caliber machine gun mount at midships. He had found the gunner and his loader standing at their mount, fast asleep. Furious, he had shaken the men awake, then gone up the ladder to the superstructure and found the key man for the rear C-WIZ mount asleep too, leaning against a bulkhead. The aft lookout had been so groggy he'd failed to realize it was the captain coming up the ladder toward him.

By the time Reisling got to CIC he was in a white-hot rage. He slammed the door open. His own exhaustion unbalancing his judgment, he shoved his way into the phosphor-lit darkness of the Combat Information Center and shouted, "Guns! Front and center!"

Lieutenant Washington walked over quickly, rubbing her eyes, which just now felt like somebody had sandpapered them open. Throughout CIC, watch personnel sat up straighter, snapped as close to attention as they could. "Here, sir! What's the problem?"

At the surface scan radar console, a thermal bloom of heat rose from behind a hill overlooking the beach. It showed on the radar as a green glow where none should have been. OS3 Harris, barely awake at the station, noticed it, but dismissed it as a ghost image.

"Guns, I just found three of your people asleep at their posts! They will be written up and court-martialed! I want you to personally inspect every position your people occupy, now!"

Jimmelle Washington hadn't been spoken to that way since officer's basic training. Further, she knew exactly why those people were asleep at their posts. "Sir, shouldn't I stand by here while we do the extraction?"

"That is precisely the lack of initiative that has so disappointed me about your performance tonight, Lieutenant Washington!" Reisling was furious now. He had not come down here to argue about orders. Nerves over the mission, exhaustion, and anger all combined to raise his voice loud enough to wake everyone in CIC out of their drowsiness. At his station, Harris snapped to full alert, and looked over the surface scan radar intently. The thermal bloom on his screen, showing on the shore about a mile away, spread to a thin line of green behind a ridge line. He ignored it in the ground clutter, staring at the screen while exhaustion fogged his mind. "People are asleep at their posts in a combat zone! There will be court-martials over this!"

Inside Jimmelle, some final reserve of control snapped, frayed by her own exhaustion and nerves. Suddenly, all the reasons she had to not argue with the CO felt meaningless. She snapped back just as loudly, "Those people are exhausted because you have run them into the ground! They are at the end of a seven-month deployment, they've been training nonstop for three days, and *you* gave them a midnight GQ drill last night and kept them up until four in the morning! Are you actually stupid enough to wonder why they're falling asleep at their posts? If you ran a machine like that, you'd be court-martialed for destruction of government property!"

Reisling, shocked into absolute silence, looked back at Washington. The young lieutenant, feeling the liberation of knowing that she no longer had to worry about her career, was about to cut loose again. The entire CIC watch section was absolutely silent.

And Leftenant-Colonel Faisal's vehicles had just crested the hill overlooking the beach.

Twelve BTR-50 armored personnel carriers were in the line, each mounting a Russian-made DSnK 12.7 mm heavy machine gun in an open-topped turret. The weapon, like the American .50 calibers, was an old design, dating from before World War Two. Firing half-inch-thick, steel-cored bullets originally intended to kill light tanks, they were too heavy to be man-portable, and were usually mounted on vehicles. Interspersed among the BTRs were four BRDM scout cars, each of which carried six laser-guided KORNET antitank missiles in a retractable mount. Running alongside them were four three-man teams of Libyan soldiers carrying the portable version of the KORNET. They found spots they believed were concealed and began setting up their launchers.

Each missile carried a six-pound shaped-charge warhead capable of penetrating fifteen inches of plate steel.

Faisal focused on the dark mass of the American ship through the sights of his weapon then, fired his red flare. It flew up, a blazing signal of death to come.

Gunners Mate Seaman Jesse Crane saw it. He'd been dozing at his .50 caliber mount on the port bridge wing of *Kimmel*. Snapping to panicked alertness, he muttered, "Oh shit," and flipped the safety off his weapon. That flare hadn't come from where the hostages were.

Captain Haddad saw it as he led his sixty men to glory. It had not occurred to him to look back and see how his soldiers, none of whom had ever seen combat, were clumping into bunches, moving forward fast and ignoring cover.

Steiner saw it from the beach. She cursed, checked the load in her shotgun, and headed for the hill.

Chief Stolchak saw it while he was sitting in the bow of his motor whaleboat, encased in khakis and flak vest and Mae West and life jacket. He wondered for a second who in the landing party had been stupid enough to light off a flare. Then he realized the landing party was dead ahead, not off to one side.

Gunners Mate First Class Shawcross saw it. He used the light to spot the first clump of Libyan troops coming towards them over distant hills. He took aim with his rifle, and flipped on the starlight scope.

It was not seen on *Kimmel*'s bridge, where metal splinter shields had been dropped over the windows. The bridge was even darker and more sepulchral than it normally was at night. At his chair, Lieutenant Commander Kendricks did glimpse a flash of red through the open door to the bridge wing. For a moment he wondered what it was.

It was not seen in the darkness of CIC. It was reported by three of the four lookouts to CIC. The OS on duty at central, his attention diverted by the fight, took a moment to answer.

The Libyan APCs opened fire in one thundering volley.

The machine guns hammered out bullets in heavy, drum-rolling bursts, sending their streams of tracer out over the ocean, reaching towards the American ship as if they were casting a web of green fire. Muzzle flashes lit the vehicles like deadly strobes. The first volley of KORNET missles launched together too, four bright tails of actinic flame leaping out over the ocean, weaving and bobbing as their gunners tried to hold their aim.

The first American to reply was GMSN Crane. He fired back in long ten- and twenty-round bursts, aiming short, then walking the impact of the tracers into his targets. As he did so, the green fireflies of tracers began passing over him, below him, to both sides of him.

Shawcross scored the first kill of the battle, dropping Captain Haddad from three hundred yards with a solid, center-of-mass shot. For a moment, he'd debated letting the man live, since if he was stupid enough to charge into battle waving a pistol, the enemy leader was an asset to the American side. He'd decided to take the shot anyway, on the theory that the Libyan grunts would lose heart without their officers. The bullet killed Captain Haddad before the sound of the rifle shot reached the Libyan soldiers. For them, it was as if Captain Haddad had spontaneously died.

In the motor whaleboat, Stolchak ducked under the illusionary cover of the gunwales of the boat. It seemed as if every machine gun in the world was firing to one side of them, then the other as *Kimmel* replied with both 5-inch guns and the two port-side .50 calibers. A blaze of gunfire erupted ahead of them as the sailors on the hill opened fire on the Libyans. The boat trip had just become a journey into a firefight.

"They're screwed!" Andrews's eyes grew wide. He

began to spin the tiller of the whaleboat. ''Let's get the hell out of here!''

''Belay that shit!'' bellowed Stolchak. ''We ain't leavin' these people behind!'' Not this time, a familiar voice almost whispered in his ear. He ignored it and drew his .45. ''Andrews, you take us to that beach! Full speed! Mayes, start busting caps with that M-60 if anything comes our way! But don't fire unless someone shoots at us!''

Andrews gave a nervous nod, and rammed the engine to full throttle. The whaleboat, not designed for speed, picked up a few more knots. Mayes shifted a toothpick in his mouth, took the machine gun off safe, and propped it on the gunwales, looking for targets.

Stolchak looked over at the captain's gig, now pulling ahead of them. At the tiller, BM2 Synder gave him a thumbs-up, then concentrated on the hostages ahead. Ensign Pullman stood beside him, rifle in hand, looking for targets. All too slowly, the distance to shore closed.

In CIC, the battle was announced by a sudden chorus of voices as reports came in, then the hammering of the bridge wing machine gun as it fired. Reisling didn't know what was going on, but he knew where his place was. In midargument, he spun and headed for the bridge.

Washington stood in the middle of CIC, and tried to sort out the hail of reports coming at her.

''Port lookout reports machine gun fire from shore, bearing 320 relative!''

''Vampire, vampire! Missiles inbound, portside!''

''Mount five-two, firing at machine guns on shore! Requesting CIC take over!''

''Belay all reports!'' shouted Washington. ''All weapons free! Fire all weapons, port side, hostiles bearing 320 relative!'' *Kimmel* shook as three of the four missles hit, blasting foot-wide holes in the superstructure. The shaped charges did surprisingly little damage against the almost nonexistent armor of the destroyer. They cut lines and cables, blew fan rooms and berthing spaces into flaming scrap. But vital ship's systems and combat spaces were deep within the superstructure, untouched.

The aft 5-inch gun crew, awakened from their nap fifteen minutes before, responded smoothly, fusing and feeding rounds into the big gun, firing under the control of CIC. The forward 5-inch gun mount, its crew staggering with exhaustion, improperly fed a shell and casing into the gun, then crushed the casing with the rammer. Screaming gunners mates shoved through the panicked gun crew and went to work clearing the jam.

A steady rain of .50 caliber bullets began hitting *Kimmel* randomly, punching through whatever they hit dead on, ricocheting off what they hit at an angle.

At the aft C-WIZ mount, the FC in charge keyed the weapon to live fire, then ducked for cover behind a life jacket locker, where the aft lookout had been huddling since the first shots were fired. The weapon cycled on, came alive, whirled to port as a second volley of anti-tank missles came in. Aiming by radar, it erupted into life with a noise like the end of the world itself. Two SAGGERs disintegrated under the hail of fire, a dragon's breath of orange tracer reaching out over the sea. One hit the boat deck, amidships. The explosion blew apart the wardroom and started a fire.

One of the KORNETs came in low, striking just above the water line outside the rec room where damage control party one waited. The shaped charge blasted a hole big enough to stick a man's head through in the hull, opening seams between the plates welded together to form the hull. Water began leaking in the seams. That was ignored as a jet of vaporized metal lanced into the ship, cutting power cables and, incidentally, killing Electricians Mate Chief Lance Morgan, who was bossing damage control party one. Other members of the party were wounded. The first call went out for stretcher teams.

On the bridge, Kendricks gave weapons free, then headed to the port bridge wing to see what was going on. That put him on the bridge wing when a long burst of machine gun fire raked it. The heavy slugs punched through the metal of the splinter shields, shattering the glass in the windows as they came through. They killed Crane, his assistant gunner, and Kendricks in passing. The port lookout, untouched but covered in blood from the death around her, was shocked into silence for a moment. Then she shouted into the phones, "The XO's dead! Get gunners mates and a medic up here!" That done, she manned the .50 caliber and wildly fired off the remaining ammunition for the weapon.

One Libyan machine gunner hosed a steady stream of green tracer through the masts of *Kimmel*. Many bullets missed. Some hit masts, radar dishes, or guy wires. In CIC, consoles began going to static.

The first infantry missile team on the beach fired. Aft C-WIZ fired in response and blew it out of the air.

In CIC, Washington tried to get a grip on the situation. "Ammo report for mount twenty-two?"

The FC at the station checked. "Down to half ammo load, still running."

"Mount fifty-one, back on line!" The forward 5-inch gun mount.

Good news, finally. "Roger that. Fire fifty-one from CIC! Fire at will!" The FC at that station took over, using the TV camera intended for direct fire with the cannon. Beside him, the FC for the aft mount had been firing steadily since the fight began. Washington wished the FC luck, because he would need it. The lightweight 5-inch gun had never been intended for pinpoint accuracy. Stability had been sacrificed for weight on the weapon, with the intention of making up for it with precision-guided munitions which, of course, had never been purchased. Hundred-meter-wide shot groups were common with the weapons. Hitting an armored vehicle with them was a matter of pure chance.

Enough of that. What did she have? The missile mounts were useless at this range. Most of the air scan consoles were dead anyway from hits to the radars. "OS1 Ingalls, take all personnel whose consoles are dead and form an emergency fire fighting team. Contact damage control central and see where they need you!"

Ingalls threw her a salute. "Aye aye, ma'am!" He turned to the CIC personnel. "All right you lazy bastards, on your feet! Grab any fire fighting gear you see! If I spot someone at a dead console, you'll have to pull my boondockers out of your ass in about five seconds!"

As Ingalls organized his fire fighting party, Washington checked the gun cameras and the remaining scans. Mount twenty-two came alive again, spotting the flares of two of the infantry KORNETs, then three more vehicle-mounted missiles being fired at them. It roared, spraying out depleted uranium slugs in an envelopment pattern, one long burst that vaporized four of the missiles, emptied its ammunition bin, and accidentally caught one of the BRDMs with an overshoot. The little APC exploded as the 20mm slugs tore through its thin armor.

Washington saw the flashes of 5-inch shells bracketing the Libyan armor on the beach, and the ricochets of .50 caliber tracer off the vehicles. Then she turned to the forward C-WIZ control, to the weapon mounted on the opposite corner of the superstructure. Located where they were, the two weapons each had slightly more than a 180-degree arc of fire, with a tiny area of overlap. Aft C-WIZ covered the port and rear of the ship, Forward C-WIZ covered the front and starboard sides. "FC3, status on mount twenty-one?"

"Full ammo load, no targets. Green lights." The FC at that station sat there, feeling helpless.

"Go to direct fire mode, tell me when you can bear on that Libyan armor! Fire only on my command! Central phone talker, get me the bridge!"

On the beach, the boats hit the sand and were instantly swamped by hostages. Several of those rescued were nearly drowned by the boats in the surf, in their eagerness to be rescued. This eagerness had been somewhat dampened when they saw the hail of fire hitting *Kimmel*, but picked up again as the destroyer fired back. The storm of small arms fire back at the hill they'd come off of decided them.

To one side, Springer checked his patient. Coltrane, attended by one of the women they'd rescued, seemed to be having a great time, talking endlessly of what a badass he was. The morphine probably had a bit to do with that, but not much.

"Yeah, so that Libyan came at me, and pow! Down he went! And once he's down, pa-pow!"

Springer grinned, looked up—and saw a Libyan soldier, his AK leveled at him. The Libyan came forward silently, a finger to his mouth indicating he wanted silence, the rifle in his hands showing the fate of whoever disobeyed. Springer cursed himself for being surprised as a second Libyan, this one with a drum-fed machine gun, moved into position where he could rake the boats with gunfire. They must have infiltrated along the rocky shore. Springer's fingers twitched as he considered reaching for his holstered .45. Survival instincts stopped him.

His weapon leveled at his prisoners, the first Libyan ignored the semiconscious sailor on the stretcher. Until the man reached up, grabbed the muzzle of his rifle, and jerked it down. As the rifle fired harmlessly into the sand, Coltrane swept his unwounded leg in a short, savage kick into the Libyan's groin. The man gasped in pain, doubled over, and Coltrane struck him on the chin with a lightning-fast-heel-of-the-palm slam to the chin that shattered his neck.

The second Libyan whirled at the gunfire, raised his machine gun. Springer beat him to the draw, emptying a clip of .45 caliber bullets into the man's chest. The second Libyan staggered back and fell into the waves as his comrade hit the ground, dead.

Coltrane groaned as he collapsed back on the stretcher and grinned, still giddy from the morphine. "Yeah, pa-pow! Down he goes! Man, this morphine is great!"

On thc hill overlooking the beach, seven sailors, one CIA agent, and a lone civilian blazed away at the Libyan infantry. The Libyans had charged them, firing from the hip on full automatic as they'd been trained. Half the Libyans died before they realized you didn't do that against dug-in troops and live to tell about it.

Halloran fired off the last two bullets in his rifle at one pesky Libyan who had a good rock to hide behind and unbelievable luck. Beside him, Richmond squeezed off a steady series of shots from his captured AK, grinning and occasionally shouting. "Take that, you motherfuckers! Come and get it! It's payback time!"

Frankly, the guy was starting to make Halloran nervous.

Steiner low-crawled up the hill, and called to him from cover. "Halloran! Everyone's on the boats! It's time to go!"

Halloran gave her a thumbs-up, and shouted above the gunfire, "You heard her! All aboard that's going aboard! Run for the boats!"

Sailor and pilot and civilian and CIA agent all jumped to their feet and ran, dumping their rifles and shotguns. Sprinting with their last reserves of energy, they waded through the waves and into the boats. The eager hands of rescued hostages and fellow sailors reached out for them, pulled them aboard. The boat engines revved up, taking them away from the beach, turning in the surf and heading towards their uncertain refuge, the distant destroyer.

The Libyans took a few seconds to realize no one was shooting at them. Then they rushed forward, weapons ready, knowing their weapons could still catch the Americans as they were getting in their boats.

Back on the hill, Halloran picked up a rifle someone had dropped and turned to face the oncoming Libyans. He'd run back a ways to fool Steiner, then ducked into hiding. Someone had to cover the retreat. With his night vision goggles, he spotted movement. Far closer than the Libyans should be. He aimed—and recognized the reversed baseball cap Shawcross had been wearing since this crazy fight had started. "You stupid cannon cocker! You were supposed to get on the boats!"

"I might say the same for you, deck ape." Shawcross leaned across a convenient rock and went back to killing Libyans, firing measured shots at the distant troops. He picked off the three lead attackers in two seconds. The Libyan charge came to a sudden halt.

Shawcross worked his chaw, spat, and found himself a rock to aim over. Now that the Libyans had cover, he would have to fire a lot of shots to score a hit. "Figured somebody had to stay here to make sure the Libyans didn't rush us. Guess I wasn't the only one."

"So what's your plan now, Halloran?" MacKenzie's voice was a hoarse bellow, coming from a bit of a ways down the hill. "Please tell me you have a plan."

A fourth voice spoke from a deep crevice between two boulders. "You guys got it all wrong! It's the white guys who are supposed to make the last stands, not the Indians!" Toombs came out of his hole, turned his M-60 towards the advancing Libyans and squeezed off a burst at a few who'd been getting too bold.

"Go screw yourself, Kemosabe." MacKenzie checked his ammunition load. "So what now?"

The wif-com at Halloran's belt squawked. "Halloran! Bravo Queen to Bravo King, respond! Over!"

Halloran picked up the radio, keyed it. The range was already getting to be too much for the little radio. "Bravo Queen, this is King. Once you return to Alpha, request air evacuation for four personnel with Sea Sprite. Do you read me? Over?"

"King, this is Queen. You are one stupid son of a bitch! Over!"

"Roger that, Queen. King out!" A rifle bullet cracked overhead.

At the gunner's position of his BRDM, Leftenant-Colonel Faisal fired his fourth missile at the American ship, trying to steady his nerves. Were the Americans using their Star Wars weapons on his vehicles? Whatever the weapon they had that sprayed orange fire, it sounded like no weapon he had ever heard. Fortunately, it seemed to be occupied with shooting his missles out of the air. It appeared to have killed one of his BRDMs only by accident.

He watched the orange tracer of his missile as it flew into the boxy structure beneath where the orange fire had come from. The weapon was silent this time, as it had been the last few times his vehicles fired missles. The explosion was satisfying, a fire breaking out where his missile struck. Around him, one by one, the machine guns mounted on the BTRs grew silent, clicking loudly as they emptied their ammunition bins. Vehicle commanders reached down to drivers who passed up fresh boxes of ammunition, but the heavy .50 caliber bullets were slow to load. He was astounded the American ship was still afloat, still firing. It had seemed every weapon in the world was firing at it, yet it simply absorbed the destruction as if it did not matter.

The cannons on the American ship continued firing harmlessly, shells exploding to the left and the right, in front of and behind them. One shot had killed one of his dismounted missile teams. Another had blasted the front wheel from one of his BTRs. Other than that, they were good only for noise so long as his men stayed inside their armor.

One of the American machine guns began firing again, orange tracers and bullets that glanced off the armor of the APCs at this range. A lucky shot from them had killed one of his vehicle commanders.

In the hills on their flank, gunfire continued. The Americans were putting up a spirited fight. Good. There would be no reason to let any of them live.

Chapter Sixteen

Reisling stormed onto the bridge twenty seconds after an anti-tank missile hit the port bridge wing and blew half the bridge crew to eternity. Splinter shields, broken glass, shattered fragments of railing sprayed as jagged metal across the bridge, killing or wounding everyone still standing. The deck was slick with blood, the bridge lit by flames from the burning lockers, the air torn with the screams of wounded and dying crew and alarms going off, as the captain of the USS *Kimmel* stepped onto the bridge, followed by the master chief.

Reisling didn't waste a second. "Master chief, man the helm!" As he spoke, he threw open the door to the starboard bridge wing, where the gunner, loader, and starboard lookout waited. "Get in here! You two, fight these fires! Lookout, man the lee helm!" He shouted up to the signal section on top of the bridge, who had been hugging the deck since machine gun fire began hitting the ship. "SIGS, get down here! Bring the first aid kit and fire fighting gear!" They moved in response to his orders, only beginning to realize that the machine gun fire from shore had stopped.

Reisling was in full command mode now, prioritizing, responding. Next priority—establish communications. He grabbed the sound-powered phone line to Damage Control Central from the dead lee helmsman, and shouted above the noise as the gunners mates began hitting the fires with CO_2 extinguishers. "DC Central, this is the CO. Damage report!"

"Sir, we have ruptured seams at frames ten, thirty-six and seventy-eight." Chief Salazar sounded normal, which didn't mean much. Normal for him was pissed off for anyone else. "Fire is out of control on the port boat deck and the helo hanger. Water main break . . ." The chief gave him a quick rundown of the situation. As he spoke, the OS who handled communications with CIC and controlled the plotting board rose up from behind the plotting table.

"Sir, Guns requests we turn thirty degree to port, immediately!"

Reisling debated a moment, mentally setting aside what Salazar was saying. Now was no time for debate. If Guns wanted it, she'd better have a damn good reason. Then he remembered that damage control central also controlled the ship's engines and propellers. All the bridge controls did was send them the message of what the bridge wanted. "Chief! Wait one!" He interrupted Salazar's report. "Port shaft all stop, starboard shaft all ahead at ten knots! Make it twenty! Master Chief, give me left, fifteen degrees rudder!"

"I'll take it from here, sir," the master chief said in a voice that brooked no argument. One of the signalmen came in the door at that moment, and slipped on the blood sloshing over the deck. In the darkness, not realizing what it was, he wiped his hands off and went to work putting out the fire in a burning map locker. The gunner mates, relieved of fire fighting duty, headed out to the port bridge wing to see if they could get the port machine gun firing again.

Reisling nodded. "Master Chief has the Conn! Damage control central, continue your report!"

Throughout *Kimmel,* sailors fought fires, treated casualties, and did the hundred and one things they'd been trained to do so often they could do them in their sleep—which, in their present condition, was exactly what they were doing. None of the missiles had opened holes below the waterline. Several shattered fire mains and other water pipes poured water into the ship. Split seams let in more water, sometimes shorting out power cables. Ruptured water lines were sealed off, auxiliary power routes brought on line. Power was cut to shorting-out lines.

The true ship killer has always been fire. On *Kimmel,* fires blazed in berthings where missile hits had sprayed white-hot shrapnel across blankets, sheets, and mattresses. They blazed in the helo hangar, where aviation fuel puddled on the floor and burned furiously. Fires broke out in passageways where fuel lines had ruptured, in a hundred and one insignificant spaces on the superstructure where tracer bullets punched through the ship's steel hide and lodged in flammable materials. Sealed off, CIC was surrounded by smoke and dozens of smoldering fires.

Through the smoke, fire fighting teams in oxygen breathing apparatus and flash gear worked with hoses or extinguishers. Sometimes they were organized teams, like the survivors of damage control team one, laying down a sheet of fire fighting foam in the blazing hangar while the flight crew suppressed the fire with low-pressure sprays of water "fog." Sometimes they were whoever happened to be there, grabbing one of the fire extinguishers scattered throughout the ship and putting out any fires they found.

In the front of the ship above the chain locker, a missile had opened a split in the seams ten feet long, widened by the pounding of the waves on the bow, pouring water into the ship. Damage Control did as their grandfathers had done in two world wars—they covered the seam with canvas and plywood, cut 4x4 timbers to wedge between it and the nearest bulkhead, then hammered it into place with wooden mallets to jam the seam closed. As they did so, dewatering teams ran hoses over the side, and began pumping out of the ship the water that was being taken on board, both by leaks and by the hose teams fighting the fires.

In CIC, Washington steeled herself to ignore the panicked cries coming over the phones, watched the angle of the ship change, and thanked Reisling for trusting his people enough not to demand an explanation. The machine gun fire from the shore had stopped—for now. She knew all they were doing was reloading the weapons. Idly, she wondered how long it would take them to reload. She watched another volley of three KORNETs coming in towards the ship as the bow came around towards the beach. The FC at the console reached for the controls to switch the C-WIZ controls to intercept.

She stopped him. "Keep it on manual. We'll need every round."

Fired at a narrower target, one of the missiles glanced off the curved bow. A second hit the forward gun turret, setting off the round that had just been chambered. The turret exploded into scrap metal, fireproof plates protecting the gun crew below the turret. The third missile flew up and hit high in the rigging. More of her consoles went to static. The noise of the explosions barely reached CIC, but they still made her cringe.

Then she compared the position of the Libyan vehicles and the firing arc of mount twenty-one.

For the first time that night, she smiled.

* * *

Leftenant-Colonel Faisal armed his final missile, and prepared to fire it at the American ship. What he would do once it was fired, he did not know. The American ship was damaged, but it did not seem to be sinking. Its commander had finally had the presence of mind to turn their front towards them to create a smaller target. Not that it mattered. At this range, the ship was still a much larger target than a tank. Beside him, the first of the BTRs to have run out of ammunition was also the first to reload. Its commander began firing again, his first burst hitting the American ship dead on.

Faisal noticed the upper portion of the ship, from where the machine guns had been firing. Belatedly, he realized that that must be the bridge. His final missile would go there. He placed the red dot of his missile sight on the American ship—then gasped.

The knob on the top of the ship's bridge was glowing, an orange ring of fire. It struck the water in front of them, moved closer with that unearthly roaring noise he had heard before. Too late, he shouted into his microphone, "Driver, reverse! Reverse—"

Aboard *Kimmel*, Lieutenant Jimmelle Washington, USN, watched the stream of tracer reach out for the Libyans, and heard the screaming of a casualty through the steel bulkheads of the ship. Her voice was an angry hiss as she said, "Eat this, you bastards!"

The General Electric Phalanx Close-In-Weapons (c-wiz) system has a magazine containing 950 rounds of depleted uranium 20mm rounds. At a firing rate of 3000 rounds per minute, it takes approximately twenty seconds to exhaust its ammunition supply. The c-wiz normally stretches this time by firing short, precise bursts at its targets. Mount twenty-one was under manual control now, however, and Jimmelle intended to use up every round of ammunition she had.

In most people's lives, twenty seconds is not very much.

Suddenly, twenty seconds became a very long time.

It was an erupting volcano, a rain of death, raking the beach and the hill with deadly projectiles that shattered rock and punched through plate steel as easily as human flesh. Some rounds struck sloped armor and ricocheted off.

Most didn't.

The BRDMs exploded as the rounds hit their spare missiles, stowed for reloads. Most of the BTRs died less spectacularly, simply riddled as the rounds penetrated their front slopes, and then, lacking the force to go back out again, ricocheted inside the vehicles. Somewhere in their flight, the shots usually passed through the crew-members of those vehicles, not appreciably slowed in their passage. Punctured fuel tanks and tracer rounds combined to start fires.

Not all the Libyans died. Even 950 rounds cannot blanket an area big enough to hold sixteen vehicles. But most of them died. The rest ran.

The four men left on the hill watched the storm of fire that wiped out the Libyan armor, and cheered as the rain of fire went on and on, as explosions roared from where they'd been watching missiles and machine gun fire pour. When it finally stopped, the silence was thunderous.

The noise shocked the Libyan troops into silence too. For about fifteen minutes, they were quiet, seemingly stunned. Shawcross fired an occasional round to keep their heads down, while the others picked up any abandoned weapons they could find and dug in. On top of the hill they had good cover and clear fields of fire. Halloran still had his night vision goggles, and Shawcross had his Starlight scope.

Then the Libyans started attacking again.

This time there was no idiotic charge. Orders were shouted in Arabic, echoing among the stones. The surviving Libyan came on in pairs, one squeezing off bursts of fire, the other moving to cover, leapfrogging. The Libyan troops apparently had no night vision gear, so the fire was still mostly wild, but every time an American fired a shot, someone sent a spray of return fire at his muzzle flash. Behind the troops, at least three light machine guns laid down cover fire, keeping up a steady rain of bullets. Now it was the Americans' turn to be rattled, to be unable to aim effectively as bullets cracked past their heads.

Halloran tried to gauge where the person shouting orders was, fired his last two 40mm rounds at the noise, using the grenade launcher like a small mortar. The order shouter kept shouting. Halloran mentally nicknamed the man "Sergeant Rock."

MacKenzie blasted one of the machine guns to perdition with his last belt of ammunition, then was down to his .45, a captured AK with half a magazine, and a shotgun. Toombs tried conserving ammunition by firing short bursts of three or four rounds, but found out that they jammed his M-60. Shawcross kept on picking people off, was nicked in the cheek, then on the hand by splinters as near misses ricocheted off stones by him. "Halloran, these guys are getting too damn good. What do we do?"

"Keep firing. The chopper is on the way!"

"Yeah, and the check is in the mail!" shouted MacKenzie.

"I'm from the government! I'm here to help you!" called Toombs.

"And I'll respect you in the morning!" Shawcross looked at *Kimmel*, saw flames on the flight deck. He whipped around his rifle, looked through his scope. He saw a blazing helicopter being pulled from the smoking hangar and shoved over the side. It hit the water and vanished beneath the waves.

He spared a glance to the east. The first streaks of false dawn were lighting the sky over the Atlas mountains. "Hoka hey yo," he muttered to himself without enthusiasm. Then he said aloud, "I sure hope they hurry!"

The boats pulled alongside *Kimmel* on the starboard side, away from the port boat deck. That meant they missed seeing the blazing, shrapnel-riddled helicopter being shoved over the side. No one could find the regular operators for the davits, to pull the boats up onto the ship. Cargo nets and Jacob's ladders were hurriedly put over the side by an improvised boat crew. Rescued hostages began scrambling up. The first person up the nets was Lieutenant Steiner, her lithe form climbing easily up the cargo net.

The hostages came onto a scene scarcely better than what they had left. Fires blazed everywhere, men and women in firefighting gear were running around seemingly at random, and orders were echoing over the 1MC as the crew struggled to save their ship. Springer led the hostages towards the mess decks, once he realized that the ward room was a smoking wreck. The mess decks were, at least, not smoking. They were, however, packed with wounded men and women screaming for help, blood puddling on the floor as *Kimmel's* other medic and various sailors did what they could to help the casualties. The rain of bullets on the port side had riddled the ship. Many casualties had been inside the destroyer, only to be hit by bullets punching through the skin of the ship.

Springer went to work. Like the other medic, he immediately found himself doing work normally reserved for doctors. Some of the rescued hostages tried to help. Most tried to stay out of the way.

* * *

Lieutenant Steiner first knew something was wrong as she looked into the smoking emptiness that had been the hangar bay. She spotted Chief Hamner dressed in fire fighting gear, and ran over to him. "Chief!"

Hamner looked over, and smiled all across a smoke-stained face. His khakis and flash gear were scorched and stained, splotched with water, foam, and purple fire fighting powder. "Ma'am, you're back! Did you get the hostages?"

"I left four people on the beach! Where's the Seasprite?"

Hamner's eyebrows shot up in surprise. "They took a missile hit in the hangar. That tore up the helo and set it on fire. By the time we got to her, it was too late to do anything but shove her over the side!"

Steiner slammed a fist against a bulkhead. "Shit! We'll have to go back to the beach! Chief, contact CIC and tell them! I'm heading back to the boat!" She went down the ladder. Chief Hamner watched, shocked into silence.

On the boat deck, the last of the landing party had come up the nets. OPS was at the net, leaning over the side. "Sink the boats and come on board! We're clearing out! Boat crew, come on board!"

"Belay that!" shouted Steiner. She ran to the net, where most of the survivors of the landing party were waiting. "OPS, the Seasprite is gone! We'll have to pull them off the beach in one of the boats!"

OPS shook his head. "Negative. Dawn is less than an hour away, by which time we have to be out of Libyan waters. Helicopters are on their way from *Savannah.* They'll evacuate the landing party."

"They won't last that long and you know it! Those choppers are still at least an hour away!"

"I will not risk this ship! That is final, Lieutenant!"

Steiner glared at OPS. "Screw you, sir." She leaned

over the rail and shouted down into the boat, "Boats! The helicopter's been can-exed! We need to go back and pull them off the beach!"

Stolchak looked up at her from the tiller of the whaleboat, cursed silently. Then he looked around at his boat crew, and at the crew of the captain's gig who had been waiting since their human cargo had gone up the side. He looked back at the distant shore.

Red tracers crossed the sky, ricochets going upwards. Someone was still back there, still fighting.

Stolchak looked back up. Steiner was already coming down the cargo net. Back on the beach were not just four sailors, but two of his own men, Halloran and Toombs. He looked up at OPS, who shouted down at him. "Boats, stop Lieutenant Steiner, bring your people aboard and sink the boats. We're getting out of here!"

Stolchak made his decision. The decision he wished he'd made years before. So many nightmares ago. Before he'd discovered that there were some things you had to do, if you were going to live with yourself. Even if they might kill you.

He picked up the loudspeaker and shouted up at OPS, "Sorry, sir! Those are my men back there! I'll take volunteers back for them! Give us thirty minutes!" He turned to face his boat crews, Snyder and Pullman watching from the other boat. The captain's gig was slightly faster than the wallowing motor whaleboat. With five crew, four passengers should just about do it. He spoke through the loudspeaker. "Dave, Ensign Pullman, I'm taking the gig! I need a volunteer crew to pick up our last four people. Everyone who isn't going, get up that net now!"

BM3 'Skater' Mayes looked Stolchak in the eye. "B-B-Boats, I done my bit t'night. This all's where I step off."

Stolchak nodded. "You did a hell of a job, Skater. Good luck to you. Leave the M-60, willya?" Mayes nodded, and joined the rest of the boat crew scrambling up the net.

Pullman brought the gig alongside the motor whaleboat and his crew jumped between the boats and went up the net. Steiner and Stolchak, carrying the M-60, leaped over to the gig. Seaman Apprentice Andrews stood at the net for a moment, looked at them. "Damn it, that crazy fuck Halloran's going to get you all killed!" He turned and scrambled up the net.

The pilot and Chief Stolchak were taken on board by Snyder and Pullman, who had waited on the gig. A moment later, a breathless Woodall joined them. Stolchak looked over at Snyder. "Dave, get us the hell out of here before we get swamped!" Snyder nodded and gunned the engine. Bobbing up and down in the swells, the gig accelerated away from *Kimmel*, headed to shore. The night sea breeze hit them again, the smell of sea and battle smoke and distant land.

Stolchak settled into a comfortable spot and barked out orders. "Okay, you jack tars, battle stations! Share out the ammo equally, and keep a weather eye out for our people! Ensign, get on the horn to *Kimmel* and see if you can get us some gunfire support." He grinned and pulled out a pack of cigarettes. He tapped out and lit an unfiltered Camel, then offered the pack to Steiner. "Cigarette, ma'am? If we're pulling one dumbass stunt, we might as well make it two."

She took one and cupped it against the wind as Stolchak lit it with his battered Zippo. "Thanks, Boats. Don't mind if I do."

They headed towards the distant shore.

On the mess decks, the confusion was as bad as ever. Though the ship was no longer being fired on, casualties were still coming in. All the crewmen knew first aid and the two medics were doing a heroic job, but the big .50 caliber bullets that had raked the ship inflicted unbelievable wounds. Now other casualties were coming in. Smoke inhalation, burns, electrical shocks. Every table, every bench had its human cargo.

Mess Specialist First Class Davis finally realized what effect the spectacle was having on the hostages, and that they were getting in the way. He unlocked the chief's mess and led the hostages in there. Majors carried in the young girl he'd been staying close to since the rescue.

The girl's mother was still upset by the scene they'd just left. She gently took her child from Majors's arms, and looked at him with wide eyes. The girl smiled at Majors, then looked beyond him and yelped, "Daddy!"

A man in civilian clothes, his face stained by smoke, came in the door. "Sorry, pumpkin. Daddy got lost on the way here." He gathered the girl into his arms and extended one hand to Majors. "Thanks. I appreciate what you did." The CIA agent shook the man's hand, then dropped his arms to his sides as he looked at the reunited family. He suddenly felt very lost.

The father glanced back at the howling chaos on the mess decks. "Though it doesn't seem much better here. Are these people going to get through this?"

Majors nodded and spoke in his most reassuring tones. "I know it's pretty wild out there, but these people are good. Amazingly good, all things considered. They know what they're doing." He looked at the family a second more, then looked away before things got uncomfortable. Tried to figure out what to do next.

Tosado leaned in the door to the wardroom. "Majors! They're heading back to the beach to get the last guys! If we hurry, we can catch them!"

The two men ran for the boat deck.

Tosado was wrong. They arrived too late to catch the boat, but just in time to see a rifleman riddle the whaleboat with bullets to sink it. Majors stood on the deck for a moment and looked out over the waves. The eastern sky was beginning to lighten. "Good luck, you crazy Irishman. And your little dog, too."

A smoke-stained chief stuck his head out of a hatch and looked over at them. "You two, get over here! I need somebody to run OBA canisters up to the helo hangar! Tosado, you show him where to go! Move!"

They moved.

On the beach, things were going badly.

The Libyans continued firing at muzzle flashes. This worked pretty well, as they had plenty of ammunition while the Americans were all running short.

Huddled behind a rock that seemed way too small, Halloran listened to bullets chip stone above his head. The taste of cordite gagged his throat. The batteries in his night vision goggles had died five minutes before. Without looking up, he tried to follow the course of the battle by sound. The AKs were easy to spot, as all of them were firing on full auto. The M-14s made a solid crack as they fired. The booming of Toombs's shotgun was distinctive.

As he listened, Halloran heard bursts of fire to three sides of them and felt a chill run down his spine. "Toombs, MacKenzie, Shawcross! We're being flanked! If we stay up here, they'll catch us in a crossfire! Head for the beach!"

The other three shouted replies. Halloran crawled down the back of the hill, jumping to his feet in a running crouch as soon as he felt he could. He came to a good piece of cover and aimed his rifle to one flank. Sure enough, bursts of automatic weapons fire. Wishing he still had his goggles, he fired a few aimed shots at the muzzle flashes. Hitting anyone would be a miracle under these conditions, but hopefully that would make the Libyans take cover, slow down their pursuit. He ducked under cover and low-crawled away from where he'd fired. Seconds later, return fire ricocheted off the stones he'd been behind.

There was a solid-sounding *Bang!*, then a much bigger explosion nearby, scattering small stones everywhere. A rocket-propelled grenade, he guessed. The Libyans were close enough to use them now. Designed to kill tanks, the antitank rockets also let enterprising soldiers act as light artillery. He crawled faster and tried to recall how long it took to load the damn things. To one side, he heard an AK firing on single shot and hoped it was MacKenzie. Ahead of him, a shadowy figure moved, whistled. "Yo, Halloran, that you?"

Toombs. Good. "Yeah. Where's MacKenzie and Shawcross?"

"Back past me, I think. Let's stick together." Toombs came out of the darkness, down to the shotgun, a pistol, and several of the blocks of C4 they'd brought along. "Anybody past you?"

"Negits."

"Good." Toombs lit the fuse on the C4 and lobbed it away from them with one heave of a massive arm. It exploded four seconds later. The two sailors jumped up and ran down the hill. As they ran, Halloran said, "You probably didn't hit anybody!"

"Confusion to the enemy, G! Just fuckin' with they minds!"

"Sounds good to me!" Halloran threw his last two grenades as he ran. They kept running, down the hill and across the road. As they crossed, an automatic weapon fired behind them. Ricochets hit all around.

Something slammed Toombs in the side. He grunted and fell down into the roadway in full careen, tumbling like a broken doll. Halloran grabbed the man's collar and pulled with all his might. The two men tumbled off the road more than they ran and crawled to cover. There they stopped. Halloran probed Toombs's side. "Where does it hurt, Tombstone?"

"Right side. Feels like somebody laid me upside the short ribs with a bat!" Toombs gritted his teeth as Halloran probed, and waited for the bad news. Strangely, the pain was fading now. Shock, he thought. I'm going into shock. His best friend had died that way after a shooting at a party. Felt no pain as he died.

Halloran probed a little more, chuckled.

"What you laughing for, motherfucker?"

"It was just a ricochet. Didn't even get through your vest. I'll bet it cracked some of your ribs, though. Here, have a souvenir!" Halloran handed him a bullet, still warm from its passage, flattened where it had bounced off the road or some rock. "Remember, without kevlar, life itself would be impossible."

"Thanks G. Mah'fucker still hurts like a bitch." They both returned their attention to the fight. Halloran looked over to where the machine gun had fired at them, saw the pumpkin-sized muzzle flash of a shotgun near it. Seconds later, carrying two AKs and his sawed-off shotgun, MacKenzie came out of the darkness.

Halloran whistled at him. MacKenzie looked for the noise, came over, and took cover beside them. "Anybody need a rifle?"

Toombs grunted and reached out. "Thanks. This shotgun ain't worth shit out here in the open."

"You gotta be one of us sneaky redskins to use them." MacKenzie grinned, handed over the rifle and a couple of spare magazines. Then he said in a mock Scottish accent, "Either that or a proper Scotsman, so ye ken how tae use the bonny hills for cover!"

Laughs were running pretty thin just then, but the joke got a chuckle or two. Then they all looked out and watched for the muzzle flash of an M-14. Toombs asked, "So where the hell is Shawcross?" They had no answer. Behind them, they could hear the waves hitting the shore. Back on the hill, gunfire continued.

Including the flat crack of an M-14, firing steadily.

Automatic fire answered every shot, tracers raking the top of the hill. Halloran suddenly realized what was going on. ‘‘Damn it! Shawcross is still up there!’’

There was a moment’s quiet in the group. Then Toombs checked the load in his newly acquired rifle and tried to rise. ‘‘Okay, let’s get him out of there.’’ He grunted with pain as cracked ribs ground against each other.

Halloran shook his head, trying to figure out a way even as he knew it was impossible. Then he said the hardest words he’d ever had to say. ‘‘Negits to that. We’d walk right into a crossfire. They’re closing in on him now. I give him five minutes before they plaster him.’’

MacKenzie looked at him, teeth gritted in sudden, helpless anger. ‘‘Fuck you! That’s Shawcross up there!’’

Halloran nodded. ‘‘And he knew exactly what he was doing when he stayed up there. He’s buying us time. If we go back, he’s dying for nothing.’’

The gunfire continued, the cracks of the rifle lonely sounds against the thunder of the AKs. Then a voice rose above the noise, a familiar voice roughened by dust and smoke. Singing.

‘‘The minstrel boy to the war is gone.
In the ranks of Death you will find him!’’

The voice was raspy from cordite fumes and dust and exhaustion. Shocked, Halloran suddenly realized it was Shawcross, his voice carrying all the way to the road. A tune Halloran had learned in his youth. ‘‘The Minstrel Boy.’’

‘‘His father’s sword he has girded on,
and his wild harp slung beside him!’’

As the storm of fire on the hilltop increased, Halloran muttered under his breath, "You magnificent, fucking lunatic!"

"Land of song, said the warrior bard,
Though all the world betray thee,
One sword at least thy rights shall guard!
One faithful heart shall praise thee!"

On the hilltop, a hail of bullets struck the rocks around Shawcross. He was having a great time. The song sent the Libyans into a frenzy, which meant they were exposing themselves to fire at him. Every time their fire slowed down, he popped up and fired another shot, which coaxed another fusillade from the Libyans. Idly, he wondered how long it would take them to bring up heavy weapons to blast him out of his position. He hoped Halloran and the others had possessed the common sense to bug out. Then he wondered if any of the Libyans would appreciate his rifle when they captured it. He thought one last time about his wife. She'd understand. Then he went back to the task at hand. Buying time. He sang out again, his throat painfully dry.

"The minstrel fell, but the foeman's chain
could not bring his proud soul under."

At the base of the hill, two Libyans aimed RPGs at the American sniper. Near the shore, Halloran sang along under his breath, his face as grim as an ancestor's had been at Waterloo, as the Inniskillings died around him. Toombs watched for approaching Libyans, marveling at what he saw. MacKenzie did the same, silent tears running down his face.

"The harp he loved ne'er spoke again,
for he tore its chords asunder!

And said No chains shall sully thee,
Thou soul of love, and bravery!
Thy songs were made for the proud and free!
They shall never sound in slavery!''

The RPGs fired, blasting the stones Shawcross hid among, killing him even as they shattered his rifle. Then the Libyans threw a volley of grenades up the hill and rushed the position. Even dying, Shawcross took some of them with him as the Libyans, charging up both sides of the hill, caught each other in a crossfire.

The final shots of that volley echoed out over the hills and stones. Quiet fell in the gray predawn as the Libyans converged on the hilltop.

That was when the Americans heard the chugging of a boat engine.

They looked out to sea, tried to see in the darkness. The wif-com at Halloran's belt crackled. ''Bravo Queen to Bravo King. Come in, over.''

Halloran fumbled with the radio, keyed it. ''Queen to King, we need a light! We are on the beach!'' A red-filtered flashlight glared out of the darkness. ''I identify a red light. Over!''

''Roger on red light, Bravo King. We're coming in! Last train from Boot Hill! Over!''

''Last train, aye! King out!'' Halloran shoved the radio into a pocket and picked up Toombs by one arm. ''Mac, get his other arm and let's get the hell out of here!''

The three men half ran, half stumbled down to the beach and through the waves, abandoning their weapons. As they ran, a Libyan on the hill heard the boat motor and fired a flare out over the water. The three men scrambled through waist-deep water as the gig came through the surf, and jumped up onto the boat as eager hands grabbed them. The first few shots came from the hilltop. Sitting at the rear of the boat, puffing on a

Camel, Stolchak braced the M-60 against his hip and opened fire, raking the hilltop. "Halloran, is there anybody else?"

"Negative! Shawcross didn't make it! We got everybody else!" Halloran barked out the words, heaved Toombs out of the surf, and then grabbed a deck fitting. Steiner grabbed his vest, braced herself.

Stolchak smiled. They'd gotten them all this time, no questions. "Dave, back us the hell out of here!" The three men aboard, Snyder gunned the engines, turning sharply in the waves as bullets kicked up sprays of water around them.

Steiner gripped Halloran by his flak vest and pulled him up and over the side as Stolchak's machine gun roared. The sudden turn of the boat threw them both in to the deck, Halloran on top. He looked down at Steiner's face and grinned, glad to be alive. She grinned back.

Woodall heaved Toombs up and over the side by herself, hugged him frantically. He yelped in pain. "Let go! My ribs are broke!" She let go, and jumped back as if stung. He looked at her, smiled. "Let's try it again, a little slower, okay?"

Stolchak heard the congratulations behind him, smiled, and held down the trigger on his machine gun. It bucked and pressed against his barrel chest, spraying out fire at the shore. Then there was a sharp pain in his chest, sudden, deep within him. He kept holding down the trigger of the M-60, laying down covering fire, but now he felt weak. Finally, his fingers losing their strength, he dropped the weapon. It fell off the boat, into the white trail of foam left by the gig under full power. Vanished beneath the water.

There was a hand on his shoulder. The scent of Old Spice and pipe tobacco. A familiar voice. But now it sounded approving. "Nice work, Boats. Nobody was left behind. You got them all."

"Yeah." Stolchak smiled. It was getting quieter suddenly. The pain was fading away. Everything was fading away. All that was left was a sense of peace. "Yeah. We got 'em all."

The roaring of the engine made it difficult to hear. The breeze was picking up, the boat bucking in the waves, when Stolchak almost tumbled over the side. Ensign Pullman grabbed him and looked at him.

Stolchak's face had an angelic calm, blue eyes staring blankly up at the dawn. The front of his flak vest had one hole and a spreading red stain. "Medic!" called Pullman. The ensign pulled open Stolchak's flak vest. The others helped where they could. But once the shirt was opened and they saw how much blood there was, everyone knew. One entry wound in the center of the chest. Death had been almost instantaneous.

Pullman grimaced and closed the chief's eyes. After that, he went to work guiding them back to *Kimmel.*

Chapter Seventeen

Dawn came. The last fires were put out, the flight deck made usable. The port side was still riddled with bullet holes, while cables and the wreckage of radar dishes and antennae dangled from the masts. The bridge, its windows shattered, was open to the sea breeze as sailors from deck division mopped the blood from its decks and cleaned out the wreckage.

The first helicopters from *Savannah* arrived just after dawn. The Marines on them were furious at having missed the fight, but once landed on *Kimmel* they went to work helping put out the fires and patch the holes. Their medics and two doctors flown in with them went to work in the impromptu hospital the mess decks had become. As soon as they were refueled, the CH-47s departed, loaded with casualties. The destroyer's radars were dead, making it blind, while the rupture near the bow slowed the ship, lest the pounding of the waves knock loose the wooden bracing and widen the split in the seams. But *Kimmel* was under the protection of the *Ticonderoga* battle group now.

Lieutenant Jimmelle Washington sat down in the armory as the last of the weapons were turned in. Most of her gunners mates and FCs were still manning their weapons, and would be at them until they were much farther away from Libya.

Washington shut the door to the armory and looked at the stack of weapons that had been turned in. Many had been left behind on the beach, and the paperwork for them would be unbelievable. So would the paperwork for the weapons they'd modified. But that would come later. She opened a can of soda and sipped it as she looked at the letter Shawcross had left. It seemed very ordinary, in an ordinary, unsealed envelope.

The phone rang. She answered it. "Ship's armory, Guns."

"Guns, this is the Captain." Reisling seemed unaffected by the night. Of course. "I've talked with OPS and Lieutenant Steiner. They tell me that GMG1 Shawcross died giving them a chance to get away. If what they're saying checks out, I'm sure there's a posthumous Medal of Honor in it."

Washington looked at the letter and wondered what she would say in the letter she would send to Shawcross's widow along with it. She felt numb. "It's good to hear that, sir. He was an outstanding petty officer."

"Indeed he was." Amazingly, it took Reisling a full twenty seconds to come up with something to say. "Lieutenant—or, rather, Lieutenant Commander, some things were said last night, under pressure, that are better forgotten. I believe some discretion might be in order for the after-action reports. Don't you agree?"

She shook her head in wonder. Back to the old routine. She found herself saying, "Yes sir. I agree completely."

"Excellent. We'll talk further. I'm sure there will be

a board of inquiry after this event. Before that happens, the first chance we get, I'd like the wardroom to get together to hash it over between ourselves. But now I have a bridge to set in order. We'll be talking again, Lieutenant Commander Washington. Have a good day."

He hung up. She hung up.

She looked at the letter. Found herself pulling it from the envelope, along with a small sheet of paper, with the words "LT. WASHINGTON" on it. Eyes widening, she took the paper and unfolded it.

Ma'am—

If you are reading this, I didn't come back from the landing party. Please send the letter enclosed to my wife, along with whatever you know of how I died. Give it to my wife straight. She can take it.

"Sure, farmboy," she whispered to herself. Halloran had said that Shawcross died singing some Irish ballad, fighting to the last. She believed that.

I want you to know you're one of the best officers I ever served under, man or woman. Keep your head about you, and someday you'll be an admiral. A good one.

As for me, don't worry. If I died, I died doing what I had to do. It was what I chose to do. I went into this mission with my eyes open, and I was glad to do it. If I hadn't, I might have lived to be an old man, but I'd have always wondered what would have happened if I went. Besides, those kids needed me. It may sound crazy, but I've always dreamed of doing something like this. Now I'm going to get to do it, and if I have to pay the price, so be it. Don't look back. Please take care of my personal effects. Remember whatever lessons I taught you. And the next time you're in some watering hole, tip a glass to an ole Missouri farmboy who went to sea.

Your friend—
Harlan

She tucked the note into a pocket. Then the tears came.

Halloran and Steiner stood together on the flight deck and watched the medics load Coltrane onto the helicopter. She looked at him. "How was it after I left?"

Halloran grimaced, cocked his head. "It was . . . I don't know. I've never seen anything like it. I'll have to work it out." He looked at her. "So what about us? Was that just adrenaline talking last night? Is there anything between us, really?"

She looked back at him, grinned. "You aren't dumping me now, Seaman. Even if OPS gets you court-martialed. You are taking me to dinner at a Chinese restaurant at our first port call, or I'm writing you up for fraternization." Halloran's confusion was comical. She laughed, then looked around. Too many people were nearby. "Look, I have to get back to my quarters, see if there's anything left. Keep in touch. You'd better get out of those khakis and back into your dungarees. Reisling is going to put things back to normal as fast as he can." She left.

Halloran stood there, thinking. As he did so, Majors walked up to him. "So, Dave, how goes it?"

"Well, I'm alive, and it's another fine Navy day." Halloran shrugged and looked at the agent. "You rescued that girl?"

Majors smiled, nodded. "Yeah. But I couldn't figure out what to do then. I heard about Shawcross." Halloran had no reply to that. "So what happens now?"

Halloran sighed, turned around, leaned on a railing, and looked out over the ocean as the helicopter took off.

Wind buffeted his close-cropped gray hair. Staring into the rising sun, his eyes were pale blue crystal. "Beats me. I guess we go back to the old routine again. I go back to being a mess crank. Maybe they give us medals."

The CIA agent nodded, leaned against the railing too. "They'll probably pull me off here in a day or two for debriefing. I won't even get a medal." He thought a moment, closed his eyes, and let the breeze caress his face. "But just once, I got to be a hero. I saved a little girl, and a lot of other people, from certain death. That's pretty good."

Halloran nodded. "That's my problem. After what we've done—Jeez. We fought terrorists! We rescued hostages! I organized a commando raid and told off my CO and got rescued under fire! What can I ever do again to compare to that? What will I ever do again in my life as important as what we did last night?"

There was a moment of silence as the ship cut through the waves, the sea breeze picking up. Another helicopter closed on them, preparing to land.

Majors opened his eyes and looked at the gray-haired seaman. "You could do it again."

Halloran looked back at him.

His laughter echoed out over the waves.

Cruising the Mediterranean on the seventh month of a six-month deployment, the guided missile destroyer USS *Kimmel* headed north over waves turned to molten copper by the sunrise.